TRIPLE FACTOR

OWEN SELA is a British author who lives in London. Celebrated for his fast-paced thrillers – *An Exchange of Eagles* was an immediate bestseller – *Triple Factor* is no exception. It is not only a story of compulsive suspense, but also an informed inside view of the deadly games which take place every day in the corridors of industrial power.

OWEN SELA

Triple Factor

FONTANA/Collins

First published by William Collins Sons & Co. Ltd 1982
First issued in Fontana Paperbacks 1983

Copyright © Owen Sela 1982

Made and printed in Great Britain by
William Collins Sons & Co. Ltd, Glasgow

To my little friend
RICHARD
for more than you know

It was still winter and at seven in the morning, Zurich was embalmed in a grey murk, as Berndt Manninger edged the mud-stained Duesenberg along the narrow confines of the Rennweg and stopped directly behind the Hoffman Bank.

In response to his coded ringing of the bell, a grilled door was opened. Manninger stepped into a steel shuttered elevator and went up to the top floor, where amongst wall to wall carpeting and discreet lighting, Dr Alois Hoffman had offices of restrained sumptuousness.

Hoffman was a large man, accustomed to wearing suits of funeral black. A gold watch chain spread across his ample belly and his round face was faintly porcine, with an expression of smugness. Dr Alois Hoffman knew a lot about money and everything about banking. In Zurich, that was more than enough.

Manninger threw himself into a chair, his ears still humming with the sound of the engine. He'd hardly slept and eaten almost nothing since he'd left Hellenthal on the 21st. His mouth tasted stale, and his cheeks were irritated by two days' stubble. His body ached from the arduous mountain climb. 'Alois, do you think I can have some coffee and cigarettes?' He took out a crumpled pack and held it up. 'Exclusivs.'

'Yes, yes, of course,' Dr Hoffman said, and ordered coffee, rolls and cigarettes, while Manninger took two envelopes from his pocket and laid them on the desk.

'My will,' he said. 'I have appointed your bank as executors.'

5

'We are privileged,' Hoffman said formally. 'I will personally ensure that your trust in us is not misplaced.'

A clerk arrived with coffee and rolls. Manninger bit hungrily into a roll and said, 'Read the will, Alois.'

Hoffman hesitated. 'It is not usual. Wills are – '

'Read it now,' Manninger snapped.

Hoffman stared in controlled surprise. He'd never seen Manninger so tense or so irritable. He had never seen Manninger with hollowed cheeks and smoke grey circles around reddened eyes. Manninger's long face was pale, the lines around his mouth and nose deeply etched. There was something manic about the hard glitter in his blue eyes.

'Read the will,' Manninger said tiredly. 'I haven't much time.'

'I, Berndt Manninger of Villa Manninger, Hellenthal, hereby revoke all former testamentary dispositions and declare this to be my last will and testament.

1 I give devise and bequeath to my wife Elisabeth Manninger:

(a) The ownership of the property known as Villa Manninger in the village of Hellenthal and the contents thereof and

(b) For as long as she shall live the income from all shares and other like investments directly owned by me which are presently in the custody of the Hoffman Bank, Zurich.

2 The ownership of the said shares and all other assets directly or indirectly owned by me shall pass to such of my direct descendants who shall be able to prove their entitlement according to the terms and conditions set out in a letter deposited by me today with the Hoffman Bank, Zurich, provided that prior to making such claim the claimant shall have attained the age of 21 years.

3 If such claim is made during the lifetime of Elisabeth

6

Manninger the ownership of the said shares and all other assets directly or indirectly owned by me shall be divided equally between such claimant and the said Elisabeth Manninger.

4 If no such claim be made against my executors within a period of thirty-five years and six months after my death the ownership of the said shares and all other assets directly or indirectly owned by me shall pass absolutely to my wife Elisabeth Manninger.'

'This is most unusual,' Hoffman said. 'There are assets we do not know of. Elisabeth does not inherit for thirty-five years. And the claimant has – '

Manninger tapped the second envelope. 'To prove direct lineage and present you with the founders certificates of Sopadep and Perpetua.'

Sopadep and Perpetua were two Swiss companies which controlled Manninger's assets and the industrial processes he had devised. Hoffman remembered that six months ago, Manninger had taken the founders certificates from the bank's custody. 'And who has these certificates now?' he asked, angered at Manninger's apparent lack of trust.

Manninger gave him a tired smile. 'It is dangerous for you to know that, Alois.' He sighed. 'Germany will shortly be defeated, and then they will do what they did in 1918 – seize our technology as war reparations.'

'But your rights to the processes are safe here in Switzerland,' Hoffman said. 'And you have friends amongst the Allies.'

'There are other processes,' Manninger said, 'which I have been working on since my son's death. They are far more valuable than anything Perpetua or Sopadep owns.' He looked thoughtful. 'As for my Allied friends, I am seeing Raison Tearkes here in an hour. I hope to persuade him to give me some kind of indemnity, in exchange for the use of these new processes.'

'And can Tearkes do that?'

'The question is whether he will.' Manninger explained that at the outbreak of war he had sold various processes to Tearkes and others on the secret understanding that the processes would be resold to him, at a fixed price, at the end of the war. Those processes had helped the Allied war effort, were worth millions, would be worth much more in peace time. 'It is in Tearkes's interests to have me tried as a war criminal, to have my assets confiscated.'

Hoffman looked concerned. He'd known Manninger for seventeen years, and while they had never been friends, there was a closeness betwen them. 'So why tell Tearkes anything at all?'

'It is a chance I have to take,' Manninger said, his grin transforming his face into a death's-head. 'I need my freedom.'

Hoffman knew Tearkes and didn't like him. Throughout the war Manninger had met secretly with Tearkes and other Allied industrialists, usually at the Hoffman Bank. He said, 'Tearkes will not help you.'

'He will have to,' Manninger said, tiredly. He told Hoffman how he had kept records of his meetings with Tearkes, records of the extent of Allied involvement with German industry throughout the war. 'If I tell Tearkes those files exist, that they will be part of my defence if I am tried as a war criminal, he'll have no alternative but to do what I want.'

Manninger put down his coffee and lit a cigarette. 'So now you know why I cannot tell you where these things are hidden, and why I have arranged my affairs in such a way that neither Elisabeth, nor my daughter Ingrid or any of her children can acquire control of the assets during the useful life of the processes. I do not want Elisabeth or any of my descendants being manipulated or hunted because of these processes and these files.'

'And you think that if they have no control, they will be left alone.'

8

'I hope so.'

'Do you realize, Berndt, that if Elisabeth dies before she inherits, your estate will be administered under the intestacy laws, that most of it could be taken by the state.'

'I realize that,' Berndt Manninger said softly. 'I hope everyone else does.'

At four thirty that afternoon, Gestapo Officer Dieter Asch stood inside the control building at Schaffhausen and watched the red, mud-stained Duesenberg ease through the Swiss border post. A few hours earlier, he'd received a telephone call from Zurich. In halting German, the caller had told Asch that for the past five years, Berndt Manninger, one of Germany's best known and most important industrialists, had been meeting with Allied intelligence in Switzerland. The caller gave a list of dates, which Asch had checked with the records of the Border Police and found correct.

He had promptly reported the call and his findings to Gestapo Headquarters in Berlin, and now had in his possession an order to arrest Manninger and escort him under armed guard to Berlin.

As Manninger's car approached the raised barriers on the German side of the border, Asch looked at the four armed men who stood beside the windows. He hoped Manninger would be sensible, that there would not be any shooting, and stepped out of the building.

A border guard was standing by the rolled down window of Manninger's car, hand extended for the necessary documents. Through the windscreen Asch glimpsed the well-built figure of a man in his early fifties, his cheeks flecked with stubble, his eyes hollowed and surrounded by dark circles. Manninger looked exhausted. Asch walked up to the window and shouldered the guard aside.

'Herr Manninger, Geheime Staats Polizei. I have a warrant for your arrest.'

Manninger's tired smile turned into an expression of wide-eyed horror. With a sharp bark the engine burst into life.

That fool of a border guard should have taken the ignition key, Asch thought, as he hurled himself at the window.

A gear graunched as it meshed, the door cannoned into his shoulder. Asch spun and fell on to the roadway. Smoke pouring from its shrieking tyres the car shot forward, turned and bounced over the opposite pavement.

'Halt!' Asch cried. 'Halt or we'll open fire!'

The car was too wide to make the turn. Its front wing clanged against a pylon. It reversed frenziedly back into the road.

Asch clambered to his feet and waved to the men in the control hut. They rushed out in an untidy line, Ernte submachine-guns held loosely at their waists.

Manninger had got his car straightened and pointing towards Switzerland.

'Halt!' Asch cried again.

The car streaked towards the Swiss border.

'Fire!' Asch shouted, his voice drowned by the crackle of gunshots.

A tyre burst. The high-pitched ricochet of bullets against metal was accompanied by the sound of a long tearing skid. Then there was a horrendous clang as the car smashed into the row of pylons and stopped.

In the momentary lull that followed, Asch heard a peaceful trickling sound, like water in a brook.

He raced up to the car. A front wheel hung lopsidedly. Its proud radiator was a mass of jangled metal. He wrenched open the door. Manninger was lying against the seat, pressed into it by the large steering wheel. Blood trickled from his mouth and nose and beneath the stubble his face was an ashen grey.

With the help of the guards, Asch eased Manninger on to the pavement. He could see that the man's chest was badly crushed, that a bullet had caught him in the shoulder and another in the lower back. He lowered his head to Manninger's and whispered, 'Try to hold on. There's an ambulance on the way.'

To his surprise, Manninger's eyes flared open. There was a wild gleam in them. 'Zurich is not the source,' Manninger said, his words followed by a choking stream of blood.

Manninger coughed and spoke again. 'The source is Hellenthal. Hellenthal and the devil. The devil in the scriptures.'

Manninger was delirious, Asch thought, watching him choke in his own blood, watching Manninger try to sit up, then fall back on the pavement and go very still.

1

Dwight Khouri, Vice President of the Imtra Bank sat in his twelfth-floor office overlooking Manhattan's Pearl Street and thought about violence. He was not essentially a violent man, but soon, he was going to hit somebody, hard. Very hard.

The restlessness was like a fever gnawing at his gut. He wanted out. He wanted something different. It wasn't banking, he told himself. It was him.

He picked up the newly restrung Head and swung it viciously, the way a man prepares to hurl a hammer. His office was large enough to swing a tennis racket, and as it swished viciously to and fro, he recalled that his coach recently had occasion to tell him there was no need to hit short balls into the next county. He was big. He was strong. He knew all he had to do was lean into the shot to get all the power he needed. But lately, he'd kept swinging. Because he wanted to hit somebody. Hard.

Dwight Khouri was over six feet and just under one hundred and seventy pounds. When he hit people, they stayed hit. Not that he'd hit anyone for years. But the way to do it had been instilled deep inside him and he knew that all he'd lost was some timing and a little speed.

He threw down the racket and picked up the little glass framed case containing his Silver Star. Major Dwight Khouri. At twenty-seven he'd been one of the youngest Majors in the whole goddam army. He'd have been a fucking hero, if that was a war with any heroes. Not that it concerned him. He'd done what he'd done, and because he'd had to, and because he'd wanted to. And in that, he'd followed his father. They were the only two of a long line of immigrant Khouris to give something back to America.

Dwight stared at the case and thought of the jungle. He didn't miss the jungles of Vietnam, neither did he want to spend weeks living off K-rations, smelling like a coyote, wearing the same sweat- and mud-encrusted uniform. What he missed about Vietnam was not the jungle, but the war, the sense of purpose; the realization that everything mattered and you lived or died by your own decision, by your own mistake. The jungle hadn't been sterile, hadn't been cotton wool. Everything had meaning because everything was to do with survival.

Not like Manhattan. Not like banking.

You need a holiday, his half-brother Sami had said. A holiday, and a good woman. Sami was thirty-two, three years younger than Dwight, looked ten years older, was shorter, tubbier and happily married, with two appealing children and a wife he seemed to love. Sami liked what he was doing. He'd worked at the Imtra Bank since he was eighteen. Dwight envied his contentment.

All right, in a month he would take that holiday. He would go to Tampa with its mid-August temperatures in the low nineties and he would spend five hours a day on those slow, green clay courts driving himself beyond exhaustion, hitting short balls with precision and purging himself of violence. As for a good woman, he'd thought he'd found that in Jackie and that hadn't worked. The war and death in the jungle had taught him the impermanence of things, especially relationships, and there was no place in his life for a good woman.

Meanwhile, there was a month to go. Meanwhile, his intercom squawked that Dr Rasul Quassim, as was his habit at ten o'clock every renewal day, was waiting to see him.

Dwight went around and sat behind his wide, Scandinavian desk and prepared to receive Quassim. Banking was so predictable, he thought, so comfortable and measured. It was the most appropriate occupation for a spy who wanted in from the cold. If being out of the cold was what he wanted.

Dr Rasul Quassim was small and bony, nervous as a goat

14

on the edge of a cliff, moving with a kind of hunched obeisance, as if he wished to compress his already diminutive figure into nothingness. Quassim chain-smoked. There was a day's growth of dark stubble on his skeletal chin and he had a disconcerting habit of shaking his thighs while he sat.

The files at the bank showed Dr Rasul Quassim managed the investment portfolio of PA Investments Inc. There was little information on record besides that, though Dwight knew that Rasul Quassim came from Tifrit in Iraq, the town which had the honour of fostering President Sadam Hussein and most of Iraq's ruling junta. Dwight suspected that PA Investments and Rasul Quassim were a front for the investments of Iraq's surplus petro-dollars. But he never investigated that.

Neither did anyone else. Two years previously, America had broken off diplomatic relations with Iraq. If, until the breach healed the Iraqis wanted to invest in the United States, the American government was happy to let them – provided they were discreet.

And Dr Rasul Quassim was the soul of discretion. His office was at an accommodation address, his mail sent care of the post office. And every month, on every renewal day, he called at the Imtra Bank, at precisely ten o'clock.

In fact, there was little need for Quassim to present himself so scrupulously at the bank. His instructions could just as well have been transmitted by letter or phone. But at precisely ten o'clock on every renewal day, Quassim would sidle into Dwight's office, as if to convince himself the bank was still there.

Today, as on every other renewal day, they went through the same routine. Quassim smoked two Camels, sipped at his mint tea, spoke about the weather, a television serial which apparently held his undivided attention, and the latest response of his stomach ulcer to treatment that seemed increasingly outrageous.

'You should invest longer term,' Dwight said. 'You should invest in something more profitable than bank deposits.'

Quassim lit another cigarette, shook his legs thoughtfully and looked mournfully out of the window at the towering hulk of the Chase Manhattan Building. 'Renew deposits please for twenty-eight days,' he said.

Dwight picked up the phone and passed on the instructions to the investment department. Within seconds eighteen million dollars would begin circulating around the American banking system.

Big fucking deal.

2

The *estancia* was one hundred and fifty miles south of Buenos Aires on the edge of the pampas, by the sea. Here the air was moist and tangy with salt, the monochrome brown of the wide plains lightened by patches of green and the monotonous landscape broken by trees of chinaberry and eucalyptus. And sometimes, from the splendidly incongruous Bavarian chalet in the middle of the *estancia*, you could see flamingoes.

Johann knew where the flamingoes nested. As a boy, each winter he had watched them nurse their young, watched the awkward egrets grow to stagger drunkenly through the reeds. He had photographs of the flamingoes, black and white, out of focus snapshots taken with a Brownie, clearer pictures with the Agfa he had been given when he was fourteen, magnificent colour enlargements from pictures taken with a Rollei. Johann hadn't been near the flamingoes' nesting place for some years. He wondered if it was still there, and was sad because he knew that on this visit he did not have the time and that he would not return to the *estancia* before mid-summer.

Johann Neumann was in his late thirties and remarkably

good looking, with the static, sculptured features of a Greek bronze. A halo of curly blond hair and an angelic mouth gave him the innocent look of a choirboy, an innocence belied by his eyes which had an unwavering, brilliant hardness, and depending on the light were sometimes brown and sometimes violet. It was the kind of face one occasionally saw on the inside of a glossy magazine, advertising aperitifs, lean, perfectly defined, assured, remote.

Johann looked down the long oak table that filled the centre of the room. Karl Muller, Klaus Altman, Dr Manfred Fendt and at the head of the table, the heavily built, ramrod stiff figure of Heinrich von Kassel. These four were all that were left of the *Alte Kameraden*, all that were left of those hundreds who had escaped to South America at the end of the war to build a new Reich. Four old men. Soon all of them would be dead. The empty, throne shaped, red cushioned chairs flanking the massive table were like gravestones.

Everything he was, Johann reflected, everything he would be, he owed to the *Alte Kameraden* and to von Kassel. Von Kassel had brought him to Argentina, von Kassel had selected him from the other children and taken him to live on the *estancia*, von Kassel had brought him up as if he were his own son. In a low voice that carried the length of the room, Johann said, 'In six weeks, Elisabeth Manninger will inherit.'

He looked at each of the other men in turn. All of them knew the terms of Berndt Manninger's will. Thirty-five years ago, in order to preserve his estate for his wife and his direct descendants, Berndt Manninger had placed his vast fortune in trust. For as long as she lived, his widow, Elisabeth, was entitled to the income from the Manninger estate. The assets comprising that estate however only passed to her if she survived Manninger by thirty-five years and six months, and *if* within that period, no direct descendant of Berndt Manninger attained the age of twenty-one *and* claimed ownership of the assets by presenting to the Hoffman Bank in Zurich certain documents testifying to Manninger's ownership of the corporations whose assets comprised the estate.

'Once Elisabeth Manninger inherits,' Johann continued, 'the Manninger fortune is lost to us forever. As you all know, for many years, Elisabeth Manninger has been demonstrably of unsound mind. She cannot properly dispose of anything she inherits, and on her death, the Manninger fortune will pass to the Swiss government and the Hoffman Bank.'

'What I do not understand,' Fendt said, eyes blinking nervously behind rimless lenses, his voice high-pitched and querulous, 'is why, if we knew all this, we have not previously taken steps to secure the Manninger inheritance.'

Johann looked to the head of the table where von Kassel sat motionless. Von Kassel knew why they had not been able to act before. It was von Kassel who should explain this to the comrades.

Slowly, von Kassel nodded his close-cropped head, indicating that Johann should make the explanation.

Johann said, 'As you know, the Manninger assets administered by the Hoffman Bank are nominally owned by Swiss corporations. The assets are, in effect, Swiss, and being Swiss, have since 1945 been immune to seizure as war reparations. If at any time over the last thirty-five years, we had attempted to claim those assets, we should have had to show that those assets belonged not to the Swiss corporations, but to Manninger. That the assets were German.'

'So what's happened now?' Fendt asked. He had travelled to this meeting from the far north of Brazil. He was tired and irritable and could not see why he'd had to travel two thousand miles to discuss this obsession Heinrich had with the Manningers.

'Three months ago,' Johann said, 'the Swiss passed a Statute of Limitations. No more war reparations. Hitherto undiscovered Geman assets could be distributed to the legal heirs.'

'It was hardly necessary to bring me all the way from Manaus for this,' Fendt said testily. 'If matters are as you describe them, you should claim the inheritance.'

Johann flashed von Kassel a glance before he said, 'Not as long as Elisabeth Manninger is alive. Under the terms of Manninger's will, any heirs share the assets jointly with Elisabeth Manninger.'

'So?'

'So, Elisabeth Manninger must be eliminated, before she inherits, before we make our claim.'

A heavy cloud of silence descended on the room. Fendt removed his spectacles and polished them assiduously. Altman turned a pencil ceaselessly round and round in his stubby fingers. Karl Muller lit another Gauloise before he said, 'Enough is enough. Let the fortune go. We do not need it.'

Johann kept his gaze averted, fixed on the table. 'You do not need it,' he said, softly. 'Your time is nearly run. But we, my generation, and those that will come after us, we need the Manninger inheritance. The inheritance is rightfully *ours*.' Slowly Johann raised his head and looked at the wall above von Kassel's head.

'My father was a war criminal,' he continued, allowing the memories to flood back.

Johann had been five years old before he realized who his father had been, and that he had not gone to bring peace, but had been running away from the Americans. He clearly remembered the day he'd learned that. It was the day when some of the older boys had demonstrated with a cat how the Americans had hung his father by the neck until he was dead.

Johann looked up at Muller, the former Head of the Gestapo, at Altman, who had run the Gestapo in southern France, at Fendt who had been in charge of the experimental hospital at Auschwitz. 'There are people who know me as my father's son, people who even today will not receive me or shake me by the hand.' Johann's lips curled in contempt. 'Germans!'

Johann looked directly at Altman. 'Your children disown you. Outside our community they call themselves by other names,' At Muller. 'Your son dare not leave South America.' And Fendt. 'Even here, your son claims he is passed over for promotion because of who you were.'

'It will pass,' Fendt muttered.

'When?' Johann looked at each of the men. 'Do I have to be as old as you before I can call myself by my father's name? How many generations must pass before we cease denying who we were? What do you talk to your grandchildren about? Do you tell them who you were and what you did? Or was all that madness?'

'Enough!' Muller cried. 'We've had enough talk. Let us put the matter to the vote. I say we have no need of the Manninger inheritance, we have no need for any more violence.' He glared defiantly at Johann as he raised his hand.

Dr Manfred Fendt replaced his glasses and also raised his hand.

Klaus Altman held the pencil between his fingers, as if it were a cigarette, tapped its end softly on the pad in front of him. 'I cannot agree with you,' he said. 'We must think of the future.'

Johann let his gaze drift up the table to von Kassel. Everything depended now on von Kassel.

'It wasn't madness, Johann,' von Kassel said slowly. 'It was a magnificent dream.' He paused, staring into space, the aggressive line of his jaw softened by reminiscence. Von Kassel had come to Argentina in 1936, posing as a businessman escaping from the Reich, in reality, creating an intelligence network whose scope went far beyond the inevitable war and the end of it, which looked to fifty years hence when Germany would need to expand beyond the borders of Europe.

But fate had decreed it should not be so, that the countries which should become satellites of the Reich had become instead, their refuge. In forty-five years the world had changed. Germany was divided; the Fuhrer dead and reviled. Nationalism was no longer a vital force. The world had grown smaller, divided by vague philosophies and held together by unlikely alliances. And wars were no longer won on battlefields but in boardrooms. Economic might had proved the ultimate weapon.

And he, Heinrich von Kassel, had forged such a weapon. From the ruins of the Reich he had created an economic force that knew no territorial boundaries. He had imbued it with strength and the soldierly principles of loyalty, courage, discipline and fear of God. And now, at last, the time had come to reach out and grasp the very essence of power.

The Manninger fortune consisted of more than mere investments. Before he died, Berndt Manninger had created certain vital industrial processes, processes which could halve the world's consumption of energy and double its food production; processes which were not only valuable in themselves, but which would give their owners undreamed-of wealth, undreamed-of power. The men, the governments, who today paid tribute to Mecca would soon turn to the Gemeinschaft in South America, would revere it and respect it, as today they revered and respected the oil-rich Arabs.

The community, his community was worth millions, their tentacles spread throughout Latin America and Europe. Due to his genius, when the Gemeinschaft obtained the Manninger processes, it would take its place amongst the industrial giants of the world: Exxon, General Motors, AT & T. The community, his community would be accepted, courted, honoured, perhaps even loved. And the world would pay tribute to German genius and finally admit that for forty-five years, *they had been wrong*!

With a sigh, von Kassel turned his attention to the men in the room. 'Elisabeth Manninger will be eliminated,' he said, his voice rough.

Johann felt his heart surge with relief, his shoulders go slack. He pushed his shaking hands under the table, as Fendt and Muller lowered their arms.

'Then, so be it,' Muller said and lit another Gauloise with a flourish that was as symbolic as a washing of hands.

'What about the girl?' von Kassel asked, the wide scar that split one saturnine cheek turning slowly livid as he thought of her. The girl! Marit von Rausenberg, the granddaughter of Berndt Manninger, the only child of Manninger's daughter, Ingrid, the only direct descendant and only legal claimant to the Manninger fortune. Slowly von Kassel shook his head. He should have ensured that the girl had been more thoroughly disciplined, that she had been broken before he'd allowed Joachim Myrdhal to take her to Germany. He should have anticipated more fully the dangerous influences in Germany that could erode the values he had so patiently instilled into her at the *estancia*. 'Without the girl we have nothing,' he said.

Johann laughed confidently. 'Don't worry about Marit,' he said. 'I saw her in Munich last week. She is happy to co-operate. After all, Marit is one of us. She is a child of the damned.'

Von Kassel looked doubtful as he unrolled a Partagas. 'In that case, my son,' he said, 'you must go to Zurich and do what has to be done. I will meet you there, afterwards.'

3

In his stiff-soled shoes and off-the-peg GUM suit, Pyotr Voskov felt like a peasant as he walked along the strip of thick red carpet that led from the door to the ornate desk of Economics and Planning Minister, Feliks Andronov. The desk was tall and very wide, its panels carved and inlaid with mother-of-pearl, its top covered with soft, red Morocco. Krupskaya Lenin had once used that desk.

As he walked the interminable length of the carpet, Voskov kept his eyes fixed on the massive frieze above the Minister's head, which depicted a muscular, shirt-sleeved, eight-foot-tall

Lenin exhorting a line of shadowy workers to follow him through the panelled ceiling. Minister Andronov was nothing if not a patriot.

Educated at the Trotsky (now Brezhnev) Workers Institute in Kublin, a former union leader and manager of a ball-bearing factory, Andronov had risen to his present eminence through scrupulous adherence to the Party line. His concept of the Western democracies had been formed at the age of sixteen from Lenin's *Imperialism, the Highest Form of Capitalism.* Nothing had happened since to alter Andronov's concept. He still looked upon the Western democracies as degenerate, corrupt and hostile. He viewed the policy of economic detente forced upon him by Russia's technological inadequacies with suspicion. Most of all he distrusted people like Pyotr Voskov who spent all their working lives living and dealing with Western politicians and industrialists.

Which was why Pyotr Voskov had taken the precaution of wearing a Russian suit which felt like a sack, and stiff-soled Russian shoes that pinched his feet. Which was why that day Pyotr Voskov felt like a peasant. A nervous peasant.

Pyotr Voskov was the Head of the East-West Trade Bureau. He was a big, well-fleshed man in his late thirties whose father was Chairman of the Administrative Organs Department of the Central Committee and effective political chief of the KGB. The East-West Trade Bureau had offices in London, Paris and New York and Pyotr Voskov cheerfully accepted the sacrifice that compelled him to live nine months a year in the decadent West.

Three days ago, Andronov had abruptly summoned Voskov to Moscow. And for three days, Pyotr Voskov had worn his GUM suit and stiff-soled shoes and waited to be admitted into the Minister's presence. Now, as he limped along the strip of red carpet, Voskov told himself he had nothing to worry about. His work was without blemish and his father was one of the most powerful people in Russia. Nevertheless, a small, disquieting voice kept reminding him that he was in Russia, that he didn't have to do anything wrong to be punished, that his own disgrace might be the first indication of his father's fall from power. When he stopped before Andronov's desk, Voskov's pendulous lips were very dry.

Andronov was a small, sleek-headed man, with hands that were surprisingly pale and delicate. Now, as he closed the file he had been reading and rested those small, perfectly shaped hands on the red cover, he reminded Voskov more than ever of a lizard waiting to snatch a dragonfly out of the air.

Andronov indicated he should sit in one of the armchairs arranged in a semi-circle four feet away from the desk, at which Krupskaya had once sat. 'I have just seen a delegation of Western bankers,' Andronov said. 'They are anxious that we should intervene in Poland.'

Pyotr sat uncertain whether any comment was required.

'Yesterday,' Andronov continued, 'I saw the British and American economic attachés. They hinted we should not get involved in Poland. Tell me, comrade Voskov, how I should interpret these messages? Tell me, what do your friends in the West really want?'

'I have no friends in the West,' Pyotr said quickly, knowing even as he said it that his denial would do little good if Andronov and his cohorts ever got into the Politbureau. He told Andronov how democracy was an impractical system, that it had neither central core nor direction and was in essence a series of temporary compromises between disparate interests.

He gave Pyotr a tight smile, revealing three shining teeth of pure, stainless steel. 'That is why I have summoned you to Moscow. I have a plan. I want you to help me.'

Pyotr felt relief surge through him like water from a burst dam. He arranged his face into an expression of polite interest. 'I am always at your service, Minister,' he murmured.

Andronov's smile widened momentarily and then was gone. 'What is our total debt to the Western banks?'

'Not much. About three point five billion dollars.'

'No, no. I mean the total debt. The total COMECON debt?'

'About ninety billion dollars.'

'And how is that made up?'

'Poland with its twenty-three billion dollars is the largest. Then there are the community banks, IBEC and IIB, with nineteen and ten billion respectively. Hungary must owe about ten billion, Yugoslavia, seven point five, Rumania, four point two –'

Andronov held up his hand. 'Enough.' He thrust his narrow face across the desk at Pyotr. 'Tell me, comrade, what do you think will happen if we and those whom we influence default on their loans?'

Pyotr made a quick calculation. Andronov was talking of ninety billion dollars. Ninety thousand million dollars! A phrase he had heard in America floated across his brain. The shit would hit the fan.

Quietly he explained. Under Western banking law, if anyone defaulted on a loan, the loan and interest had to be written off. Both balance sheets and profit and loss accounts would be depleted. The lending ratios of the banks – and that included the majority of the big Western banks – would be affected. Other loans would have to be called in. Interest rates would rise. Businesses suddenly deprived of working capital would go bankrupt. There would be panic. Other countries might default. Banks would collapse. The entire Western economy could spiral frenziedly to destruction. 'But it won't come to that,' Pyotr said. 'Before things got that far, governments would intervene.'

'And what will governments do?' Andronov asked.

'They will change laws. They will print new money. They will subject us to diplomatic, cultural and propagandist pressures. They will intensify their embargoes. They might even go –'

'But they won't go to war,' Andronov interrupted. 'And to do any of these things will take time, is that right?'

Pyotr nodded.

'So if we move quickly, none of these things will happen?'. Pyotr stopped nodding.

Andronov tapped his slender fingers impatiently on the desk. Then he said, 'Suppose, just suppose, that on a certain day in September, we announce the cessation of all interest on capital payments. What then will happen to the dollar?'

'It will sink like a lead weight in a fish pond.'

'And gold?'

Pyotr looked up at Lenin. 'It will go through the ceiling.'

Andronov rested his head against the back of his chair. He looked well satisfied. 'Then, comrade, that is what we shall do.'

Pyotr's mind raced. A short-term collapse of the dollar and an escalation in the price of gold would enable Russia to buy the food it needed at bargain prices. Properly organized, they could be in and out of the markets in three days. Afterwards there would be recriminations, but no permanent damage.

'I would like you to arrange this for me,' Andronov said. 'I would like you to submit your plan to me in two days.' Andronov came round from behind his large desk.

He really was quite a tiny little man, Pyotr thought, as he got to his feet. 'Of course, Minister,' he said.

He savoured the experience of being taken by the Minister's hand and escorted to the door. It had never happened before, and probably would never happen again.

At the door, Andronov released him and for the first time since Pyotr had known him looked vaguely embarrassed. 'Tell me, comrade,' he asked, shyly. 'What do you think of my plan?'

'Minister,' Pyotr said with feeling, 'you are a genius.'

4

All that afternoon Pyotr Voskov sat in his office working out how Andronov's plan could be implemented. The trouble was that it was myopic, which made it a nonsense plan, a no-win plan. As soon as the West realized what had happened and why, all trust in the financial integrity of Russia and the Eastern Bloc would cease. Western investment would be curtailed and sales of technology stopped. Russia's economic development would be set back twenty years – and all for fifty million tons of wheat!

Pyotr gave off a small sigh. What else could one expect from a person whose knowledge of economic theory had been gleaned at a Workers Institute in where was it – Kublin. Pyotr's own early education had been at an exclusive school for the children of senior bureaucrats, and from there he'd proceeded to Moscow University and graduated with the Lenin Prize for Applied Economic Theory and the Malyshev Award for Economic History. It was his duty to ensure that if Andronov's plan was implemented, Russia would be safe.

To succeed, Andronov's plan had to have a greater objective than the mere buying in of the year's wheat shortfall cheaply. And the plan had the potential to achieve that greater objective. Properly developed and implemented, the plan could be enlarged to obtain a stranglehold on Western industry, to give Russia permanent and unfettered access to the technology it sorely needed.

Pyotr lit a Marlboro and wondered if he dared do it. He would have to work alone. There was no one he could trust, and if he succeeded, he could allow no doubt as to who the real architect had been. If he succeeded, Pyotr thought, the Politbureau would have no alternative but to dismiss

Andronov and his bunch of union veterans who still believed they were fighting the White Armies. The Politbureau would have to appoint a Minister of Economics who was familiar with the ways of the West.

Pyotr Fyodorovich Voskov, Minister of Economics and Planning of the Union of Soviet Socialist Republics. Pyotr liked the sound of that.

His office was a four-roomed affair on the sixteenth floor of a modern tower block overlooking Kalinin Prospekt. Apart from Pyotr's own room, and a small cubicle where his staff of four middle-aged ladies brewed tea, the rest of the office was taken up by files. Files on every foreign investment project in the USSR. Files on every foreign investor.

Now Pyotr summoned the four middle-aged ladies to his room and asked them to produce a list of every foreign company that had investments in the USSR, and which was controlled by less than five entities.

The list did not take long to prepare. Most of the companies trading in Russia were giants: the Ford Motor Company, Montedison, Davy Powergas GmbH, Creusot Loire, Imperial Chemical Industries. Giant corporations were best equipped to deal with giant bureaucracies, and there were only seven companies that could be described as being controlled by a few people, four of these being specialist suppliers of components with no permanent base nor large investments inside Russia. Pyotr saw that the other three companies had combined to form a consortium to construct three aromatic plants in Omsk, Ufa and Gorky.

Pyotr had the file on the consortium brought to his office and dismissed the ladies. He remembered the consortium had been headed by Topf Industrie of Frankfurt and recalled meeting Topf at the outset of the negotiations, a man in his early seventies whose career had begun in the early 1920s with Inter-Chemie AG. Topf had built Inter-Chemie into one of Germany's largest chemical corporations, then initiated the formation of the Aktiegesselschaft, that enormous German cartel that had dominated European industry between the wars. For his efforts in aiding Hitler's war machine, Topf had been sentenced to seven years at Nuremberg, although he emerged after three to create Topf Industrie. Pyotr remembered Topf as cautious, pedantic and punctillious and that he was the controlling shareholder in Topf Industrie.

The second member of the consortium, Vickery Industries Limited was headed by Sir Bernard Vickery, and though its shares were quoted on the London Stock Exchange, the majority of the holdings were owned by the Vickery family trust. From the file, Pyotr saw that Vickery's financial commitment had been less than twenty per cent, and seemed to have compensated for this by the provision of personal and technical services.

The largest contributor to the consortium had been SummiTco. SummiTco had contributed over five hundred million dollars, more than half the consortium's financial requirement. However, there was little information on the file about SummiTco, except that its headquarters were in Miami, and that it was run by Raison Tearkes. The file showed that neither Tearkes nor any SummiTco representatives had ever visited Russia. Intriguing, Pytor thought, that the largest contributor should leave everything in the hands of Topf, and walked out into the main office and picked up copies of the *Wall Street Journal* and the *Financial Times*. SummiTco wasn't listed in either of the papers. Pyotr looked up a recent edition of *Who's Who in Business*. Nothing.

He wandered into the ladies' cubicle and picked up a stack of back numbers of *Fortune* magazine. There, an hour later, he finally found Raison Tearkes.

Tearkes was featured in an article appropriately entitled, *America's Invisible Rich*. Opposite the lead page were postage-stamp-sized photographs of America's private rich. Pyotr stared at the photograph above the caption, which read, *Raison Tearkes, 64, SummiTco Holdings Inc, Miami. Holding company with diversified investments. $500–650 million.*

Tearkes was a stern-looking man, with a weathered face, a

thick, silvery moustache and a close cropped semi-circle of white hair. It was a hard face. The mouth had a ruthless curve to it; there was a look of careful calculation in the eyes. A right son of a bitch, Pyotr thought, a mean, no nonsense son of a bitch.

The body of the article contained a history of SummiTco which had been built on the ruins of the US Styrite Corporation, a company which had once held the world monopoly of a lightweight metal, styrium. In 1953, the US Styrite Corporation together with Willard and Raison Tearkes had been indicted with having conspired to fix prices, divide the market and control the output of styrium. The forty-two charges were the longest in Anti-Trust history; the penalties the most severe since the passing of the Sherman Act. The company was ordered to cease those practices and dispose of those processes through which it had controlled the styrium market for thirty-three years. The two Tearkes and the company were fined a total of $3,474,500 and Willard Tearkes was sentenced to three years in jail.

An hour after the judgement was delivered Willard Tearkes had shot himself. The already depressed stock value of the US Styrite Co had plummeted and as competitors had rushed to buy the company at a fraction of its true worth, Raison Tearkes had to liquidate the Tearkes fortune.

One by one, he had disposed of the assets of Tearkes Holdings, the company created by his father to invest the family profits. The investments in rubber were the first to go, then coal, then the vinyl flooring company, the food processing operation. In the end, all that was left was an electronics company which nobody wanted, a ridiculously expensive synthetic oil process and a minority stake in a pharmaceutical company. In less than three months, the Tearkes fortune, which had taken nearly sixty years to accumulate, had virtually disappeared; and while Raison Tearkes was not exactly bankrupt, by his own estimate, he was pretty damn close to it.

Then followed what *Fortune* described as a saga of triumph

over adversity that would have made even Horatio Alger blink. Raison Tearkes consolidated his cash and what was left of his investments, and changed the name of Tearkes Holdings to SummiTco. With help from a friendly banker, he acquired the pharmaceuticals company. In 1956, riding a wave of confidence following the company's announcement of a new type of birth control pill, Tearkes took SummiTco to market. A year later, in one of those manoeuvres that Pyotr never quite understood, he acquired a light aircraft company. It was the start of the boom in executive air travel. One light aircraft company became two. The electronics company announced a new form of transistor, the pharmaceuticals company, a new drug for stomach ulcers. In 1959, using the time honoured technique of buying companies out with their own cash, Tearkes acquired the Twinsburg store chain, and promptly used the value of their real estate to acquire a pinball and slot-machine manufacturing concern. Other acquisitions followed rapidly, companies dealing in computer software, terminals and controls systems, construction, another pharmaceutical company, an oil refinery, each acquisition producing new assets which in turn could be used in an ever-expanding circle to acquire still more assets.

During the years 1958 to 1968, SummiTco's reported earnings per share averaged a phenomenal 32.3 per cent. In 1969 it fell to half that, in 1970 to 6.96 per cent. In 1971 and 1972 SummiTco showed negative returns. Financial experts commented that SummiTco was too highly geared. Shareholders complained that performance had declined and growth that was dependent on acquisitions was neither safe nor productive. Business consultants wrote that large, diverse groups were inefficient.

In 1973, helped by appraisers taking a doomsday view of the oil crisis, Raison Tearkes bought out every single outside shareholder. SummiTco became his personal property, with no obligation to make public filings of financial information.

In the years that followed, SummiTco was reorganized.

Unprofitable acquisitions were disposed of and Tearkes's personal control over his empire grew tighter. The rapid succession of acquisitions ended. Over the past seven years, Tearkes had bought carefully and discreetly into new growth industries, micro computers, memory circuits, satellite TV, in every case, acquiring only a large shareholding and the right to influence the companies' policies.

Pyotr tore out the article and put it away carefully in his briefcase. Raison Tearkes and SummiTco were ideal for what he had in mind. All he had to do was arrange for Tearkes to co-operate, and Pyotr felt sure he knew how to achieve that.

That evening, Pyotr dined with his father at Palkins. And the next day, having given Andronov what he wanted, Pyotr had his Paris office arrange a meeting with Raison Tearkes.

5

Raison Tearkes stood amidst the lush foliage of the roof garden watching the red and white SummiTco Bell Ranger flutter over the island. He was a big man, tall and raw boned with vast triangular forearms protruding from his pale cream safari jacket. His face was obscured by the shade of a wide-brimmed hat and a massive pair of sunglasses, the discernible skin of his face and neck thick and brown, patchworked with creases that had the texture of roughened bark. Standing a few feet away from Tearkes was a guard. Both men were hidden from the helicopter by the foliage and almost hidden from each other.

The mansion in whose roof garden they stood, and the island on which the mansion was built, belonged to Tearkes. His grandfather had first bought the island in 1896 and it had remained in the family until 1953. In 1965, Tearkes had re-purchased the island. He'd rebuilt the mansion and re-opened the styrite mines on the west of the island. There was little styrium left on the island and an even smaller demand for it. But still, Tearkes kept the mines going, and every night an electric sign, the size of a drive-in movie screen, was lit up. It faced the mainland and defiantly proclaimed UNITED STATES STYRIUM LIVES!

The mansion was a massive, thirty-roomed structure, three storeys high and enormously wide, its white walls yellowed by heat and salt, the paint on its military green shutters beginning to flake. Tearkes had completed rebuilding the mansion six years ago and had since used it as an alternative to the SummiTco headquarters in downtown Miami.

Most days the helicopter darted frenetically between the island and Miami, ferrying worried-looking executives and earnest-looking businessmen. But on Friday afternoons, the traffic diminished. And on this particular afternoon, the helicopter was carrying only a single passenger.

Tearkes watched the helicopter bubble brightly over the palm trees and descend to hover level with the roof garden. The Russian was tall, plump and round shouldered, huddling morosely into a tan, epauletted raincoat and looking nervously at the ground. Tearkes wondered what the hell Pyotr Voskov wanted.

Tearkes waited for Voskov in the boardroom. It was a vastly spacious room, occupying the entire second floor of the mansion. Wide windows ran along three sides of it, and at one end was a raised concrete platform, separated by a movable glass screen. Behind the screen was a huge fan-shaped console, before whose constantly winking lights an ever changing team of girls maintained constant communication with SummiTco's varied business interests.

Above the console was a semi-circular bank of television screens, each linked to separate share information services in Frankfurt, Paris, Zurich, London, Hong Kong, Tokyo, Los Angeles and New York. At that time of the day, only the American exchanges were open, and the screens connected to them flashed out the information in a series of flickering green figures.

Tearkes usually worked at a large mahogany desk below the platform, beside which was a computer terminal of the kind used at airline ticket counters. Opposite Tearkes's desk were two comfortable leather armchairs, and at the far end of the room, a large pinewood table, surrounded by eighteen cane armchairs, covered with highly coloured cushions. It was an impressive room, combining luxury, grace and space-age efficiency.

As Tearkes expected, Voskov was unable to hide his awe.

Voskov's eyes kept wandering along the length of the room, unable to cope immediately with its size and blend of styles, his attention drawn irresistibly to the goldfish bowl display of technology above Tearkes's head. Tearkes remembered how he had once driven the ageing, but still lusty, president of Conco Aircraft to distraction, by having a smooth-legged girl walk between the displays throughout an entire meeting. Tearkes fought back a laugh. He'd got Conco Aircraft and randy old Elmer Tuttle hadn't got the girl.

'Take off your coat and sit down,' Tearkes said, giving no indication where the Russian should sit.

Pyotr dabbed at his forehead with a monogrammed handkerchief. The flight had been bumpy, the landing like riding a roller-coaster. Then guards had surrounded him and rushed him across the lawn, up two flights of stairs and along a baking hot terrace into this room. He was perspiring and out of breath, and his stomach was still somewhere near his throat.

Nevertheless, he forced himself to take off his coat, to sit down and remain completely still until his breathing returned to normal. Nothing in the *Fortune* photograph had led him to expect so very big a man. Even seated, Tearkes looked tall. And seated, standing or lying down, he was massive. Pyotr couldn't help staring at the width of those shoulders and the size of those forearms splayed with menacing casualness on Tearkes's desk. Tearkes could lift that

34

desk as if it were a matchbox. And if it came to it, he could probably lift that concrete platform with all its Disneyland fantasy of gadgetry. 'I am the Head of the East-West Bureau,' Pyotr said formally. 'We are responsible for all trade between the Soviet Bloc and the Western group of countries.'

Tearkes didn't say anything.

'We, that is to say, my government and the East-West Bureau wish to congratulate you on the exemplary manner in which the factories at Omsk, Ufa and Gorky have been completed.'

Still Tearkes didn't say anything. Not only had the *Fortune* photograph given no indication of Tearkes's size, it had not indicated the brute force of his presence. The man was like a massive slab of radioactive rock, still, but charged with lethal energy. 'There are some other projects which I feel you might be interested in,' Pyotr said, feeling uncomfortable at the sound of his own voice. 'Mutually profitable projects.'

Tearkes stared silently at the Russian with his big soft face, full mouth and rounded jowls. Voskov was wearing a Cardin lightweight, no less, and beneath the inch of Hathaway shirt cuff, there was a gold banded Piaget. A Commissar in fancy threads, Tearkes thought, then catching a whiff of the man's aftershave, a bloody fancy boy, who was opening his Gucci briefcase.

'Leave it,' Tearkes snapped. 'Show those papers to Bruno Topf. Topf deals with Russia.'

'But Topf does not own a company that manufactures computer tape drives,' Voskov said. 'A company that is in serious trouble.'

Tearkes came slowly erect in his chair, freezing his face into immobility. The fancy boy Commissar had done his homework. Data Comp, SummiTco's computer data storage subsidiary, was in trouble. The market for tape storage had stopped growing, and the big manufacturers had hit back at Data Comp's compatible storage systems with new designs. A crash programme to move into disc storage had cost millions, without any tangible result. In two years, Data

35

Comp had turned from a high profit earner to an unsaleable liability that was bleeding SummiTco dry. 'What's your interest in data storage systems?' Tearkes asked.

'We have many old computers in Russia,' Voskov said. 'We understand that your company's storage systems are compatible with the systems produced by the major computer manufacturers, and that your company's product is cheaper.'

'That is correct.'

Voskov flashed him a shy smile and opened his briefcase, without interruption. 'Our Economics Ministry estimates the market for tape storage drives at eight hundred and fifty million dollars annually.'

Which meant, Tearkes calculated, with no re-tooling or re-designing necessary, profits of somewhere between twenty-five and forty per cent, between two hundred and three hundred and fifty million dollars.

'We are looking for a source of supply,' Voskov said, and thrust a sheaf of papers across the desk. 'I have here, heads of agreement.'

Tearkes looked at the papers quickly. It was a perfectly standard agreement guaranteeing three years' purchase of tape drives at a price in accord with Data Comp's current price structure. Tearkes felt his relief replaced by suspicion. It was unlike the Russians not to check out other sources of supply, unlike any large buyer not to negotiate a special price. 'The agreement looks fine,' he said, non-committally.

'But as is stated in clause thirteen of the agreement, there is a pre-condition.'

Tearkes nodded while Voskov took out another piece of paper. 'The original of that condition is deposited in a bank in Switzerland,' he said. 'The condition requires that you, SummiTco and all its subsidiaries co-operate fully in the Zolata Project, and that this agreement only becomes effective if the Zolata Project is successful.'

'What the hell is the Zolata Project?' Tearkes asked.

Voskov replaced the paper in his hand with another.

'Some friends and I – we wish – how do you say it – to diversify our investments. We wish to acquire some banks. We would be grateful for your assistance.' Pyotr slid the typewritten sheet across the desk to Tearkes.

Slowly Tearkes drew the paper towards him, then casually allowed his eyes to glance down at it. Glanced, and stared in amazement. *'Banks to be acquired'*, he read. *'United States: Bank of America, Citicorp, Chase Manhattan, Manufacturers Hanover, J P Morgan.'* Jesus! The five biggest banks in the U S of A! *'United Kingdom: Barclays, National Westminster. Germany: Deutsche Bank, Dresdner Bank, Kommerz Bank.'* Tearkes looked up at Voskov. Voskov was staring mildly out of the room at the private marina where the SummiTco motor yacht rode high in the water. *'Switzerland: Union Banque Suisse. Belgium: Banque de Bruxelles, Banque Lambert.'* This dude Commissar was out of his head. All he was trying to do was buy thirteen of the largest and most prestigious banks in the world.

'It's impossible,' Tearkes said.

'Nothing's impossible. Do you realize that it would only take the OPEC countries fifteen years to buy every single share quoted on every single stock exchange in the world?'

Tearkes turned to the computer and typed out a request for the net worth of Voskov's shopping list. 'Who are your friends?' he asked. 'Arabs?'

'The others involved are people like me, people planning for their retirement.'

Tearkes had a lunatic vision of the entire Politbureau retiring to the West and administering its banks; Comrade Brezhnev at the Bank of America and Premier Kosygin sharing control of the Chase Manhattan with David Rockefeller. 'Why banks?' he asked, 'when for the kind of money you're going to need, you could by *both* Exxon and Mobil.'

'We seek respectability,' Voskov said, piously.

And influence, Tearkes thought, and information. The Russian government was going to acquire thirteen of the West's biggest banks. And why not? Banks were a sound investment. Banks exercised influence. Banks had access to confidential information, especially in Europe where they were allowed to be large investors in major corporations. But if the Russian government was involved, why was Voskov talking to him and not to the Moscow-Narodny? 'You'd better tell me who else is involved,' Tearkes said. 'If there are others, I want names.'

'I will give you that information, later.'

Tearkes looked down at the computer screen. 'That little lot will cost you around thirty-five billion dollars, give or take a couple of million.'

'Less,' Pyotr Voskov said, confidently. He explained that they didn't need to acquire all the shares in the banks. All they had to do was buy around five per cent of each bank, which because of the spread of shareholdings would give them the influence and control they wanted and also preserve their anonymity.

Tearkes listened carefully. Voskov's scheme had a brutal obviousness, a devastating simplicity. The acquisitions were only a matter of organization, timing, corporate camouflage and of course, money. The possibilities afterwards were endless.

Banks. Money. Influence. Power. Tearkes saw the equation clearly. Wealth, influence and knowledge could be used to generate more wealth, more influence, more knowledge. Progress would be geometric. It would be rapid, startling. He'd done it before, parlaying a million dollar company into something three hundred times its size. And now he would have more than a million to play with. He could involve the consortium and turn tens of millions into hundreds. In less than a year they would be bigger than Exxon. And after that, there was no limit to what they could do. 'Why talk to me about this?' Tearkes asked.

'Because you know how these things are done. You have experience in the secret acquisition of companies.'

'So have countless others.'

'But you are the only one that I know who hates the government and the business establishment, who seeks revenge for what they did to your father and the US Styrite Corporation in 1953. You are the only person I have found, and believe me, Mr Tearkes, I have researched this matter very thoroughly, who combines this lust for revenge with the necessary skill, ruthlessness and ambition. You are not content with having built SummiTco into a large private company, are you, Mr Tearkes? You want to see SummiTco take its place amongst the industrial giants. You are beyond money, Mr Tearkes, but not beyond ambition.'

'And you,' Tearkes retorted, angrily. 'What do you get out of this? A dacha on the Black Sea or do you mean to defect?'

Voskov patted his ample thighs lightly and smiled. 'No, Mr Tearkes. I do not mean to do that. You see, if that Zolata Project succeeds, I will be the new Minister of Economics and Planning. Which means that in three years, when I am forty-one, I will be the youngest member of the Politbureau. Which means that in approximately fifteen years, I will also be its most senior member.'

'You,' Tearkes breathed. 'You the supreme head of Russia!'

'I too am ambitious,' Voskov said.

'And how will you find the two billion dollars you need to get these banks?'

'Much less,' Pyotr said. 'You see, soon an event will occur that will drive the value of bank shares – how do you say it – into the ground.'

'What event?'

It was Voskov's turn to go silent.

Not a surprise nuclear attack, Tearkes decided. A nuclear attack would depress all shares, permanently. So, a conventional war in Europe? No, that wouldn't necessarily depress bank shares; it could even raise them because of anticipated inflationary profits. So it wasn't war, at least not the shooting kind. 'When will this event take place?' he asked.

Voskov pursed his lips tightly together and shook his head. 'I have to be sure of you.'

'Is it one event?'

Voskov nodded.

'Occurring over what length of time?'

'A few minutes.'

Tearkes wondered what could happen in a few minutes that would depress the share prices of the world's leading banks. What was it that linked Chase Manhattan, Morgan Guarantee, the National Westminster and the Union Bank of Switzerland? What was it that linked all banks? Money. So it had to do with money. Not only money, lending . . . interest . . . that was it. Tearkes said, 'You bastards are going to renege on your loans,' and saw Voskov's bulbous eyes blink open, very wide. 'That's what you sons of bitches are going to do. Renege on your loans.'

Slowly, Vokov nodded. 'I know when, and I know how. Without that information, everything I have told you is useless. Now, will you help me or will you not?'

'All right,' Tearkes said, 'but I have one condition.'

'Mr Tearkes, if that contract is implemented, you will make nearly a billion dollars in three years. That is the only condition.'

Tearkes said, 'There is nothing wrong with making a second billion. I want SummiTco to participate. Also Topf, Vickery and Brassard.'

Voskov thought rapidly. Once Tearkes had started to implement the scheme, he could participate whether Vokov liked it or not. 'Participate? To what extent?'

'Forty per cent. All investments, expenses and profits to be divided between us on that basis.'

'I must have control,' Voskov said.

'You will have control.' Tearkes explained how the banks'

40

shares would be acquired by nominee companies in Switzerland, Luxembourg, Cayman and the Bahamas and how each of the companies would be owned as to sixty per cent by a company Voskov would incorporate, and the remainder by Sabator SA, a Swiss company. 'There will be agreements between your company, Sabator and the nominee companies,' Tearkes continued, 'giving you unfettered access to all information received by those companies and of course, as the controlling shareholder, those companies will be subject to your direction.'

Voskov thought about that for a moment before he said, 'That will be acceptable.'

Voskov remained on the island for another two hours, while Tearkes hand-wrote an agreement which they both signed and described how the scheme would operate. When Voskov left, he was certain he'd made the right choice in Raison Tearkes, and that his plan would work.

Tearkes too was certain that the plan would work. But he had no intention of leaving Voskov in control of it, nor the Russians influencing Western industry. Soon after Voskov left, he placed three telephone calls to Bruno Topf, Sir Alex Vickery and Odile Brassard, and asked them to meet with him in London in three days' time. Then he called Gerhardt Hoffman at the Hoffman Bank in Zurich and arranged a meeting there in four days' time.

'So you know,' Hoffman said, nervously.

'Know what?'

'The Gemeinschaft is preparing to make a claim against the Manninger estate. One of their lawyers has just left my office.'

Tearkes had a feeling of dangling over empty space. Manninger had been finished with years ago, his ill-gotten fortune doled out to his crazed widow in dribs and drabs, his processes and his files lost for ever.

The files! Manninger had maintained duplicate files on Brunhilde. Those files would implicate not only himself, but every other allied businessman who'd worked together with the Germans throughout the war! And not only businessmen. Governments!

The Gemeinschaft had to be stopped. But how? Soon after the war, the OSS had tried to find the files and failed. He and the consortium had already tried to find the files and also failed. He'd bought the Hoffman Bank hoping to find where Manninger had secreted his files and discovered that Hoffman didn't know any more about them than he did.

Those files had to be found. Every inch of Switzerland had to be scoured if necessary. But he couldn't do it. Neither could the consortium. To find those files and dispose of them would require greater authority than he or the consortium commanded. Governmental authority.

Tearkes thought he should get the CIA after those files. After all, he had influence with the CIA and dammit, he had a Presidential order for the destruction of the files. The case went beyond his own need, and the CIA could safely be involved. God dammit he would use them. After all, they owed it to him.

6

The next day, Pyotr flew to London and on Sunday he met with Valeri Gursev, the Head of the Moscow-Narodny Bank. Andronov had already cabled Gursev to expect Pyotr on a vital and very secret mission. In view of the mission's total secrecy, Gursev insisted they met away from the Russian Embassy, the Moscow-Narodny Bank and Gursev's home in the Russian Trade Delegation compound off Highgate's West Hill.

So for an hour and a half that Sunday afternoon, Pyotr and

Gursev walked on Hampstead Heath. Pyotr, loathing all forms of exercise, hated every minute of it.

Pyotr told Gursev 500,000 ounces of gold were already in transit to the Moscow-Narodny in London and Zurich. Immediately following Andronov's announcement, Gursev was to commence selling the gold. The fall in the value of the dollar was expected to balance out the levelling-off effect of putting so much gold on the market in a short time, so substantial profits were expected.

Pyotr himself would look after the currency transactions. Starting tomorrow, Gursev was to begin converting six hundred million dollars' worth of the bank's Euro-dollar holdings into Japanese and European currencies. The mixture should be weighted in favour of the pound sterling, which, because of its underlying oil base, was expected to depreciate less than the other currencies.

Why not sell the dollar short? Gursev enquired. To Pyotr's irritation, he began to explain what he meant. All the bank had to do was to enter into a number of agreements, promising to sell six hundred million dollars on the day of Andronov's annoucement. If the dollar fell, all they would have to do was go into the market, buy the dollars they needed and deliver it to the purchasers.

'That won't work,' Pyotr said. 'Firstly, to have so many contracts outstanding on that day would draw attention to us. Secondly, we don't know how much the dollar will fall on that day. Thirdly, we still are going to be left with dollars. My way is better.' In retaliation, he explained.

They would sell their dollars now and acquire other currencies. Once the dollar fell, they would go into the market and buy dollars, hopefully acquiring their six hundred million dollars, for four hundred million worth of foreign currency. Alternatively, they would go all the way and exchange their entire stock of foreign currency for dollars, converting their six hundred million dollars to say, eight hundred million, which if the dollar recovered,

43

following a settlement between America and Russia, would then represent a profit of two hundred million.

Pyotr went on to explain that Moscow had decided that the gold and currency transactions be kept separate to reduce the chances of the scheme being discovered by the Americans. Gursev was to deposit the proceeds of the Euro-dollars with the Mozche Bank in Geneva, for the account of the East-West Trade Bureau.

'And if I refuse,' Gursev snorted.

'Then, comrade, I suggest you start packing your bag for Moscow.'

The next day in Paris, Pyotr instructed his staff to change all their purchase contracts into dollars, and their sales contracts to sterling, marks, Swiss francs or gold. When, later that day he met an Iraqi arms-buying delegation for lunch, he insisted they made all their payments in gold, and the next afternoon in Frankfurt, had Germany's largest importer of vodka agree to make payments in marks.

On the Thursday of that week, Pyotr was in Geneva feeling slightly dyspeptic from the travelling and nervous strain. He spent the morning with Dr Bieler, the Chairman of the Mozche Bank who could hardly suppress his enthusiasm when he learned that his bank was to be the recipient of six hundred million dollars' worth of assorted currencies and nearly two million dollars' worth of gold. Pyotr instructed Bieler to loan out the money on twenty-four-hour call, and hold the gold to his order. He had fifty thousand dollars transferred to the account of Sabator SA at the Hoffman Bank in Zurich and asked Dr Bieler to buy him a company.

Like all good Swiss bankers, Dr Bieler had a company ready, waiting and raring to go. The company was called Blissan SA, and it took only minutes for the formalities to be completed and details of the company to be telexed to the Hoffman Bank in Zurich.

That Monday, Tearkes flew to Washington, where he

lunched with Randall Hopner in the chandeliered elegance of the Madison's Montpelier restaurant.

Hopner was a man of about Tearkes's own age, with a lived-in, comfortable-looking face. He had worked with Tearkes in the OSS Economic Division. He had joined the CIA at its inception, and done tours in Korea, the Middle East and Vietnam. He was now a Deputy Director of Operations, four years away from retirement.

'I thought you couldn't stand Washington,' he said, in his nicotine strained voice.

'I like Washington,' Tearkes replied, sipping his vodka martini. 'It's the crap artists who live in it I can't take.'

'So what's brought you here? Something important?'

'Dead right, Hop.' Hopner had been Tearkes's personal assistant at the OSS, and had never been known as Randall, or Randy. One of the standing jokes in the Dulles office in Geneva had been, 'Have Hop step over here.'

'It's Brunhilde,' Tearkes said and looked around him. None of the tables near them were occupied.

'Brunhilde was a long time ago.'

'Long time or not, it could still bust a lot of people. It could make a lot of governments, including ours, look damned silly.'

'Okay, so what's happened with Brunhilde?'

Tearkes looked round again and leaned across the table. 'Had a call from the Hoffman Bank in Switzerland. Someone's looking for the Brunhilde files. Someone who could be Russian.'

'The Manninger files?'

Slowly, Tearkes nodded.

'What chance do you think they have of finding the Manninger files?'

Tearkes shrugged. 'Who the hell knows? It was all so long ago. But they could be lucky.'

'We should have made those files a priority in 1945.'

'We did,' Tearkes said, thinking of the chaos of post-war Europe, of everyone's anxiety to get home and the disbanding of the OSS. 'And we goofed. So now we've got to go after the Manninger files. You've got to help me get them, Hop.'

'Me?' Randall Hopner said. 'No way.'

'The hell you mean, no way. We were promised immunity. We were promised that Brunhilde would be buried. I don't know if you realize it, Hop, but half of Western industry is on the line here. And all the fucking governments of the so-called Free World.'

'Let's not exaggerate,' Hopner said, placatingly. He toyed with the menu as a waiter placed fresh drinks before them.

'You know SummiTco's involved in Russia,' Tearkes said. 'Think of what the Russians could do to SummiTco with that information, what they could do to everyone involved in Brunhilde who's now trading with Russia.'

Hopner put down the menu. 'I can't okay an operation in Switzerland on my own,' he said. 'Switzerland is a highly sensitive area, and the Swiss are highly sensitive. Any Swiss operation would have to go before the Operations Advisory Group, and on something like this, bet your life they'd refer it to the National Security Council, which means the President will get involved.'

'Look, Hop, I'm not asking for a fucking invasion. All you need is a few top guys from your funny money section. They know how these things are done. They'd be able to find out where Manninger buried his files, without the Swiss knowing anything. For Christ's sake, if I was still with the outfit, I could do it myself.'

'Times have changed,' Hopner said. 'We're much more structured now.'

'And you're all scared of stepping out of line.'

'Look at it my way,' Hopner said. 'What do I tell these guys over at OAG and the White House? "Hey fellas, I'd like to run a small operation in friendly, neutral Switzerland so I can pick up some files that we left behind in 1945?" Sorry, the files make a lot of big names in industry look pretty damn terrifying and the Russkis are after it. You know what our people will say? No cover ups. And as far as Pennsylvania

Avenue is concerned, those bloody businessmen deserve everything they get.'

'Tell them about the governments. Tell them about the British and the French snowing the Russkis with their office boy delegations, while the bigwigs were trying to do a deal with Hitler. Tell them about our people moving oil through – '

'Rab, you've got to understand one thing. This is going up to the White House and those boys really believe in open government. As far as they're concerned, if Chamberlain or Daladier or even our own beloved FDR screwed up, then the world has a right to know. I am not saying they're right or they're wrong. That's just how they think.'

Tearkes picked at his goose liver pâté without appetite.

Hopner said, 'I'm sorry. I'd like to help, but I know it won't work.' He speared a prawn out of the cocktail. 'How are things down on the island?'

Tearkes ignored the question and ate determinedly in silence.

Hopner said, 'I wish you wouldn't take this personally, Rab. There's really nothing I can do.'

'For Christ's sake! The Agency, the government owes us this. Don't you realize what we did? Throughout the war we traded with Germany! And do you know why we did that? Because we were asked to, by the government. Oh sure, some of us made a few bucks out of it, but we were the guys who found out about Peenemunde and the heavy water plant in Norway. We were the guys who bought the strategic material the Allies needed, paid for the design of advanced weaponry. We were the guys who persuaded German industrialists to sabotage their own plants and hinder Hitler's war effort. Now, we're going to be crucified and you tell me there is nothing you can do, and I shouldn't take it personally!'

Hopner sighed. 'Five years ago, ten, I'd have ordered half the Agency into Switzerland. But things have changed. We were publicly castrated by that Senate Committee, Rab. We don't breathe, without asking permission.'

'All that may be true,' Tearkes said, 'but you're turning me

47

down right here and now. You won't even talk to the Agency about it.'

'That's because I know what the Agency's answer will be. It isn't as if you've given me something to sell. If you had a legend, a cover story . . .'

Tearkes gulped furiously from a glass of water and attacked the filet mignon. Half-way through he asked, 'How do those shitheads feel about energy?'

'Frustrated. They've told the people all they can about the crisis. The problem is no one really believes them. No one really believes this is something that cannot be solved by the oil companies and the mighty American government.'

'Tell them about the Manninger processes,' Tearkes said. 'Tell them about his hydrogen engine, his non-chemical fertilizer, his work on geo-thermal energy.'

'We're not far away from all of that,' Hopner said. 'It's going to interest them, but they aren't going to risk diplomatic protests from Switzerland for it.'

Tearkes put his fork down and stared across the table at Hopner. 'Tell them about his mass-energy conversion and re-use of thermal by-products.'

'I will,' Hopner smiled. 'If I knew what the hell it was.'

'Energy,' Tearkes said, 'all forms of man-made energy consists of the transformation of mass into energy by heat. For example, gasoline is exploded by tiny electric sparks which release energy to drive the pistons of an engine. It is a tremendously wasteful process. At the time of his death, Manninger was working on making the process less wasteful, on extracting more energy from a given mass. In other words, with the application of the Manninger process, we could halve the gas consumption of the monoliths we all drive and the Manninger process not only applies to motor cars; it applies to heating, to aircraft, to anything that converts oil into energy. At one stroke, we halve our energy needs.'

Hopner reached for his drink. 'Is all this true, Rab?'

'I saw Manninger the day he died. He wanted to deal. Certain processes for his freedom. Certain processes so he would not be tried as a war criminal.' Tearkes shrugged. 'I told him I couldn't guarantee anything. You know how it was then. Unconditional surrender and keeping Uncle Joe Stalin happy. Manninger showed me his papers on the Mass-Energy Conversion. I put it all in my report.'

'And?'

'No one was interested. In 1945, no one dreamed of an oil crisis. My report was destroyed with the rest of the Brunhilde files.'

'And this process is in Switzerland?'

'With Manninger's Brunhilde files.'

Hopner pointed vaguely in the direction of the White House. 'If we find this process, how quickly could it be put into operation?'

Tearkes shrugged again. 'Manninger told me the process was fully developed. He wouldn't have lied about a thing like that. So I'd say it could be in use within three months to a year.'

Hopner pushed away his plate. 'I think I can sell them a limited operation. One man, perhaps two.'

'You're joking, Hop. You're going to need ten to fifteen men at least.'

Hopner shook his head. 'It's got to be low key. We can't risk upsetting the Swiss, and we can't have our Arab friends getting suspicious. Don't worry, Rab. We've got new, fancy ways of doing things now. With computers. The guy we're going to pick will be tailor-made for this job. He'll be pure gold. I promise you, he'll be better than fifteen men picked the old way.'

Tearkes said doubtfully, 'If that's the best you can do.'

'Even if I could get fifteen men,' Hopner said. 'This is still the approach I'd take.' He clicked a cigarette into life. 'Elisabeth Manninger is still alive, isn't she? Getting the processes could mean a deal with the Germans – the old Germans – you know who I mean?'

'Sure.'

'No government, no government agency can officially be

involved in such negotiations, not in an election year. Can I tell them SummiTco will front the operation?'

'Yes.'

Hopner pulled deeply at his cigarette. 'You're on the level with me, aren't you, Rab? I mean you're not using the files as a cover for the processes?'

'Of course not,' Tearkes snapped.

Hopner gave him a crooked smile. 'In that case, I suppose you wouldn't mind signing an agreement undertaking to license the processes at a miminal cost to all persons and organizations recommended by the Department of Trade.'

'I'll sign the agreement,' Tearkes said. Then he added, 'If it's to be a SummiTco operation, you'll need a SummiTco case officer.'

'The company wouldn't like that,' Hopner said. 'He's going to have to know Agency procedures, make Agency contacts.'

'The person I have in mind, is Sam Kamas,' Tearkes said. 'He's spent a long time with the Agency. He knows how they work.'

'The company may buy that,' Hopner ventured.

'They'd better,' Tearkes said. 'It would look pretty damned stupid if a SummiTco operation is run from Langley!'

7

The mansion lay deep in the Hertfordshire countryside, surrounded by a small acreage of parkland. It had been built in the late nineteenth century for a royal courtesan, had passed over the decades from noblemen to the carriage trade and was now owned by Sir Alex Vickery. Raison Tearkes reached it punctually at noon.

He'd flown overnight from Washington, his large frame uncomfortable in the wide first class seats. He had slept only fitfully and despite a bath and a large breakfast at Claridges, felt frayed at the edges. He wasn't, he told himself climbing out of the powder blue Rolls-Royce Sir Alex had sent for him, as vigorous as he used to be.

The other members of the consortium were waiting for him in the library, Sir Alex fussing over drinks, Bruno Topf crabbed into a leather armchair near the magnificent fireplace, and Odile Brassard aggressively erect on the only upright chair in the room. The consortium had held together for over sixty years. Willard Tearkes had worked with Andre Brassard and Reginald Vickery, and even during the war they had all worked together with Bruno Topf.

Topf was the only survivor of the old cartel. He had become crafty with age, narrow and cautious and Tearkes knew his loyalties were divided between two, no three Germanys and that he was obsessed with his own failing health and his struggle to keep control of Topf Industrie. Bruno should have been put out to grass a long while ago, Tearkes reflected. But Bruno was there, Bruno was still part of the consortium. For better or worse he had to work with Topf.

'Bonjour, Raison.'

'How are you, Odile?'

Their smiles were pure plastic. Tearkes eyed Odile Brassard's mannish brown blazer with distaste. He felt uncomfortable with Odile Brassard, and felt certain the aversion was mutual.

'Vodka martini straight up.' Sir Alex was holding a glass out to him, chin thrust up in the manner of a cocky bantam-weight, as if challenging Tearkes not to like his drink.

'Thanks, Alex.' Tearkes knew Sir Alex had little imagin-ation. Sir Alex had spent his life consolidating what his father had created, expanding from solid foundations. Tearkes wondered if he could now be persuaded to risk all, to take the long view and leap upwards in the dark.

Sipping his martini, he sat down on the broad leather sofa opposite the fireplace. Sir Alex made good vodka martinis. As soon as Sir Alex had joined him on the sofa, Tearkes told them of Voskov's plan.

As he expected, Odile Brassard was the first to react. '*Sacre Bleu!* We make a great financial coup, *no!*'

'I can't say I'm keen on the idea of the Russians having access to all this information.' That was Sir Alex.

'Four hundred million dollars,' Bruno Topf said. 'Where are we going to find four hundred million dollars? We are already fully stretched in Russia.'

Their reactions were what he had anticipated, Odile's petty cupidity, Alex's weak-willed caution disguised as concern over wider issues, Topf's mean practicality.

'We can sell dollars short and buy gold forward on margin,' Tearkes said.

'Bravo, Raison! When do we do it?' Odile Brassard clapped her hands together. Tearkes looked away. Girlishness did not suit her.

'How much profit would we make?' Sir Alex asked.

'After taxes,' Bruno Topf said. 'Taxes in Germany are high.'

So, as he'd thought, they were all interested. 'We can't simply go in and out,' Tearkes said. 'If anyone ever finds out we helped the Russians take control of our major banks, we could be charged with treason.'

'Oh dear,' Sir Alex said, while Bruno Topf glared from beneath drooping lids.

Odile Brassard said, 'But obviously you have a way around that.'

Tearkes suppressed his irritation and forced his lips apart in a tight smile. He said, 'We duplicate Voskov's plan. We put up a billion four to his six hundred million. We take control.'

'*C'est magnifique*, Raison, but all of us together do not have that kind of money.'

Tearkes said, 'If we dispose of the Russian project, we'll pick up half a million dollars.' He ignored Topf's restless shifting in his chair. 'We put up forty million for four hundred million worth of dollar contracts and gold, and on the day if the prices move thirty-five per cent, we make a clear profit of a hundred and forty million. Double that, and we make two hundred and eighty million dollars in a day. Think about that.'

They did, pleasantly, until Topf said, 'It's still a long way from a billion four.'

'So we sell what we have, we borrow as much as we can. Somehow we find the money.'

Sir Alex asked, 'Why, Raison? Why should we risk everything we've made?'

'Because we have been given a unique opportunity, the opportunity of gambling on a certainty. We must maximize this opportunity. We must take control of the banks.'

'We are not bankers,' Topf said.

'If we have to take control of something, why not oil?' Sir Alex asked. 'The profits of oil companies are larger than those of banks.'

Banks, money, influence, power; patiently Tearkes explained the equation. Controlling banks, they would have opportunities for greater profit. Controlling banks, they would have the funds for the acquisition and elimination of competitors. Tearkes said, 'We buy, we pledge what we buy, and buy some more. We turn ten million into twenty, twenty into forty. Size is the name of the game. Look at the oil industry, controlled by four corporations. The automobile industry, five and that'll get smaller. You want to buy yourself an airline, whom do you go to? Boeing, McDonnell Douglas or Lockheed. You want a big computer, how many companies can you go to? Three.'

'We should compete with quality, not size,' Topf said.

'That's a lot of crap, Bruno. Why did Hoechst and Bayer and BASF and a few others get together to form I. G. Farben? Why did you help create the Aktiegesselschaft?'

'Economics of scale,' Topf muttered.

'Economics of scale be damned. You guys wanted muscle, muscle to buy cheap, muscle to sell high. You wanted industrial muscle to control labour, financial muscle to control sources of finance, political muscle to run governments your way.'

'None of that is true,' Topf said.

'And in any case,' Odile Brassard said, 'none of this can happen. Our governments will never let us eliminate our competitors.' She smiled and added unkindly, 'I believe in your country there is something called the Sherman Act.'

Tearkes felt a nerve in his temple start to throb. Deliberately, he occupied himself with placing his glass on the floor. Then he said, 'What if the Sherman Act was repealed?'

They looked at him in amazement. 'You can do that?' Sir Alex asked.

Tearkes smiled confidently. 'Democratically elected governments are susceptible to public pressure,' he said, 'which is another way of saying that politicians are concerned only with their own skin. And what is public opinion? It isn't the four of us sitting here and saying taxes are too high. It's some soft core radical going on television and saying businessmen aren't taxed enough. It's journalists saying that America, the richest country in the world, should not have any poverty. It's politicians looking for causes that will bring them the most votes.

'We aren't simply going to grow big,' he continued. 'We're going to grow wide. We're going to *make* public opinion. We're going to buy newspapers, we're going to buy television stations.' He paused and laughed, harshly. 'We'll even manage to buy a politician or two.'

'But why do any of this?' Sir Alex enquired. 'We all have enough.'

'But will we keep it?' Tearkes challenged. 'The future is big government and big business. We do not fit into that scheme of things. We are going to be driven out of the market place. We have to grow in order to survive.'

Sir Alex said, 'I don't quite believe that.'

Tearkes flashed him a tight smile. 'Let me prove it to you.' He looked from Sir Alex to Odile Brassard and Bruno Topf. 'I have already begun to dispose of SummiTco's assets. In a few days I will be able to invest nearly seven hundred million dollars in the Voskov plan. You people are in or out. And if you're out, you take the consequences.'

Odile Brassard said, 'You mean you will find other partners. You will acquire us and eliminate us.'

Tearkes's smile was like ice. 'There's only the brave and the dead, Odile,' he said. 'You know that.'

Silence descended on the room, finally broken by Odile Brassard asking, 'Are our investments fixed to the contributions we make now?'

'No. All of us have always been prepared to buy and sell.'

Odile Brassard said, 'In that case, Brassards will contribute one hundred and seventy-five million dollars.'

'What about you, Alex?'

'Interest rates are penal,' Sir Alex said.

'Are you in or out, Alex?' Tearkes's voice was harsh.

Sir Alex Vickery shrugged. 'I suppose we're in. We've been in everything together.'

Tearkes turned to Bruno Topf.

Topf said, 'I don't trust the Russians.'

'Oh come, come, Bruno,' Vickery said. 'We've done business with the Russians before.'

'I know,' Topf said, sadly. 'I was the one who arranged everything with this Voskov. I was the one who went seven times to Moscow. And I can tell you the water in Moscow does all sorts of things to your stomach. I suffered for all of you, for Russia, and yet when this Voskov has a proposal to make, he comes not to me, but goes to America.'

Tearkes thought he could do without Bruno Topf, but before he could speak, Vickery intervened. 'It doesn't matter where Voskov went. We're all in this together. One for all, all for one, that's how it is, how it's always been.'

'Voskov went to Raison because he knew I wouldn't buy this crazy scheme. I know too much about Russia. In 1939 –'

'You in or out, Bruno?'

Topf shifted in his chair to face Tearkes. 'I'm an old man,' he said. 'I have no reason to risk everything again. Besides, I don't like this scheme. I think it's crazy. I think you, all of you, will ruin yourselves. I am out.'

'It means you're out for good, Bruno.'

'Which in my case is no more than five years.'

Tearkes said ominously, 'But you have to come in. You see, you already know too much.'

'And whom should I talk about it with? I have no wife, I see my two sons twice a year. My co-directors cannot wait till I die to modernize Topf Industrie.' He paused and lowered his eyes. 'Besides, if I wanted to participate in such a scheme, who else would I do it with except you?' Slowly Topf got to his feet and left the room.

Tearkes remained another hour with Odile Brassard and Alex Vickery, adjusting their contributions and running through the mechanics of the scheme. That afternoon, he left for Zurich.

In Zurich, Gerhardt Hoffman told him of the receipt of fifty thousand dollars expense money from the Mozche Bank and of the incorporation of Blissan AG. Tearkes spent that evening arranging for five companies to be incorporated, for bank accounts to be opened, for references to be filed with stockbrokers and with other banks and gave Hoffman instructions as to how the one thousand four hundred million dollars he would shortly receive should be dealt with. Then, he asked Hoffman about the Germans.

'I haven't heard from the lawyer since,' Gerhardt Hoffman said, and swallowed nervously before he told Tearkes that the lawyer was one Johann Neumann with offices in Munich.

'What exactly did he say?'

'That he represented a claimant to the Manninger estate. That all the proof required by Manninger's will would shortly be provided and that meanwhile, I was not to dispose of or charge any of the Manninger assets.' Hoffman winced at the remembered slight. 'Neumann seemed to know all about Manninger's will.'

'And since then, you've heard nothing?'

Hoffman shook his head.

'What could the effect of this claim be on the estate?'

'The claimant will share jointly in the estate, unless Elisabeth Manninger dies first.'

'And what has the claimant to do to obtain the inheritance?'

'Provide evidence of kinship and the founders certificates of the two Manninger companies, Sopadep and Perpetua.'

'Which Manninger hid before he died,' Tearkes said.

Hoffman nodded.

Together with the Brunhilde files, Tearkes thought grimly.

Tearkes spent the rest of that week in Luxembourg, in Cayman and in Nassau where he incorporated more companies, opened more bank accounts and left a series of detailed instructions. When he returned to the island a message from Randall Hopner confirmed that the operation to find the Manninger processes was already under way, and Sam Kamas was in charge.

8

Sam Kamas looked through the computer print-outs, studied the input data and stared morosely at the Chief Programmer's note confirming that the programme had been rigorously re-checked twice and that the computer itself had been cleared of any malfunction. Whatever the computer said, Kamas wasn't sure this guy Khouri was the best. Khouri had left the Agency three years ago. Kamas didn't like working with ex-professionals. He pulled the print-outs to him and read them for the fifteenth time. The computer knew more about Dwight Khouri than his own father.

Khouri had been born in February, 1946, the eldest son of Mark Khouri and his German war bride, Trude. According to the computer, his childhood had been an unremarkable combination of mumps and measles, adolescent wrangles, discreet academic success, a good record at non-team sports and a teenage affair with a girl called Mary Ellen Wielgosz.

Kamas didn't like that bit about non-team sports. People like that usually tended to go their own way.

In 1966, Khouri had graduated from New York State and spent the following year bumming around Europe. That didn't look too hopeful, either. Having got whatever he needed out of his system, Khouri had returned home and trained as a CPA. On the day he'd qualified, he'd been drafted.

Khouri had spent three years in Vietnam. He'd proved to be an excellent soldier and had come out of the war as a Major with a Silver Star.

That, at least, looked hopeful.

After Vietnam, Khouri had joined the Financial Operations Division of the CIA. He'd been good at his job, demonstrating an exceptional flair for the combination of financial skill and convoluted secrecy the job required, and when four years later he'd resigned to go into the family banking business, he'd been tipped for the post of Division Chief.

Kamas wondered if Khouri's resignation had to do with the breakdown of his marriage. Four years previously, Khouri had married Jackie, the ravishingly beautiful socialite daughter of Senator Nathan Rivers. The computer knew all about the man's marriage too. Khouri was no socialite and Jackie Rivers no housewife. Ten months later, they had been amicably divorced.

Khouri was now a Vice President of the Imtra Bank. He earned just over a hundred thousand dollars a year, had a mortgage for thirty-five thousand and current debts of just under seven hundred. He was six foot two and weighed a hundred and seventy pounds. According to the photograph obtained from Personnel, he'd inherited his mother's thick, straight, blond hair and deep-set blue eyes, his father's rounded face and an expression of boyish innocence that belied his experience in the jungles of Vietnam and the even denser forests of the CIA.

Kamas grunted and pulled the surveillance reports towards him. He'd had a six-man team on three eight-hour shifts tailing Khouri since the previous Wednesday. They had followed Khouri from his brownstone by the East River to the bank, followed him to lunch at Oscars (that was Wednesday), to his tennis club (Thursday), and on Friday he'd collected a girl from an apartment on the East Sixties and taken her to spend the weekend with him.

The girl was a fashion model named Melanie Stevens, who, in the photograph taken by the legman, was a pretty, elfin-faced creature, with a walk like a ballet dancer's. Khouri and the girl had gone shopping Saturday morning, played tennis all Saturday afternoon and gone to a movie on Saturday night. On Sunday, they'd lunched with Khouri's parents.

Kamas pushed the reports away. There was nothing there

that wasn't normal. Perhaps that was it. This guy Khouri was too damned normal.

He picked up the phone, dialled the White House and asked for Jeb Anderson. 'I've re-checked everything,' he said. 'Looks like it'll have to be this guy, Khouri.'

'There's nothing wrong with Dwight,' Jeb Anderson said. 'Except he's been away from the game for four years.'

'If we're putting only one man in, we need the best,' Kamas said.

'It sure looks like you've got him.'

Kamas said, 'I'd like to check out on him some more. I'd like to check out on this Stevens girl.'

'It's your job,' Anderson said. 'Be quick about it.'

'Two days,' Kamas said. 'In two days, I'll bring him in.'

'No,' replied Anderson. 'I'll do that.'

9

That Sunday was a fine one in Zurich. In the sanatorium where Elisabeth Manninger had spent most of her life, warm afternoon sun slanted over manicured lawns; nurses in crisp grey uniforms carried trays of cakes and sandwiches, while old ladies sat talking, dozing, and taking tea.

A nurse emerged on to the terrace behind the lawn, a smooth-faced girl in her early twenties, with a bulky figure that filled the antiseptic lines of the uniform. She stood for a moment on the terrace, narrowing her eyes against the sun, then walked, a little hesitantly at first, then with increasing confidence, to a group of three ladies seated beside the rockery.

Frau von Heissler was the most vital of the three. Only sixty-two and in full possession of all her faculties, she had

60

elected to live in the home rather than be a burden to either of her sons. A stocky, well fleshed woman, she had the features of a patriarchal bulldog and her stubby, ring-encrusted fingers flashed as she emphasized point after point to her perennial companion, Frau Putterschoorn.

With her wheelchair turned slightly away from them, and oblivious to their conversation was Frau Elisabeth Manninger. A frail stick of a woman, she looked more seventy than fifty-five. Her face was wrinkled and hollowed, her once full mouth drooped in pendulous despair, her large luminous brown eyes stared unseeingly at the rockery. A half eaten sandwich and a partly drunk cup of tea were on the tray slotted into the front of her chair, and she did not move when the nurse clasped the rubber-tipped handles of her wheelchair.

'Frau Manninger,' the nurse said softly, bending her head to the old woman's ear. 'You have visitors.'

Frau Manninger moved to pull the shawl of Bruges lace more closely around her narrow shoulders.

'There are people to see you,' the nurse repeated, a little more loudly, a little more firmly.

'Here let me,' Frau von Heissler said and tapped Frau Manninger on the knee. 'Elisabeth you have visitors. Isn't that nice? Come, smarten yourself up to meet them.'

Frau Manninger looked blankly from Frau von Heissler to the rockery.

'Visitors, Elisabeth, visitors.' Frau von Heissler shook her head and turned to the nurse, rolling her eyes in mock anguish. 'It's no use when she's in one of these moods. Better tell them to come another time. Perhaps she'll be better tomorrow.'

The nurse smiled, mechanically. 'They have come a long way.'

'Perhaps later then, after dinner. She might be herself then.'

'They might bring her out of her mood,' the nurse said, and abruptly tilting the wheelchair, wheeled Frau Manninger away.

Frau von Heissler watched them go. 'It's no use,' she called after them. 'No use at all when she's like that.'

Frau Manninger felt the wheelchair bump over the uneven turf, heard the cup rattle against its saucer on the tray in front of her. When the nurse stopped at a convenient table to remove the tray, she glanced briefly at the girl. A pretty girl. Heavy in the face, but good bone structure and what lovely hair underneath the cap. Once, her hair too had been blonde and glistened in the sunlight. Berndt had loved her hair. Loved all of her. She had been beautiful. Once.

She remembered the carnival and the procession. She'd ridden in a float covered in flowers and festooned with red and black banners. She'd been the prettiest girl in Hellenthal, the carnival queen, the year she'd met and married Berndt Manninger.

The nurse was hurrying her across the lawn. She could feel the chair bucking underneath her and turned to protest, but by then they were round the corner of the building, out of sight of the others and she forgot. Visitors? The only visitors she had were the men from the bank. She did not want to meet those nasty men from the bank. The last time the young man had been most abusive when she had refused to sign those silly papers.

She pulled her shawl more tightly around her shoulders and thought of the time before the bombing. Those had been good days. Fun. Picnics on the Rhine. Parties. Seventy people had come to her wedding. Minister Goebbels had been there with a pretty young actress, and Minister Speer. The Fuhrer had sent a hundred red and white roses and a tea set of Sèvres china. Good days, before the bombing and the rationing. Good days when she had been safe. Berndt had kept her safe. It was afterwards that the bad things had happened.

She opened her eyes. The nurse was taking her away from the house towards the forest. She didn't like the forest. She had her room on the far side of the building where she did not have to see those dark, brooding, menacing shapes. She turned her head. '*Fräulein.*'

The nurse kept pushing her. Ignoring her.

'*Fräulein, ich mag der Wald nicht.*'

'*Die Freundin,*' the nurse said and patted her on the shoulder.

'*Nein, Fräulein, nein.*'

The nurse smiled a peculiar, rigid smile.

They were under the trees now, bouncing along a rutted path. The nurse was pushing her faster and faster, the rubber-tyred wheels bouncing on the stones and jarring out of the ruts. Frau Manninger felt herself being shaken, nearly thrown out of the chair. She gripped the arms tightly.

'*Fräulein, bitte . . .*'

Her mouth was dry and the tip of her tongue rubbed the serrated cracks on her lips. With a frightening heave the nurse skidded the wheelchair off the path and into the trees. Twigs snapped under their progress, branches snatched at her clothes. She opened her mouth to scream, but had no breath. She felt her heart pounding furiously inside her chest, filling her throat. A great ball of pain swelled inside her. Pills – she must have her pills.

Her lips moved soundlessly.

They were slowing down, the wheelchair lurching instead of bouncing. They were on one side of the clearing moving towards the trees and the tangled undergrowth. She felt the pain inside her subside, felt the clammy sweat congealing on her hands and feet. They stopped and there was a brief silence. Then the rapid crackle of breaking twigs. The sound of someone running. Slowly she turned her head.

'*Fräulein . . .*'

Her mouth began to tremble. She raised her hand to it and bit down on her finger. She wanted to scream, to cry. What had the silly, foolish nurse done? Her heart was pounding, its drumming filled her ears. There was the pain again, deep and swelling . . . the pain . . . when she got back to the –

There was something moving in the trees ahead of her. Someone. Shapes of men. Six men. She would call out. Her mouth froze in a silent scream.

Three of the men wore long brown leather coats, the other three, black uniforms. It was summer and too hot for coats. She'd seen those coats before, those uniforms. It was an illusion, a bad dream! SS! Gestapo! But that was long ago. There was no SS, no Gestapo now. They were coming out of the trees towards her. She made herself small in the chair.

She cowered in the chair, the men towering above her, crowding out the light. Men. Men who had done terrible things to her. She knew nothing. She could tell them nothing. They must stop hurting her. She couldn't bear the pain. Not any more. Not the lash on her bare feet, not the sharpened sticks under her fingernails, not the abuse and the kicks and the blows and the tightened handcuffs.

Please!

Elisabeth Manninger was trembling violently in her chair, her body covered with icy sweat. Her breath came in sharp, dry gasps and the pain within her chest was swelling, growing, stifling. Pills. She must have her pills. She could hardly breathe.

'We have come back to you.' The men were speaking to her. 'You might have thought it was over. You were wrong. It is beginning again. Now.'

One of the men was pulling a mask from his pocket, an obscene, smiling, jester's mask. They were pressing her trembling body to the chair. One of them was wrapping the Bruges shawl around her throat.

No, she screamed, silently. No!

'Remember Fasching night, Frau Manninger?'

She heard their laughter, cruel, scornful, beating at her eardrums, mingling with that cruel laughter of long ago. Hands were pawing at her, leather-gloved fingers lifting up her face.

'If you do it for Manninger, you can do it for us.'

Elisabeth Manninger gave a strangled scream. The horrible, leering, cardboard faces were all around her. She remembered her prison cell, the six men, drunk and wearing masks, holding her down on the bed, smelling of sweat and beer. Six of them, tearing at her clothes, stripping her naked. It was Fasching, the night before Ash Wednesday. They had held her and taken her, again and again. They had been worse than animals.

Traitor!

Spy!

Manninger's whore!

'Oh God, no. No!' She opened her mouth. She was choking. They were choking the air out of her. The pain in her chest was sharp, knifing, intense. They were pressing the masks to her face and they were laughing louder and louder.

Nein!

10

Dwight Khouri came into his office that Monday, feeling quite relieved. A month had passed and though he was still swiping short balls into the back netting, he hadn't hit anybody. That morning, as soon as he'd finished his meeting with Dr Rasul Quassim, he was leaving for Tampa.

Dr Quassim came punctually at ten, and if he was surprised at the sight of a banker in jeans and sneakers, he didn't show it. He sipped his mint tea and lit two cigarettes in quick succession. His ulcer was worse, he said and he'd missed last night's episode of *Dallas*.

Dwight thought Quassim was more than usually nervous. The pace at which he swung his knees together was definitely *ralletando*, and he hissed as he drew at his cigarette. Dwight said, 'You should seriously consider investing in something other than bank deposits. I have here a portfolio – '

Quassim's knees went into high gear. His Adam's apple bobbed like a float on a fast moving stream. 'Sell dollar,' he said, hoarsely.

Quassim was talking of selling eighteen million two hundred and seventy thousand three hundred and ninety-two dollars and ninety cents. 'All of it?' Dwight asked.

Quassim nodded.

Dwight tried not to look mystified. 'And what would you like me to exchange the dollars for?'

Quassim frowned, and for a moment Dwight thought he would close his account and disappear as mysteriously as a Bedouin in the night. Except Quassim wasn't Bedouin. He said, 'Buy other currencies.'

'I couldn't recommend that. The pound is over-valued, the mark is heading for a fall, the yen is too susceptible to,' Dwight lowered his voice piously, 'oil prices.'

'Buy gold.'

'You do not earn interest on gold.'

Quassim scratched his ear thoughtfully. 'Sixteen million dollar gold. One million English pound. One million German mark.' Quassim's knobbly face was set, the lips under the day's growth of stubble, firmly pressed together. His mind was firmly made up.

'As you wish,' Dwight said and phoned instructions through to the Foreign Exchange and Bullion Department.

Quassim ground out his cigarette and stood up.

'Same time next month,' Dwight said.

For a moment, Quassim hesitated. Then he said, 'Perhaps so. If God wills.'

Dwight waited until the Foreign Exchange and Bullion Department confirmed his instructions had been carried out, scribbled the address and phone number of Harry Hopman's Tennis Camp on his blotter, picked up his bag and made for the door.

The phone rang.

He looked at his watch. Ten thirty. He wasn't due at the airport till twelve.

The phone rang again.

Officially, he was supposed to be in Florida. He'd cleared

his desk Friday and come in only to go through the ritual with Quassim.

The phone rang again.

The hell with it. It was probably Sami double checking he'd completed the Liban Syndicate loan agreements. He picked up the phone.

It was Sami's secretary.

'The Liban agreements are with Adele, in Legal,' Dwight said.

'There's a call for you,' Sami's secretary said. She sounded excited. 'The switchboard put it through to us.'

'I'm not here,' Dwight said. 'I'm in Florida.'

Sami's secretary said, 'Mr Khouri, it's the White House.'

Dwight let the bag drop from his hand. He knew no one at the White House well enough to call and couldn't think of anyone at the White House who would call him. 'Dwight Khouri,' he said into the phone, dropping his voice two octaves.

'Hi there, Dwight! This is Jeb Anderson.'

Now that was a voice from the past. Jeb Anderson had been Dwight's immediate superior at the Agency. He'd resigned shortly after Dwight, to go into politics, and was now a Presidential aide. 'Hello, Jeb,' he said. 'You've just bumped up my status here six notches. The whole office thinks I'm talking to the President.'

Jeb Anderson laughed and asked, 'How quickly can you get to Washington?'

Dwight grinned. The White House hadn't changed Jeb. Jeb still got to the point fast. 'In three weeks,' Dwight said. 'I'm just off to Tampa on holiday. You caught me going out the door.'

'Washington's on the way,' Jeb Anderson said. 'And it can't wait three weeks.'

'What the hell is *it*?'

'Why don't you get down here and find out?'

Dwight's mind raced. Had someone found something funny in the books? Or did they want to talk about a past operation? But if so, what was the hurry? 'I've got to get away,' Dwight said. 'New York's like an oven and I'm going round the twist. For a whole month I've been trying not to belt somebody.'

Anderson said, 'I might have a cure for that. Why don't you stop off in Washington and talk. It will only take an hour or two, and if you don't like what we'll talk about, you can go on to Tampa. There's a Pan Am flight that leaves Washington at six thirty.'

Jeb Anderson didn't bullshit. Which was why Dwight liked him and they'd got on so well at the Agency. So if Jeb said he could walk, he could walk. 'Give me a clue, Jeb. What do you want to see me about?'

'Can't talk on an open line. Come to Washington.'

Dwight felt a shiver of excitement, a stirring of curiosity. There was an undercurrent of anxiety in Jeb's voice. And Jeb was calling from the White House. So whatever *it* was, *it* was important and urgent. What?

'And if I say yes?'

'I'll say thank you.'

'You'd better write that, Jeb. In large letters. I'll get the eleven-thirty shuttle from La Guardia.'

'I'll have a car meet you,' Jeb Anderson said.

11

The car was a long, black Cadillac with darkened windows, and the uniformed chauffeur told him that Mr Anderson was running a little behind schedule, so would Dwight mind seeing a Mr Sam Kamas. Dwight said he didn't mind. The chauffeur opened the rear door for him and put his bag away in the boot.

The limousine took him straight to the Executive Office Building where Kamas had a room on the fourth floor that looked as if it was rented by the hour.

Kamas was a squat, powerfully built man, all chest, shoulders and hirsute arms. He was in his late thirties, with dark, crisply curled hair and a squarish face, most of which was obscured by an aggressive moustache. He sported a heavy gold bracelet, a watch with a capped leather face, and a heavy chain and gold-plated dog tag rested in the hairy V of his open shirt.

Macho, Dwight thought, and that was not all he disliked about Sam Kamas. Kamas's sun tan was too even, the smile under the heavy moustache too bright. But most of all it was the eyes, Dwight decided. They were a dark brown, the colour and texture of frozen mud. Whatever else he was, Sam Kamas wasn't playing at being macho.

'Where is Jeb Anderson?' Dwight asked.

'He'll be along as soon as I've finished briefing you.' Kamas's thick eyebrows rose enquiringly. 'Coffee? A drink? I think I can find a bottle of Chambolle Musigny if you want it.'

From the way he pronounced it, Dwight knew the man hadn't heard of the wine before. 'What my file doesn't state,' Dwight said, 'is that I do not drink burgundy before lunch.'

Kamas shrugged and grinned, walked over to a table and turned on an electric kettle. 'And you like your coffee black.'

Dwight watched him scoop instant coffee into two mugs. There was an economy about Kamas's movements, and he walked with a balanced, slightly splayed gait of a *judoka*.

Kamas placed the coffee before Dwight, walked round the barren desk, and in one fluid movement sat down, opened a drawer and pushed a folder across to Dwight.

Inside were the buff sheets of an analysis submitted with the National Intelligence Daily.

'Read that,' Kamas said. 'It'll give you the background.'

It had been years since Dwight had seen a National Intelligence Daily or any of its attachments. The National

69

Intelligence Daily was prepared by the Directorate of Intelligence for members of the Cabinet, and only rarely were its contents disclosed to anyone below Cabinet level.

Dwight picked up the report and saw that even though it was an edited extract, it still bore its original Cabinet level classification. The report was headed *Gulf War: Economic Consequences on the United States*, and was dated the previous Thursday.

A terse summary at the head of the report stated that Iraq had been stockpiling arms and that within weeks the current border conflict with Iran would escalate into a full scale war. So that was why Rasul Quassim had switched to gold, Dwight thought and immediately put Dr Rasul Quassim out of his mind.

Dwight finished reading the report and said, 'What do you want me to do? I'm not an oil man, I'm a banker.'

Kamas ignored his question. 'What do you think of the scenario?'

'That Saudi Arabia will go belly up? I think that's very likely. The only question is when? This war could do it. A push from our Russian friends could do it. Khomeini could do it.'

'If that were to happen in the next five years, we and the free world have had it. We are all going right back to zero.'

'But aren't we cutting down on the use of oil? Aren't we developing alternative sources of energy?'

'Sure, sure,' Kamas said, 'fossil fuels, nuclear power, solar energy. Sure, we're trying, but we're going to be dependent on oil for the next fifteen years.'

'That long?'

Kamas nodded. 'How long has it taken Detroit to produce a more fuel efficient car? Four years, five, and that is merely adapting existing technology. Just think how long it would take to replace all the automobile engines in the world, all the aircraft, all the ships, all the factories, all the homes using oil for heating, with an alternative source of fuel. Looking at it that way, even twenty years doesn't seem enough.'

'Okay,' Dwight said. 'So we're in trouble. What else is new?'

'If the Saudis go down the chute, we're not in trouble, Dwight. We're dead.' Kamas leaned forward across the desk and gave Dwight a knowing smile. 'Would you believe me if I told you there was a way we could get out of this mess, a way *you* could end our dependence on Middle Eastern oil?'

'Why don't you get to the point?' Dwight asked.

'Okay. Ever heard of a man called Berndt Manninger?'

Dwight shook his head.

'Manninger was a German technologist, an expert in synthetics. Oil, fertilizer, magnesium, plastics, rubber – you name it, the Manninger factories had a hand in producing it. Some of our people who were around at the time believe that without Manninger, Hitler could not have gone to war.'

'So you want me to find this genius? Is that it?' Dwight looked at his watch, then out of the window, thinking that as soon as Jeb Anderson arrived, he would make his excuses and leave.

'Berndt Manninger is dead,' Kamas said. 'He was shot by the Gestapo in 1945.'

Dwight shifted restlessly in his chair. 'Drop by the next time you're in New York, Sam, and we'll re-run the Second World War.'

Kamas appeared not to have heard him. 'Apart from coal and steel, Germany had few raw materials. Before the war, most of what they needed had to be imported. Before the war, those imports could be stopped, and those imports were dependent on the goodwill of the British Navy. Do you see what I'm getting at Dwight?'

'Quite frankly, no.'

'In the 1930s, Germany experienced what we and the rest of the world are experiencing now. A drastic shortage of natural resources. Dependence on unreliable foreign suppliers. Dependence on sea lanes that could easily be blockaded. The Germans licked that problem, Dwight. With the help of men like Berndt Manninger they licked that problem to such an extent, that they were able to go to war.'

Kamas was a most unlikely historian, Dwight thought, and wondered who had briefed him; wondered also, why, if the background was so important, he was being briefed indirectly.

'The Germans resolved their problem in two ways,' Kamas continued. 'By the production of synthetics – and by developing processes that extended the use of such raw materials as they had.'

'Take styrium, for example. For years the United States had been the largest producer of styrium. We mined it, we refined it, we sold it. Then around 1928 or 1929, along comes Manninger with an electro-chemical process for creating styrium ore. A process that extracts eight times as much styrium from the ore as previously. And within two years, Germany, that is to say, Manninger, becomes the most important producer of styrium in the world.' Kamas leaned forward across the desk and fixed his muddy brown eyes on Dwight.

Dwight thought he'd detected an expression of sincerity in Kamas's stare. 'No one needs styrium any more,' he said.

'That's right. But we sure need that process and the principle behind that process. You get what I mean? The principle of extracting more metal, more energy, more anything from a finite supply of natural goods.

'Some time between 1941 and 1945,' Kamas continued, 'Berndt Manninger developed a process which enabled him to extract more energy from a given mass. What that means, in layman's terms, is that he could make a car go twice as far on a gallon of gas. Whilst I believe the process is mainly applicable to oil, it can be applied to gas, electricity or any other source of energy. If we had that process, Dwight, we could produce all the energy we need from a quarter of our resources. In the first year alone, we could halve our oil consumption.'

'Jiminy cricket!' Dwight breathed. If its oil consumption was halved, the United States would become self sufficient in oil. It would become an *exporter* of oil. It would no longer pay eighty billion dollars a year to the OPEC countries and the Middle East would lose its strategic importance and the need for an American military presence. If there was such a process, it would have profound consequences, it would completely alter the balance of power, it would make America strong again . . . if there was such a process.

'Is all this true?' Dwight asked.

Kamas placed his hand on his heart. 'Absolute gospel,' he said.

'In that case, why are you talking to me? I'm not an engineer. You need to send an engineer to Germany for this.'

Kamas smiled and shook his head. 'No, Dwight, we need you. We need you to go to Zurich.' Still smiling, he pushed a manila folder across the desk to Dwight.

12

Dwight opened the folder. The paper inside was dry and brittle, its edges turning brown, the typescript a faded bluish grey. The front page bore the stamp of the Economic Division of the Office of Strategic Services, and underneath was typed in block capitals: SUMMARY OF INVESTIGATION INTO MANNINGER INDUSTRIE.' The report was dated 27 April 1946 and the investigating agent had been one Calvin W. Dooley.

Dooley had begun his investigation in May 1945, when the Economic Division of the OSS was scouring Germany for industrial processes and industrial assets. With a team of six, Dooley had spent four months poring over surviving records and patiently listing the operations carried out in the various Manninger factories. Apart from synthetic oil, Manninger Industrie had produced an improved plastic for aircraft canopies, manganese for the munitions factories, gasoline additives, lubricants and a toughened plastic that could replace metal. Manninger had devised a means of combining berylium with copper and nickel to form alloys that were stronger and easier to work with, had produced a cement carbide that was more efficient and longer lasting than high speed steel.

But nowhere amongst the company's records had the investigating team been able to find who owned the processes. Dooley and his team had descended on the German patents registries. There, also, they'd drawn a blank. There was nothing registered in the name of Manninger Industrie or any of its subsidiaries, nothing relevant that was registered in the name of Berndt Manninger.

And that was not all. Every Manninger engineer and technologist that was interrogated spoke of other processes. In the last years of the war, Berndt Manninger had run his industrial empire from the Swabian village of Hellenthal. And there, or so everyone said, he had developed different processes, processes so far reaching and revolutionary that industry could be forever changed. According to Manninger's former employees, he had spent his last years working on alternative sources of energy, on new forms of heating; he had experimented with plants and devised a means of making crops fertile all the year round, he'd developed new ways of extracting protein. But no one knew exactly what or where the processes were.

In the fall of 1945, Dooley's team had been disbanded. But Dooley had continued the investigation alone. Patiently, he'd worked out the processes Manninger had required for the creation of his industrial empire and worked his way through the patent records again. At the end of three months he had discovered that every process Manninger had used was registered in Germany, but not in Manninger's name. Every process was registered in the name of a Swiss company, Perpetua AG.

In Switzerland, Dooley found that Perpetua itself was

owned by a Liechtenstein anstalt, Sopadep. He'd also found that Perpetua had no offices of its own and that its affairs were administered by the Hoffman Bank in Zurich.

And there, amidst the overstuffed leather chairs and wooden panelling of Alois Hoffman's office, the trail had ended.

Alois Hoffman had freely admitted that his bank had represented Perpetua. Perpetua was a Swiss company he pointed out and Switzerland had been neutral throughout the war. Any attempt to seize its patents as war reparations would be strongly resisted, not only by the company, but by the Swiss government.

Alois Hoffman regretted he could not discuss the affairs of Berndt Manninger. He was unfortunately bound by the laws of bank secrecy, the breach of which could put them both in prison. In response to Dooley's persistence however, he had stated that the bank did not directly or indirectly control any processes invented by Berndt Manninger in the last three years of his life.

That information had only served to make Dooley more enthusiastic and three days later he was arrested by the Swiss. Given the alternative of a twenty-year prison sentence for economic espionage or leaving Switzerland immediately, Dooley had left.

But he had not abandoned the investigation. In March 1946 he had gone from Switzerland to Germany, looking for the Manninger heirs, believing that once he located them, once they attempted to claim their inheritance, he would be able to show that Perpetua was a Manninger front and that its assets should be seized in reparations.

In Essen, and Ludwigshafen and Hellenthal, Dooley had discovered that Manninger's first wife had died, and that shortly before his own death, Manninger had remarried. In February 1945, Manninger's widow, Elisabeth, had been arrested by the Gestapo and tortured, as a result of which she had suffered a mental breakdown and was now in a semi-permanent catatonic state in a sanatorium outside Zurich.

Manninger had a son and daughter by his first marriage. The son, Dieter, had died in Russia. The daughter, Ingrid, had after her mother's death, lived with her maternal grandparents near the Manninger factory in Oppau. The grandparents had been killed in a bombing raid, and the girl arrested two days after her father's death and sent to Ravensbruck.

The records at Ravensbruck had been partially destroyed at the end of the war. Dooley studied them, talked to survivors and came away with conflicting stories. There were two women however, who clearly remembered a young, blonde Aryan girl being brought to the camp shortly before the end of the war. She had not remained there long, they said. Two days after her arrival, she had been taken out of her punishment cell and shot.

Dooley's report ended there. Dwight shut the folder and passed it back to Kamas. 'What happened to Dooley?' he asked.

Kamas was already pushing another folder at him. 'In the summer of 1946, the OSS was disbanded. Dooley was recalled to America and had to find himself another job.'

Dwight opened the second folder. Dooley had found himself a job with the Treasury, working as an investigator with special responsibility for the location and seizure of Nazi assets.

In 1948, Dooley had been searching for the missing funds of the Reich Main Security Office. He was certain that the funds had been got out of Germany somehow and knew that at the end of the war there had been an unusually high number of submarine movements out of bases near Cadiz and that after the battle for Germany had begun, a squad of three long-range Condor aircraft had been transferred to a base in southern Spain. Checking this information in Spain, he had come across a former German double agent, who in exchange for three thousand dollars was prepared to talk. According to the agent, the submarines and aircraft had been used to ship the assets of the Reich Main Security Office to

Argentina, where an accommodation had been made with the Perons.

Dooley had immediately headed for Argentina, but there he had found little. The Perons were in power and any investigation was dangerous. Whatever Nazi assets existed were deeply and securely buried.

His only consolation was a man called Querillin, a Harbour Master in the port of Buenos Aires, bitterly opposed to the Perons and, Dooley suspected, a secret Communist. Querillin *knew* things.

At the end of April 1945, he had supervised the unloading of a submarine that had docked at an *estancia* south of Buenos Aires. The *estancia* was owned by a German immigrant, one Heinrich von Kassel. In addition to the booty that had been unloaded from the submarine, Querillin swore that a young woman had disembarked from it. The woman still lived on the *estancia*, Querillin said, and her name was Ingrid Manninger.

Dooley had attempted to penetrate the *estancia*, had been discovered by von Kassel's guards and savagely beaten. He had then been returned to America where he had spent the next four months in hospital

Dwight shut the folder and passed it back to Kamas. 'What happened next?' he asked.

Kamas shrugged. 'Nothing.'

'You mean to say another agent wasn't sent? We didn't make diplomatic representations?'

Kamas gave him a pitying smile. '1948 wasn't a good year to go looking for Nazis in Argentina,' he said. 'In 1948, we decided that Communism was a greater threat than Fascism. In any case what could the United States protest about? That a German girl who had played no part in the war had emigrated to Argentina?'

'But couldn't we have done something about von Kassel?'

'Von Kassel emigrated to Argentina in 1936. As far as the Argentinians were concerned, he was just another businessman.'

'And was he?'

'We suspected that he was a German agent. We knew that he had been in the German Army, that he'd organized the first SS Officers' Training School. But all the records showed was that he'd been invalided out of the army. And that was the end of it.'

'Until now?'

With a brief knock on the door, Jeb Anderson entered. 'Dwight, it's good to see you.'

Dwight shook Anderson's hand. In the four years since he had left the Agency, Anderson had aged about ten. The once prematurely grey streaked hair was now almost completely silver and there were fine lines at the corners of his eyes and mouth. The mouth itself was thinner and there was a new wariness in the eyes. Jeb Anderson looked a driven man.

'You look well, Jeb,' Dwight said. 'Government suits you.'

'It's twice as easy as banking.' Jeb's smile lit up his face and suddenly he didn't look so old or so harassed.

Anderson walked away and leant against the wall by Kamas's desk. Dwight remembered Jeb Anderson hated sitting down at meetings. Once he'd said, supporting walls was the only exercise he had time for. 'Well, Dwight, what do you think so far?'

The top of Anderson's shoulders and the back of his head was pressed against the wall. His arms were folded loosely across his chest and he was looking at Dwight sleepily from beneath half closed lids. Moment by moment he was growing more like the Anderson Dwight remembered, casual, relaxed, alert.

'I think you're chasing rainbows. Nazi treasure went out with B movies.'

'Those processes exist.' There was the barest trace of irritation underneath the matter-of-factness in Jeb's voice. He rolled his head towards Kamas. 'Has Dwight seen the will yet?'

Kamas slid another folder across the desk to Dwight.

'Do you – ' Jeb began. 'Of course you read German.'

Dwight took out a photocopy of Berndt Manninger's will from the folder. It was a strange document.

There were the usual clauses appointing executors, providing for their fees and giving them discretion to change the investments under their control. The will was one and a half pages long and dated 23 February 1945. For someone as wealthy and influential as Berndt Manninger, it was a surprisingly simple document.

Deceptively simple, Dwight thought. The only asset specifically mentioned in the will was Manninger's house in Hellenthal. The other assets were only known to Manninger and the bank or Manninger and . . . someone else. Clearly the bank had knowledge of and control over those Manninger assets which had been deposited with them. Clearly also, Manninger had trusted the Hoffman Bank to a limited extent, because other assets had been secreted elsewhere. The processes?

Dwight looked across the room at Jeb. 'All right. I'll buy it. Manninger left something in Switzerland. You want me to find it for you?'

'Right on the button, old son,' Kamas said.

'It won't work,' Dwight said. 'The trail is thirty-five years old. If anyone could have found these processes, it would have been Calvin Dooley, soon after the war.'

Dwight saw Jeb Anderson looking at him and stopped. The silence in the room grew. Kamas picked at his nails. Jeb remained leaning against the wall. 'You can succeed where Dooley failed,' Anderson said.

Dwight asked, 'Why don't you wait until Elisabeth Manninger inherits and buy the processes from her?'

Anderson sighed. 'Three reasons,' he said slowly.

'One, we don't have the time. Two, the processes are not with the Hoffman Bank – and we know that for a fact – so Elisabeth Manninger won't get them. Three, Elisabeth Manninger died yesterday.'

'Died? How?'

'Died naturally,' Sam Kamas said. 'She was an old lady.'

Jeb Anderson said, 'We'd like you to go to Zurich, Dwight. Manninger meant those processes to be found. He must have left a trail.'

'A trail that's thirty-five years old,' Dwight said. 'Maybe by now they've built an office block over the place where Manninger buried the processes, or more likely, a bank. Are there any other Manninger heirs?'

Anderson smiled thinly. 'If you find the processes, they will talk to you. If they have them, you talk to them. Offer them anything, but get those processes.'

'What made you pick me?' Dwight asked. 'A retired bagman.'

'You know Switzerland, Dwight. You know how Swiss banks work. For Christ's sake man, you're a banker yourself!'

'I've never run a field operation before,' Dwight said. 'As you know, Jeb, all I'm good at is shifting money and bribing the odd revolutionary president.'

Anderson said, 'You've done more than that. Anyway, this isn't a field operation. It's a bank investigation.' He smiled. 'It'll get you away from behind that desk, and maybe it'll stop you hitting somebody.'

Kamas said, 'The computer said you were the best man for the job. You could be back here with the processes in a week.'

Dwight asked, 'How many other agents are involved?'

'None.'

'For Christ's sake, Jeb! If these processes are so important you need a whole team out there. You need people in Germany, in Switzerland, in Argentina. This whole thing's impossible.'

'Ideally,' Anderson said, 'I'd have half the CIA looking for those processes. That's how important it is. But we can't have a whole platoon of agents tramping through Switzerland. It upsets the Swiss and puts their cows off their feed. Besides, this has to be kept very, very quiet. You might have to make a deal with former Nazis, Dwight. And if that were to happen, the fewer who know the better.'

Dwight asked, 'Who else knows of this operation?'

'Apart from us and the President, only a few high-ranking officials, and none of them know you exist.'

'What kind of back-up is available?' Dwight asked.

'Sam will be following you to Zurich.'

Dwight did not look at Kamas. 'What about money, access to the information pool?'

'You name it,' Anderson said. 'You've got it.'

'How about ten thousand dollars up front, another thirty sent to me at the Imtra Bank in Zurich?'

'That's fine,' Anderson said.

'Do I get direct access to you?'

'Sure.' Anderson scribbled a number on a pad and showed it to Dwight. 'That'll find me, any time of the day or night.'

'What if I run into trouble?' Dwight asked. 'Do I get to carry a weapon?'

'You can have anything up to an M-16. You can also have nursemaids, if you want them.'

Dwight leaned back in his chair and stretched out his legs. He stared down at his jeans and sneakers. 'Is there anything I can't have?' he asked.

'The President is personally concerned with the outcome of this operation,' Anderson said softly. 'We believe those processes could make a significant difference to the future of America.'

The toes of his sneakers were worn smooth and streaked with grime from the courts. 'I was going on holiday,' Dwight said. 'To play tennis in Tampa.'

'We'll take care of that,' Kamas offered.

Jeb Anderson said, 'I'm asking you on behalf of the President. If you want to, I'll fix it so we go over to the White House and have the President ask you himself.'

'You're kidding,' Dwight said, but he knew Jeb Anderson wasn't, and that he had no come back. The President asked and the President got. He looked up at Jeb Anderson and grinned. 'You want to know something, Jeb? Sometimes, both banking and tennis get dead boring.'

An hour later, Dwight was hurrying to Dulles, in the back of the Cadillac, clutching the attaché case Kamas had given him containing the ten thousand dollars.

He had cancelled his holiday arrangements and signed a one-time Agency contract, in which he named his father as next of kin and in the event of an accident asked the Agency to notify Sami first.

As Kamas had assured him, it was simply routine.

13

Dwight reached Zurich early the next morning. On the second floor of the luxurious terminal building, he hired a car, checked the address on the map he'd asked for, and drove to the Streuli Sanatorium, where Elisabeth Manninger had died.

The sanatorium was on the opposite side of the city, a cluster of neat, low roofed buildings, standing on the side of a hill, separated from the picture postcard village of Streuli by a stream and a surrounding wall of pale yellow brick.

It was a comfortable place, restful, undoubtedly expensive, more a discerning hotel than hospital. Dwight gave the wholesome-looking receptionist a business card and a few minutes later was ushered into the presence of Senior Resident Physician, Dr Armand Flacker.

Flacker was a large, solid, well scrubbed Swiss, wearing a crisp, white surgeon's gown over a pale grey business suit. He was in his mid-forties, his high forehead wrinkled in supercilious comprehension as he studied Dwight's business card, held in long, white fingers, whose nails seemed to be manicured twice a day. 'Good morning,' he said, '*bonjour, grüss gott, buongiorno.*' He put down the card and looked condescendingly across the desk at Dwight, head tilted back, languid eyes half closed, a half smile playing around the corners of his soft mouth.

Smart-arse, Dwight thought, and said, 'Good morning, *gutenmorgen, Flacker seen-sang, tso sun.*'

The titillation at the corners of the mouth became a proper smile. Flacker asked, 'What was that last one?'

'Good morning, Mr Flacker, in Vietnamese,' Dwight said. 'Very useful if you want to find the way to Saigon.'

Dr Flacker tilted his chair forward and rested his elbows on the desk. 'You were in Vietnam?'

'Yes.'

'And you are a banker?'

Dwight nodded.

'And what does the Imtra Bank have to do with the late Mrs Manninger?'

Dwight told him that one of the Imtra Bank's largest customers, the Capital Mutual Assurance Co of Omaha had a large policy on Elisabeth Manninger's life. As Dwight was coming to Switzerland on business, they had asked him to verify the fact and circumstances of Elisabeth Manninger's death. 'It's normal where large policies are concerned,' Dwight said. 'Pure routine.'

'Pure routine,' Dr Flacker repeated, softly. 'Tell me, Mr Khouri, in English, German or Vietnamese, do you know a lawyer from Munich called Johann Neumann?'

Dwight shook his head.

'Johann Neumann saw me yesterday about Elisabeth Manninger. And now there's you. Funny, isn't it, when the poor lady was alive, no one came, except twice a year the gentlemen from the Hoffman Bank. Now she is dead, two people arrive within twenty-four hours. Tell me, Mr Khouri, what makes Elisabeth Manninger so popular?'

'Money,' Dwight said. 'I believe Mrs Manninger was quite wealthy, even wealthier in death than in life. Mrs Manninger was insured with the Capital Mutual for a quarter of a million dollars.'

'So much?' Flacker lifted eyebrows like tufts of dried grass, his condescension barely concealing suspicion. 'When was this policy taken out, Mr Khouri?'

'Oh, many years ago, 1944, '45, something like that, when she married Berndt Manninger. I believe it was effected through Switzerland, and the policy was quite small when it was issued. But over the years with the compound interest and undrawn bonuses it has grown. As the insurance people always say, from little acorns . . .' The story was unlikely enough to be credible. 'What did this German lawyer want?' he asked, hoping to prevent Dr Flacker thinking too much about the Capital Mutual Assurance Co of Omaha.

'Same as you. The Manninger estate.'

'I am hoping to increase the value of the estate.'

Flacker gave a sarcastic nod. 'The German represented certain beneficiaries of the Manninger estate. He wanted to ensure that none of Mrs Manninger's personal property was disposed of without his consent.'

'And what did you tell him?' Dwight asked, setting his face into an expression of anticipatory admiration.

'To talk to the Hoffman Bank or get a court order.'

'That was very clever of you,' Dwight said, looking around the office. Dr Flacker's medical degrees were prominently displayed on the wall above his head; a row of glass jars containing human organs preserved in formaldehyde were neatly arrayed on the top of a low cabinet filled with medical textbooks. Becoming a doctor had obviously been the highpoint of Flacker's life. And here he was, at the peak of his career, comforting rich old ladies waiting to die. Dwight wondered whether Flacker compensated for that by being excessively rude to his subordinates.

'I could tell you to do something similar,' Flacker offered. 'But you are lucky. I like Americans.'

And welcome to the world's smallest fan club, Dwight thought.

'Do you know Rudi Frenzak?'

Dwight shook his head. All he needed now was to find the Poles had an interest in Elisabeth Manninger's estate.

'He's a dentist,' Flacker said, his expression conveying mild surprise that Dwight hadn't heard of him. 'He lives in Los Angeles. He is married to my sister.'

Dwight murmured something about America being a huge country.

Dr Flacker appeared not to have heard. 'You must visit him the next time you are in Los Angeles. He is very famous. Film stars go to him.' Dr Flacker sighed, perhaps wishing that there were a few film stars at the Streuli Sanatorium.

'I could always take him a message,' Dwight offered. 'Or if there is anything you want to send . . .'

'No,' Dr Flacker said, briskly. 'I am going there for my holiday next year. Tell me, is Los Angeles very expensive?'

'No,' Dwight smiled. 'Not compared to Zurich.'

That settled, Dr Flacker asked, 'And what is this verification you have to make?'

Dwight made a great show of pulling out a notebook and pen. 'How did Elisabeth Manninger die?'

Flacker opened a drawer and took out a piece of official-looking paper. 'This is her death certificate,' he said, looking down at it. 'It says that Mrs Manninger died of a coronary occlusion, or in simple words, a heart attack.'

Dwight religiously noted that fact in his book. 'Did Elisabeth have a history of heart trouble?'

'She had a heart condition, yes. We discovered it five years ago during her bi-annual check up. It was not however serious, and recently appeared to have stabilized.' Flacker gave a massive shrug. 'But you can never tell with a heart condition. A slight shock, a change of diet, the weather even, can bring about an attack.' He told Dwight that Elisabeth Manninger had died the previous Sunday afternoon, around tea time. She'd been taken to the woods and had expressed a wish to remain there a while. When Nurse Haberstrom had gone to collect her, she was dead. She died peacefully, without any pain.

'Why was Mrs Manninger here?' Dwight asked.

'She was,' Dr Flacker paused, choosing his words carefully,

'not entirely sane. For long periods she would drift away from reality, and if she lived outside the sanatorium, she could, in one of these states, walk in front of a bus or a train without knowing it. It is something that afflicts the very old.'

'And how old was Mrs Manninger?'

'Fifty-five. But in her case, the affliction was not caused by senility. At some point in her life, Mrs Manninger suffered an enormous shock – a shock that literally drove her out of her mind. We tried everything we knew to bring her out of this state. But nothing worked.'

'What was that experience?'

Flacker hesitated. 'Whatever it was, it happened during the war. I don't think it would be professional for me to discuss it with you.'

Dwight closed the notebook in tacit agreement. 'I wonder if I could have a few words with the person who found her. Nurse . . .'

'Haberstrom,' Flacker finished. 'I will see if she is free.' He picked up a phone from his desk and spoke into it. Replacing the receiver, he gave Dwight a superior smile. 'She is coming. You will find that she speaks excellent English. We have patients from all over the world here.'

Nurse Haberstrom was in her mid-thirties, a fresh complexioned, motherly-looking woman, with a robust air of Swiss healthiness. She listened carefully as Dr Flacker explained the purpose of Dwight's visit and agreed to answer Dwight's questions and take him to the spot where Elisabeth Manninger had been found.

Walking across the carefully nurtured lawn she said she had come on duty at half past six the previous Sunday. Having discovered that Frau Manninger was not in her room, she had checked with Frau von Heissler, the patient Elisabeth Manninger had been friendliest with. Frau von Heissler had informed her that Elisabeth Manninger had been taken to the woods to meet some visitors.

'Was that usual?' Dwight asked. 'I mean, meeting people in the woods?'

'On Sundays, it is usual,' Nurse Haberstrom replied. 'On Sundays, visitors come, and if it is good weather they go to the gardens and the woods.'

'Is there a record of visitors?'

'No. It is not necessary.'

They walked into the forest and stood under the threaded shadows of the larches. The marks where the wheelchair had left the track and been pushed into the clearing were still clearly visible.

'Who brought Mrs Manninger here?' Dwight asked.

'On Sunday afternoons we have . . . *gastarbeiters* – other nurses. We do not have treatments on Sundays, and because we do not always work on Sundays, we have other . . .'

'Temporary nurses,' Dwight said.

'Temporary nurses, that is right.'

'So the nurse who brought Mrs Manninger here was a temporary?'

'Yes. She should not have left her here, but I suppose she thought Frau Manninger's friends would bring her back to the main building.'

'Do you have the nurse's name?' Dwight asked, staring at the flattened grass around the spot where the wheelchair had stood.

'It is in the office,' Nurse Haberstrom replied.

Dwight stood staring at the flattened grass, then walked softly across it and went into the thicket beyond. There were broken twigs, the breaks still fresh, two cigarette ends. A number of people had been here, had waited in this clearing. At least four or five people, Dwight estimated.

Dwight squatted and began pulling at the undergrowth with his hands. 'Do many people use these woods?' he called.

'Only the patients and the staff, and if it is nice, on Sundays, the visitors.'

'Do you know how many people visited Mrs Manninger last Sunday?'

Nurse Haberstrom frowned. 'It would be unusual if it were more than two.'

Dwight continued searching. There was nothing more to show who had been in the clearing with Elisabeth Manninger. He shifted on his haunches, side-stepped uncomfortably, suddenly saw something glint beneath the brambles. He reached forward and picked it up, stared fascinated at the silver badge in his palm. It was the kind of thing that was worn on epaulettes and a shred of black thread still dangled from the pin. The badge was shaped like two parallel z's.

Parallel z's or twin bolts of lightning. The symbol of the SS!

Dwight got to his feet. There was no SS now. There had never been an SS in Switzerland. But he was holding an SS badge in his hand. Something torn from an epaulette. Someone had been here recently in full death's-head regalia.

Dwight walked thoughtfully back to the clearing.

'You want to go back to the office?' Nurse Haberstrom asked.

'You told me there was a patient Mrs Manninger was friendly with. A Frau von . . .'

'Frau von Heissler.'

'Yes. Is it possible for me to speak to her?'

'I will see,' Nurse Haberstrom said, and led the way purposefully towards the sanatorium building.

Frau von Heissler was an imperious-looking woman, with a double stranded pearl necklace across her ample bosom and a trickle of cream dribbling from the corner of her rouged mouth. She was, she explained, having her customary mid-morning snack, two cream cakes and coffee.

Nurse Haberstrom introduced Dwight to her.

Dwight politely refused Frau von Heissler's offer of coffee.

'Mr Khouri is from the insurance company,' Nurse Haberstrom said.

Frau von Heissler gave Dwight an angry stare. 'There is no use in insurance,' she said, bluntly. 'Elisabeth had no family.' She turned majestically on Nurse Haberstrom. 'I have reported that stupid girl,' she cried. 'She should never have taken Elisabeth to the woods. Elisabeth hated the woods. She

88

was in no mood to receive visitors. I told that stupid girl to have the visitors come back later, but she wouldn't listen. She just took Elisabeth away.'

'Do you mean Mrs Manninger did not want to see these visitors?' Dwight asked.

'She didn't want to see anybody,' Frau von Heissler said and took a sad mouthful of cake.

Afterwards, in the administration office, Nurse Haberstrom looked for the name and address of the temporary nurse. She said, 'You must not take Frau von Heissler too seriously These patients, they all dislike something. Today it's the woods, tomorrow the food or another patient. They're old. They can't always control what they do or say.'

'I envy you your fortitude,' Dwight said.

Nurse Haberstrom took a card from a file, scribbled a name and address on a sheet of paper and handed it to Dwight. The nurse who had taken Elisabeth Manninger to the woods was Ilana Jarusovic and she lived in a village called Rilswil.

Dwight went straight from the sanatorium to the funeral parlour in the village. It was a sombre place, with large opaque windows filtering out the bright sunlight. A gloomy man dressed in black conducted Dwight to a chapel at the back where Frau Manninger lay coffined. Two candles glowed feebly at the head of the coffin beside a crucifix. She lay small in her shroud, and looking very frail. There was a tinge of blue about her face and despite the expertise of the mortician, her brows remained raised, the jaw slightly stretched.

For a long time, Dwight stared at the body. There was a small scrape on Elisabeth Manninger's middle finger, that might have been made by the pin of a brooch, or an SS epaulette badge. And it seemed, looking at Elisabeth Manninger's face, that at the moment of death she had been overcome by fear.

14

Rilswil was a few kilometres from Streuli, pretty, the kind of place tourists stopped in for lunch and afterwards remembered as typically Swiss. It was small and picturesque, a huddle of timbered houses clustered round a church, a moss-covered stone fountain in the Marketplatz, a small railway station surrounded by grey picket fencing and two cafés with brightly coloured awnings spread over the pavement.

Ilana Jarusovic lodged in one of the cafés, and apparently paid for her board by working as a waitress six evenings a week. The proprietor told Dwight she wasn't in the café, she was out walking, and would be back shortly before her shift began at four. Dwight could wait or he could drive towards Streuli. She'd been seen walking in that direction and Dwight would probably meet her on the way.

Dwight left, driving slowly out of the village. Rilswil was surrounded by farmland, gently undulating hills neatly quartered by hedges and fences, dotted with farm houses built of dark timber. About a kilometre from the village Dwight stopped, got out of the car and looked over the hedges. Everything was peaceful, still and very green, the fields deserted except for the solitary figure of a woman walking briskly across a pasture forty yards away.

Dwight found a barred gate, climbed over it and went to meet her, feeling incongruous and hot in his jacket and tie, his leather soled shoes slipping on the uneven surface beneath the smooth grass. Ilana Jarusovic came towards him confidently, the wind pressing her dark cotton dress against her body, outlining large breasts and hips, ruffling her hair into bright golden streaks. She had a round, childish face, a regularity of feature that made her look unremarkably pretty. As Dwight approached she greeted him with a polite *Guten tag* and altered direction.

'One moment, Fraulein,' Dwight called and moved after her.

She looked sideways at him, her body tensed in sudden fear.

'Dr Flacker sent me to talk to you.'

Instantly, the girl relaxed.

Dwight showed her a business card. 'We are making a few enquiries about Frau Manninger. I understand you were with Frau Manninger when she died.'

Immediately, fleetingly, her shoulders hunched, her ruddy cheeks momentarily lost all colour. Her tongue darted over dry lips. 'There must be some mistake. I was not with Frau Manninger when she died.'

Dwight fell into step beside her walking in the direction she had chosen, back towards the road. 'My mistake,' he said, soothingly. 'No one was with Elisabeth Manninger when she died. You were the person who took her to the woods, isn't that right?'

The girl nodded vehemently as if she didn't trust herself to speak.

'Why did you take her to the woods?' Dwight asked.

'To meet . . . people. There were visitors for her.'

'How many visitors?'

'Thr – I don't remember, three or four men.'

'Men? Not her family?'

A vehement shake of her head. 'No, they were from the bank.'

'Which bank?'

The girl stumbled, checked herself before she replied. 'I don't know.'

'The Hoffman Bank?'

She kept looking down at her flat heeled shoes. 'I don't know.'

They walked closer together along a small ridge. 'Why didn't you fetch Frau Manninger afterwards?'

'I'd thought . . . I'd thought the visitors would bring her back to the main building.'

'Shouldn't you have checked before you left? Frau Manninger was an old lady and helpless.'

'I – I told one of the other nurses where she was. I was in a hurry to leave that day. I was meeting someone and – '

'Whom did you tell?' Dwight asked fiercely.

She started at the anger in his voice. 'One of the others . . . one of the other nurses.'

'A staff-nurse or one of the Sunday girls?'

'I don't remember who it was.'

Dwight stopped, turned, swung his hand round open palmed. His palm caught her on the cheek, spun her head round, pushed her off balance. Her feet scrabbled along the side of the ridge. Her arms flailed. She lost her balance and fell on all fours. 'Who *paid* you to take Elisabeth Manninger to the woods?' Dwight asked, quietly.

The girl crouched on her knees and elbows, a hand distractedly stroking her reddened cheek. Slowly she shook her head in a mixture of shock and refusal. A large tear rolled down her cheek and over the back of her hand.

'Elisabeth Manninger died because of your neglect!' Dwight said, raising his voice. 'If you hadn't left her she wouldn't have died.'

'No,' the girl sobbed. 'No! They said they wanted to talk to her. They promised they would bring her back.'

'Who?'

'The men from the bank. Not Hoffman's Bank, another one. They wanted to talk business with Frau Manninger, and the only way they could do it was by meeting her in secret in the woods.'

Dwight stooped and helped her to her feet. The mark of his blow had left three thick stripes on her cheek. She stood in front of him, still crying, the backs of her fists thrust into her eyes, like a child.

'How did the men contact you?'

A man had picked her up at the bus stop the previous week.

He was a *gastarbeiter* like her, from near Zagreb. He had got quite excited when he'd learned that she worked at the sanatorium. He worked for a bank, he'd said, and his employers would give her a thousand francs if she could arrange for them to meet with Elisabeth Manninger. At first she hadn't wanted to do it. But the man had sworn that no harm would come to Elisabeth Manninger; that the meeting was in Elisabeth Manninger's interest. That morning he had given her five hundred francs and told her she could keep it whether she helped them or not.

'And the rest of the money?'

'He met me on Sunday evening, after I left the sanatorium.'

'Did he bring you back to Rilswil?'

'No. He handed me the money in an envelope and drove away.'

'What kind of car was it?' Dwight asked.

'A red one.' She paused, thinking, wiping the tears from her face with the back of her hand. 'It had Zurich plates.' She stared blankly past his shoulder.

'Describe the man.'

'He was about your age, fair-haired, ordinary-looking. His suit had shiny patches at the knees and elbows, and his Slavic had a funny accent.'

'Funny how? Because of dialect?'

'No. It wasn't dialect . . . it was as if Slavic was not his first language.' Her eyes widened in realization. 'The man was – '

Dwight heard a sharp parting of air, saw the girl's mouth open in a silent scream, saw her face open. A deep, spouting hole appeared below her left eye, spraying him with blood and slivers of bone. Her head rocked sideways, the bright golden hair snapping straight as she wheeled, arms outflung, seeming in death to evade Dwight's outstretched arms. Her feet slid down the side of the ridge, her body crumpling as she slipped, folding itself towards the earth. She hit the earth in silence and lay still, lying on her side, a child asleep.

Except she wasn't asleep. Dwight knelt beside her, then

threw himself flat as another bullet whirred above his head. Her eyes, open in frozen surprise, stared blankly at him. A red wash of blood flowed unheeded down her cheek.

A bullet thudded into the earth two feet from him. Dwight pulled himself round behind the girl's body and turned to look.

The field was empty, an open expanse of grass flecked with the brown of mid-summer heat. Beyond the field was a tree-covered hillock. Behind him, a hedge screening the field from the road. He looked at the road, then back at the dead girl, looked along the field. The shots had come from the hillock. Someone was there amongst those trees with a high powered rifle and a telescopic sight.

Someone who had already killed. Someone who was going to kill him!

Dwight lay motionless by the girl's body. If he could get to the hedge, to the road. He calculated angles of fire. He could sprint the five yards to the hedge, lose himself in the undergrowth beside it. But from the hillock, the gunman would have a clear view of the road, the benefit of a target conspicuous against an open expanse of tarmac.

He saw sunlight glint on metal, glimpsed a shadowy figure flit between the trees.

Dwight turned and ran, moving as the gunman moved, pulling his legs under him, sprinting crouched for the hedge. Three steps, four, he flung himself face down into the undergrowth. A bullet ripped through the hedge. Dwight pushed himself forward, rolled, allowed himself to slide down into the ditch.

He lay there breathless, momentarily out of sight and safe. A car rushed past on the road above him, its tyres giving off a whirring sound. His heart leaped as the sound of the engine faltered. They'd seen the girl. Seen the gunman. Then the engine resumed its steady throb. The sound diminished in the distance.

Dwight remembered the field was obscured from the road. Even if someone glimpsed the girl lying in it, her face was turned away from the road. They would imagine she was asleep in the sunshine. He had to do something. On all fours he crawled along the ditch for a few yards, stopped and cautiously raised his head. The girl still lay there. The hillock seemed deserted in the bright afternoon sun. Was the gunman still there? Or was he making a stealthy approach along the road? If the gunman got to the road, he was finished.

His heart hammered furiously against the wall of his chest. Rivulets of sweat trickled down his face and arms. He risked another look at the hillock. Silent. Deserted. Perhaps the anonymous killer had gone. Slowly, Dwight raised his body on his hands, pulled himself half-way out of the ditch. He saw a dark blur of movement, a bright glint of sunlight on metal. He dropped back into the ditch as a bullet smacked into the hedge three feet above him.

Dead leaves oozed damp under the weight of his hands and knees. Twigs snapped. A bird took off in front of him with a startled flapping of wings. If only he could reach high ground. If only he could –

He heard the sound of trickling water and hurried along the ditch. The ditch followed the curve of the road. He crawled rapidly along it, stopped at the end where a small gash of earth led to a small stream. The stream ran at right angles to the ditch, diverted underneath the road by a large iron pipe four feet in diameter. He could easily crawl through that pipe.

Dwight looked across the stream to the right. On the further side of the stream was a small clearing, beyond it tangled undergrowth and trees that edged the field. Dwight followed the line of trees. If you can't run, fight. Well, little chance of running or fighting. The trees were separated from the hillock by a bare expanse of pasture.

Dwight remained motionless, studying the trees, studying the hillock. There had to be something he could do, some way he could lure the gunman from his cover. Then he saw it. A constant glint, too large to be sunlight reflected off a gun barrel and motionless so as to appear part of the forest. Dwight shaded his eyes and looked into the bright silver glare. A large rectangular shadow lay behind the gleaming blob. A shadow that was absolutely still. A car! The gunman's car!

Dwight rose to a crouch, poised like a runner on starting blocks. Then still crouching, he ran over the top of the bank and threw himself on hands and knees into the water. The water was ice cold. The shock of it made him gasp. His knees and elbows jarred on slimy rock, as on all fours he scrambled across the stream, then sprinted across the clearing, and threw himself face down into the undergrowth.

For a while he lay there, allowing the water to run from his clothes, feeling his feet squelch inside his shoes. When he'd got his breath back, he dragged himself deeper into the undergrowth and ran his hands down his arms and legs, squeezing off all the surplus water. Then quietly, he got to his feet and peered at the hillock. Satisfied he had not been seen, he moved into the forest.

For three years he had lived in jungles. For three years his survival had depended on an ingrained ability to move over dead foliage with the softness of a serpent, and to travel like a shadow through trees and undergrowth. It all came back as he moved instinctively from shadow to shadow, his sliding feet making no more sound than the gentlest of breezes.

Dwight stopped ten feet from the car. A muddy BMW sedan, its yellow paintwork mottled with shadow. The car was unoccupied, and through a tenuity in the pattern of the trees, Dwight could discern the gunman on the hillock, squatting crouched behind a tree trunk, weapon tucked beneath his armpit, pointing loosely at the field.

Dwight moved deeper into the forest, filled his hand-kerchief with a collection of pebbles. Then moving closer to the car, he picked up three larger stones.

He walked to within five feet of the car, examined the forest on the further side of it. Then he flung a stone through the driver's window. The sound of shattering glass was startling.

He flung a stone through the windscreen, another through the rear window, rushed across and yanked open the door. Quickly he released the seat back and tilted it forward, studied the angle at which it rested against the wheel, stooped and adjusted the bottom of the seat. When he had got the required angle, he locked the seat in place and wedged the back of the seat against the horn with a vicious blow from his fist.

The horn blared. Birds scattered into the air. The continuous, single note pealed into the afternoon like a siren.

Dwight scurried into the trees and waited.

The gunman could not afford to ignore the car. Before the battery expired, that single, continuous blaring would bring someone into the field, into the woods. The gunman would either have to walk away from the hillock or take a chance and return to the car.

The gunman decided to return to the car. Moments later, Dwight saw him emerge from the trees, sprint down the hill, a tall, athletic-looking man in black trousers, black turtle neck sweater, partially covered by an army camouflage jacket. He had a black, woollen ski cap pulled over his head, and there was a brief glint of blond hair as he ran across the open expanse and came into the forest.

Once he got to the trees, he moved more cautiously, gun fanning the air in front of him. Dwight waited motionless, breath slipping softly over his tongue. The gunman slowed, dropped into an ungainly crouch and approached the car.

He stared disbelievingly at the shattered windows. Then as Dwight expected he turned to look at the direction from which the stone had come. Dwight hurled the pebbles in his handkerchief into the undergrowth.

The man jumped, whirled the gun round in the direction of the noise, then stood frozen, peering into the forest.

Dwight moved silently from where he was crouched, eased himself around the car, his hands raised shoulder high in front of him, the cutting edge of his palms outwards.

A split second before those palms crashed down on either

97

side of the gunman's neck, he heard the sharp explosion of breath as Dwight contracted his stomach muscles to give more force to the blow. Then the hands like flying steel wedges were on him, driving deep into the roots of his neck, a great grey cloud of paralysis filling his lungs, locking his mouth open, spilling the gun from his nerveless grasp.

The gunman fell face forwards with a quiet thumping sound. Dwight turned him over on to his back, took his wallet from the camouflage jacket. There was just over five hundred German marks in it and a thousand Swiss francs, a driving licence and two credit cards in the name of Rolf Hausen. All the documents gave an address in Munich.

Dwight knew the man would be unconscious for hours, that if he recovered, he would never talk normally again. He opened the car door and pulled the seat away from the steering wheel, and in the unnerving silence that followed, he could hear his pulse drumming in his head. He decided he wouldn't involve the Swiss police. Involving the Swiss police would mean explaining what he had been doing in that field with Ilana Jarusovic, and the clear instructions from the Agency were that what the Swiss didn't know, they wouldn't complain about.

Dwight slipped the money, the licence and the credit cards into his pocket. Then he hurled the wallet into the undergrowth and set off to walk back to his car.

Dwight drove towards Zurich, till the trembling of his hands forced him to stop. All the while he had been in the field and crawling silently through the trees, all the while he had been coping with the gunman instinct and training had taken over and he had felt nothing. He had been in a state of total absorption, his entire being focused on a single physical objective.

Now it was different. The steering wheel vibrated in his hands. His shirt was clammy with sweat. He wanted to scream, to beat his head against the windscreen. He was frightened, he was terrified. He felt utterly alone and completely helpless. He wanted to crawl under the seat and hide. Desperately he clung to the wheel, pressed his damp forehead against the back of a clenched fist, feeling the dull burn at the back of his eyes and his dry mouth opening and closing in a soundless phrase. Jesus help me! Oh God help me . . . help me . . . help me . . .

15

The next morning, the Bahnhofstrasse was at its elegant, summer best. Sunlight glistened on displays of watches in Omega and Piaget, on traceries of fine lace in Sturzenneger, on blocks of gold in the shaded windows of the Swiss Bank Corporation. The large shady trees lining the pavement were in luxuriant frondescence, and blue trams bustled along the centre of the street with a drone of electric motors.

Yet, as Dwight walked to the Hoffman Bank, he could not share the brightness of the day or the exhilaration of the shoppers and tourists crowding the elegant window displays. He felt jaded, lethargic, hollowed by a brutal emptiness. He was too long out of strategy, too long out of training. And he had lost the habit of blind faith. Dwight knew that once an agent began to make value judgements, he was dead. The whole point of training was to avoid judgement, to react instinctively, with deadly expertise. As he had reacted to the German. And if he was to go on, if he was to survive, he had to fight the terror and revulsion that followed the action. He had to overcome it. He had to overcome *them*.

Dwight started to walk quickly along the Bahnhofstrasse, so quickly that he was almost running. Action, he knew, provided its own deliverance.

The Hoffman Bank was situated half-way down the street in a discreet, two-storeyed building of glass and concrete.

Instead of gold in its windows, there was a list of share prices, and outside its heavy swing doors, a commissionaire in a frock coat, who led Dwight to a bespectacled matron of no more than thirty years.

The matron looked at his business card with respect. Dr Hoffman would see him straight away, she said, and as he followed her to the elevators, Dwight reflected that in Switzerland there were still two classes of people, bankers and others.

Gerhardt Hoffman was a sullen man in his mid thirties, smugly corpulent with a large aggressive head on a short neck, thinning sandy hair and bulbous blue eyes. He reminded Dwight of a bellicose frog.

His office was large and flamboyantly ponderous, with a huge desk and heavy reproduction furniture on wall to wall carpeting, a wallpaper of grey flecked design to better display his garish modern prints, and a portrait in oils, which if the bellicose pomposity was any indication, was of Hoffman's father.

'I am afraid I am not going to be of very much use,' Hoffman said, modestly. He spoke a peculiarly unaccented English, that was probably the result of hours of practice with records. 'You see, I did not personally know Berndt Manninger. He was a friend of my father's — ' Here Hoffman looked up respectfully at the portrait. 'An extremely wealthy man and very suspicious.'

Manninger had been a customer of the bank since 1929. His affairs were run through two companies incorporated in Liechtenstein, Sopadep and Perpetua. 'But we were merely bankers, you understand.' Hoffman bared large teeth in an ingratiating smile. 'We did not control the companies. We played no part in their administration.

'As you know,' Hoffman continued, 'we are the executors of Berndt Manninger's estate. It is a responsibility we have carried out to the utmost of our ability. We have, I think, administered the investments wisely. We have at all times kept Mrs Manninger informed of our activities, and of the income available to her.'

'I understand Mrs Manninger was not entirely sane,' Dwight said.

'Perhaps so. But the information was always presented to her, and we were always available to answer her queries. As far as the processes you are interested in are concerned, we know nothing about them. They were not left with us. We believe Manninger's will clearly indicates that if they ever existed at all, they were deposited elsewhere.'

'And you have no idea where?'

Mournfully, Hoffman shook his head.

'What happens now that Elisabeth Manninger is dead?'

'The other heirs must prove their inheritance.'

'And how would they do that?'

'According to the instructions Manninger left with us, the heirs must first prove their kinship in the conventional way, and also produce to us the *Zessions* of the companies – the founders certificates.' Hoffman explained that every Liechtenstein anstalt had a founders certificate, certifying the existence and ownership of the company.

'And where would they find this? In the Companies Registry at Vaduz?'

Hoffman shook his head. 'They must produce the originals.'

'Has any claim been made against the estate?' Dwight asked.

Hoffman shook his head. 'Not so far.'

'But you are expecting a claim to be made?'

Hoffman gave an expressive shrug, which clearly said that whether a claim was made or not made, was nothing to do with him.

Dwight asked, 'In the thirty-five years since Manninger died, have you or the bank made any attempt to find these *Zessions* or Manninger's other assets?'

There was the right touch of incredulousness in Hoffman's smile. 'We are bankers, Mr Khouri,' he said. 'Not private detectives. It is not our business to trace the Manninger assets.'

No, Dwight thought sourly, as long as you are sitting on the Manninger fortune and collecting your commissions and interest, it isn't your business.

'You are being surprisingly candid,' he said, even though he felt nothing of the kind. 'Why?'

'I am not telling you anything I shouldn't,' Hoffman said. 'In telling you that we do not have the Manninger processes, I am not breaching any laws. You see, Mr Khouri, a number of people, Americans particularly, misunderstand our laws of bank secrecy. They believe that they were created to help people hide money and the proceeds of criminal activities. That is not the case. The bank secrecy laws derive from deep belief by our people, that a man's banking affairs are his own business. Anyone who comes here, who is not a criminal, is entitled to the protection of those laws, just as a Swiss citizen visiting America is entitled to the protection of American law. Our law of bank secrecy has existed for over three hundred years. We would not want anyone to besmirch our name by spreading rumours that we pass these laws so that we may have the benefit of Nazi inventions. The Hoffman Bank does not have the processes you seek, Mr Khouri. The Hoffman Bank does not know where they are.'

All very moral and above board, Dwight thought, and asked, 'How did the bank receive its instructions from Manninger?'

'From Manninger himself. I suppose though, in exceptional circumstances, certain of his trusted associates would have been authorized to give us instructions.'

'Do you recall any of these trusted associates?'

Hoffman smiled apologetically. 'As I told you, it was before my time.'

Dwight questioned Hoffman a little further, but Hoffman either did not know, or the answers were too specifically connected with the Manninger estate and therefore governed by the bank secrecy laws.

'Do you know of anyone who would want to kill Elisabeth Manninger?'

Hoffman thrust his hands wide. 'Mr Khouri,' he said with genuine incredulity. 'This is Switzerland.'

A few minutes later, Dwight left, with an irritating feeling of having learned little that he did not already know, and that beneath Hoffman's blandness, there was a sense of anxiety, and a carefully suppressed hope that matters which had been buried would remain so. If ever there was a Swiss demonstrating neutrality, Dwight thought, Dr Hoffman was it.

The matron met Dwight outside Hoffman's office and escorted him to the ground floor. 'Have a nice day, Mr Khouri,' she said, flashing him a business-like smile. 'Enjoy Zurich.'

'I will,' Dwight replied. That afternoon he was attending Elisabeth Manninger's funeral.

The cemetery was on a hill outside Streuli, a walled-in enclosure of neat tombstones, slabs of black and white marble and small crosses arranged in precise rows. In Switzerland even death was ordered, with just so much space for each person and commemorative tablets of a pre-determined size and shape. Dwight hurried along the gravelled path towards the group by the open grave at the north end, deliberately late to avoid the rigours of a long service on a hot afternoon.

'*Dies irae! Dies illa!*'

The chant hung on the still afternoon air. So the shop girl who had married Berndt Manninger had been Catholic. Dwight hurried between the tombstones and edged into the gathering. He recognized Dr Flacker and Nurse Haberstrom, Frau von Heissler with a pinched-faced companion who dabbed at her eyes constantly. Gerhardt Hoffman was there sweating profusely in his dark suit, a few other old ladies from the sanatorium, younger people with them who looked as if they were medical staff. Altogether there weren't many people to mourn the passing of the last of the Manningers.

The coffin had already been lowered, the tapes on which it had been cradled slack along the bare earthen sides. An old priest stood at the head of the grave, a frail, gloomy figure in surplice and black chasuble. Behind him were two altar boys in black surplices and a small choir from the village.

The chanting faded and stopped. The priest began the last prayer for the dead. The only Manninger heir was about to be finally laid to rest. The last of the Manningers.

Standing on the right of the priest, in the position of chief mourner was a young woman, her face obscured by the veil suspended from her black, pillbox hat. From the slimness of her body, the firmness of her breasts and legs, Dwight reckoned she was in her early twenties. She was flanked by two burly men, all shoulders and rock-jawed faces, and eyes that looked neither at the priest nor the coffin, but stared expressionlessly at the congregation.

The priest blessed the grave, scooped up earth in a trowel and handed it to the woman. Mechanically, she stepped forward and stood for a moment, looking down at the coffin. Then she emptied the trowel over the coffin and followed the soft thuds of falling earth with a small bouquet of white roses she carried.

The priest turned to her, spoke a few words and moved away. The mourners shuffled forward. Dwight felt himself pressed towards the front of the line, skirting the open grave. Dr Flacker shook hands brusquely with the veiled woman. Gerhardt Hoffman made a great show of sympathy, taking both her hands in his, lowering his great head confidentially over hers. Frau von Heissler grasped the girl to a heaving bosom.

Dwight stood in line behind nurse Haberstrom. He watched the nurse walk up to the girl and say a few words of consolation. Beneath the veil, the girl's face was pretty, with a tip-tilted nose and pert chin, a soft wide mouth and level grey-green eyes, dry as a bone.

Nurse Haberstrom stepped away. Dwight moved forward, aware of the grey-green eyes fixed on him, totally disinterested. Her hand, when he took it, was firm and dry.

Afterwards, Dwight waited with the mourners near the cemetery gate, where a black Mercedes was parked. The girl and the two bodyguards came towards them and climbed into the Mercedes. It pulled away majestically into the road.

Dwight climbed into his own car and set off after the Mercedes. The road was narrow, the Mercedes was travelling slowly, and he picked it up without difficulty. When they reached the main road to Zurich, he settled in behind it, closing up as they entered Zurich and driving past it when they parked in a side street in the pedestrian area of the Bahnhofstrasse.

Dwight drew ahead and double parked illegally, watched them walk past him to the Hoffman Bank. Their business there was predictable, he reflected. After the funeral, the reading of the will.

When Dwight got back to the Baur Au Lac, Sam Kamas was in the lounge, nursing a vodka-tonic in which the ice had long since melted. He looked appreciatively around the lofty, panelled room and said, 'Christ, you bagmen types live well.'

'Always have,' Dwight said, sitting down opposite Kamas. 'The Agency likes us to stay in the best hotels and fly first class. They feel it reduces temptation.'

'Increases it, more likely,' Kamas said and looked at Dwight's tie. 'Been paying your last respects to Elisabeth Manninger?'

'Not exactly,' Dwight said. Apart from a slight reddening of the eye, Kamas seemed unaffected by the flight from Washington. He told Kamas he believed Elisabeth Manninger had been murdered and showed him the SS badge.

Kamas examined it closely. 'Could be a coincidence,' he said, without conviction.

'Sure,' Dwight agreed and told him about the killing of Ilana Jarusovic. He handed Kamas Rolf Hausen's credit cards and driving licence. 'No one told me I was going to be shot at.'

'Hell, Dwight, we didn't think it would get this heavy. Okay, what do you want me to do? You want me to get you some protection?'

A waiter approached. Dwight ordered coffee for himself and a fresh vodka-tonic for Kamas. 'I think I'll be a hero,' he said. 'Can you get me a Colt Python chambered for a .45 magnum?'

'Sure,' Kamas said and looked keenly across the table at Dwight. 'You think they'll bring out the Panzers?'

Dwight gave Kamas a half smile. 'Perhaps,' he said, 'but seriously, I think when you get our people in Munich on to Hausen, you'll find he's a pro. If that's what they're using, I'd like to know I could stop them with the first shot.'

'I'll get you the Python,' Kamas said.

'Thanks. There's something else you should know. There is a Manninger heiress, complete with two very large bodyguards.' Dwight told Kamas about the funeral and following the Manninger heiress back to the Hoffman Bank.

Kamas flashed him a tight grin. 'Don't worry,' he said. 'I'll sort them out.'

16

The *Da'Irah* was taller and over a hundred feet longer than any other yacht in Nice's Port Lympia. It had a swimming pool at each end of its promenade deck and a helicopter landing pad; its masts bristled with communications antennae, and it was fitted with the latest computerized navigation system. Its stateroom was a lavish extravaganza of polished teak and gleaming brass and its kitchen was staffed by a chef from the four-star Le Savoy. The *Da'Irah* had cost forty million dollars.

Which only confirmed Raison Tearkes's opinion that Taimur Sa'ad was pretty damned stupid.

Taimur Sa'ad was an Arab, a confidant of kings and ministers, a friend of Western bankers and industrialists. Three years before, a news magazine had euphorically described him as a bridge between two opposed and mutually suspicious cultures. The reality was more mundane. As the incorporation papers of his Monaco based holding company described him, Taimur Sa'ad was a commission agent.

Everywhere in the Middle East, Taimur Sa'ad had a brother, a cousin, a cousin's cousin, a friend. For the right sort of *bakshish* he could fix the sale of a platoon of tanks or a squadron of fighter aircraft; he could influence the award of tenders for the construction of hospitals, high rise dwellings and airports. Sometimes. If God willed.

Two years before, when Taimur Sa'ad had attempted to acquire two Californian banks, God had not willed. There had been a vociferous public outcry followed by demands for an investigation into his business affairs and calls for his expulsion from the United States. It was then that Raison

Tearkes had introduced him to the art of discreet corporate acquisitions, and since then Tearkes had remained a trusted, but unpaid advisor. Taimur Sa'ad did not know it now, but Tearkes had come to collect.

'What happened in Cairo?' Tearkes asked, puffing at a low-tar Winston.

'A ballsup,' Sa'ad replied. At close quarters he was much less impressive than his press photographs. He was shorter and fatter, his round, darkling face with its oleaginous black eyes and natty, co-respondent moustache revealing not the inscrutable intelligence and romantic mystery so beloved of gossip columnists, but the wariness, vacuity and hesitant avarice of a con-man running out of luck. 'The Egyptians started acting over land the way you Americans did about banks.'

'Word gets around, Taimur,' Tearkes remarked and gave his host a rat-trap of a smile. Sa'ad had been planning to invest his ill-gotten gains in a six-hundred-million-dollar tourist development near Cairo. If that had been aborted, Sa'ad was inundated with cash. 'How's business otherwise?'

'Fine.' Then realizing that Tearkes knew a lot about his affairs, added, 'Not so good. Too many people believe the lies your newspapers printed about me.'

Tearkes said, 'The problem is, that too many people believe you do not have influence in the Middle East, any more.'

'That's not true,' Sa'ad exclaimed. 'King Khaled, Prince Fahd – look, why don't we fly to the Middle East tonight? You'll see how they treat me in Riyadh, in Kuwait, in Bahrein. You will see – '

'Cut the bullshit,' Tearkes snapped. 'The fact is that for two years you have taken your commissions and not delivered. For two years, you have not been *able* to deliver.'

'Lies!' Sa'ad shrilled. 'You must not believe these people, Raison. You are my friend. You must not listen to bazaar rumour and gossip by jealous, envious, greedy people. You know how things work over there. Deals take years to set up.

We have a different time scale from you Westerners. If people will be patient, I will give them what they want.'

Tearkes kicked away the foot-stool and got to his feet. 'Hogwash!' he shouted. 'I didn't come here to be conned by a two bit gyp-artist. I came here to talk about a deal that will get you out of the shit you are in, in America and your goddam desert kingdoms.' Stubbing out his cigarette on the antique Asfahar carpet, Tearkes turned and stalked disdainfully to the door.

'Raison, wait! Stay and talk!' Sa'ad's podgy hand tapped gingerly on Tearkes's massive biceps. 'I promise I won't lie to you. Stay for dinner. I shall have the chef prepare a steak diane like you have never had before. And I have some excellent Chateau Rothschild on board.'

Tearkes tried to ignore that last exquisite irony, and allowed Sa'ad's fluttering hand to restrain him.

Sa'ad pointed out of the stateroom window where two golden girls gambolled by the pool. 'In from Paris this morning,' Sa'ad said. 'I'll give them both to you, Raison. Please stay.'

Tearkes picked a chair in the centre of the stateroom and sat with his back to the window. 'What I've come to tell you,' he said, 'is that the Mid-East, like you, is running out of time.'

'We know that. Don't worry, Raison, we know that.' Sa'ad lowered himself on to a stool beside Tearkes's chair. 'That's why we're trying to industrialize so quickly. That's why we're building houses, factories, ports. That's why we are looking so desperately for other investments for our petro-dollars. We know that all we have left is twenty years.'

'Five years,' Tearkes corrected. 'If you're lucky.'

'Five! Even the most pessimistic of the oil company futurologists talks of ten to twelve years. Five is absurd.'

Tearkes told Sa'ad about the Manninger process.

Sa'ad sat still, incredulous, horrified. He lit a cigarette after a dozen nervous flicks at a gold Dunhill, and asked, 'If what you say is true, why haven't you people gone after this process before? Why didn't you start looking for it in 1973?'

'Because Manninger's widow, Elisabeth Manninger was alive,' Tearkes said. 'She was not in a fit mental condition to assign her interest in the process to anyone. The American government is proposing to find the process and deal with the Manninger heirs.'

'In that case, we shall stop them,' Sa'ad announced. 'We shall reveal to the world that the American government is buying trade secrets from the Nazis.'

'Which rumour the American government will promptly deny and buy the process through a CIA proprietary.'

Sa'ad buried his fleshy face in his hands. 'Is what you are telling me true, Raison?' he asked.

'Yes,' Raison Tearkes said.

Sa'ad's fingers kneaded at his cheeks, his body swayed rhythmically backwards and forwards in an agony of indecision. 'Why do you tell me all this?' he asked, plaintively. 'Don't you know that I must convey this information to my government?'

'I know that,' Tearkes said. 'The point is whether your government will believe you, or think this is another of your sordid schemes.'

Sa'ad raised his head and looked at Tearkes, wide eyed with anxiety. 'They will -- ' he started to say.

'You know they won't, Taimur,' Tearkes said. 'Now here's what I want you to do. I want you to buy the process. Yes, buy it. And then give it to your government.'

'How much will this cost?'

'Three hundred million dollars,' Tearkes said.

'Three hundred mill --! You must be crazy, Raison. I don't have that kind of money. And even if I did, I wouldn't go around giving it away.'

'You have the money, and you will make a present of the process to your government,' Tearkes said. 'It is the only way you can restore your credibility with them. And without that credibility, you're finished.'

'Three hundred million,' Sa'ad muttered disconsolately. 'Raison, you don't know what you're doing to me. Three hundred million! I suppose you're right. But how do I get the processes? How do I know they're authentic?'

'I will get them for you,' Tearkes said. 'After all, I am advising the American government.'

Sa'ad's face clouded threateningly. 'Why are you doing this for me? For us?'

'Because,' Tearkes said, 'there are no profits in a free share-out of technology. Because my own investments in oil are substantial. Because I hate the American business and government establishments, and because I need three hundred million dollars.'

Without allowing Sa'ad the time to interrupt, he explained how Sa'ad's investment would be protected. Sa'ad would pay the three hundred million in amounts Tearkes would designate into the separate accounts of certain corporations at various banks. Tearkes had brought with him under-takings from those banks confirming that they would ensure that the monies in those accounts would only be used for the acquisition of certain currencies and stocks, and that if the three hundred million dollars had not been discharged within three years, the banks would transfer the monies held by them and the stock certificates to Sa'ad or his designees. In Sa'ad's books the three hundred million dollars would be treated as a loan to SummiTco, repayable within three years, and guaranteed by Tearkes personally, SummiTco and every single corporation involved in Tearkes's scheme. The rate of interest would be two per cent above the Euro-dollar monthly rate.

'So your money will be quite safe,' Tearkes concluded, 'and earning more than you get out of it presently. If within the three years, I deliver the processes to you, the loan gets cancelled.'

'But Raison, I don't want to lend you three hundred million dollars. I don't want to buy the processes.'

'Look at it this way,' Tearkes said, reasonably. 'Do you really have a choice?'

✤

Dwight drove the rented Mercedes along the autoroute to Vaduz, his eyes crinkled against the brightness of the mid-morning sun. Soon after he'd hit the autoroute, he'd alternated driving excruciatingly slowly with winding the Merc up to near its maximum speed. No other vehicle had complemented his extraordinary manoeuvres, and now he felt reasonably certain that he wasn't being followed. But even so, as he cruised at a steady eighty, he mechanically noted the position and speed of other vehicles. With sharpshooters around one couldn't be too careful.

That morning Kamas had given him a Colt Python chambered for a .45 Magnum cartridge, and suggested he keep on and hang tough. Dwight puzzled over Kamas. So far, Kamas had done all that could have been expected of him, but there were times when Kamas had displayed areas of ignorance, unusual for a case officer in charge of so vital a mission. Dwight had a worrying feeling that Kamas was in fact being run, that his case officer was not Kamas, but someone else.

Deciding to raise the matter with Anderson when he got back to Zurich, Dwight allowed his attention to drift from Kamas to the exigencies of the journey. The autoroute had been extended since he'd last driven to Vaduz, and he knew if he missed the turn-off he would end up in Austria. Dwight slowed and drove scanning the blue and white signs until he spotted the ones marked, Vaduz, Liechtenstein, Buchs and changed lanes, feeling the car lean precariously as he entered the banked exit curve too quickly.

Vaduz looked more prosperous than he remembered, more business-like, a fungus of parking meters clouding the main square between the two streets that were the town. There was a huge, new, cream and black building at one end housing the post office, the stamp museum and, inevitably more banks. Dwight drifted into the square, parked and walked up the steps to the road and into the Commercial Registry.

The clerk who saw him said it was unusual to give

information to personal callers. If Dwight would write, the matter would be attended to in due course.

Dwight produced his banker's business card. He had come all the way from New York for this information, he said, and he needed to be back in Zurich with that information by three o'clock. If he could not get the information, a whole series of complex negotiations would fall through, and there was no legal requirement that the information could only be transmitted by post, was there?

The clerk admitted there wasn't, retired grumbling and returned twenty minutes later with photocopies of the companies' registrations.

Dwight took the copies to the Café Engel, two blocks from the Registry, had coffee on the terrace while he read the extracts. Both companies had been formed in 1929, by one Peter DuBuois, a lawyer, with an address in Tschaan, a few kilometres away from Vaduz. Then came the interesting thing. Each company was owned seventy-six per cent by the other, and in each case, the remaining twenty-four per cent were held equally by Peter DuBuois, Karl Haller, an employee of the Hoffman Bank, and Herren Mollwo, described as a salesman, with an address in Ludwigshafen, Germany.

Dwight put the papers away and sipped at this coffee. Every company incorporated in Liechtenstein had to have a resident of the principality on its board. Peter DuBuois had obviously fulfilled that function for Manninger. Dwight studied the pencil note on one of the extracts, which said that DuBuois now lived in Malbun, a small village near Vaduz. Dwight decided to see him.

'A banker?' DuBuois asked belligerently. 'Why should I talk to a banker?' DuBuois lived in a small wooden house in the village. He had come out to the gate to meet Dwight, a shambling figure in crumpled jersey and baggy trousers, unshaven and with a fetid smell about him. 'Bankers take and never give,' he said and spat out a yellow stream of phlegm.

Dwight told him he was looking for information about the two Manninger companies, Perpetua and Sopadep.

'Why should I talk to you?' DuBuois grumbled. 'Why should I talk to anyone?'

'Because you're still a lawyer,' Dwight said. 'Because your professional responsibilities do not end when you retire.'

DuBuois coughed and spat again, before he led Dwight into a cluttered living-room, full of stuffed birds in glass cases. He lived alone, DuBuois said. His wife had died three years previously. A woman cleaned for him three times a week, but she had not come today. He waved a thick veined hand apologetically at the mess.

Dwight refused tea, coffee or an aperitif, watched silently as DuBuois fumbled for the bottle of ruby port and poured a large measure of the sweet, brown liquid into a stained glass. DuBuois obviously had a drink problem, and was at the stage where he had ceased keeping up appearances. His trousers and sweater were stained with mud and food, his boots covered with grime. The glass cases containing the stuffed birds were covered with a fine film of dust; a hobby in which he had lost interest.

'You are an American banker, yes?' Behind the thick-lensed spectacles, the eyes were blank, the narrow face with the pink, stubbly cheeks, devoid of interest. DuBuois spoke for the sake of speaking, the sound of his voice reassurance against loneliness.

Dwight said he was an American banker, yes, and he was negotiating for the purchase of Sopadep and Perpetua, which was why he had come to see DuBuois, who was a director of both those companies.

'Director!' DuBuois laughed harshly. 'I shouldn't be a director, still.' He explained that in his life-time he had been a director of over six thousand companies, and had never directed any one of them. His function as a director was purely nominal. 'All I ever did was sign papers when I was told to. Hoffman should have taken me off the boards of Sopadep and Perpetua when I retired from practice.'

Dwight asked if it was the Hoffman Bank which really controlled the companies.

DuBuois explained that the Hoffman Bank was the connection between him and the true owner.

'So who gave you instructions then? Karl Haller?'

DuBuois shook his head. Karl Haller was merely an employee of Hoffman. And there was no way Dwight could speak to him. Haller had died five years ago. His name too should have been removed from the board of directors.

Perhaps Herren Mollwo controlled the companies then, Dwight suggested, Mollwo the salesman from Ludwigshafen.

DuBuois's eyes brightened. He pinched his lips firmly together and looked out of the window where a telecabin rose silently over the peaceful pastures of Malbun. DuBuois's hands tightened around his glass. 'How important is this information to you?' he asked.

'So important,' Dwight said, 'that I would like to retain your professional services to find out about these companies. What would you say to a retainer of two thousand five hundred francs?'

DuBuois drank swiftly, licked a trickle of port from the corner of his mouth. 'Three thousand,' he said.

Without a word, Dwight counted out the money and laid it on the table between them.

DuBuois tore his gaze away from the pile of notes and said, 'Mollwo was the working nominee. He was the one who brought instructions to the bank.'

'Did you ever meet Mollwo?' Dwight asked.

DuBuois nodded. 'There were times when he would bring me instructions direct.'

'From Berndt Manninger?' Dwight asked.

DuBuois pursed his lips and remained silent. There were times when even retired lawyers remembered their professional obligations.

'Sopadep and Perpetua,' Dwight said, 'own each other. How did the true owner exercise control?'

DuBuois raised a grubby forefinger. 'Under Liechtenstein

law, the person who controls the company, the person who can appoint and dismiss directors, the person whose instructions the local representative is bound to carry out, the person to whom the assets of the company belong, is the holder of the *Zession*, the founders certificate. Those who are on record as directors and shareholders have no powers, except with his consent. The directors and shareholders of record can do nothing without the *Zession*.'

'And that person was Berndt Manninger,' Dwight said. 'Do you know where the *Zessions* are?'

DuBuois let out a small giggle. 'No. And I don't suppose anyone else knows either. That is why Haller, Mollwo and I are still shown as directors. Without production of the *Zessions*, we cannot be removed, nor can anyone else be appointed.'

'Perhaps Mollwo has the *Zessions*,' Dwight said. 'Do you know where he is?'

'I must point out, kind sir, that I have not been concerned with the affairs of these companies for many years.' He looked thoughtfully at the pile of money. 'When I last heard of Mollwo, he was in Germany.'

'Where in Germany? Try to remember where.'

DuBuois's face puckered in concentration, the eyes beneath the steel-rimmed glasses screwed shut, the small mouth worked rapidly. 'Hell – Hellesheim, Helle something. It was somewhere in Swabia.'

'Hellenthal,' Dwight suggested, softly.

DuBuois shook his head. 'Perhaps. I honestly don't remember.'

Dwight drove thoughtfully back to Vaduz, parked the car in the square and decided to lunch at the Real. After lunch he would return to Zurich and then go looking for Mollwo in Germany. He'd start his search at Hellenthal, the village in which Manninger had spent the last years of his life. Even if Mollwo was no longer there, someone would remember him. Someone would remember Manninger.

With a start of surprise he recognized the woman, standing hands on hips, outside the Commercial Registry. He recognized the long, slim legs, the trim figure, the oval face with those intriguing grey-green eyes. The intriguing grey-green eyes were staring angrily at the glass door of the Registry on which a cardboard sign unequivocally announced: *Geschlossen*.

Dwight approached her, switched on his most innocent and engaging smile, and said, 'Hi there!' He pointed to the notice. 'That says they're closed. You'd better have lunch and come back later.'

The girl's eyes flared, a light of recognition, a flash of anger – or was it fear? 'I can read German better than you can,' she snapped. Her English was lightly and delightfully accented.

'On the other hand,' Dwight said, tapping his coat pocket, 'I might have the information you want. Sopadep and Perpetua, isn't it? Why don't we have lunch at the Real?'

The girl looked at him thoughtfully, then came to a rapid decision. 'Not the Real,' she said. 'Somewhere outside Vaduz.'

'I know just the place,' Dwight smiled.

Without another word she brushed past him and led the way to a dented, cream Porsche 924 illegally parked outside the Registry.

17

Johann Neumann felt his world was coming apart. First, Rolf Hausen had crawled back to Munich, his throat and neck so badly crushed that he was barely able to speak. Then, Marit had informed him that Gerhardt Hoffman was refusing to co-operate. Johann had rushed to Zurich only to find Klaus and Karl wandering about the Hotel Carillon like two lost sheepdogs and Marit embarked on a journalistic foray of her own. And now here was Gerhardt Hoffman, full of some inner joy and secret confidence, baring large, squarish teeth in a placatory smile.

Despite his worry and his irritation, Neumann began gently. 'Marit tells me there are some difficulties about Elisabeth Manninger's will.'

The startled expression of a man who has walked into a glass door flitted across Hoffman's plump features. 'There are no difficulties,' he said, cautiously. 'We are bound by the rules of Berndt Manninger's will. Marit von Rausenberg must prove her claim. She must find the *Zessions*.'

Johann stared at Hoffman in silence. What Hoffman said was legally correct. But that was not what Hoffman had agreed to do. After the death of Alois Hoffman, who now looked down on them so primly from the wall over his son's desk, Gerhardt Hoffman had accepted their approaches, had used their help to finance the expansion of the Hoffman Bank and had agreed to be friend as well as banker.

'Is it essential that Marit von Rausenberg prove ownership?' Johann asked.

'Yes,' Hoffman said. 'I am sorry, Johann, but I have my duty to carry out. I, the bank, we are bound by the terms of Berndt Manninger's will. However difficult, however tiresome, however inconvenient it may be to implement the provisions of that will, it is our duty to see that the conditions attached to that will are implemented.'

Alois Hoffman couldn't have put it better, Johann thought, bitterly. 'Of course, you must preserve your integrity as a banker,' Johann said, sarcastically. 'But if people knew how rigid you were, if certain customers felt that the best you could do was interpret the law strictly, they might seek more flexible arrangements elsewhere.'

Hoffman's mouth drooped, his eyes filled with the sadness of a professional mourner. 'It would be quite sad, Johann, if this small disagreement means that you feel obliged to take your account away. Your account has been an important one. We value your custom enormously. But we value our principles even more.'

'It would not only be my company's account,' Johann said, curtly. 'I mentioned others. Topf Industrie, for instance.' Johann knew that the account of Topf Industrie was enormous and constituted about eight per cent of the bank's turnover.

Hoffman slumped resignedly. 'If that is how it must be, so it must be.'

Johann struggled to keep his face expressionless. He knew Gerhardt Hoffman was highly ambitious. Hoffman's relationship with the Gemeinschaft had been cemented by their introduction of accounts, the largest of which was Topf Industrie. An account the size of Topf Industrie would not easily be replaced. Gerhardt Hoffman could not contemplate such a loss so passively unless he already had more profitable alternatives. 'Who are your new friends, Gerhardt?' Johann asked, softly. 'What are they giving you that we aren't?'

Hoffman said, 'You're talking nonsense, Johann. There are no new friends. All I am doing is my duty as a banker.'

'You're lying,' Johann snapped. 'Tell me who you are working for? Don't you realize, we can pay you more than they can?'

Hoffman's smile was pacific. 'Johann, Johann,' he murmured. 'No one has bought me. I am only acting the way any banker should.'

'And what is this?' Johann demanded, producing a copy of that morning's *Neue Zuricher Zeitung* and pointing to an advertisement on the financial page, calling separate meetings of the owners of Perpetua and Sopadep, for the purpose of recording any opposition such owners might have to the sale of the companies' assets. According to the notice, an offer totalling twenty-five million dollars had been received by the Hoffman Bank for the assets of those companies. Appropriate notices had been sent to the last known addresses of the shareholders, containing the Hoffman Bank's recommendation for the acceptance of the offer.

Unless the Hoffman Bank was informed to the contrary prior to the meeting, it proposed to exercise its trustee powers and accept the offer. The meetings were to be held in exactly fourteen days' time.

Hoffman did not bother to look at the advertisement. 'It is our duty to convey such an offer to the owners,' he said. 'As the owners have not been in touch with us for some time, it is our duty to insert such an advertisement.'

'But the way this is worded, if the owners don't object, you will sell!'

'In the absence of the true owners,' Hoffman said sanctimoniously, 'we have a duty to protect their interests.'

'Whom are you selling to?' Johann demanded.

Hoffman's smile was tight. 'You know I can't tell you that. Look at it from my point of view, Johann. We are trustees. We have to act in the best interests of our client. There can be no question of our refusing an offer nearly three times the known asset value of the companies.'

'Known asset value?' Johann repeated sarcastically.

'If we reject such an offer or allowed it to lapse, the true owner of those companies could one day sue us for negligence.'

'Marit von Rausenberg is the true owner of those companies,' Johann cried. 'You're trying to cheat her out of her inheritance.'

Hoffman said carefully, 'Marit von Rausenberg is only entitled to the Manninger inheritance after she has complied with the provisions of Berndt Manninger's will.'

'You bastard!' Anger, white hot and blinding, seized him, surged over him in wild, suffocating waves.

His body moved. He got to his feet and moved towards the desk, fists clenching. He was going to drag Hoffman's corpulent carcass to the floor, he was going to kick him deep in the belly and groin, he was going to pound that complacent face into a bloody pap.

Hoffman was looking at him, leaning back in his chair, curious, smug, unafraid. 'You bastard,' Johann whispered again, and thought, Heinrich. Heinrich would not want him to kill Hoffman. Killing Hoffman, assaulting Hoffman, would endanger everything. Hoffman may have been bought slug-like body and mercenary soul, but they needed him. In the end, after they had disposed of the other contenders, they would need him. And Heinrich would never forgive him if he ruined everything now.

Johann stopped and leaned forward, placing his hands on the edge of Hoffman's desk. They trembled. 'Should you not include the Manninger processes in your valuations?' Johann asked, tightly.

Hoffman's smile was bland. 'Rumour! Gossip! There isn't one bit of hard evidence concerning those processes. As far as this bank is concerned, those processes simply do not exist.'

Dwight clung to the grab handle as the girl hurled the Porsche full bloodedly up the curves. She drove well, if fiercely, attacking the mountain as if it were an enemy. Close to, she was bigger and more strongly built, the initial impression of waif-like slimness created by the length of her legs, and the contrast between width of shoulder and narrowness of waist. Her body, splayed out against the high backed seat in the modern laid-back driving style, was athletic, her stomach almost concave. Long sprinter's muscles rippled along her legs as her feet pumped at the pedals, and her bare, cream complexioned arms, stretched out to the wheel, made Dwight think of steel cables under silk.

Her face was wide and strong, stolidity relieved by a degree of cuteness in the triangular, dimpled chin and the snub, tip-tilted nose. Her mouth was firm and sensitive, its corners tucked into the tiniest of dimples and in the bright afternoon sunlight the wide apart eyes were a definite, tigress green. Her high brow was lined with concentration, and her expression one of tuned-in intensity. There was something sensual about her remoteness and her controlled aggression.

He made her slow down for the turn into the restaurant's narrow drive, tensed involuntarily as she defiantly skidded the Porsche on to the gravel of the small car park and stopped with locked wheels, inches from the stone wall supporting the restaurant terrace.

There was only one other car in the park, and despite the brightness of the day, the terrace was empty. She marched briskly ahead of him across the gravel of the car park and up the broad sweep of stone steps at the head of the drive. Dwight caught up with her as she reached the wide, paved landing, lined with massive stone vases and statuary. 'There's a good view of the town from here,' he said, conversationally, turning to look down along the steep sides of the valley, its pastures dotted with grazing cattle and beyond it a ribbon of grey river meandering beyond the stacked roofs of Vaduz.

But the girl was gone, shouldering her way through the chest-high saloon doors at the front of the restaurant.

Inside, she ordered Campari and soda, lit a mentholated Kool and said, 'I am Marit von Rausenberg,' and looked at him with a contemptuous curiosity.

Dwight introduced himself, and told her he was a director of the Imtra Bank in New York.

'And what is the interest of the Imtra Bank in the Manninger estate?'

'We have an important customer, who wishes to buy certain industrial processes which he believes are part of the estate.'

There was a momentary, brilliant flash in those deep-set eyes. Then she snapped, 'Is there anything you Americans don't want to buy?' And lowered her furious glance to the menu.

'Right now,' Dwight said equably, 'we aren't buying Iranian carpets or Cuban cigars.'

She sniffed scornfully and snapped the menu shut, her choice of food swiftly decided. 'You'd better show me the information you got from the Commercial Registry,' she said in a matter-of-fact voice.

Wordlessly, Dwight passed her the company reports and watched her read them, eyes darting across the pages, jaw thrust out in concentration. When she'd finished, she left the reports on the table and stood up. 'Thanks for the information,' she said. 'I think I'll pass on lunch. Do you want a ride back to Vaduz?'

Dwight ignored her question. 'I saw DuBuois this morning,' he said. 'The man who is the local director of the companies.'

For a moment she stared at him, eyes smouldering thoughtfully. Then she sat.

A waiter approached her and she brusquely ordered the day's special of grilled red mullet, lit another cigarette impatiently as Dwight scanned the menu.

Apart from a group of four men drinking beer, the restaurant was empty. Bright sunlight shone through its plate glass windows, streaming over spotless tablecloths with gleaming cutlery.

'Tell me about DuBuois,' she said, as soon as the waiter had left. She was tapping a ring set with two small emeralds against the side of her glass, and Dwight wondered why she was so tense and so anxious to be somewhere else. It couldn't all be him, he thought, and told her about Karl Haller being dead and the *Zessions* being lost.

The waiter brought their food, and she began to eat, impatiently.

'I can help you find the *Zessions*,' Dwight said. 'Banks have access to a surprising amount of information, you know.'

She put down her fork, dabbed quickly at her mouth, swallowed rapidly and said, 'And what would you want for your help? The processes?'

Dwight shook his head. Already, the girl was half-way through her meal. 'All we want is the right to bid for the processes,' Dwight said.

'How very altruistic,' she said, sarcastically. 'And being American, you know you'll outbid everyone else.'

'It's a free market,' Dwight said.

She swallowed quickly, and took a sip of water. 'And what will you do with the processes once you've got them? Tell the world how brilliant your inventors are? Tell them how the people who found synthetic rubber, aluminium and berylium, have now discovered a panacea for the energy shortage?'

'I don't know what you're talking about,' Dwight said.

'Don't you? I suggest you read some unbiased works on recent economic history. You might find out for yourself how many so called American inventions were actually German.'

'Don't be ridiculous! No one's stupid enough to make false claims like that!'

'They did,' Marit said quietly and went on with her lunch.

Dwight asked, 'What do you know about the processes?'

'Not very much. Except that they are valuable and that they could change our whole way of life.'

'You're going to need money to develop those processes,' Dwight said. 'To market them. You're going to have to lease your interest in those processes to someone, someone capable of exploiting them to their fullest.'

'I'm sure you Americans would have no difficulty in doing that,' Marit said. 'You will take the processes, you will exploit them, and then you will exploit us.' She put down her knife and fork and leaned her elbows on the table. 'You'd better get one thing straight, Mr Khouri. Those processes are German, not American. And they're staying German.'

Dwight leaned back in his chair, unsure of how to cope with this unexpected outburst of nationalism. 'Everything's becoming more international these days,' he said placatingly.

'Yes,' Marit snapped. 'Like Ford of Cologne, and General Motors of Dusseldorf.'

Dwight decided to leave it. There was no point antagonizing her, and in any case, neither of them had the processes or the *Zessions*. 'How are you related to Berndt Manninger?' he asked.

'He was my grandfather.' Her eyes wandered disinterestedly about the restaurant. 'My mother was Ingrid Manninger.'

'And the von Rausenberg?'

She seemed jolted into attention. She laid her knife and fork on the plate and pushed it away. 'My father was Paul von Rausenberg,' she said, slowly. 'He flew with the Luftwaffe. He scored twenty-one kills in the battle for Britain.'

Dwight felt his spine prickle at the defiant ring in her voice. He looked at her cautiously. She was sitting very erect, palms face downwards on the table, chin thrust forward challengingly. She met his gaze with steady disdain.

'You live in Zurich?' Dwight asked, half hoping.

'I work for *Event* magazine in Munich.'

That settled it. *Event* was a lavishly illustrated fortnightly magazine published by the Myrdhal Group, and Joachim von Myrdhal was well known for his reactionary views, and believed to give aid and comfort to extreme right wing organizations. If she was with them, she had to be a neo-Nazi. Dwight fingered the SS badge in his pocket, incredulously. If she was one of them, if she was involved in the search for the Manninger processes, she must have been part of the plot to murder Elisabeth Manninger.

Dwight looked down at the table. The time to accuse her of murder was after the processes had been found. Meanwhile he had to find some way of getting her, of running and controlling her. '*Mein mutter war Deutsch*,' he said, remembering the joke about the Jewish businessman, who in tendering for a large Arab contract had been asked if he was Jewish, and replied after some thought, 'Not necessarily.'

Her eyebrows arched in surprise. 'Did you get that out of a phrase book?' she asked, in English.

'*Nein, nein. Ich spreche Deutsch.*'

For the first time since he'd met her, she smiled. 'And you do it very well, Mr Khouri. Do you speak any other languages?'

'Vietnamese. It's very useful if you want to find the way – '

She was looking over his shoulder, her eyes wide with shock, her face pale as the tablecloth.

Dwight turned. Her bodyguards were marching through the restaurant, massive and threatening, their bunched shoulders bouncing against each other, their double breasted jackets hanging open, their battered faces rigid with hostility.

'Invite them to join us,' Dwight said, still looking at the men.

She didn't say anything.

The bodyguards stopped a few feet from the table. One of them crooked his finger at Marit. *'Fräulein, kommen Sie, bitte.'*

Dwight turned to look at Marit. She was crouched in her chair, staring helplessly at the men. All the vivacity had drained from her face. She looked hopeless and resigned. Avoiding Dwight's eyes, she picked up her handbag and walked towards them.

Dwight watched her fall in between them, watched them place massive arms above her elbows and push her between them to the door.

Dwight stared at the trio, confused. Yesterday, at the funeral, these men had been her protectors. Now she was terrified of them. Now they were her captors. If they were all on the same side, why did she have to be forced?

He flung a hundred-franc note on the table and walked out after them. Perhaps the men belonged to another faction in the neo-Nazi community. Perhaps there had been a double cross. He recalled the look of utter hopelessness on Marit's face, her uncharacteristic, abject surrender. No, she knew the men, she knew who and what they represented. He came into the small lobby three feet behind them, paused while they pushed through the small, slatted, saloon doors. The men still gripped her by the arms and she walked meekly between them with lowered head. Dwight looked past them, along the drive. And then propelled himself forward.

Parked across the entrance to the drive was a large saloon with darkened windows. Its rear passenger window was half lowered and the slender barrel of an automatic rifle protruded from it.

'Down!' Dwight shrieked, hurling himself through the wooden doors. The bodyguards whirled, free hands darting underneath their jackets. Dwight glimpsed Marit's face, white and rounded with surprise. Then he launched himself off the paving in a shallow dive, felt his shoulder cannon into Marit's waist, wrapped his arms around her and pushed her down on to the paving stones at the head of the steps.

Marit screamed. Her heel caught him in the stomach. He lay on her, arms pressed around her waist, his head pressed against the backs of her thighs. He felt the long muscles tense against his cheek. 'Keep down!' he gasped.

Then there were two shots, twin spits of flame from the protruding barrel, two nearly simultaneous snaps in the still afternoon air.

'Get behind the vase!' Dwight shouted, pulling himself away from Marit, moving in a low crouch to the side of the stairhead, pressing himself against the stone balustrade. Freed of his weight, Marit was turning, rising to her hands and knees.

'Down!' Dwight snapped, reaching out a hand along the floor, pulling a leg from under her, dragging her face down out of the direct line of fire.

'Keep still,' he said, urgently. One of the guards had fallen forward, lay face down on the steps. The other lay on his back on the landing, a bullet hole drilled into the centre of his forehead, his double breasted jacket thrown open revealing the workman-like butt of a Luger, still in its shoulder holster.

'Keep still,' Dwight repeated, crouching over Marit, feeling her body trembling violently underneath his fingers. The car reversed away from the entrance, started to turn at an angle to the road, giving the assassin in its passenger compartment a clearer angle of fire. Through the half lowered window Dwight glimpsed a shadowy figure wearing a black turtle neck and a black balaclava.

He had to do something now. Within seconds the car would be in position, the gunman's line of fire uninterrupted. Over the balustrade and across the terrace? No time for that and anyway the terrace was exposed. He pushed Marit further behind the massive stone vase. 'Whatever you do, don't move,' he said and threw himself sideways, rolling on his shoulder in a shallow cartwheel, pulling himself round with his chest across the dead bodyguard.

He whipped the Luger out of the holster, flicked off the safety catch and keeping his body pressed to the floor, raised his arm and fired rapidly in the direction of the car. He heard the high whine of a bullet richocheting off metal, a shattering of glass. Then with a sharp screech of tyres and a muted roaring of a large engine, the car was gone.

Dwight picked himself up and ran across to Marit. She was huddled against the base of the vase, face white and frightened, tears striping the grime on her cheeks.

'Let's get the hell out,' Dwight said kneeling beside her.

She looked at him in terror, her eyes fixed on the gun in his hand. 'What are you doing with that gun?' she cried, her voice breaking.

'Later,' Dwight said. 'Now move.' He grabbed her shoulder, heard the sharp rip of cloth as she pulled away.

'Leave me alone!' she cried.

Dwight plunged his hand into her hair and pulled her upright. Behind him he heard the swing doors clatter, turned with the gun arm outstretched. A man in a black coat and bow tie scuttled back into the restaurant.

'Move!' Dwight shouted and pushed her in front of him, jammed the barrel of the gun into her back and thrust her down the steps. Half running, half walking, he propelled her before him across the car park to the Porsche, freed her hair and yanked open the passenger door.

'Get in!' he ordered and jabbed her in the stomach.

She gasped and sat backwards, falling across the seat.

Dwight rushed around, opened the driver's door and threw himself into the seat. He grabbed her handbag, emptied its contents, snatched the keys and started the car.

He flung the transmission into reverse, shot the car backwards away from the wall, the open passenger door swinging away from Marit's legs as he did so. As he braked, she leaned forward, held the door away from her outstretched legs, pulled herself into the car and slammed the door.

Dwight ground into first, spun the car around in a gravel-shedding slide, bounced along the drive, shot the car across the road and began to drive quickly away from Vaduz.

'Where are we going?' Marit gasped.

18

'Where are we *going*, for God's sake!' Marit cried for the sixth time.

Dwight heard the brittle break of hysteria in her voice, tore his eyes away from the streaming, switchback mountain road and looked at his watch. 'Austria,' he said.

'I don't want to go to bloody Austria! I want to go to Zurich!'

Dwight hit the brakes. The steady flow of road and trees and fields slowed. The raucous roar of the engine died to a grumble. Dwight pulled in to the side of the road and stopped. They were hardly ten minutes from the Austrian border. 'You're going to Austria,' he said, his voice thick as porridge, feeling his hands begin to tremble against the wheel.

She sat huddled into the seat, one hand over her stomach. She had collected the contents of her handbag from the floor, and it now leaned lopsidedly against her feet. She was frightened and angry. There was a dark smudge on her cheek that might have been a bruise, a streak of dirt across her nose. 'You – you can't make me.' There was self-doubt in the hesitation. And anger.

Dwight gripped the wheel tightly. God damn it, he couldn't let it happen now. He dare not get out of control. He had to *do* something. 'Who were the gunmen in the limo?' he asked.

'I don't know.'

'Their car. Did you recognize their car?' He had to keep the questions coming fast. As long as he was talking, thinking, he wouldn't break up.

'No.'

'What about the two men who were killed?'

'What about them?'

'Stop playing games, woman! Who were they? Why were they killed?'

'I don't bloody know.'

'Surely you knew who they were?'

'They were my bodyguards – hired men – professionals from Hamburg.'

'Who hired them? Why?'

'It's got nothing to do with you.'

Dwight looked at his watch. Twenty-five minutes had elapsed since the shooting. Already, the border could be closed.

'We're going to Austria,' he said, tightly, knowing only that Austria was in the opposite direction to Zurich, that the gunmen had followed Marit's bodyguards, that Marit's bodyguards had come from Zurich.

'I've told you I'm not going to Austria!'

'Those killers came from Zurich,' Dwight said, tiredly. 'They'll be waiting for you in Zurich. And if they miss you, the police certainly won't. Liechtenstein has no frontier with Switzerland, did you know that?'

'I've got nothing to hide from the police,' Marit said, and stared blankly through the windscreen.

'You'll be safe in Austria,' Dwight said.

Without a word, she opened the car door.

Immediately, instinctively, Dwight moved, the decision made a split second before his hand flashed between the seats, its fingers folded over into a flying wedge, as hard and lethal as blued steel. He twisted his arm as the blow caught her beneath the ear, felt her head whip sideways with the impact. Her legs straightened convulsively, then went limp. Her body slumped against the seat.

Quickly, Dwight leaned over and pulled the door shut. He

tilted the seat into a reclining position and strapped her into it. Then taking a Kleenex from the box on the rear seat, he moistened it with saliva and sponged the dirt from her face. When he had finished, he flung the used tissues out of the window and drove rapidly towards the Austrian border.

Somewhere between Feldkirch and Tschagguns, she recovered consciousness. She gave a long sigh and her eyes fluttered open. 'Oh God, I feel sick,' she said and gagged.

Dwight stopped the car, eased the seat upright and handed her a bottle of mineral water. She took two pensive sips, belched and sipped again. Slowly, the colour returned to her face. She grimaced and felt the spot beneath her ear where Dwight had hit her. 'You bastard,' she said. 'You hit me.'

Dwight started to drive again. He'd had a bad moment at the border when the *Feldpolizei* had wanted to talk to Marit, another after Feldkirch, when he'd begun to worry that he'd hit her too hard.

'Where are we?' she asked, quietly.

'Austria.'

She sighed and slumped against the seat. 'Where are we going?'

'To a place called Tschagguns. I have friends there. You will be safe.'

'Kidnapping me won't help you get the processes,' she said. 'In fact, without me, no one will get anything.'

Dwight pulled round a dawdling Fiat, sitting four square in the middle of the road. 'I'm not kidnapping you,' he said. 'I'm simply taking you into protective custody. You can go back to Zurich as soon as it's safe.'

Dwight pulled off to Tschagguns, drove past the railway crossing and up the hill, turned before the village and drove out past empty pastures to a tall, old house obscured from the road by a screen of tall firs.

'What the hell is this place?' Marit demanded, roused from her lethargy.

'It's what they call a safe house. Frau Stecher is an old friend. She will look after us very well.'

'I'm not going in,' Marit cried. 'You stay if you want to. I'll drive back to Zurich.'

Dwight turned off the engine, reached over and ran his fingers down her cheek. 'You can walk in or I can carry you in,' he said. 'You choose.'

She flashed him a look of unmitigated hatred and climbed out of the car, slamming the door behind her.

Frau Stecher was a bobbing balloon of a woman, wearing a shapeless sack of a dress. She flung open the door, joyously, seized each of Dwight's hands successively in both of hers, called to her husband, Willi, to run downstairs and see who had come. Button black eyes wandered neutrally over Marit, noted her pallor, noted that all the luggage they had was the small rucksack which Dwight carried, and betrayed no surprise when Dwight asked for a twin-bedded room.

She led them up the stairs, panting and pausing occasionally to flick away invisible specks of dust, an empty-handed Willi sheepishly bringing up the rear. She flung open the door of a room at the top of the stairs, fluffed the beds, threw open the bathroom door, assured them they would be very comfortable and that there were no other guests, then bustled down the stairs, promising to send up food and wine.

Marit went and sat nervously on one of the narrow beds, her knees pressed together, fingers twisting in her lap. 'I'm not going to sleep in the same room as you,' she said.

Dwight looked across at her, over the rucksack he was unpacking. 'You're staying,' he said. 'With me. In this room.'

'But – but – '

'I'm not getting into bed with you,' Dwight said. 'If that's what you're worried about.'

'Oh go to hell!' she cried.

Dwight handed her a parcel from the rucksack. 'You'll find some toilet articles in there and a change of clothing. Go and have a long shower. It'll make you feel much better.'

She looked from the opened bag to him. 'When did you

get this? Or do you always travel prepared like some bloody boy scout?'

'I bought it in Feldkirch,' Dwight said. 'While you were asleep.'

With an angry click of her tongue, she carried the bag to the bathroom, stopped outside the door and asked, 'When can I have my things back?'

'When you're ready to go back to Zurich.'

She stepped into the bathroom and pulled the door noisily shut behind her.

As soon as he heard the sound of the shower, Dwight picked up the phone from the battered table by the window and gave the operator Kamas's emergency number in Zurich. The operator took a while to connect him, but Marit was taking a long shower.

'Sam,' Dwight said urgently, as soon as Kamas came on the line, 'you got a scrambler or something you can put on?'

'Sorry old son. The people here don't go for that kind of thing.'

'Okay. I'll have to give it to you in clear. Hold your breath.' He told Kamas what had happened at the restaurant.

Sam Kamas said, 'Phew!' then, 'Do you know who they were?'

'No,' Dwight said. 'All I know is they had an Armalite.'

'Bloody Nazis,' Kamas said.

'I don't think so. The girl's all Sturm und Drang und Horst Wessel.'

'Could be the fucking Ivans,' Kamas said. 'They had a line to the processes at the end of the war and could be after them now Elisabeth Manninger's dead. How're you getting on with her?'

'Badly,' Dwight said. 'She hates Yanks.'

'How long can you hold her?'

'Maybe twelve hours, maybe twenty-four.'

'Think you can use that boyish charm of yours to convince her we're not so bad?'

133

'Not much chance of that,' Dwight said. 'But I can try to find out her team's game plan.'

'Good boy,' Kamas said. 'Meanwhile, I'll talk to a few people and find out if it's okay for you to get back here.'

'One more thing,' Dwight said, and asked Kamas to have the Mercedes collected from Vaduz and make sure the Colt Python was removed from its glove compartment before it was returned to Hertz.

'Will do,' Kamas said. 'Now, where are you staying?'

Dwight told him.

'Okay. Expect me for breakfast tomorrow. And Dwight, I like my eggs sunny side up.'

Marit felt the water sting new life into her. Her cheek throbbed with remembered pain and there was a slight soreness in the pit of her stomach. Bastard, she thought angrily, then again with less vehemance, bastard. She thrust her head outside the shower curtain. Yes, that had been a phone ringing. She could hear his voice now rumbling indistinctly on the other side of the door. She wrapped a towel around herself and walked dripping to the bathroom window.

It was small and square and high. She fetched a stool, stood on it and looked out. The bathroom and bedroom were on the side of the house, separated from a wooden barn by a small, paved alley. Dwight had parked the Porsche in the alley, out of sight of the road. Its sleek roof glinted invitingly at her.

She opened the window and looked down. Nothing but sheer wall between her and the ground. To the left a drainpipe. She calculated the distance. Four, maybe five feet away. She eased her shoulders through the window. A squeeze, but no problem in reaching that drainpipe. It looked new too, so no problem shinning down it either. She looked to the left, to the end of the alley. A small vegetable garden and Willi stooping over a wheelbarrow and cabbage plot.

She could do it, she thought, excitedly. She could get away.

It would take her less than a minute to get into her clothes. In five minutes at the most, she could be speeding towards Zurich.

She heard a clang below her and peered out cautiously. Frau Stecher had come round the side of the house and was tipping refuse into the row of trash cans at the end of the alleyway. Marit looked down again. The drainpipe stopped short of the ground and skirted a window. A kitchen window, with a large fan stuck in the middle of it. A faint smell of cooking reached her nostrils. Hadn't he said Frau Stecher was bringing food and wine to them? So she was in the kitchen and Willi in the garden.

She looked down again at the drainpipe. Once out of the bathroom, she had no cover and she'd have to jump the last few feet to the paving. No, she couldn't do it without being seen by Frau Stecher, Willi, or both.

So what? She was younger and faster than they were. She could reach the car before they did. But she'd lose time looking for the spare key. They'd catch up with her then. They would certainly raise the alarm.

She drew her head back, thoughtfully. If they stopped her escaping, she was finished. He would make sure she didn't get another chance. She didn't want him knocking her unconscious again. Or locking her in a room. Or worse, tying her to a bed. She couldn't stand that again. The memory made her tremble.

She shut the window and climbed down off the stool. Better to wait till a more favourable opportunity presented itself. They couldn't watch her day and night, and she didn't have to escape. All she had to do was get to a phone.

He was still talking as she walked back to the shower. She held her face to its soothing spray. Oh God, she was tired of running. The list of places she had run to were endless. Bariloche, Buenos Aires, Munich, Zurich even. All she had inherited was fear.

She screwed her eyes shut against the water, and tried not to think of that afternoon, tried to forget that Klaus and Karl were dead. They were real gangsters, they had boasted, and promised to take good care of her. Poor, vain, fools. When it came to it, they hadn't been able to take care of themselves. If not for the American, she too could have been – she began to tremble at the thought – she could have been dead, with a bullet through her forehead, like Karl.

She scooped water away from her face and thought, it was all her fault. Or was it? Klaus and Karl were bombastic, stupid, violent men. If they had not died in Vaduz that day, they would have been killed in Hamburg or Munich. But they were dead and she was responsible. If she had not childishly evaded them at the hotel that morning, if she had not been determined to show Johann and the others that she could work better alone, if she had not been determined to find out things for herself, if she had carried out orders . . .

Orders! She braced her arms against the sides of the shower cabinet to stop herself falling. It wasn't her fault. They must believe that. They must believe that all she was trying to do was get away from Klaus and Karl for a morning. They must believe that she had been frightened, confused and *forced* to accompany the American. She could show them the mark of his blow on her head. She'd been forced!

Her shoulders slumped. They wouldn't believe her, unless she escaped. Not unless she called the number she'd been given for emergencies like this.

She turned off the shower, stepped out of the cabinet and dried herself. She opened the parcel he had given her and laid out the clothes. Two pairs of brassieres, size 34. Her size. Two pairs of silk panties, her size again. Two pairs of nylons and an off the peg dress in pale cream, size 12. Her size.

She slipped into the panties and fastened the brassiere. How had he known? Perhaps he had interfered with her while she was unconscious. No, that wasn't so. Subconsciously she knew he wouldn't have done that, and in any case he had been concerned with his own problems. Perhaps he bought underwear for his wife.

Wife! He didn't look married. He was more likely one of the

modern types who believed in live-in girl-friends, whose underwear he bought.

Shit!

When she came out of the bathroom, he was standing barefoot by the bed nearest the centre of the room, his parcel of clothes in one hand, a glass of wine in the other. On the plain wooden table by the window was an open bottle of red wine, a second glass and a packet of Kool.

'Feeling better?' he asked.

Marit ignored him, walked over to the table and lit a cigarette.

'Have a drink,' he said, as if they were in a hotel bar. 'The food will be up shortly. Meanwhile, I'll have a shower.' He walked across the room, stopped and turned. 'That door is open,' he said. 'Feel free to walk about the house. But don't try to get away. Don't go near the car. Willi will stop you, and he won't be polite about it.'

'Go and have your shower,' she said tightly and turned away from him.

When she heard the sound of the running water, she reached out across the table for the phone. Then stopped. Whatever else he was, he wasn't a fool. For all she knew, he'd turned on the water and was waiting for her to touch that phone. She drew herself erect and walked out of the room. Yes, she had been right. There was a phone on the landing. She picked it up and dialled. Damn. There was no direct line. The operator was asking her what number she wanted.

Quickly, she gave it to him. 'Please hurry,' she said, softly, 'it's very urgent. No, don't ring back. I'll hold.'

She waited, feeling the receiver grow damp with sweat from her palm, the thud of her heartbeats echoing like a giant metronome in the middle of her head. She didn't dare to move, or breathe. Any movement, any noise, would attract their attention.

Then she heard the repeated buzz of a ringing tone, a voice. '*Guten tag,*' followed by the number. Johann's voice!

'Johann, this is Marit. There's been trouble. Klaus and Karl were shot outside Vaduz. I've been kidnapped, by an American.'

'Where are you?'

'I'm in Austria. Outside a village – '

The connection was suddenly cut. Willi's voice came on the line. 'Excuse me, Fraulein, that phone is not working properly. If you want to make a phone call, use the one in the room.'

The line whirred in her ear.

19

Marit walked unsteadily back to the room. The hiss of the shower had stopped, but she could hear him moving about the bathroom. She lit a cigarette and sloshed more wine into her glass. Willi would report she'd made a telephone call, long before Johann could trace the number and get to Austria.

So what should she tell him? That she was calling a girl-friend? Absurd! Checking with the Hotel Carillon for messages? Equally absurd. The devil with it! She didn't have to make excuses. He couldn't expect her to allow herself to be passively abducted. He must know she would try to get help, to escape.

The important thing, she told herself, was that Johann knew. Johann knew she'd made the call, knew that she hadn't betrayed them.

'Hey, don't drink any more of that crap!'

She turned, startled. Lost in thought, she hadn't heard him emerge from the bathroom.

'I've got some proper wine for us.'

Glowing from the shower, his collar length blond hair all tangled, he was walking across the room to the rucksack, boyish and innocent as a fifteen-year-old on a picnic. She watched him fish around for one of those Swiss Army knife things, open the bottle and produce fresh glasses from a cupboard over one of the beds.

'It'll be a bit sharp to begin with,' he warned, handing her the half filled glass, 'but I promise you, it'll get better.'

There was little brutality in him now, no sign of the savage expertise he had demonstrated on the terrace at the restaurant outside Vaduz. He was smiling at her and raising his glass.

'Let's declare a truce,' he said.

Marit sipped the wine, silently. It was, as he had predicted, a bit sharp.

In the shower, Dwight had decided that soft was the only way to play it. Soft, loose, friendly. Her confidence had to be won. She had to be convinced that she'd been brought to Austria for her own good. Soft, easy, friendly, but not too friendly. This was a job, and she was an accessory to the murder of Elisabeth Manninger, to the killing of Ilana Jarusovic, and if Rolf Hauser had been good enough, to his own death as well.

He finished dressing, opened a second bottle of burgundy and carried it to the table. Willi came in, followed by a bustling Frau Stecher. The table was covered with a vivid red and white check cloth, plates were laid. Trays holding bread, an enormous salad, schnitzels and French fries were fetched. Frau Stecher insisted that if they wanted anything more, all they had to do was ask. They sat down to eat.

In complete contrast to her rapid lunch, Marit picked delicately at the food.

'Those gunmen in the limo were Russian,' Dwight lied, deciding to shock her into receptiveness. Russians had a Frankenstein effect on the German psyche.

It worked. The green eyes flared. Her listlessness was replaced with a cautious curiosity. 'How do you know?'

'They weren't your people were they? And they weren't ours.'

She leaned forward across her plate, her eyes searching his face. 'Who are you?' she asked in a harsh whisper. 'Who are you, that you know these things?'

Dwight decided to tell her the truth, 'I'm with the CIA,' he said.

The colour flooded her face, abruptly she turned away, pushing her plate aside with the back of her arms. 'That's all I bloody need,' she cried. 'The fucking CIA!'

'It's all right,' Dwight said, soothingly. 'I'm not one of those people who tried to assassinate Castro with a poisoned cigar. I'm administrative. Finance.'

'I don't care what you are,' she cried, getting to her feet. 'I'm not having anything to do with the CIA.'

'We're already involved,' Dwight said, quietly. 'You're involved.'

She looked down at him, eyes blazing. 'What the devil do you people want?'

'Your grandfather's processes,' Dwight said. 'We want to buy them, for the American government.'

For a moment, Marit stared at him angrily. Then she said, 'You told me you were a banker.'

'That's right. I worked for the CIA, in their Financial Division, many years ago. They pulled me out of retirement to help locate your grandfather's processes.'

'Why now?' Marit asked.

'Because the world needs them now.'

She pursed her lips and gave him a scornful Pffft. Then she sat down, sideways across the table from him, and lit a cigarette. 'The processes are not for sale, Mr Khouri. So you'd better take me back to Zurich.'

Dwight shook his head. 'Not until I'm certain that Zurich is clear of KGB hit men.'

She turned and blew a cloud of smoke across the table. 'I don't need your protection,' she said. 'There are others who will take care of me.'

'Sure,' Dwight said. 'And look what happened to them this afternoon?'

'You're a bastard,' she said. 'A grasping, unfeeling, bastard.'

'My poor old dad would be most upset to hear you say that,' Dwight said, mildly. He concentrated on cutting the schnitzel. 'Who were those two men? Why were you so frightened of them?'

'I wasn't frightened of them,' she said, tersely.

'So who were they?'

'They're nothing to do with this,' she said. She told him she'd been doing a story on drugs, for *Event* magazine. She'd got certain information about a big dealer, and the magazine had received death threats. So when she'd had to come to Zurich to clear up her grandfather's estate, they'd provided her with bodyguards.

A likely story, Dwight thought, and decided not to push it. One of his instructors, out in 'Nam, had once said there were three basic techniques of interrogation. Hard soft, soft soft, or hard hard. Hard hard was impossible, if he wanted her co-operation. Hard soft would have to wait, at least until Kamas arrived. So all he had was soft soft and the rest of the evening to find out who she was, who her associates were, and what game they were playing. 'Were you born in Germany?' Dwight asked.

'No, Argentina,' she replied, instinctively.

'Where in Argentina?' He leaned across and filled her glass with wine.

'What's this got to do with anything?'

'We're going to have to spend some time with each other,' Dwight said, 'before our people make it safe for you to return to Zurich. I thought we may as well get to know each other.' He told her that he was born in New York, that his father had married a German at the end of the war, and that he owned the Imtra Bank.

'What made you join the CIA?' she asked, still not looking at him.

'I wanted a lot of financial experience, fast.' He told her that he'd been drafted for Vietnam, soon after he'd qualified as an accountant. He'd wanted to catch up on the years he'd missed, and the CIA was one of the largest and most versatile corporations in the world and needed the most up to date accounting techniques.

She looked at him, quizzically. 'That's the weirdest reason I've heard for anyone joining the CIA,' she said.

'I guess I'm kind of weird.' Dwight smiled, self-deprecatingly. 'Tell me about Argentina. Tell me about the place you were born.'

The place was La Plata, a large and elegant Spanish city twenty miles from Buenos Aires. It was a major seaport, exporting oil, grain and refrigerated meat. And within its three square miles was a magnificent museum of National History, a university and Argentina's largest oil refinery.

Marit had lived in a large house near the Parque Riaola. They'd had servants, and in the mornings, Marit had been woken by the chatter of monkeys and the cry of birds from the nearby zoo.

There was a large German community in La Plata, and she'd been educated at a German school. At school, she had excelled in languages – she spoke German, Spanish, French and English – and enjoyed sport. She'd won numerous trophies for sprinting and jumping, played tennis and hockey, and skied since she was eight.

Dwight stopped eating while she spoke, leaned across the table, interested. She seemed to have had a comfortable, pleasant, secure childhood. She'd been an only child. He couldn't quite see her conspiring to murder. 'Tell me about your father,' he said. 'You told me he flew with the Luftwaffe.'

'Yes.' Challengingly.

Dwight topped up their glasses. 'Neither of us were born when that war ended,' he said. 'Let's not fight it now.'

Marit looked away thoughtfully, then lit another cigarette. As long as she kept talking about irrelevant matters he would not ask her about Johann and the others. If she pretended to be friendly, they would keep drinking, and with the mixture of alcohol and conversation, he might relax and give her an opportunity of escape.

She told him her father had been an engineer, and that when she was sixteen, they had moved to Buenos Aires. It was something to do with a pipeline that ran from La Plata to the southern docks at La Boca.

'Is your father still alive?' Dwight asked.

Her face clouded. Nine months after they'd moved to Buenos Aires, her father had been killed in a stupid accident. He'd been taking a short cut across the dockyards to his office, when he'd been run down by a shunting engine.

'And when did you decide to become a journalist?'

It was soon after her father's death, Marit told him. She'd taken a job on *Salimos*, a newspaper which was really a weekly listing of what was happening in Buenos Aires. A year later, she had moved to Bariloche, where she had worked on a local German paper for two years. There, she had won a scholarship sponsored by the Myrdhal Group and come to Germany.

'And your mother?'

'She died four years ago,' Marit said.

'And now, will you return to Argentina?'

She gave him a quizzical smile. 'Who knows?'

They spoke for a while about other things. Dwight discovered that she was still keen on athletics and played tennis three times a week. He got a small measure of sympathy when he told her his own tennis holiday had been cancelled, because of the hunt for the processes.

'When did your mother go to South America?' Dwight asked.

Marit frowned. 'I don't really know.'

'Would it be 1945?' Dwight persisted. 'Just after the end of the war?'

'It could have been. Why is that important?'

'It isn't. It's just something that intrigued me when I was

143

reading our file on Manninger. According to that file, your mother was brought to Argentina by submarine.'

She stiffened. Her expression became wary. 'I wasn't aware that my mother was so important.'

'According to the file, the submarine docked at the ranch of a man called Heinrich von Kassel. Do you know Heinrich von Kassel?'

'Heinrich von – ' Her face momentarily twitched – momentarily seemed to go a ghastly yellowish white. Dwight thought she would scream. Then she raised a cigarette to her trembling lips. 'No,' she gasped. 'No. I don't know anyone of that name.'

'Know anyone by the name of Rolf Hauser?'

'No.'

This time the denial was genuine.

'Why do you ask me these things?' she asked, suddenly furious.

'It's just because Mr Hauser tried to kill me,' Dwight said. He told her about the incident in the field outside then he took the SS badge and placed it on the table between them. 'Seen one of those before?'

'Of course,' hauteur now replacing her original panic.

Dwight told her he'd found the badge near where Elisabeth Manninger had died.

'You're bloody crazy!' she shouted at him. 'That's what you are! Crazy – First you bring me here against my will to save me from some Russians. Now you try to tell me that the SS murdered Elisabeth Manninger!' She jumped to her feet and made for the door. 'I'm not staying here a moment longer!'

Dwight moved between her and the door.

She stopped short of him, not wanting to touch him.

'You're not going anywhere,' Dwight said.

She stared at him, her face flushed and angry. Then she drew herself erect. 'I'll stay,' she said, quietly. 'I'll stay, because I have to. But from now on, I'll not say another word to you.'

She turned and walked to the bed.

Dwight went and sat down by the table, poured himself more wine. 'Okay,' he said. Idiot, he'd pushed it along too quickly. She was coming along nicely, when he'd had to start with the whole Nazi thing. Perhaps when Kamas came, he'd be able to relate better to her. He took a gulp at the wine. 'You can use the bathroom first,' he said.

Sam Kamas put down the phone and turned to the two men in the room with him. 'Looks like Khouri's saved your ass,' he said.

The house had been opened yesterday, and the room still smelt musty. It was a gloomy room, narrow and high, like the house, dark green shutters still pulled down over the windows and illuminated by a spray of yellow shaded bulbs in the middle of the ceiling.

Jerry Vaslav, crouched on the low chair by the desk, pulled deeply at his cigarette. His fingers and the edges of his drooping moustache were stained khaki from the weed. He was a short, barrel-chested man. His receding forehead ended in a patch of cropped brown hair which gave his head an odd, pointed appearance. He had close set, narrow eyes and a stainless steel ID bracelet was clamped to one large, hairy wrist. 'We'll go and finish the job, now, Sam,' he said quietly.

'No,' Kamas said. He'd already decided it was better that Dwight find out what the other side was doing. 'I'll bring them in tomorrow.'

Karoly Lorincz, whom everyone knew as Cary Lawrence said, 'Come off it, Sam. We'd have wasted him if Khouri didn't fuck up. Didn't you tell Khouri what was going on?'

Kamas stared at Cary in silence.

Cary's wide, blue, unblinking eyes returned the stare. Cary was younger than Vaslav, taller, slimmer, with the tenseness of a coiled whip about him. His face was squarish, regular featured, with a fine head of wavy hair. He was good looking, until he smiled, when he revealed a mouthful of rotting gums and stumps of teeth. Now he touched the parting in his hair and said, 'Bastard nearly drilled me.'

Kamas wondered how long it would be before Cary snapped. He said, 'I'll bring them in tomorrow. What we do then depends on what Khouri has found out.'

Cary walked over to him and leaned over the desk. Kamas tried not to turn his head away from that fetid breath.

'We could have taken her, you know,' he said. 'We took the guards, didn't we? Didn't we, Sam?'

'It was the girl who was important,' Kamas said and reached for the phone. He waited, finger poised over the dial, until they got up to leave. 'Stay in the house and keep out of sight,' he warned, 'until I tell you it's safe.'

When they left he dialled Otto Geier. 'Otto, Sam. There's a Mercedes,' he gave Otto Geier the registration number, 'in the lot in the middle of Vaduz. I'd like it returned to Hertz at the airport. You'll have to take off the steering lock and give Hertz some story about losing the key. Also, there's a gun in the glove compartment. I want that returned to me.'

'Sure. I'll leave right away. These things are better done at night.'

'You'd better send someone,' Kamas said. 'I've got something else for you to do. Two guys got wasted in Vaduz today. Germans and I think they're pros. I want you to find out who they were and who hired them. Also see if you can find out what our friends in the force are doing about it.'

'No problem,' Otto Geier said.

20

Marit raised her hand from beneath the quilt and looked at the pale green glow of her watch. Twenty after twelve. She lowered her hand, gently. Eight feet away from her she could see the curved ridge of his body, turned on its side, facing away from her. From eight feet away she could hear his deep, even breathing.

It wasn't a sham. She'd been listening to that steady sound for over forty minutes. Jet lag, nervous strain, physical and mental activity and nearly three quarters of a bottle of wine had sent him to sleep almost as soon as he'd got into bed. Marit lay, looking and listening, trying to remember what she'd read about sleep patterns. Only one fact came through. Sleep patterns were individual, and those of people undergoing time change, unpredictable.

She sat up quietly and swung her legs off the bed, placed her feet lightly on the floor and waited, listening. There was no change in the pattern of his breathing. Quietly, she let her feet and ankles take her weight, stooped and picked up her shoes from the floor, then stood up in one, rapid moment.

So far, so good. So far, she could pretend she was going to the bathroom. Holding her breath, she transferred her shoes to her right hand, thrust her left leg forward and leaned over him. He was still sound asleep. Gently she ran her left hand, palm upwards, underneath his pillow, until her patiently exploring fingers felt the cold outline of the key. Gripping it between her fingers, she withdrew it from underneath the pillow, and still not daring to breathe, eased herself up-right.

She placed her feet together, turned and scooped up the clothes she had left neatly folded at the foot of her bed.

Then she took her first step, a soundless transfer of weight. A second. Underneath the threadbare carpet a board groaned. She felt the room come alive with sound, and stood petrified. But he didn't move. His breathing remained unaltered. She took another step forward.

She reached the foot of his bed and moved sideways past it, feet lightly brushing the carpet. Past the bed she stopped, studying him, then stepped diagonally backwards and bracing her weight on the rearward foot, turned. Three more large, stealthy steps, and she was at the door. She ran her fingertips over it, placed her index finger above the keyhole as a guide, and slid the key in, as gently as if she were threading a needle. With a barely audible rasp, she felt the lock take hold, felt the key tighten in her fingers. Quietly, she turned it. After the first click when the key engaged, the lock slid back in oiled silence. She leaned her weight on the door handle, pulled gently. The door came softly open. When she thought the gap was wide enough, she slipped through it on to the landing.

The landing was bathed in the pale light of a three-quarter moon, filtering through the stained glass windows. She put down her shoes and slipped into her clothes. Then, carrying her shoes, she reached for the banister at the head of the stairs.

She went down the stairs with agonizing slowness, trying to blend the sounds her feet made with the creaking of the house. When she reached the bottom of the stairs, she turned along a narrow corridor, walked quickly on flattened feet to the kitchen. The door was shut, warped. It dragged as she opened it, making her heart leap, her body go rigid with fear.

But nothing happened. No one heard the door, or if they did, believed it was something to do with the house movement. She went through the kitchen with its white Formica tops gleaming in the moonlight. The back door was locked and latched.

The latch was a cumbrous affair, the heavy strip of iron wedged into a rack. There were circular marks on the door where its motion had scraped the wood, and the iron latch had been shoved tightly into the rack. Determinedly, Marit wrestled with it, her fingers moving the strip up and down, struggling to ease it in silence. Each time it moved, it stayed further from the bottom of the rack, made the subsequent movement fractionally easier. Marit's fingers felt stiff with the continual motion, a narrow ribbon of pain ran all the way from her knuckles to her elbow. But she couldn't stop. She had to keep working at the latch. And every second was precious.

She did not know the habits of the household. At any moment, Frau Stecher or Willi could come down for water, a smoke, or to lay out food for the next day. Or he might wake and come looking for her.

Gradually, she felt the latch move in wider arcs under her furious fingers. There was sweat trickling over her scalp and down the centre of her back. Move, you infernal thing, she muttered, breathing fast and deeply through her mouth. She felt as if she had been running a long distance over uneven ground and the bloody thing wouldn't give in.

She jabbed the heel of her hand underneath its small knob, hit upwards at it. At first nothing, then a small scrape of metal on wood. She jabbed at it again. Again. Harder. It moved. Once more. Again. The latch jumped free with a clatter that she felt must wake the whole house.

Marit forced herself to stand by the door, not moving. The sound of the freed latch was similar in quality to the other sounds of the house. That single wooden note would alarm no one. But that sound, followed by running footsteps . . . Marit concentrated on moving the latch quietly out of the way. She looked up at the ceiling, towards his room. No sound came from there. She released the latch and felt for the lock. The key was still in it, a long thin affair and it moved stiffly.

She felt the long key twist in her fingers, as the lock fought it, felt the lock move with it, heavy and solid at first, gradually becoming easier. The lock sprung open with a sharp *thwock*, the sound of a single stone dropping on wood.

She couldn't wait now. She opened the door and stepped outside.

Moonlight bathed the steps and the yard with its small greenhouse along the wall at the end, bathed Willi's neat vegetable plots, looking like long graves. She felt the cement, hard and cold under her bare feet and hurried down the steps on to the grass, slippery with dew.

The Porsche was a black gleam in the shadows of the house and barn. Marit knew he had left it unlocked, through carelessness, or more likely, to save time if they'd had to leave in a hurry. She clicked open the latch of the driver's door and slipped into the seat, bent across and felt underneath the carpet in front of the passenger seat, until her fingers grasped shaped metal – the spare key fastened to the metal floor pan by a magnet. She brought herself upright and pulled the door against the body, not shutting it. Then, using the built-in pencil torch in the key, she found the ignition switch and turned it half-way. She pressed a switch and allowed the electric window to hum slightly downwards, in order to reduce the air pressure inside the car. Then she pulled the door gently towards her, until the latch clicked.

She sat there, heart racing, certain her departure must have been noticed. Then, taking care to keep her foot off the gas pedal, she turned the ignition key fully. The engine caught and fired at once, its note rising and falling quietly, as the fuel injection system settled down. She turned on the parking lights, slipped easily into bottom gear, and foot resting lightly on the throttle, eased the car out of the shadows and up the drive.

She drove quietly until she reached the road. There she shut the door properly, rolled up the window and drove quickly towards the Swiss border and Zurich.

A few miles further on, she came to an all night gas station. While the tank was being filled, she put on her shoes and took her handbag from the boot. Having checked that her passport and money were there, she asked to use the phone.

Johann answered on the seventh ring.

'I've got away,' she told him, still not believing it herself. 'I'm about ten miles east of a place called Tschagguns. I should be in Zurich in about four hours.'

She heard Johann say, 'That's good.' Then he asked, 'What about this American?'

'He's still in the house in Tschagguns.'

'The house of Frau Stecher?'

Marit wondered how Johann knew, then realized that he had managed to trace her call. 'Yes,' she said.

'You come back to Zurich,' Johann said. He gave her a Munich car registration number. 'If you are spotted by two men in a black Mercedes 350 with that registration, don't try to evade them. Stop and tell them who you are, that you have spoken to me and that you are on your way back. If they want to check with me, that will be all right. Otherwise, tell them to go on to Tschagguns.'

'But what's the point, Johann? I'm free. I'll be in Zurich in a few hours.'

She heard Johann laugh softly. 'It's not your concern, my dear. Now, do as you're told and get back to Zurich as quickly as you can.'

Marit thought furiously. Who were these men? And what were they going to do in Tschagguns? What was Johann trying to do? 'Johann,' she said, 'let me send these men back. The man who kidnapped me, the American, he's with the CIA.'

'I know,' Johann said.

'You're not going to do anything to upset the CIA, are you?'

'I'm doing what has to be done,' Johann replied tersely. 'Now get off that phone and get back to Zurich.'

From his imperative tone, she knew there was no point in arguing. Johann had decided. Johann was responsible for all of them. He had more information than she had, and had from boyhood been trained to do what was right. But still, she felt uneasy. 'If these men in the Mercedes intend to stop me,' she said, 'I'd better know their names.'

'Rolf Hausen and Manfred Huber.'

'I'll see you soon,' she said.

'I'll look forward to that.'

Marit got back into the car and drove towards Zurich, trying not to think of the two men speeding on their mysterious mission to Tschagguns, telling herself that Johann was in charge, Johann was right. In any case, what could she do? Go back and warn him? All he would do was knock her unconscious and perhaps use Karl's Luger on Johann's messengers. She remembered how decisively he had acted that afternoon. He would undoubtedly do so again, because banker or not, he was a trained operative.

She pressed her foot down on the gas. The road was deserted and the hell with speed limits. She slipped a Bruce Springsteen cassette into the player and turned the volume up loud. She was free, and soon she would be back with the people to whom she belonged.

The miles roared past beneath the car's speeding wheels. The drone of the exhaust was comforting. She began to feel sleepy and lit a cigarette. In forty minutes she would be at Feldkirch and soon after that, the Swiss border.

She wondered if the Swiss police would want to question her about the shootings. No, she thought, if that were so, Johann would have asked her to stay out of Switzerland. Johann had obviously seen to that. A replay of the afternoon's shooting rolled through her drowsing brain. She saw Karl fall, Klaus go over backwards, his arms above his head, his jacket flung upwards. She felt the American's weight on her body, pressing her to the concrete. 'No!' she screamed above the eight lane cadence of the music. The road came sharply into focus, the powerful headlights carving a yellow swathe, straight at a fence. Oh God, she had dropped off. Her foot pounded the brake desperately, her hand snaked for the gears. Then she was heeling the car around, feeling all four wheels breaking, feeling herself thrust against the door as the car drifted sideways. Then somehow, she was round, travelling too quickly along a short straight. She felt herself thrown forward as she braked sharply, then gently eased the car around the next corner.

Her heart was thudding, her mouth was dry. She leaned back in the seat and forced herself to concentrate. Feldkirch, Vaduz, Zurich. That's what she had to think about. Leave the American to solve his own problems. He'd have done the same to her. But that afternoon, he had saved her life . . . so what? He hadn't done it for her, he'd done it for the processes.

Then the name Rolf Hausen flashed across her consciousness, like lightning streaking across a thunderous sky. The American had said Rolf Hausen had murdered . . . he'd shot and killed the girl in the field. He'd tried to *kill* the American.

And if that was true, Elisabeth Manninger had also been murdered.

She couldn't believe it! Johann wouldn't have authorized that. Heinrich wouldn't have let him. They were business-men, not killers. And why kill Elisabeth Manninger? Why kill anyone?

But if it were true, the two men in the Mercedes were going to kill the American. That was impossible. Johann wouldn't kill a CIA agent. But then he wouldn't have killed Elisabeth Manninger either.

She remembered the SS badge in the American's hand. He couldn't have known he was going to meet her that day. He couldn't have carried it on the off-chance that he would meet her and convince her that Elisabeth Manninger had been murdered.

It's not true, she thought despairingly and stopped the car.

But if it was true, what could she do? She dare not disobey Johann. She'd already disobeyed him once, by leaving the Carillon, and because of that, Klaus and Karl had been killed. If she disobeyed Johann now, there was no end to what he would have done to her.

She remembered the raw pain across her buttocks, the repeated sting across the soles of her feet. She remembered the humiliation of being stripped naked, of being held helpless, the unendurable horror of being forced to lie in her own filth for day after day. She remembered being forced to recant, to promise. No! She could not stand that again. Not for anything. Not for anyone.

But if she did nothing, she would be an accessory to murder. God knew, she might already be an unwitting accessory to two other murders. She could not allow that. This was the kind of thing her father had fought and in the end died for. She could not allow it. Not even if Johann wanted it. Not even if Heinrich wanted it.

She had to warn the American. She had to get him out of the house. She would return, she would take the gun. She would warn him. She would help him to escape, then leave him somewhere safe and return to Munich tomorrow. She would explain everything to Joachim.

He would protect her from Johann.

She slammed the car into first, gunned the accelerator and pulled it round in a tyre shredding U-turn and drove quickly back to Tschagguns.

21

Marit coasted the unlit Porsche down the drive and allowed it to roll into the shadow of the alleyway. Removing her shoes, she clicked open the car door and moved swiftly round the back of the house into the moonlit yard. Her toes curled as she went up the cold cement steps and into the kitchen. She had to move quickly, silently. In the corridor beyond the kitchen she stopped and listened. There was no sound, except that of her own breathing and that of her own thudding heart.

She tiptoed along the corridor, clutching the bottom of the banister rails. At the stairs, she took her weight on her arms, lifted herself over the first two stairs and lowered herself gently on to the third. She did it again, raising herself, lowering herself, taking her weight on braced legs. Again and again till she was two steps from the landing. There she paused for a moment collecting her breath, then went up the steps and across the landing, and very, very gently, opened the door of the room.

He was still there, turned on his side, his long figure a dark pile underneath the quilt. Feet sliding over the carpet, she approached the bed. The time for caution was nearly over. She yanked open the drawer of the bedside table and took out the gun.

He moved with a swift, rustling sound. His arm snaked out, but she was able to jump clear of it. 'It's me, Marit,' she said, fumbling with the gun as he came upright. 'Don't move. I've got something to tell you.'

He came upright, swinging bare legs off the bed, his eyes bright ovals in the pale half light.

'There are two men coming here after you,' she said. 'Get dressed and I'll take you wherever you want to go.'

'Don't be – What have you been doing?'

'Never mind. Get dressed.'

Dwight pressed his fists to his temples, his brain still wrapped in the cotton wool of sleep. He hadn't realized how tired he'd been until he'd stretched out on the bed, and then he'd gone out like a fused bulb. And now, Marit was dressed. She was barefoot and holding the gun. She wanted to take him out of the house. His heart beat faster as he realized it was a trap.

'Get dressed,' Marit repeated, her voice low and urgent. 'Move.'

She was a good actress. She'd sneaked out of the room and summoned help. That help was waiting outside the house. The men who had killed Elisabeth Manninger and Ilana Jarusovic. Her friends!

He calculated the distance between them, noticed she was holding the gun without any confidence and wondered whether she'd have the courage to shoot. He tensed himself for the leap. In six feet and two seconds he'd find out.

Then he heard it. And from the way she stiffened and half turned towards the window, she'd heard it too, a continuous, rolling, crunch noise, the sound of tyres rolling over gravel.

'They've come,' she said. 'Get out through the back door.' Gun still vaguely pointed at him, she had backed up against the window. Quietly, so as not to alarm her, Dwight stood up and took three steps forward, where he could keep his distance and look out of the window.

A black Mercedes had drawn up in front of the house, its dark bulk illuminated only by the narrow crescents of parking lights. Two men were walking from the car to the front door, one of them a short, chunky, barrel-chested character, walking as if his feet were mounted on springs and the other, taller, leaner, a black balaclava over his head, and a white circle round his neck, like a clerical collar.

'Give me the gun,' Dwight said.

'No. There's not going to be any shooting.'

'Don't be silly, Marit. The man with the white neck brace is Rolf Hausen. He's a professional killer.'

'There's not going to be any shooting,' Marit repeated. 'I'll go down and talk to them. I'll send them away.'

'Do you know Hausen?'

'No.'

'Then forget it. Hausen's a professional. He won't let you interfere. He'll shoot you if he has to.'

'He won't,' Marit said confidently and slipped past Dwight to the door.

There was no time to persuade her, and she was too far away for a crippling blow.

'Give me the gun,' he said. 'Don't you realize that if you can't send him away, I'm going to be dead?'

For a moment that seemed like eternity, she hesitated. Then she said, 'No shooting.'

'Not unless I have to,' Dwight promised.

She gave him the gun and went out of the room.

Dwight watched her go down the moonlit stairs, his mind

racing, checking and rejecting alternative strategies. The men were at the front door. The only way they could get to the room was up those stairs. He went out to the landing and opened the bedroom door wider. Then turned and stared into the room. If he stood in the shadow between the door and the window, he couldn't be seen from the stairs. He'd have a direct line of fire down the stairs, and he could also cover the window. He heard Marit fiddling with the lock of the front door, hurried back into the room and crouched in the shadow.

Even though she'd been expecting them, Marit nearly screamed when she saw the men, two black shadows crouched on either side of the door, the moonlight whitening their faces and reflecting off the weapons they carried.

'I am Marit von Rausenberg,' she whispered. 'Johann told me to expect you. Let's go.'

The taller man said, hoarsely, 'Where's the American?'

'Johann's changed his mind,' Marit said. 'The American is to be left alone.' She saw Hausen's eyes dart past her into the gloom of the lobby. His face was frightening, the moonlight emphasizing the shadow under high cheekbones, an almost lipless mouth like a razor slash and large staring eyes that were blank as a dead man's.

'How do we get to the American?' Hausen asked, his whisper sounding as if it were strained through cardboard.

'He's to be left alone,' Marit repeated, her insides twisting as she realized Dwight had been right, that they weren't going to leave him alone.

'Get to the car, lady.' That was the second man.

'No,' she whispered. 'No.'

Hausen grabbed her with a movement as quick as a striking snake. She was yanked forward out of the door, an arm seized, twisted behind her and forced up the middle of her back. Pain exploded all the way down her shoulder. 'No!' she screamed. 'Dwight!' Then Hausen's hand was across her mouth, forcing her head against his body. The pressure on her arm increased. She could feel his body against hers, thrusting her forward. 'Move, sister,' he muttered hoarsely in her ear.

Dwight heard Marit's scream, saw the shorter man leap sideways through the doorway, land on the balls of his feet in a tight crouch. He'd never stormed a building before, Dwight realized; all the man's experience had been gleaned from television. Dwight pressed his back against the wall and waited, gun held in front of his chest, pointing down the stairs.

The man came crawling quickly up the stairs on all fours. Dwight allowed him to get half-way up before he fired.

There was a vivid, orange flash, a sharp snap, followed by a yelp of pain and surprise. Something light and solid clattered down the stairs, followed by a succession of heavier thumps.

Dwight saw the man sprawl at the foot of the stairs, saw him flounder as he tried to gather himself up on all fours. Thrashing wildly and uttering a succession of animal grunts, the man rolled to the door, one hand pressed to a shattered shoulder.

One down, one to go, Dwight thought, standing up and moving to the window. Outside Hausen and Marit were half-way to the car. Dwight poked out a pane of glass with the gun barrel and fired deliberately high, forcing Hausen to loosen his grip to get at his own weapon.

'Run, Marit, run!' he shouted and fired again. He saw Hausen and Marit struggle round, then she was free, sprinting for the shadow of the alleyway. Dwight fired again, the bullet ricocheting off the car with a whining twang. Hausen loosed off three shots at the window, turned and dived for the car. He was already starting to reverse when his companion lurched up to the rear door and dragged himself inside. Dwight put a shot through the windscreen of the car as it spun round in a wild arc, then he bounded down the stairs and out of the front door.

The car was gone with only an ugly scar of tyre tracks on

Willi's lawn and a faint odour of gasoline and cordite to show that the men had ever been there.

Dwight turned and walked to the alleyway where the Porsche was parked, the gravel pressing into his bare feet and making him wince. As he approached the alleyway, the engine of the Porsche burst into life and settled down to a throaty burble. It was parked, he saw, in the opposite direction to which he had left it.

As he approached it, the car lunged at him. Unable to move smoothly because of the pain of the gravel against his bare feet, he jumped clumsily, found himself wedged between the rear wing of the car and the wall of the barn. The driver's door opened.

'Put the gun on the floor, Mr Khouri,' Marit said. 'Or I'll scrape you off the side of that wall.'

Dwight looked down and realized just how vulnerable he was. He laid the gun at his feet.

'Now push it where I can reach it.'

Dwight did so, saw Marit's hand reach out of the car and pick the gun up from the floor. The door shut. He heard the hum of an electric window being rolled down. 'I'm leaving,' Marit said. 'You can come with me or wait here and pray those men don't come back.'

Dwight shivered as a light breeze blew through the alleyway. 'I'll go and get some trousers on,' he said, 'and bring down our things.'

As he reached the open front door, he heard the engine die, the sound of voices inside the house. Crowded together on the stairs were Frau Stecher and Willi, her enormous frame outlandish in a vividly flowered nightgown and rollers; Willi equally incongruous in warm up suit and nightcap.

'Herr Dwight!' Frau Stecher screamed in a rich combination of outrage and fear.

He heard Marit enter behind him and turned. She was still carrying the gun.

'Burglars,' Dwight explained; going up the moonlit stairs.

Frau Stecher looked from him to Marit, and the gun in Marit's hand.

'Herr Dwight, we want no shootings here.' Willi moved meekly behind her, to let them through, and they followed him and Marit suspiciously to the landing.

Dwight hurried into the room and returned to the landing with his wallet. 'There has been some damage,' Dwight said, pressing ten thousand schillings into Frau Stecher's hand. 'This should more than cover it, and don't involve the police. If you do you'll have to pay tax on that.'

Frau Stecher allowed herself to be mollified. 'You must understand, Herr Dwight, we don't want any trouble.'

'There won't be any,' Dwight reassured her and returned to the room.

Marit still held the gun in her hand. 'Come on,' she said, her voice almost breaking with tension. 'Get your shirt on and let's go.'

She insisted that Dwight drove, while she sat huddled in the passenger seat, gun cradled in her lap, hard rock blasting out of the cassette player. They would go to Germany, she decided, and once they got there, she would leave Dwight at a convenient motel.

Speeding along the empty road, Dwight knew that her decision was not entirely altruistic. The trip to Germany would take at least two hours, enough time for Hausen and his wounded companion to scamper back undetected to Zurich or wherever they'd come from. But still he had two hours to work out an alternative strategy, two hours to devise a way of holding her. He wished she had a different choice of music. The constant beat drove all thought from his mind, and confirmed his belief that since the Beatles, pop-rock had gotten worse.

He kept the Porsche at a steady eighty, giving himself space to think. She hadn't been implicated in the murders of Elisabeth Manninger and Ilana Jarusovic. Now, he was sure of that. No one who had conspired to murder those two women would have come back to warn him. And she had come back. The way the Porsche had been parked had confirmed that. She'd sneaked out, made contact, discovered that Hausen was on his way, and returned to warn him. Murderesses didn't do that.

He reached across and lowered the volume of the cassette player. 'Now do you believe me?' he asked.

She looked at him in startled annoyance. Then, hand reaching out to the cassette player, 'Believe what?'

'About the deaths of Elisabeth Manninger and Ilana Jarusovic. About Rolf Hausen.'

She turned up the volume slightly. 'That isn't important,' she said, defensively.

'But it is, Marit. It's important for you. If your people killed· Elisabeth Manninger and Ilana Jarusovic for the processes, what will they do to you? The moment Hausen gets back to Zurich, they're going to know you've betrayed them. Whether you have or not, doesn't matter. They will think you have.'

'They can't get the processes without me,' Marit said. There was a harshness in her voice, a high-pitched note of fear.

Dwight flashed a glance at her out of the corner of his eye. Her body was tense, shoulders hunched, the gun gripped between both hands as if it were her only salvation.

'And what happens afterwards,' Dwight asked, 'when you are no longer needed?'

'It's got nothing to do with you,' she said.

'There's only one thing you can do now,' Dwight continued, knowing she was worried, knowing she was frightened.

'What's that?' Her voice was small, barely audible.

'Get the processes first. Once you have them, no one's going to threaten you. Once you have the processes, you can afford all the protection you want.'

She turned up the volume of the cassette player.

Dwight waited till the tape ended. 'I can help you get the processes, in twenty-four hours.'

'How?'

'I think I know where they are. They're in Germany. And I think I know who has them.'

'And you will go and get them?'

'Not much point in that. The processes are useless without the legal heir.'

For a while she played with the ejected cassette. Then she said, 'I've told you before. I'm not interested in dealing with the CIA.'

'You don't have to involve the CIA. There's you and me in Germany. We can pick them up tomorrow. All I want is for you to allow my government to bid for them.'

'No,' she said.

'For heaven's sake, Marit, be reasonable. We can make you the highest offer.'

'I'm not interested in being rich,' she said.

'That's beside the point. Anyone you sell them to, will finally have to deal with us. We are the biggest market, we are the largest consumer. We have the most advanced technology, and in the end we will buy them. No German company can ignore America. You need us too much.'

She slipped a cassette into the player, allowed the music to fill the car. Then suddenly, raising her voice above the music, she said, 'No deal, Mr Khouri. As soon as we get to the autobahn I'm going to drop you off at the first motel. I'll get the processes my own way.'

'You won't,' Dwight said. 'Don't you realize, Marit, that within forty-eight hours of dropping me off at this motel, you could be dead. That if it hadn't been for fortuitous circumstance, you could be lying on a slab between Klaus and Karl.'

A violent tremor ran through her. 'Don't,' she muttered, 'don't talk about that.'

'Face facts,' Dwight shouted. 'The processes are all that anyone's interested in. Without that you're dead.' He saw the pale yellow gleam of a call box beside the road and skidded the car to a stop.

'What the hell are you doing? Drive on!' She waved the gun threateningly.

Dwight turned off the engine and handed her the key. 'Call your friends in Zurich,' he said. 'Tell them you're going after the processes yourself. Tell them you don't want any more killing. Listen to what they say.' She looked hesitatingly from him to the call box.

'Go on,' Dwight said. 'Convince yourself who they really are.' He opened the door and stepped out of the car. A wind rustled through the trees, and in the woods beyond the road there were subterranean rustlings. She would do it, or she wouldn't. If she didn't, everything was lost. He stood, feeling his heart pounding slow, filling his chest. Do it, he willed, silently. Marit, please do it.

A spasm of excitement ran through him, as she opened the door and marched, white-faced, to the call box. He stood outside while she dialled and gave the operator the number of her credit card.

Marit heard the phone ring three times before Johann answered. 'Johann, this is Marit. Hausen and his companion tried to kill the American. I stopped them.'

'You did what?'

'I stopped them. We don't have to kill to get what we want.'

'Marit, you don't understand.' Johann's voice was low, persuasive. 'That American is very dangerous. He's with the CIA, and they're trying to take the processes away from us. He has to be eliminated.'

Marit could feel her knees tremble, could feel the receiver clammy in her hand. 'And who else has to be eliminated, Johann? Elisabeth Manninger, Ilana Jarusovic?'

'You don't know what you're talking about, Marit. Where are you?'

She remained silent, trying to control herself, feeling as if everything was breaking up inside her. The American had been right. They had killed Elisabeth Manninger. They had killed the young girl. What was she involved in? What were they doing in her name? Her father, she thought, her father would never have gone along with it. War was one thing, cold-blooded murder something else.

'Where are you, Marit? Marit, will you get back to Zurich? Now!'

'I'm not coming back to Zurich,' Marit said, her voice trembling. 'I'm going to find the processes. Then we'll talk.'

'You can't find those processes without us. You need us.'

Marit remained silent.

'You're betraying us.' Johann's voice was soft again, controlled. 'You're betraying us to the Americans.'

'No, Johann,' Marit said. 'I'm only doing things my way. I'm going to get those processes without any more violence.'

'Traitress!' Johann's tone was cold. 'You have betrayed us! You have nowhere to hide. Remember that. You have nowhere to run. Wherever you are, we will find you. Wherever you are – '

With a trembling hand, Marit put down the receiver. She felt her legs going and hung on to the telephone mount for support. Her body was covered with a cold, clammy sweat and her breath was coming in shallow gasps. Oh God, what had she done? What was she going to do?

She heard the door of the booth open and turned, panic stricken. The American was standing outside, his face concerned. 'You all right, kid?' There was a surprising comfort in the strength of his voice.

Marit nodded. 'Let's drive on,' she said.

They picked up the autobahn near Memmingen and found a motel east of Ulm.

'Get one room,' Marit said. 'I want to talk to you, and I don't want you sneaking out and calling in the whole bloody CIA.'

They were given a sparse, characterless room on the second

floor, with two narrow bunk beds at right angles to each other, a small square table in the space between them, a picture window and a small bathroom with a shower. Dwight bought coffee and a half-bottle of brandy and took it to the room.

Marit looked indifferently around her and sat on a chair by the table, slumping forward on her elbows, staring at the patterned Formica top. Dwight brought glasses from the bathroom, poured out a brandy and coffee.

'Drink that, and you'll feel better.'

She drank moodily, and in time, the colour returned to her cheeks. She'd been badly frightened during that telephone call, Dwight reflected. When he'd gone to the booth to collect her, she'd been cowering with fear.

'Why do you want to help me?' she asked.

'Because I think the world needs those processes. And it has a better chance of getting them through my side than yours.'

'At a price?'

'There's always a price. Only our price will be lower than anyone else's.'

'Are you saying that if you help me get the processes, I should give them to you?'

'No.' Dwight shook his head vehemently. 'All I want is you allow us to buy them. If someone outbids us, that's our hard luck. We aren't going to take them away from you, if that's what you're worried about.'

'And you say we can get these processes in twenty-four hours?'

'I said I think I know where they are. I think we can get them within twenty-four hours.'

She looked directly at him. 'All right. I'll try it. But only you, you understand. I won't be involved with the CIA. I won't have you making telephone calls and reports to your friends. It's just you and me.'

Dwight grinned. 'So who needs the CIA?' He leaned across and rested his hands on hers. 'Why are you so frightened of your people? What will they do to you?'

'They've already done all they can,' she said and stood up. 'What are we doing tomorrow?'

'We're going to Hellenthal, to look for Herren Mollwo.'

'Who's he?'

'He was one of your grandfather's most trusted employees. In Agency terms, he was the runner between your grandfather and the Swiss. I think your grandfather left the *Zessions* and the processes with him.'

She closed her eyes and nodded. She looked desperately tired. There were dark rings around her eyes, and her mouth was turned down at the edges in despair. Dwight couldn't help it. He stooped down and kissed her lightly on the lips.

Her mouth opened, her head thrust back in surprise. Then to his surprise, her lips responded, moved quietly under his, then pulled away.

'We'd both better get some sleep,' she said.

22

That morning for the first time, Pyotr Voskov heard Raison Tearkes laugh. Pyotr had dreaded this breakfast meeting in Tearkes's suite at the George V. Tearkes was a cantankerous old buzzard, and old buzzards tended to be especially cantankerous first thing in the morning. Pyotr remembered the brusqueness in Tearkes's tone when he'd said they couldn't meet at any other time, because Tearkes was taking the Air France Concorde back to the States that morning.

Putting away devilled kidneys and scrambled eggs, with toast, and an appetite that matched Pyotr's own, Tearkes explained that he'd created thirteen subsidiary companies, all jointly owned by Sabator SA and Blissan. And he didn't give a damn about thirteen being unlucky.

Two of the companies, he said, were incorporated in

Monaco, three in Luxembourg, two in Switzerland, three in Cayman and three in the Bahamas. The Monagasque and Swiss companies would acquire the holdings in the British and Belgian banks. The Luxembourg companies would acquire the German banks, the Cayman and Bahamian companies the five American banks. The Union Banque Suisse would be acquired by the Monaco companies.

Pyotr saw the sense of no company acquiring anything in the country of its incorporation.

Tearkes explained that on the day, there would be a certain lack of precision about the acquisitions, and that after the bank shares had been acquired, the companies would have to exchange holdings amongst themselves.

'As long as we don't get too imprecise,' Pyotr said.

'That depends on you,' Tearkes said and explained that the entire operation would be controlled from Zurich, where a complicated communications network was being installed in a house he owned on the Uetliberg. 'You'd better give me the day, comrade commissar,' he said and though he laughed, there was a gleam of blued steel in his eyes.

Pyotr hesitated. The date was the only control he had over Tearkes. 'I'd better check the documents first,' he said and looked nervously at Tearkes.

Tearkes paused momentarily in his eating. 'Of course.' He brought a pile of documents over to the table.

Voskov went through them carefully, checking the incorporation of the companies, the confirmations of bank accounts, the deposits of monies, the acknowledgement of instructions from bankers and brokers. When he'd finished he said, 'The thirtieth September. The date is the thirtieth September.'

'That gives us just about enough time. Can you be in Zurich then?'

'Of course,' Pyotr said and laughed.

The phone rang. Tearkes reached a large hand to it. 'Yes – hello, Sam.'

Pyotr saw Tearkes's face go dark with fury.

'You've identified what?' Tearkes cried. 'Who the hell's she? . . . You don't say! The *granddaughter* of Berndt Manninger! Well stuff me stupid!'

Tearkes began to beat the handle of his fork against the table. Pyotr thought he looked more composed now. Pyotr heard him say, 'You did what? That's good, Sam.' He listened for a while, then his face darkened again. 'Where the fuck did the heavies come from? . . . Oh Jesus Christ! . . . Have you talked to Bruno? . . . Has anyone talked to Bruno?' Tearkes's hand was shaking. The colour had drained from his face and there was an ugly white circle around his mouth. Pyotr knew he was looking at a very frightened man. 'This screws everything up.' He started to beat the fork against the table again.

'Did you say you can fix it? . . . Yes that'll be fine . . . I'll wait here till it's over . . . I'm going to tell him why . . . no reason, I just feel like it . . .'

Pyotr saw Tearkes's eyes rest on him and freeze in recognition.

'Sam, I'm in a meeting, let me call you back . . . Oh, go ahead then . . . the hell you mean, disappeared! . . . Can't you do something about it? . . . All right, I know they're running you tight on this. Get some outsiders . . . Why the hell should it take three days? . . . Oh, I see.'

Pyotr felt Tearkes's gaze rest on him. There was something calculating in his look.

Tearkes said, 'Sam, why don't you leave this with me? I think I can sort it out.' Tearkes put the phone down and swigged a mouthful of coffee. Then he looked across at Pyotr and smiled. 'Comrade commissar,' he said, 'I'd like a favour.'

'What?' Then Pyotr remembered that putting Tearkes under obligation meant gaining an advantage. 'Go ahead and ask. Ask anything.'

'I'm told your father is pretty high in the KGB?'

'My father is not in the KGB,' Pyotr said. 'My father is Chairman of the Administrative Organs Committee which directs the KGB politically.'

'Can you – him – have the KGB do something for me?'

'I think so,' Pyotr said.

Tearkes said, 'There are two people I need to find, two friends who disappeared in Switzerland yesterday. A man and a woman.'

Pyotr breathed out slowly. That was simple enough to arrange. But he wondered if that would solve Tearkes's problem. If Tearkes was in trouble, he was in trouble. 'As it so happens, I am leaving for Zurich this afternoon. If you give me the information I can have our people look for your friends.'

Tearkes scribbled a phone number and handed it to Pyotr. 'When you get to Zurich, call that number and ask for Sam. He'll tell you everything you need to know about these persons.'

'And what should we do when we find these people?'

'Tell Sam.'

'We could look after them, if it would help,' Pyotr said. 'After all, we wouldn't want anything to go wrong now, would we?'

Hellenthal lay in a valley of the Swabian Alps, a long and lovely straggle of half timbered houses spread out along the raised bank of a narrow and winding river. At first sight it seemed as if the houses with their wooden frames and exposed beams criss-crossing the upper storeys, the church with its onion-shaped dome, the narrow pavements and the old town hall with its dormer windows, had remained unchanged for centuries.

But as they drove into the village, Dwight saw that progress had come to Hellenthal. Many of the houses had been converted into shops with plate glass windows set under the timbered eaves, with freezers, televisions and radios mingling incongruously with the old butchers and bakers and *weinstuben*. A railway line crossed the road before the village, running along the river bank to the Bahnhof with its two exposed platforms and curved roof. On the opposite bank of the river was a row of modern, three-storey buildings, painted grey and running the entire length of the village. Through the uncurtained windows one could see strips of fluorescent lighting, a large open plan office and vast areas filled with machinery. Signs along the walls, on the roofs and suspended in gaps between the buildings in vivid yellow neon, proclaimed, 'Schoeller Werke'.

'The Manninger factory used to be there,' Marit said, stopping the car so he could get a good look.

Dwight experienced that vague sense of disbelief that comes to people actually seeing what they have read about. Manninger had worked in those buildings. He had looked up at those same shaggy hills. Here, by this placid stream he had developed processes that later, men still killed for. 'Your grandfather owned that factory?' He couldn't quite keep the wonder out of his voice.

'Not exactly that factory,' Marit said. 'My grandfather's factory, the whole village in fact, was bombed at the end of the war. It was what they called a curtain raid, wave after wave of heavy bombers. Nothing was left afterwards. The Schoeller Werke was built after the war, around 1950, I think.'

They parked the car and walked through the village. Marit pointed out the flower shop, now rebuilt, where Elisabeth Manninger had worked, the church also rebuilt, in which she had been married. The church was large, separated from the street by a wide piazza, with benches, trees and a small fountain that wasn't playing that morning.

'You've been here often?'

'Once, when I first came to Germany, four years ago.' She hesitated, thinking about his unspoken question. 'I was brought here and shown the Manninger inheritance.' A sullen expression descended on her face. They walked on in silence.

At the end of the village they turned over a narrow, iron bridge. This was the oldest part of the village, the streets laid with cobblestones, and with ancient houses pressing closely on either side. On a corner past the iron bridge they came to the village *weinstuben,* a cheerful-looking building with a line of muddy cars and two earth-stained tractors parked on the kerb outside it.

Inside, there was a large, horseshoe-shaped bar in the centre of the room. To the left of it were a dozen tables, set for lunch with spotless tablecloths and gleaming cutlery. The tables to the right were bare, exposing freshly wiped, dark wood. There were only nine customers, all men, all aged about sixty or so, some in open shirts, frayed trousers and calf length boots, the others in business suits of pale blue and grey, all standing on the right of the bar. They looked at Dwight and Marit with friendly interest.

Dwight led Marit to the bar and stood with her close to the group of men. He ordered two beers and smiled at the men politely.

'I'm looking for a man called Herren Mollwo,' he said when the barman placed two foaming tankards on the polished wood. 'Do you know him?'

The barman stopped wiping his hands on the front of his apron, reached across and carefully dabbed at the wood where the frothy head had overflowed. 'I don't know him,' he said. 'He doesn't drink here.'

'Where does he drink?'

The barman glared at him, balefully. 'I don't know and I don't give a shit!'

Suddenly the atmosphere in the *weinstuben* became tangibly hostile. Marit felt it too and moved closer to Dwight. Dwight looked across her at the men. They were staring at him with set, stony faces, and eyes that were hard and expressionless.

'Do any of you know Herren Mollwo?' Dwight asked.

The men seemed embarrassed by the directness of the question. There was a turning of heads, a shifting of eyes. Tankards of beer were raised nervously. Then one of the men, a brawny fellow with coils of wiry grey hair curling from his open-necked shirt, asked, 'What do you want with Mollwo?'

Dwight said, 'I am a banker concerned with the estate of

Berndt Manninger. This lady is Berndt Manninger's granddaughter.'

As Marit turned to face them, nine heads swivelled slowly. Nine pairs of eyes looked at her with interest, with guarded watchfulness. The eyes probed her, examining her closely.

The man who seemed to be their spokesman asked, 'And what does this Herren Mollwo have to do with Berndt Manninger?'

'Mollwo used to work for Manninger.'

The man looked from him to Marit with casual contempt. The others had moved closer together, their tankards held like weapons. In a moment, Dwight thought, they would attack him, attack Marit.

Then the man who seemed to be their leader, spoke. 'We know no one of that name.'

'What about Berndt Manninger? Don't any of you remember Berndt Manninger?'

The man looked away. 'That was a long time ago.'

These men had to remember Manninger. They'd all been born within a five-mile radius of the village, they'd all grown up in it. The Manninger factory had been the biggest thing in Hellenthal, and there was not one of them who could not have known of it; perhaps one or more of them had actually worked in it.

'You!' Dwight pointed to the oldest and feeblest-looking man amongst the group. 'You must remember Berndt Manninger. You must remember the Manninger factory on the other side of the village.

The man looked confusedly around him. Then the leader said, 'He doesn't remember anything. He's strange,' and tapped the side of his head, significantly.

Everyone except the old man burst into laughter.

There was relief in that laughter, Dwight thought. But more than relief, cruelty and scorn. Scorn that was not directed at the old man, but at Marit and at him. 'But surely one of you remembers the factory on the other side of the village?'

'Perhaps so. Look mister, why don't you go and look at that factory. You might find Berndt Manninger there.'

Again the chorus of laughter, louder this time, harsher. Encouraged, their leader went on, 'Or you might try the Villa Manninger.'

The laughter grew to a crescendo. From behind them, the barman joined in with a deep throated guffaw. Dwight looked from the men to Marit. She was staring at them, her face tight with anger. 'You fools,' she cried over the bray of their laughter. 'There's nothing there!'

The men's laughter increased. Tears rolled out of their eyes. They waved their tankards in the air.

Dwight took Marit's arm and led her out of the bar.

'I don't understand it,' Marit said, furiously. 'My grandfather built a factory here. He gave them work, he paid them good wages, he taught them skills. And now, no one wants to remember him.'

'The war was a long time ago,' Dwight said, soothingly. 'Perhaps they blame your grandfather for the bombing.'

'He didn't bomb Hellenthal. You people did!'

Dwight changed the subject. 'What was so funny back there, about the Villa Manninger?'

'Why don't you drive up there and see for yourself?'

'Okay,' Dwight said. 'After lunch we will.'

23

It was lunchtime also in Frankfurt. In his office on the seventeenth floor of the Topf Industrie building, Bruno Topf looked with distaste at the packet of cucumber and cottage cheese sandwiches his housekeeper had made for him. Once again, Bruno Topf was on a diet. Cottage cheese and cucumber sandwiches on thin slices of rye bread, a tomato and a glass of milk. That was no way for a man to live. Bruno Topf thought longingly of pickled ribs of pork and cabbage in sour cream washed down with hard cider and finished off with Black Forest gateau dripping with dark chocolate.

He ate like a peasant, his doctor said. He weighed a hundred and ninety pounds and was only five feet six, his protruding belly barely disguised by the chunky, double breasted suits he wore in the style of forty years ago. Food! He craved food! Real food, not this mush. With a sigh, he reached for the sandwich.

The phone rang, the green instrument which by-passed the switchboard and whose number was known only to a few important people. Unwrapping the sandwich, Topf reached across the desk for it.

'Bruno?'

There was no mistaking the hard, western twang of that voice, the clipped flatness of vowel. There was no warmth in the voice and Topf dropped the sandwich on the desk, spilling white flecks of cottage cheese over the dark leather. He let the sandwich lie there. Topf had lost what little appetite he'd had.

'Bruno, what have you been up to?'

'Up to! Nothing. Everything's the same as usual.'

'The Rausenberg gal. Whose idea was it to put two men on her?'

Whose idea? It hadn't been his idea. But how did they *know*? 'It was – it wasn't – I thought with all these kidnappings – the Red Brigade and so on – she needed protection. You're going to need her, Raison. She has access to – '

'Your men are dead, Bruno. They were killed last afternoon.'

Klaus and Karl dead? That was impossible! He'd been assured they were the best, that they had a record of violence that stretched from Hamburg to Munich. No one could have killed them. Bruno Topf licked his thick lips furiously. Someone had killed them and he knew who

'They left a bait open to you, Bruno. We found out. By tomorrow the Swiss will also have found out.'

'Thank you for telling me,' Topf spluttered. 'Thank you for the warning. I'll do something about it right away.' He had to call Johann. 'Don't worry,' he spluttered into the phone.

'I'm not worried, Bruno,' the voice said.

'Yes, yes, of course. You have nothing to worry about. Nothing. I thought it would be a good idea to give the girl some protection. Keep her safe, you know, just in case you needed her.'

'You're lying, Bruno. You have betrayed us to the Gemein-schaft.'

'No, no! You're mistaken! Your sources are contaminated! I have proof – '

'Goodbye, Bruno,' Raison Teakes said.

Topf stared at the instrument whirring softly in his hand. They couldn't do it to him. He was too important, too powerful. They *needed* him.

He reached for the intercom to ask his secretary to cancel all his appointments for that afternoon and the next day. He would leave Frankfurt, immediately. He would go to the lodge in Westphalia. No one knew of the lodge. They'd never find him there. Once he got to the lodge he would arrange for his protection, and he would call them and make his peace.

He could hear the intercom buzzing in the outer office and remembered that his secretary had slipped out for half an hour. Topf got to his feet and walked over to the door. He would lock his office. His secretary would be back in twenty minutes. In twenty minutes the staff would be back from lunch. And once there were people in the building, no one would dare do anything to him.

His office door opened with a soft click. Bruno Topf gave a little leap, emitted a little scream. A man stood there, a hat pulled low down over his forehead and wearing, despite the heat of the day, a heavy overcoat. A sales representative, Topf thought wildly. It was a sales representative who had lost his way in the empty building and approached the only room that had seemed occupied.

'Who are you?' he asked, surprised that his voice sounded so shrill.

'Bruno Topf?' the man asked in a mellow, friendly voice.

Topf nodded violently. 'No,' he said. 'Yes. It was all a mistake.' He padded back towards his desk. 'I promise you, it is all a mistake, a misunderstanding. I can explain everything. Wait while I call – '

There was an orange flash from the man's coat pocket, a smell of cordite and of burning cloth.

Then everything went.

After lunch, Marit and Dwight returned to Hellenthal, drove to the end of the village and crossed the iron bridge. They drove past the *weinstuben* and through the oldest part of the village without stopping, reached the road beyond the village and began to drive up the mountain.

Marit drove slowly, looking carefully about her. After a while she braked and turned on to an unmade track. Tangled undergrowth clawed at the sides of the Porsche. Its tyres churned up loose stones and at one point they had to drive into the ditch to circumvent a gaping hole in the track. The track was little used and no motor vehicle had been down it for a long time.

At the end of the track was a high wall, its plaster peeling, stained yellow and brown by time and dirt, the deep red scars of its brickwork exposed. In its centre was a tall gate, brown with rust, above which an iron scroll announced, 'Villa Manninger'.

Marit stopped the car and turned off the engine. Dwight walked to the gate. It was padlocked and secured by a heavy chain. A notice stuck in the driveway proclaimed that entry was prohibited and the tops of the walls were lined with savage spikes and sharp edges of broken glass. Dwight pressed his face against the ancient bars and looked.

Beyond the gates were the remains of a gravel drive, now

overgrown with weeds and sliced by runnels of brown earth. It had been a magnificent drive once, sweeping from the gate in a wide circle up to the small hill on which the house had stood.

There was no house now, not one wall, not one door or window, no part of its framework left. All there was, were mounds of brick and timber and broken glass. Dwight wondered why no one had bothered to even salvage the materials.

Beside him, Marit murmured, 'My name is Ozymandias, King of Kings: Look on my works, ye Mighty and despair!'

Dwight turned to her. 'Why has this place been abandoned?'

Marit shrugged. 'My grandfather's German assets were confiscated by the Nazis. Their successors have elected to keep it and they leave it like this to demonstrate how anti-Nazi they all really were.'

Dwight caught the bitterness in her tone and chose to avoid an argument. 'I'd like to go in,' he said.

'You can't. Didn't you see the notice? Unauthorized entry is forbidden.'

'I've seen the notice,' Dwight said. 'I still want to go in. Come.' He took her hand and led her alongside the wall where there were faint traces of an old path.

'Why do you want to go in?' Marit asked.

Dwight couldn't explain why. It was a feeling he had, a crazy kind of intuition. A lot had happened within those walls, and while he knew that after all these years there would be no evidence, he felt if he stood where Manninger had once stood, he might learn something.

'I just want to,' he said to Marit.

She looked at him quizzically. 'You're a strange one,' she murmured and raised her face to him. Then she gave him a heart-stopping smile and said, 'All right, Davy Crockett. Lead the way.'

Dwight took her hand and led her along the pathway. After a few yards the pathway disappeared under tangled thicket, undergrowth and creepers. Dwight moved into the forest looking for a way around.

'Let's go back,' Marit said. 'Let's go to the Town Hall.'

'This won't take long,' Dwight said and pulled her deeper into the forest. It was at once so similar and so unlike the Vietnamese jungle. The trees were taller and grew closer together, only the faintest glimmer of sunlight penetrating their matted branches. The ground underfoot was moist and soft, dead branches and scrub intertwined with a carpet of decaying leaves. In Vietnam there had been heat and humidity, white pools of sunlight. Here there was perpetual twilight and a dampness that chilled the bone.

They had only covered a few yards, but already he had lost sight of the wall. They were surrounded by the trees, cut off, ringed by restless stirrings and frantic bird calls. Once or twice Marit stumbled, her soft cry, the crash of her feet, accompanied by rapid whirrings and flutterings about them.

If Manninger had been seeking solitude, he had undoubtedly found it here, Dwight thought. In Manninger's time motorized transport had been scarce and access from the village would have been restricted. The village itself, Dwight recalled, was isolated, would have been more isolated then, cut off from the surrounding area by inaccessible roads and the mountain. Had it only been the death of his son that had driven Manninger to seek solitude? Or had it been something else, a realization perhaps of his own mortality? Or had Manninger been seeking refuge, driven from Berlin and his industrial headquarters on the Rhine by a difference of opinion with the Nazis?

Ahead and to the right of them, there was a sharp crack, the sound of a twig snapping. But Dwight knew it was not only that. Something was moving in the forest ahead of them. That twig had snapped under weight.

Dwight's grip on Marit's hand tightened, stopping her. For a moment they stood there, listening to the rustling of the forest. Dwight peered through the curtain of trees. He could see no one.

But someone was there. He was sure of it.

Abruptly he pulled Marit round, started to walk quickly back the way they had come. There was a rushing noise behind them, as if the wind was sweeping through the trees, followed by individual crashing sounds that were not of the forest. Pushing Marit ahead of him, Dwight looked over his shoulder, saw something flicker between the trees. A man. Men. Three or four of them moving rapidly through the forest.

Dwight caught up with Marit, took her arm. 'Run,' he said, pulling her with him.

Behind them the sound of the moving men grew louder, the sound of feet pounding on dead leaves, of bodies crashing through undergrowth. Dwight turned. There were four of them and they had abandoned all attempt at concealment. They were running underneath the trees after them, and two of them carried rifles held sideways across their bodies.

'Who are they?' Marit panted.

'It doesn't matter. Keep going!'

The banging and the crashing grew louder. They had to reach the car, Dwight thought. The men had no transport and once they reached the car, they would be safe. Ahead of them he could see the dappled light at the edge of the forest. Beyond that was the pathway and the wall. Once they got there, they could move more quickly, they would be safe.

Half dragging, half pushing Marit, he tore through the undergrowth, ran easier as they neared the edge of the forest, feet padding over the packed mass of dead leaves. Sunlight leapt and danced giddily as they raced under the last of the trees and on to the path.

'Faster,' Dwight cried as they sprinted down the path, leapt over a fallen tree trunk, sprinted alongside the wall and burst into the clearing in front of the gates. They could hear shouts behind them, a sustained pounding of feet.

Safe, Dwight thought, skidding to a stop, simultaneously with Marit.

Marit gave a little scream.

Lounging against the hood of the Porsche were two men, heavily bearded and wearing open shirts, with thick trousers tucked into battered leather boots. Each man cradled a pump-action shotgun. Each weapon was pointing casually at Marit and Dwight.

The men came away from the car, quickly lifting the barrels of their weapons, indicating that Dwight and Marit should stand still and raise their hands.

Dwight did as the men wanted, listening to the sounds of their pursuers drawing closer. There was no escape, no alternative. He tried not to look at Marit's tense face.

The others jogged into the clearing, two of them carrying shotguns. They were all dressed alike in farming clothes, and there was a family resemblance about them. They were not KGB, Dwight thought. Marit's people probably, or they were being kidnapped.

With a brusque gesture, one of the men indicated that Marit should move away from Dwight. The men were too far in front for Dwight to do anything, and now a third man moved diagonally behind him and Marit, covering them both with his weapon. Dwight couldn't do anything. He couldn't take chances with shotguns. He watched with helpless fury as three of the men walked slowly round Marit, inspecting her. Then two of them grabbed her hands and pulling them behind her back, bound them firmly together. Then, a black bandage was pulled tight around her eyes.

It was over, Dwight thought, looking at Marit's bound, blindfolded figure. They'd been found and taken before the search had even begun. What was it he had said last night? Outwit and outrun them! All he'd done was lead Marit into the hands of the enemy, whoever they were.

One of the guards approached him and gestured to Dwight to lower his hands and place them behind his back. Dwight did so and felt the rope fasten his wrists together expertly. Before they placed the blindfold around his eyes, he saw an ancient Mercedes sedan lumbering up the track towards them, a relic of the last war and very definitely the kind of motor car old Nazis would use.

Dwight felt himself being pushed through the darkness into the back of the Mercedes. He could feel Marit's body beside him, felt himself thrust closer to her as two men got in on either side of them. As they drove away, Dwight heard the roar of the Porsche starting up behind them.

He tried to keep count of the number of curves they took, tried to make a mental note of the distance. It was hopeless. The old car shuddered and groaned, wheezed up and cruised silently downhill with turned-off engine. The frequent turns disoriented him and he had no idea in which direction they were travelling. All he knew was that they climbed more often than they descended, and that the last part of the journey had been over an unmade road.

24

Dwight sat in the artificial darkness created by the blindfold, ears straining, striving to identify every sound, every silence. After the car ride, they'd walked a short distance over packed earth and dead leaves. He had heard the rustle of branches in the wind, the stirrings of the forest, surmised they were in a clearing. They'd been led up a flight of wooden steps and across a boarded platform into a room that smelled of machine oil and freshly cut wood. From the hollowness of the sounds, from the way the pounding of boots on bare boards faded, Dwight deduced the room was large.

Their captors had been greeted by another man, speaking in a deep voice and in a language that wasn't German, but a dialect close to it. So far, there had been no attempt to communicate the news of their capture to anyone. All of which indicated that their captors were local people, villagers with a grandiose scheme of holding Marit to ransom.

Dwight tried to recall the faces of their captors. Men in their late twenties and early thirties, wearing clothes designed for use rather than decoration. They had looked more like farmers than revolutionaries. There had been a family resemblance about the men, brothers or cousins, obviously. Dwight remembered stories of kidnappings by men such as these, but those had taken place in Sardinia and Sicily, where tradition and culture were markedly different. He began to plan how he could convince the men that Marit was not worth holding for ransom.

Marit, he knew, was not far from him. He had heard her protests when the men had searched her and emptied the contents of her handbag. Dwight too had been searched, his pockets emptied, their contents now being silently examined. He could sense the presence of men standing near him. Then in response to an unseen signal, someone tugged at the bandage binding his eyes and pulled it away.

Dwight blinked at the painful brightness of the afternoon sun. They were in an area partly enclosed by movable screens, part of an enormous room that ran the entire width of a wooden building. The whole area was lined with piles of freshly cut logs, stacked to the roof, and at the furthest end of the room was an angled, wide belt connected to brutal-looking sawing machinery.

They had been brought to a sawmill somewhere in the forest. The partitioned-off section they were in was some kind of an office. Marit was seated a yard away from him, flanked by two men, her blindfold also removed, her hands still bound. Seated behind a narrow desk was the leader of the group, an enormously wide man with massive shoulders, a chest like a water butt. He looked in his late fifties or early sixties, his face weathered and wrinkled like crumpled leather. Above the deep ridges of his forehead, his spiky brown hair was speckled with grey, and the fingers holding

Marit's passport were thick as fence pegs, calloused and scarred.

The man looked from Dwight to Marit, his gaze enquiring, suspicious. 'I am Herren Mollwo,' the man said. 'You've been looking for me. Who the devil are you?'

She said, 'I am Marit von Rausenberg. I am the granddaughter of Berndt Manninger. We believe you can help us locate part of my grandfather's estate.'

Mollwo looked at her closely, compared what he saw with the photograph in her passport. 'You say you are Marit von Rausenberg,' he said slowly. 'This document seems to confirm that. But passports can easily be forged. You could be someone masquerading as Marit von Rausenberg.'

'I am not,' Marit snapped.

Mollwo gestured to the oldest of the other men. He stepped forward, opening a small brown paper packet, and one by one thrust a series of photographs before Marit's face.

'You know these people?' Mollwo asked.

'That's Dr Manfred Fendt,' Marit said, identifying the first photograph. She frowned. 'And that I think is Lucien Wehling. I believe he died a few years ago. That's the lawyer, Heinz Gunther, and that's Klaus Altman.' She took a deep breath and stared at the photograph of a man in uniform, his braided cap tilted rakishly over one eye. 'That – that's my father, Paul von Rausenberg.' She looked steadily at the next photograph. 'Gestapo Chief Muller,' she said, flatly. 'Captain Moritz Gruber – he's dead, too. I don't recognize this man. That's Rudolf Bayerlein and that's Karl Schumann.' Her face suddenly went pale, and her hands twisted helplessly against the rope. Then she controlled herself, and in a tight voice, said, 'That's Heinrich von Kassel.'

The man put the photographs away.

'That was very good,' Mollwo said. 'You got everyone right and spotted our fake.' He stared at her with a look of cold fascination, as if she were some rare artifact he had

183

discovered on a walk in the forest. 'Where were you born, and when?'

'La Plata, Argentina. 11 February 1956.'

'And your mother was . . .'

'Ingrid Manninger.'

'When did she go to Argentina?'

'I – I don't know.'

'Where did you live in Argentina?'

'First La Plata, then Buenos Aires, and after my father died, in Bariloche.'

'When did you come to live in Europe?'

'Four years ago.'

'And what do you do here?'

'I work for *Event* magazine. I live in Munich.' Defiantly she gave Mollwo her address and telephone number.

'*Event* is a Myrdhal publication, is it not?'

'That's right.'

'How well do you know Joachim Myrdhal?'

Marit coloured. 'Very well.'

Mollwo scrutinized her thoughtfully, meeting Marit's defiant stare with a distant calmness. Then suddenly he said, 'Free her.'

While Marit's bonds were being severed, Mollwo came round the desk with hands outstretched and stood before Marit. As soon as she was free, he took her wrists in his big, calloused hands and massaged them. 'Welcome to my house, Fraulein von Rausenberg,' he said, fighting to keep his voice even. 'Welcome, daughter of Ingrid Manninger and grandchild of my friend.' He took her shoulders and looked into her face with a tender, happy-sadness. 'I have waited thirty-five years for this,' he said. 'For thirty-five years, I have waited to discharge my trust.' He bit his lips to suppress his emotion. Then, in a more level voice, he said, 'I apologize for the manner in which you were brought here. You must understand there have been others seeking what your grandfather left, and all of us, including the people in the village, have had to be very careful. And very suspicious.'

Dwight tugged quietly at his bonds. It was all over for him. Despair chilled his gut. They were all in this together, he thought, bitterly, watching Mollwo purring over Marit like a cat let loose in a cream factory. All he had done with his great plans was to lead Marit back to them.

Fool! You should have checked Mollwo first. You should have knocked the girl unconscious instead of trying to win her trust, should have got Kamas to Germany or wherever and sent a team to Hellenthal to investigate Mollwo. That was how he would have played it, had he been in 'Nam. That was the sensible way to play it. That was how the five-star agent the CIA had pulled out of retirement *should* have played it. Instead of which he was now seated tied to a chair, while his conduit to the Manninger processes was welcomed back to the bosom of the Nazi Party.

Bloody hell! He had to think of the present. He had to think of a way of breaking free. The ropes holding his wrists wouldn't budge. And Mollwo was looking at him with the dispassionate curiosity of a farmer studying the weather.

'Tell me about this American,' Mollwo said to Marit.

'Why don't you let him tell you himself? He speaks fluent German.'

Mollwo's look became at once more interested and more hostile. 'What is your concern with Berndt Manninger?'

'I am a banker – ' Dwight began.

'He also works for the CIA,' Marit said.

You're a great help, Dwight thought, with friends like you who needs enemies, and stared blankly at the wall in front of him, as he'd been taught to do. Christ, she must have seen him coming. She'd never left them. Her attempt at saving him was only a ploy –

'And what does an American banker and the CIA have to do with this?' Mollwo was back behind the desk now, his massive shoulders hunched, his weathered face set like granite.

'Tell him the truth, Dwight,' Marit said. 'Tell him everything you told me.'

Next time I need advice from you, I'll find a hangman, Dwight thought and said, 'We represent the American government. We believe that part of the Manninger estate consists of certain industrial processes. We wish to buy those processes.'

'And what will you do with them, once you've got them?'

'Develop them, exploit them, make them available to the rest of the world at a fair price.'

'A fair price. How interesting. A fair price that will hold the rest of the world to ransom.'

'No,' Dwight said. 'We didn't do that when we were the largest exporters of oil. We aren't going to do it now.'

'That sounds very good,' Mollwo said. 'But haven't things changed since then? Haven't you seen how wealthy certain nations have become through exercise of an oil monopoly?'

'We are more sophisticated and less greedy than they are,' Dwight said. 'We realize that our prosperity depends on having prosperous trading partners.'

'So the Marshall Plan was an act of self-interest?'

'Let me quote you a Lebanese proverb,' Dwight said. 'True generosity springs from a selfish heart.'

A flicker of amusement crossed Mollwo's face. Then he said, 'Do you have some document, some proof that you are working for the government and not for some large American company?'

Dwight shook his head. 'We don't carry documents like that. But I can prove I am working for the government.' He looked over at the telephone. 'Have the operator get you the White House in Washington.' Mollwo's jaw dropped in amazement. 'Yes,' Dwight repeated, 'the White House, and ask for Jeb Anderson. He's an assistant to the President. He'll confirm whom I'm working for.'

Mollwo gestured for Dwight to be freed, and still staring incredulously picked up the phone and asked the operator for the call. 'Why do you carry a gun, Mr Khouri?'

Dwight told him about the shooting outside Vaduz.

Mollwo darted concerned glances from one to the other of

186

them. 'The Russians,' he said, slowly. 'I don't understand that at all.'

The phone rang. Mollwo picked it up, and satisfied that he was connected to the White House, passed it to Dwight.

Dwight asked for Jeb Anderson.

'Just one moment, Mr Khouri. I believe Mr Anderson's left, but I'll try to locate him for you.'

Jeb Anderson just left. That was the kind of luck he needed. There were a series of clicks and whirrings, of distant voices faintly heard, of connections being made and cut. Then the girl was on the line again. 'I have Mr Anderson for you.'

Jeb Anderson sounded hurried. 'Dwight, I was just leaving for Camp David.'

Dwight let out a breath he didn't know he had been holding. 'Jeb, in a few moments I'm going to pass you on to a Mr Mollwo. Will you inform him of my status with the Agency and the Imtra Bank?'

'Hang on, Dwight! Who is this guy? Is your line secure?'

'You've got a plane to catch and I've got a job to do,' Dwight said and passed the phone to Mollwo.

Mollwo covered the mouthpiece with his hand. 'How do I address him?'

'Just call him Mr Anderson. He's used to that.'

'*Gruss Gott*, Mr Anderson,' Mollwo said with heavy formality. 'This is Herren Mollwo.' Mollwo sat erect in his chair wearing an expression of defiant humility, as if he'd just been pulled over by a traffic cop.

From the way Mollwo's eyes wandered thoughtfully over him, Dwight knew that despite his reservations, Anderson was confirming his status.

Suddenly Mollwo cleared his throat, took his eyes away from Dwight and frowned at his desk. 'I have one question. Does your government want to *buy* the processes?'

Dwight couldn't decipher what Anderson said, but Mollwo rephrased the question, 'Your government, not an American company?'

Anderson obviously said yes, because Mollwo looked

187

satisfied and said, 'No, there is nothing else. Goodbye.' He looked thoughtfully at Dwight for a long time before turning to Marit and saying, 'So you two met only yesterday.'

Marit and Dwight looked at each other in synchronized surprise, that it had been as recent as that.

'Yes,' Marit said with a small smile.

'And the two men who were killed? Who were they?'

'Bodyguards,' Marit said.

'You hired them?'

Marit hesitated. 'They were hired for me.'

'Who by?'

Marit looked down at her shoes. 'That isn't important,' she said.

'On the contrary, my dear, it is extremely important. Who hired those guards? Who else is involved?'

Marit looked rapidly around the room as if looking for a means of escape. Then she said, 'Can we talk privately?'

'Of course, my dear,' Mollwo said and led her outside the mill.

The afternoon sun sloped through the trees, the day already beginning to cool. An erratic breeze snatched at their clothes and made the branches sigh as Mollwo led her across the clearing and into the forest.

His splay-legged gait was deceptively brisk and he moved with a lightness incredible in so big a man. There was something basic about Mollwo, Marit thought, a deep-rooted strength, an oak-like solidity that inspired confidence. He was raw earth and rock, central core. Marit could sense why her grandfather had trusted him so completely. She'd felt an immediate empathy with him, the moment he'd come round his desk and massaged her wrists, with those big, calloused hands.

'The bodyguards were from *Der Spinne*,' Marit said.

'*Der Spinne*,' Mollwo repeated, thoughtfully. 'Von Kassel, Muller, Altman, Fendt. They are all that are left, aren't they?'

Marit nodded. 'All that are left of the *Alte Kameraden*.'

'And you want the processes for them?'

Marit looked down and stopped walking. She drew a rough circle over the dead leaves with the point of her shoe. 'They're all I have,' she said softly. 'They brought my mother out of Germany and took her to Argentina. They raised her from the time she was sixteen. After my father's death, they supported us. They gave me work, they sent me here, to Germany. It is because of them that I am alive, that I exist.'

'Was it for you they did all this, or for the processes?'

'I'm not the only person they have helped. They have done a lot for the exiled German community.'

'All they do is look after their own,' Mollwo muttered. 'Do you know of Operation Feuerland? No, I don't suppose they talk of it in Argentina. Operation Land of Fire. It was authorized from the office of the Deputy Fuhrer himself. The transfer of the assets of the Reich, so that out of the ashes of the old Reich, a new Reich would rise like a phoenix. Bormann himself directed that your grandfather should be transported to Argentina. Your grandfather didn't want to go. That was one reason why he transferred his processes out of Germany. He did not want to be part of this new Reich.'

'No one's interested in that any more,' Marit said.

'I know that, and I despise them for it. They used the money to line their own pockets, to create their own businesses. *Der Spinne* is really a large business organization, is it not?'

Marit nodded. 'It is the Adler Gemeinschaft.'

'And if they get the processes, they will grow bigger. They will be the largest and most important corporation in the whole world. They will be wealthier than many countries, and nations will make obeisance to them. They will no longer be war criminals but war heroes. That is what they seek from you, is it not? That is why they nurtured you for twenty-four years. That is why they took your mother out of Germany, why they nourished and educated you. None of it has anything to do with what you are, but who you are.'

Mollwo placed his hands on her shoulders and looked into her face. 'You must not allow the processes to go to these men, my child, men who profited from the ruin of the Fatherland, men who were prepared to kill your grandfather for his processes, the men who brutalized his wife so that she could never make any claim to the Manninger Estate.'

'What do you mean, brutalized? Elisabeth Manninger was injured in the bombing of Hellenthal.'

'No, my child. She was deliberately driven mad. She could not be killed because the inheritance would revert to the state, which would have meant the Allies. And she could not be allowed to inherit. So Muller had her arrested and systematically tortured. And when that did not work, he had his thugs repeatedly perform the most grotesque sexual assaults on her.'

'Oh no,' Marit cried. 'It isn't true! It can't be true!'

Mollwo's face was set like stone. 'I collected her from the Gestapo afterwards,' he said. 'I arranged for her hospitalization and transfer to Switzerland.'

'Oh God!' Marit sobbed, her mouth breaking, her shoulders heaving, tears rolling down her cheeks. 'Oh God! Will it never end?'

She felt Mollwo's arms around her, strong and comforting. 'There, there, my child,' he murmured. 'It was all over, long ago.'

'No,' Marit cried, burying her face in his shoulder. 'It isn't over! Don't you see, it isn't over yet!'

Sobbing, she told him about the SS badge and Dwight, the killing of Elisabeth Manninger and the young girl in the field outside Rilswil. She told him about Johann, how she'd hoped that through him there would have been an end to the inhumanity and the violence. She wanted to give the processes, not to the *Alte Kameraden*, but to the community. She wanted to see the money used for hospitals and schools and for new business ventures that would provide employment and bring prosperity. Most of all, she'd wanted to use the processes so that the children of the damned would once again take their place in the world.

'In Argentina, we are tolerated,' she said. 'In Europe, we are despised for what our parents were. There are countries which we are prohibited from entering, there are people who seek to degrade us and destroy us. I wanted all that to end.'

Mollwo said, 'You will not achieve any of that through von Kassel or this Neumann.'

'I know that now,' Marit said and dabbed at her eyes.

'But you can still do it through other ways. When you get the processes you can give your community hospitals and schools that it needs. You can show the world that a child of the damned need not be damned forever.' He took her face in his hands. 'We will help you,' he said. 'We will be your family, and your bodyguards and your friends. But now, let us go back. There is a lot I have to tell you, and many things you will have to do, before you obtain the processes.' He released her face and taking her arm began to lead her back to the sawmill.

'You mean you don't have the processes?'

'No,' Mollwo said. 'All your grandfather left me was the means through which they could be found. You will have to find them, and this American with his ability to use a gun, and his contacts in banking and intelligence could be very useful.'

'How?' Marit asked.

'Firstly, he will protect you from the *Alte Kameraden* and others. Secondly, to find the processes, you're going to need the help of someone with a knowledge of banking, someone able to penetrate Swiss banks, someone who is a trained investigator.' Mollwo stopped and stared thoughtfully at the trees. 'My sons and I could protect you, but we would be useless at coping with financial matters.'

'Why don't I simply engage a lawyer?' Marit asked.

'The lawyer you need doesn't exist,' Mollwo replied. 'For reasons which I will tell you when we get back to the mill, you have to locate those processes within the next two weeks. So your lawyer has got to be able to devote the next two weeks to finding the processes, he's got to be fit enough to do a lot of travelling, he's got to be rich enough or moral enough not to change sides, and he's got to be able to cope with people threatening him, beating him up, or even shooting at him. I don't think you will find a lawyer like that today or even next month.'

'But I don't want to sell the processes to the Americans.'

'I don't think you have much choice, child,' Mollwo said, a hint of reproof in his voice. 'Do you realize the effect of those processes when they are developed and marketed? They are going to put certain countries out of business. They're going to deplete the value of the oil industry by half or two-thirds. The oil industry is a three-hundred-billion-dollar business, Marit. They're not going to sit on their behinds, and allow a little German girl to make them bankrupt.'

'What could they do?' Marit asked. 'If the processes work, people will want them.'

'Big business,' Mollwo said, 'like big politics, or big trade unions, only pays lip service to the principles of democracy and free competition. The first thing they will do, is attempt to buy you out and suppress the processes. If that fails, they will create other obstacles, raise legal questions regarding the title, create an environmental lobby to protest against new chemicals given off by the processes, have the unions protest about loss of jobs. Oh, there's no end of things they will do.' Mollwo paused and looked at her, searchingly. 'And if all that fails, they will use other means. Believe me, child, that's what the world is really like. I spent a quarter of a century working with your grandfather in big business and big government. I know. So tell me again how you met this American.'

Marit told Mollwo how she had met Dwight in Vaduz, how he'd given her the information about the Manninger companies, saved her from the gunmen, knocked her unconscious and taken her to Austria, and finally brought her to Hellenthal.

'A resourceful man,' Mollwo commented. 'The kind of man we need. Now let's see if we can get him on to our side.'

25

As soon as they came in, Dwight sensed that something had happened. Marit had been crying and Mollwo looked like a man who had arrived at a crossroads and found two signposts, marked with the same destination. Marit did not look at him as she walked across the room and sat in the chair beside him. Mollwo lumbered to his seat behind the desk, from where he glowered at Dwight thoughtfully, before studying the backs of his hands as if the answer to his problem wás tattooed there.

Finally Mollwo broke the silence by saying, 'Mr Khouri, you are both a banker and an intelligence agent. Inform me please how you combine these two activities and how you came to be involved in the hunt for the Manninger processes.'

Dwight saw no harm in telling Mollwo that. He told Mollwo of his past involvement with the CIA, and of how, on his way to a tennis camp, he had been pulled in by the Agency.

'And what have you been doing since you have been in Europe? I understand you have done some detective work concerning Elisabeth Manninger's death.'

Dwight looked quickly at Marit. She was looking away from him, po-faced. She'd obviously repeated everything to Mollwo. So there was nothing to be gained by refusing to answer the question. Dwight told Mollwo about the SS badge and the circumstances of Elisabeth Manninger's death. 'Dr Flacker told me she had a heart condition. If that was known to the people who visited her that day, a heart attack could have been induced.'

'And that is what you think happened?'

Dwight nodded and told him of the murder of Ilana Jarusovic.

Mollwo was studying his hands again. Dwight couldn't tell from his expression whether Mollwo believed him or not, whether Mollwo had been involved in those killings or not.

Mollwo asked, 'Tell me, Mr Khouri, how much are you being paid by the CIA for this?'

And that was the point of it all, Dwight thought. Mollwo wanted to bribe him. 'One dollar,' Dwight said, 'and expenses.' And that was the truth.

He saw an expression of amazement cross Mollwo's face. Beside him Marit turned and stared at him, frowning. Dwight explained that his job at the Imtra Bank paid well enough for him to work for the CIA for two weeks for nothing, and that it was not unusual for wealthy Americans to work for the government for very little.

'And how much are your expenses?' Mollwo asked.

'Theoretically, they are unlimited. But for now, I have a float of ten thousand dollars, most of which you have already seen in my wallet. There's another thirty thousand I can draw on, at the Imtra Bank in Zurich. If you like, I can arrange for you to have confirmation of that.'

'That won't be necessary,' Mollwo said, and went back to studying the hands again.

For an amateur, Mollwo had handled the interrogation well. Of course, he had been helped by the fact that Dwight had found it either unnecessary or impossible to lie. But so far, Mollwo had managed to conceal the purpose of the interrogation. And Mollwo had a purpose. Dwight thought about that for a few minutes, before it struck him. Mollwo was looking for a way to recruit him. Otherwise, there was little point in the interrogation. If Mollwo wanted to prevent him going after the processes, that was easy enough. They could hold him at the sawmill until the processes had been found, they could arrange to leave him somewhere in Germany, or they could bury him in the forest.

Mollwo said, 'Mr Khouri, describe to me the operation the CIA is running to find the processes.'

'It's a small operation,' Dwight said. 'Only three people are involved. Jeb Anderson, whom you spoke to, is the person in overall charge of the operation and carries political responsibility for it. Sam Kamas is the Agency field officer. He is responsible for seeing that my reports get to the right people, for providing me with any facilities I need, and for making sure the operation is being properly run. And then there's me. I'm the one who is supposed to find the processes.'

'Just you?' Mollwo asked.

Dwight told him of the Agency reservations concerning a large operation.

'Who is this Jeb Anderson?' Mollwo asked, and listened patiently while Dwight told him everything he knew about Anderson.

'And this man Kamas?'

'I don't know much about him. I only met him on Monday.'

'But he is with the CIA?'

'It sure looks like that to me.'

'Could you find out about him?'

Dwight hesitated. That was something he'd wanted to do himself, before people had started shooting at him and he'd met Marit. But should he involve Mollwo in that? That depended on what Mollwo was trying to do. Bloody hell! What Mollwo was trying to do was so obvious it had been staring him in the face for the past twenty minutes. Mollwo was trying to use him to find the processes. That was the only point of all this talk.

But the immediate problem was the background on Kamas. Was Mollwo testing his loyalty to the Agency by trying to establish how far Dwight would co-operate, or did he really want to know? It was a time when all decisions were equal. 'I can find out about Kamas for you,' Dwight said, reached for the phone and gave the operator the number of the CIA in Langley.

The call came through quickly. Dwight gave his access code and asked for Personnel.

A voice said, 'Clint Adams.'

Dwight repeated his access code. 'I want some background on someone called Sam Kamas,' Dwight said.

'Just one moment, Mr Khouri.'

Two minutes later, Adams was back. 'What information do you require?'

'What is his status and rank within the Agency?'

'He is on temporary assignment to the Agency,' Adams said. 'He is on a one-time contract.'

'Assignment from where?'

Dwight heard the rasp of a match, followed by an inhalation. Then Adams said, 'I'm sorry, Mr Khouri, I don't think I could give you any more information. Not unless you apply personally. Mr Kamas's file is marked for restricted access, and I only gave you the details I did because of your priority code.'

'I'm not in Washington,' Dwight said. 'Hell man, I'm not even in America.'

'I'm sorry, Mr Khouri, I can't tell you more than that on an open line.'

And that, Dwight thought, was that. But not quite. The CIA's bag men were mainly first or second generation immigrants, Lebanese, Italian, German, Yugoslav, you name it, as long as they had the right contacts and knew how to move money discreetly around the world, they were in. No one quite knew why foreigners were peculiarly suited to this, unless of course the whole business of funny money was more widespread outside America.

The money men formed a separate group within the CIA, excluded, disliked and mistrusted by the average agent who was usually white, usually more expensively educated and usually protestant. Like any minority group the money men had their own sources of information.

Dwight jiggled the receiver and gave the operator a number in New York. Ten minutes later, Samir Achmet was on the line. Dwight went through the ritual exchange of Levantine pleasantry, then asked Samir for information on Sam Kamas. Fast.

Samir's non-computerized system was as efficient as the Agency's, and more revealing. 'You've got a hard one here,' Samir said. Kamas was Hungarian, and had come over in 1956, bringing with him a fluency in Slavic languages and a hatred for everything communist. He'd been ideal fodder for the Agency and within three years was in the Balkans exploiting his linguistic ability and his passion for revenge. Revenge had grown to be a habit with Kamas. He'd worked in Albania, Greece and Italy, gone into Vietnam early, been one of the top people in Phoenix, and then returned to the United States to infiltrate domestic revolutionary groups. In 1975, the Congressional Committee investigating the CIA had demanded his resignation.

Dwight felt the hair prickle along the back of his neck. 'And did he resign?'

'Yes. Sam Kamas was thrown out of the Agency in 1975. There is no way he can get back.'

'Not even on a one time?'

Samir Achmet went silent. When he spoke again Dwight had a feeling he was choosing his words carefully. 'What's seen is not always to be believed. I hear Kamas is in Europe and that he has got Jerry Vaslav with him.'

'Who is he?'

'A Hungarian, former Vietnam buddy of Kamas's, a real mean bastard. The other one, Karoly Lawrence, part Hungarian, gets very mean and nasty on coke. Does any of this make sense to you, Dwight?'

'No,' Dwight said.

'Then try this for size. He is looking for guys with combat experience. Immediate assignment, three thou a head, no questions asked. Says it's a heavy security operation.'

'A hit team,' Dwight muttered. What the hell was Kamas

up to? The operation was supposed to be low key. No more than half a dozen people knew about it. He had spoken to Kamas last night. Things couldn't have changed so quickly since.

Samir was saying, 'Even if you're starting World War Three, be careful.'

'I will,' Dwight said. 'And thanks.' He put the phone down, dazed.

'Bad news, Mr Khouri?'

Dwight nodded. He wanted time to think. He wanted to talk to Jeb Anderson.

'You have problems. Your Mr Kamas is not *Zuverlässig* – not trustworthy?'

'You could say I have doubts.'

Mollwo leaned forward and resting his chin in his palm, looked steadily at Dwight. 'Tell me, Mr Khouri, would you find it difficult to believe an arrangement between your CIA and the business community?'

'No,' Dwight said. As the Congressional Enquiry had shown, the Agency had links with organized crime. So why not organized business?

'I believe,' Mollwo said, 'that your Agency has been infiltrated. That this man Kamas represents not your Agency, but certain business interests.'

'What business interests?'

'I cannot say. But if I were looking for those who are interested, I would look in the direction of the oil community or those businessmen who many years ago worked with Berndt Manninger.' Mollwo looked keenly across his desk at Dwight. 'What are you going to do, now that you have found out your Mr Kamas may be working for someone else?'

'I can easily by-pass Sam,' Dwight said. 'I can report directly to Anderson if I have to.'

'And if I ask you to help us locate the processes, would you agree to by-pass this Mr Kamas?'

'With the information I have now, I'd have to.'

'How can you convince me that the moment you get to a phone, all this will not be relayed to Sam Kamas?'

'Knowing what I know, I'd be stupid to use Kamas,' Dwight said. 'You've got to believe that I'm working for the American government and no one else. If you don't believe that by now, then there's nothing more I can do to convince you.'

There was a long silence while Mollwo and Marit stared at each other. Then slowly, they both nodded, and Mollwo said, 'Mr Khouri, we would like you to help us locate the processes.' He paused and smiled. 'For one more dollar.'

26

Mollwo introduced the four men who had brought them to the sawmill as his sons. He had his sons set a table in the long room behind them, and a few minutes later they all sat down to a meal of black pumpernickel bread, ham and wine. Mollwo sat at the head of the table, had Dwight and Marit sit on either side of him and poured them glasses of pale, yellow Moselle.

'I owe everything to Berndt Manninger,' Mollwo said, 'and not because of all this.' He waved expansively around the room and told them that the land on which the sawmill stood and the forest surrounding it had been given to him by Manninger. 'In the war, he saved my life.'

As his sons ate furiously, Mollwo told Dwight and Marit how they had been retreating from around La-Chapelle-en-Argonne. Their company had been decimated. There were only seven of them left, two of them barely able to walk, and Manninger had taken command. Struggling between the English and American lines, they'd come across an English corporal, attempting to repair a Crossley van. Manninger had shot the corporal, then fixed the van's broken head gasket with a mixture of mud and dung, and driven it thirty miles to the German lines at Douzy.

'That is why I owe Berndt Manninger everything,' Mollwo finished. 'That is why there is nothing I would not do for him.'

Mollwo said that after the war he had lost contact with Manninger, had only met him some years afterwards, when Manninger had just completed his designs for the synthetic nitrate factory and Mollwo was ekeing out a precarious living selling agricultural machinery. 'He told me all about synthetic nitrates,' Mollwo said, 'how they would change the entire basis of European agriculture. Then he invited me to head his sales division, and suggested I got the French interested in nitrate production.' Mollwo laughed. 'Sales division! For the first four months all I had was a partially deaf lady with an insatiable appetite for chocolate. But that was Berndt Manninger. He could never think small.'

Mollwo described how he'd sold licensing rights in the nitrate process to the French, how Manninger Industrie had not only received substantial royalties on all synthetic nitrates sold in France, but had also capitalized on the sale of know-how and supervision of French production. He told them that within the year, there were four Manninger nitrate factories in Germany, and that within two years, eighty-five per cent of all synthetic nitrates sold in Western and Central Europe was directly or indirectly produced by Manninger.

'Then,' Mollwo said, 'came styrium, manganese, plastics, oil.

'They were good days,' Mollwo continued, 'we were rich, successful, admired. We were welcome everywhere we went. We were respected.'

And in 1928, the control of the Manninger companies had been moved to Switzerland.

'There was no alternative,' Mollwo said. 'Germany was in an indescribable mess with high taxes, soaring inflation and exchange control. And there were still people in Europe and

America who would not deal with German companies.' Mollwo said he had helped create the Swiss operation, worked with the Hoffman Bank and Peter DuBuois in setting up the companies, transferring holdings, granting licences and investing profits. 'But there were still parts of that operation I did not know about and which Berndt never told me of. Berndt could sometimes be a very suspicious man.'

It was about that time, Mollwo said, that Manninger had become interested in politics. Like many businessmen in an era of supra-national corporations, he could not ignore politics. He had a vision of nation states motivated by profit, of governments run with the efficiency of corporations and subsidiary to the giant cartels. It was a vision that was shared by many others. 'And in those days,' Mollwo said, 'it was an easier dream to realize. There was little of what you Americans call consumer awareness.'

The problem, however, was Germany, ineffectually governed, with private armies rampaging along its streets, with inflation rampant and burdened with a back-breaking debt of war reparations. And like it or not, the world needed Germany. It had a population of some fifty million people, it was Europe's bulwark against Communism, and its technologists were years ahead of everyone else. So Manninger and others decided to impose order on Germany, order in the form of Adolf Hitler and the most popular of political armies – the National Socialist Party.

'Did Manninger really help to bring Hitler to power?' Dwight asked.

'With the help of many others,' Mollwo replied. 'And I am not only talking of the von Thyssens and the Krupps. I am talking of other industrialists, other politicians, other governments.'

But everyone had misjudged Hitler, Mollwo continued, not only was he more opportunist than they were, he was a man who in the end could not be bought. Hitler had had his own vision, a vision of Germany restored to its rightful place in the hierarchy of nations, a Germany that was self-sufficient and free from the threat of being starved out by the British Navy, a Germany that would be the home of all the German-speaking people scattered throughout Europe. Hitler's Pan-Germanic vision was not shared by many of those who had helped bring him to power.

'So Hitler had to be removed. The excuse was Poland, at the time a military dictatorship and militarily indefensible. It was thought that threats of war would be enough. The speed of our conquest of Poland surprised and frightened everyone. Unable to cope with this mad genius who had gone out of control, the threats continued. Then came 1940 and the *Blitzkreig*. We expected the war to end quickly and for England to sue for peace. So, the old arrangements continued, between Manninger and his associates, between many others. In fact, the Allies sanctioned this participation by converting it into an intelligence operation called Brunhilde.'

Three days before he was killed, Mollwo said, Manninger had called on him at his home in Ludwigshafen. Manninger had been nervous and emphasized that no one should know of his visit. He told Mollwo that Martin Bormann and a few other important people had come to an accommodation with the Perons and devised a lunatic plan to create a Fourth Reich in Argentina. They had invited him to join them, to contribute his technological genius and the processes he had worked on in Hellenthal, since the death of his son, Dieter. At the same time he was concerned that his colleagues in the cartels, with whom he had worked throughout the war, would use the defeat of Germany to condemn him as a war criminal, and then seize his assets and confiscate the processes. Manninger had said he was going to hide everything in Switzerland. He said he was going to meet with the cartel at the Hoffman Bank in Zurich and he intended to warn them that if any attempt was made to seize what was not rightly theirs, he would expose them and their governments.

Mollwo said, "He gave me a parcel, which he said contained a photograph album and a Johannes Bruckner bible. They contained the secret of where everything was hidden. If anything happened to him, I was to keep the parcel until it was claimed by his heirs. Berndt was insistent that the parcel should be claimed. Under no circumstances was I to deliver anything to his inheritors.'

Abruptly Mollwo got up and left the table, returning ten minutes later, with a streak of mud down one trouser leg, panting slightly and carrying a large parcel wrapped in goatskin. He placed it on the table beside him and asked his sons to clear the remnants of the meal. 'On the 23rd February 1945,' he said, as if there had been no interruption, 'returning from his meeting in Switzerland, Berndt Manninger was murdered by his Allied friends!'

'Berndt Manninger was shot by the Gestapo,' Dwight said.

Mollwo was opening the parcel with tender care. 'The Gestapo fired the shots,' he said, not looking up from his task. 'But it was the cartel that killed him.'

The goatskin fell away revealing another parcel wrapped in oilskin on which there was a small leather case. Mollwo opened the case, took a long envelope from it and passed it to Marit. 'I got that some years after Berndt's death,' he said. 'It is the official Gestapo report of the shooting.'

The report was terse and to the point, signed by one Dieter Asch, a Gestapo officer with Schaffhausen Border Control. At noon on the 23rd February, Asch had received an anonymous telephone call from Zurich. The caller's German was not fluent, and he had informed Asch that Berndt Manninger had over the past five years held regular meetings with Allied Intelligence in Switzerland. Asch had verified this information, notified Berlin and been ordered to arrest Manninger.

At four thirty that afternoon, Manninger had arrived at the Schaffhausen border post. He had attempted to escape back to Switzerland, and shots had been fired. A tyre had burst, causing Manninger's car to skid into the pylons arranged to prevent escapes, and Manninger had been seriously injured.

With the help of the guards, Asch had extricated him from the wreckage of the car and laid him on the pavement. Manninger had recovered consciousness briefly, and before he died had said, 'Zurich is not the source. The source is Hellenthal. Hellenthal and the devil. The devil in the scriptures.'

Gestapo officer Dieter Asch had concluded that Manninger had been delirious.

Dwight looked from the report to Mollwo. What could Manninger have meant? *The source is Hellenthal! Zurich is not the source!* Had Manninger left the processes in Germany? 'What was Manninger trying to say?' Dwight asked, as he walked back to his chair.

But Mollwo ignored him, unwrapping the oilskin from the parcel and revealing yet another parcel, wrapped in brown paper and sealed with crusty brown wax. 'This is the parcel Berndt left with me,' he said. 'I have not opened it. The other wrappings were only for protection.'

'Open it, please,' Marit said, quietly.

Mollwo picked up a knife and cut the string, peeled away the paper and exposed the bible and the album that had been in his possession for thirty-five years. 'Now I discharge my trust,' he said, looking steadily at Marit, his large hands resting on the bible. 'I pray that you will find what is rightfully yours and that you will have the strength and the courage to use your power and your wealth as wisely as Berndt Manninger would have wished.' Gently, Mollwo pushed the bible and the album to Marit. 'My family and I are at your sevice,' he said. 'There is not one of us who would not die for Berndt Manninger or his true inheritor.'

Afterwards they sat in the partitioned-off area around Mollwo's desk and looked through the bible and the photograph album. The bible was about three hundred years old, large and heavy, with ancient printing and thick, Gothic lettering. On the flyleaf at the back of the bible there was a series of figures and letters in faded purple ink and on the frontispiece M459L4813. Dwight showed them to Mollwo.

Mollwo said, 'It's Berndt's handwriting. But I have no idea what the figures mean.'

'A car number,' Marit suggested.

'Or a map reference?'

Mollwo said, 'It could mean anything. When Berndt was thinking he had a habit of scribbling on the nearest piece of paper. That could even be a chemical formula.'

They looked through the photograph album. There were photographs of Manninger as a boy, of his parents, wedding photographs, snapshots of Ingrid and Dieter as babies and as children. There were smiling family groups and pictures taken on holiday. There were photographs obtained from newspapers and magazines, glossy prints of Manninger at official receptions, Manninger at meetings, Manninger escorting the Fuhrer around the factory at Ludwigshafen. There were photographs of Manninger with business colleagues, Manninger standing before the Eiffel Tower, before the Brandenburg Gate, on a ferry crossing the Hudson with the Statue of Liberty in the background. There were numerous photographs of Elisabeth, placid and very beautiful, numerous photographs of their wedding. The album was nothing more than a pictorial biography of Berndt Manninger. None of them could see what it had to do with the processes.

'But we will have to do something soon,' Mollwo said and reaching into his desk drawer, brought out the previous day's copy of *Neue Zuricher Zeitung*. He turned to the financial page where he had marked an advertisement inserted by the Hoffman Bank, calling a meeting of the shareholders of Perpetua and Sopadep, to consider the acceptance of an offer of the sum of twenty-five million dollars for the assets of both companies. In the absence of any notification to the contrary from the shareholders, the Hoffman Bank proposed to accept the sale offer.

Dwight found Marit and Mollwo looking at him. 'Someone's gambling on the processes being found,' he said. 'They've persuaded Hoffmans to go along with them, and if the sale goes through before the processes are found, they will have the companies and the processes for twenty-five million dollars.'

'But that's hardly a fair price,' Marit said.

'I would imagine that it is a very high price,' Dwight said, 'as things stand now. The processes have been missing for thirty-five years. It would be technically correct, for Hoffmans to place a low valuation on them.'

'How can we stop them?' Marit asked.

'By finding the *Zessions*, before the meeting,' Dwight said, 'then attending the meeting and rejecting the offer. That is the only safe way. You could take legal action to stop Hoffmans, but that would only be a delaying process. You have no legal rights until you get the *Zessions*, and if Hoffmans can show, as I am sure they will, that the offer is a good one, taking into account the value of the known assets of the companies, a court may even approve the sale.'

Marit lit a cigarette. 'So we'll have to find another way of stopping Hoffman.' She blew smoke across the desk and turned to Mollwo. 'Do you know who the buyers are?'

'I don't know,' Mollwo said, slowly. 'But I can guess. The cartel still exists.' He opened the photograph album and turned to a picture of Manninger with two men. 'Andre Brassard and Sir Alex Vickery. They knew of the processes. Now, with Elisabeth dead, they must have decided to get them.'

'But the Hoffman Bank? Would Gerhardt Hoffman conspire with people like that?'

'Gerhardt Hoffman would,' Dwight said. 'He's taking no risks at all. What he's doing is scrupulously correct. If he succeeds, his bank handles two of the world's largest companies, and that is only the beginning.'

Marit reached for the phone and asked for a number in Stuttgart. 'Let's find out what we can about Brassard and

Vickery,' she said. 'Maybe we can stop them easier than we can stop Hoffman.'

'How?' Dwight and Mollwo asked together.

'They want the processes,' Marit said. 'They'll deal with anyone they think has them.'

At that moment her call was connected and she spoke rapidly into the phone, replaced the receiver with a lot of enthusiastic *danke*'s and turned back to them.

'That was Uwe Berger,' she said. 'He's a freelance researcher, who has worked for us from time to time. He says he already has the information on Brassard and Vickery. He will meet us at the Graf Zeppelin, in Stuttgart, in two hours.'

27

Dwight drove, and as he threaded the car down the twisty mountainside he felt the heady exultation of a gambler whose luck had unaccountably turned. Mollwo had been terrific, a marvellous old man, solid as oak, firm as rock. And somehow he had persuaded Marit to abandon her Nazi friends, somehow persuaded her to like Americans. And now, thanks to Mollwo, he was the official seeker after the Manninger inheritance and the protector of the Manninger heiress.

The Manninger heiress however did not appear to share his elation. She sat beside him staring blankly at the road, wearing that expression of tuned-in concentration he was beginning to know so well. He wished he knew what she was thinking about.

Marit was thinking that by now the hunt had already begun, that men like Rolf Hausen would be wandering all over Europe, asking questions, checking hotel registers, doing everything necessary to find her. And when they found her, it would be worse. She couldn't imagine what worse could be, but she knew. *You have nowhere to run. Nowhere to hide. Wherever you go we will find you.*

As they had done before!

'You'd better tell me about the people from Zurich,' Dwight said. 'The people you're running away from.'

She started, then looked at him uneasily. 'Why?' she asked.

'The more I know about them, the safer it will be for both of us.'

She turned and stared at the road streaming towards them. When they reached the stretch of dual carriageway before the autobahn, she said, 'They're not from Zurich. They're from Argentina. They're part of the German community there, people who left Germany at the end of the war.'

'*Odessa.* Isn't that what they're called?'

'You read too many bad books,' she said. 'In 1945, these men were fugitives, from what was known as Allied justice. They took with them vast sums of money, two, three hundred million dollars, something like that. With that they bought sanctuary and did what any group of people with that kind of money would do. They invested it. They set up businesses. They bought land and property. They're not *Odessa* or *Der Spinne* or whatever you people call them. They are the Adler Gemeinschaft Corporation, which has an income of over six billion dollars a year and assets of about half of that. It is one of the largest corporations in South America and is entirely owned by former German exiles.'

And with their income and their assets one of the world's larger corporations, Dwight thought.

'As far as those German exiles are concerned,' Marit continued, 'as far as their children are concerned, Adler Gemeinschaft is more than a large German corporation, it is more than the source of their livelihood. Adler Gemeinschaft is their whole life.'

Marit went on to describe a self-sufficient, enclosed, inward-looking exile community, largely isolated from the local population and controlling that population through economic strength, a community with its own churches, clubs, schools, newspapers, theatres, and in some cases, its own armies. There was no life for an exile outside that community.

'Most of the men who founded the Gemeinschaft, founded the community, are dead. The Gemeinschaft is controlled by the survivors, von Kassel, Klaus Altman, Heinrich Muller and Dr Manfred Fendt. They're also the benevolent leaders of the community.

'From the day I knew I would inherit the Manninger estate, it was instilled into me that the Manninger processes belonged to the Adler Gemeinschaft.'

'Why?' Dwight asked.

'The why isn't important,' Marit said. 'That is how the community works. And to be quite honest, I felt I owed them that, that it was a small return for all they had done for me and my family. They brought my mother out of Germany – by submarine, as your files so diligently show – I was educated in their schools, and attended their churches. I was entertained in their social clubs, I worked on their newspapers. After my father's death, they supported my mother and me. To someone like me, a child of the damned, that community represents more than economic security. That community is my home, my country, my family.'

'But today, you decided not to give them the processes.'

'That's right. It was a decision I should have made before. For many years I have had doubts about the men who ran the Gemeinschaft. When I came to Germany, when I lived with Germans who were not part of the community, my doubts grew. I've often hoped that I would die before Elisabeth Manninger. I worried about doing what was right for the community, and I worried about the use men like von Kassel would make of the processes.

'Then, two months ago, Johann Neumann came to see me in Munich. Johann is one of the many orphans who were smuggled out to Argentina at the end of the war. His father was Director of the Reich Main Security Office, one of those so-called war criminals executed by you Americans.

'Since the age of twelve, Johann has lived on von Kassel's *estancia* and been brought up by him. Now, he is a man of about your age. He trained as a lawyer in Germany, and spends a great deal of time in Europe, looking after the interests of the Gemeinschaft. Oh yes, don't look so surprised. Europe is quite happy to deal with the Gemeinschaft, as are you Americans.

'Johann told me that he had been appointed to the board of the Gemeinschaft. He pointed out to me that most of the *Alte Kameraden* were dead and the survivors would not live for much longer. He told me that people like him and me would run the Gemeinschaft, that we could do what he'd always advocated the Gemeinschaft should do, create a fairer society for our people. And, Johann assured me, that the money from the processes would be used only for that purpose. The *Alte Kameraden* would not control it.

'You must understand that I've known Johann since I was a child. At one time, I was even in love with him. Anyway, I believed him. I was glad to do whatever was necessary to get the processes for him. I was glad to give it to him.'

Marit went silent, took a cigarette from the pack on the dashboard and lit it. 'And now he uses hired assassins. He kills, like they killed. And he will use the processes, as the others would have used them.'

Marit turned to him, sending out twin streams of smoke through her nostrils. 'I don't know who Johann will send after us,' she said. 'But I know he will have people looking for us. And I – ' her voice broke – 'and I would rather die than let them find me.'

'Why? They can't kill you. Without you no one has any chance of getting the processes.'

'They don't have to kill me,' Marit said.

Dwight slowed and looked at her. 'What have they done to you, Marit? What have they done to make you so terrified of them?'

She reached across and patted his hand. 'Perhaps, I'll tell you later. It's a long story, and there isn't enough time before we reach Stuttgart.'

The Graf Zeppelin was elegantly space-age, discreet and expensive. Uwe Berger came into the lobby five minutes after they had ordered coffee, a slightly built, prematurely balding man, neatly dressed in a pale brown suit which matched the fawn raincoat he carried over his arm.

Marit introduced Dwight as a colleague from the Munich office and Berger shook hands courteously and ordered mineral water for himself. Then, taking out a large notebook, he said he had all the information they'd need.

'Let me give you some background on Vickerys,' Berger said. 'The company was founded in 1922 by one Reginald Vickery, a chemical engineer from Rochdale in Lancashire, England. From 1906 to 1912, Vickery worked in Russia, for the German textile industry. At the time, German dye processes were the most advanced in the world, and when Vickery returned to England, he was promptly appointed Head of Research at the British Dyestuffs Company.

'Vickery had a safe war,' Berger continued. 'Too old to go into the trenches, he continued to work for the British Dyestuffs Company and then did some work for the government. At the end of the war he appeared as an advisor to the British Armistice Commission, regarding the valuation of German dyestuffs patents to be seized by the British in reparations.'

Berger leaned back against the chair and sipped his mineral water. 'Vickery pronounced those patents valueless. He convinced the Armistice Commission that without German know-how they were best excluded from the restitution settlement.

'Four years later, Vickery formed his own company, Vickery Chemicals Limited, which utilized German patents, hitherto unavailable to the British dyestuffs industry. It was rumoured that Vickery's finance came from a group of

German companies.' Berger looked from Marit to Dwight. 'And that's why people say, wars are good for business.'

Berger told them that with his privileged access to the latest German technology, Vickerys had grown rapidly, producing not only dyestuffs, but lucrative by-products such as sulpha drugs and film. Vickery had also established a close relationship with the newly formed Manninger Industrie, and became the sole British licensee for the marketing of Manninger produced synthetic nitrates, and later, styrium.

With his new-found wealth, Vickery then embarked on a series of acquisitions, and in 1930 absorbed the British Dyestuffs Company.

Vickery Chemicals became Vickery Industries and was now run by Reginald Vickery's son, Sir Alex Vickery. The company was large and prosperous. Its profits and dividends increased each year, and for all practical purposes the Vickery family controlled it.

Berger looked down at his notebook. 'Brassards,' he said, 'bears remarkable similarities to Vickerys. Like Vickerys, the company was started many years ago as the Compagnie Payes de Sureté. Its name was changed to Brassard et Fils fifty years ago. Like Vickerys, Brassards has a record of being well managed and financially healthy. It has survived wars, Euro-Communism and the loss of Algeria. Forty per cent of its stock is owned by the Brassard family.

'The company is run by Odile Brassard. André Brassard had no *fils*, and when she succeeded her father, many people thought the company would collapse or diversify into frivolous things. But under Madame Odile the company has grown at a faster rate than under her father, and the men of the Bourse have learned to fear and respect her. Madame Odile is forty-five and unmarried. Her life is the company.'

Berger smiled and said, 'I have kept the most intriguing bit of information for the last. I obtained copies of each company's most recent internal accounts statement. The similarity between their affairs is amazing. Both companies have recently divested themselves of most of their investments, both companies are getting out of dollars and both have large cash balances. Rumour has it that both Vickerys and Brassards have been trying to increase their borrowing facilities.'

Berger closed his notebook with a snap, leaned back in his chair.

'Why would they borrow if they already have large cash balances?' Marit asked.

'There are many reasons,' Berger replied. 'They may have temporarily decided to go into the money business. They may have simply lost faith in company paper. But looking at the history of both those companies, I wouldn't think it's either of those reasons. Both companies are tightly managed and aggressive. They wouldn't have money sitting around, when it falls in value every day. I believe that jointly, or separately, they're planning a massive coup. I couldn't even begin to guess what that might be.'

'Thanks, Uwe,' Marit said. 'You've been most helpful. Mark your account for my attention. I'll approve it quickly.'

But Berger remained in his chair, leaning back and smiling. 'Fair's fair,' he said. 'Now you tell me, what's the story?'

'A general interest feature on old established companies,' Marit said. 'How they've changed with the times, how they've survived various financial crises. I hope to interview Odile Brassard and Sir Bernard Vickery.'

'I thought this had something to do with Topf,' Berger said.

'Topf!' Marit's voice was strained, her face suddenly pale.

'What's it got to do with Topf?' Dwight asked.

Berger said, 'Didn't you know? Bruno Topf committed suicide this afternoon.'

'We've been driving from Munich,' Marit said in a small voice. 'We didn't know.'

Berger studied her carefully before he said, 'According to unconfirmed reports, Topf was in serious financial trouble. The old man had invested heavily in Russia, something around three to four hundred million dollars in the construction of aromatic factories, and I hear that deal has gone sour.' Berger looked questioningly at Marit. 'You're positive your story has nothing to do with Topf?'

'My story has nothing to do with Bruno Topf,' Marit said, in a strained voice.

'Why should our enquiries about Vickery and Brassard make you think we're doing a story about Topf?' Dwight asked.

Uwe Berger leaned across the table. 'Those aromatic factories,' he said. 'Topf was building them with Vickery and Brassard. And three days ago, all of them sold out their interest in that venture. Like Vickery and Brassard, Topf is exceptionally liquid. He is also selling dollars short and trying to borrow money.'

Dwight sat back in his chair, leaning away from Berger's confidential crouch. So Topf too had been a member of the cartel. And the cartel was in trouble of some kind. But he would have to think about that, and first he had to deal with Berger. 'You've given us a whole new angle for the story,' Dwight said.

Berger got to his feet. 'In that case, I've done my job.' He smiled at Marit. 'If you need me, you know where to find me.' And giving them a cheery wave, left.

They realized it was Friday evening and the start of the German weekend when they came out of the hotel. Stuttgart was an endless gleam of throbbing cars in the soft drizzle that had begun while they'd been closeted with Berger. Topf's death had merited a special edition and they bought a paper from the hotel kiosk. Marit read out the story as Dwight inched through the congealed traffic.

Topf's body had been found at around three o'clock that afternoon, when his secretary, alarmed at his prolonged silence, had forced the locked door of his office. Topf had been lying between his desk and the door, with a bullet wound in his head. There had been a gun in his hand and a suicide note on his desk. A ballistics expert had pronounced that the bullet taken from the body matched the weapon found in Topf's hand and that the angle of the wound was consistent with self-inflicted injury. Nothing had been taken from Topf's office and the only fingerprints on the gun were his. The Frankfurt police had said they were satisfied it was suicide.

The police conclusion was supported by an anonymous spokesman for Topf Industrie, who said that recently Topf had been very concerned about his health and had embarked upon an extremely rigid diet. The fact that hallucinatory states could be induced by excessive dieting was well known, and the spokesman implied that Topf's suicide was only the last and largest of a whole series of aberrations.

'It's not true,' Marit said.

'What's not true?' Dwight's brain was in neutral, stultified by the crush of traffic, the continuous starting, crawling, stopping. They'd tried two hotels without any success, and all Dwight could think of was a long, hot bath and total, absolute silence.

'Topf didn't commit suicide. He was murdered.'

Dwight looked tiredly from the mesmeric rear wiper on the Volvo estate in front of him. Marit was seated sideways across the seat, paper on her knee, the rectangular interior light above her head darkening the shadow of her face and heightening its intensity. She looked like a compressed spring, about to break loose.

Not now, Dwight thought, not when he couldn't think straight.

'Why do you say that?' he asked, tonelessly.

The traffic around him moved. Mechanically Dwight graunched into gear. He wished the man in the Volvo would turn off that damned wiper.

'Topf went through two world wars,' Marit said. 'Twice in his life, everything he'd created was taken from him. He was tried at Nuremberg and jailed for four years. He wouldn't shoot himself because his business had gone sour or his doctor had put him on a diet.'

Dwight recalled a SIAF patrol that had lived for four days

on bandicoot flesh. Hunger did strange things to people. The rear wiper of the Volvo stopped its squealing arc. Dwight felt his mind mesh, but slowly and heavily, like the ridges of a snow tyre creeping through mud. He told Marit about the SIAF patrol and the bandicoots.

'Topf's starved before,' she said, flatly.

'All right. So who did it?' Tiredly. 'Not the cartel. Topf was one of them.' He felt irritated at Marit's ferreting around, for wanting to discuss it now.

'Topf was also part of the Adler Gemeinschaft,' Marit said.

Dwight forced himself to think. Neumann's crowd had obviously discovered Topf was helping the cartel to acquire the Manninger processes and bumped him off. That was the risk anyone took working both sides of the street. 'Johann Neumann,' he said, tentatively.

'Not Johann,' Marit said, positively. 'Johann would need approval from the entire council for that, and they'd never give it. Topf was useful to all of them. He was friendly with all of them. He was particularly close to von Kassel and if they had differences they would have resolved them another way.'

'And if their differences were too great?'

'They couldn't be,' Marit said.

'Suppose Neumann acted on his own?'

'He wouldn't,' Marit said. 'Like Bruno Topf, Johann Neumann would not want to commit suicide.'

28

An hour later they found a small, family-run hotel in the woods near the Solitude Race Circuit, outside Stuttgart. A steady buzz of conversation came from the dining-room beside the reception area, where waitresses scurried busily between noisy tables bearing steaming trays of *gulaschsuppe*, *kartoffelsalat* and *schweinbraten*. Dwight carried the rucksack up narrow flights of cemented stairs to the second floor, where they'd been given two adjoining rooms. He took out the paper shopping-bag containing Marit's clothes and gave it to her.

She took it, hesitated, then asked, 'What do you do on Friday nights in New York?'

Dwight had to make an effort to remember. Last Friday, good God, last Friday seemed years ago. He'd taken Melanie home. She'd been at the studio since seven that morning, he remembered, and she hadn't wanted to do anything. They'd watched a movie on television, drunk a bottle of Beaujolais Villages and eaten a warmed-up TV dinner. He told Marit what he'd done the previous Friday night.

The skin over Marit's cheeks tightened, and her mouth became firm. 'I'd like to go somewhere tonight,' she said. 'For a few hours I'd like to forget everything that is happening to us.'

And that was a brilliant idea! An expensive, intimate restaurant in Stuttgart, preferably French, a nightclub afterwards . . . Dwight knew they couldn't do it. Hunted people did not go into crowded restaurants or smooch on dimly-lit dance floors. Not when they had no means of recognizing those hunting them and certainly not when the hunters were professional killers.

'You're paranoid,' Marit snapped.

Dwight shrugged. 'So, paranoids live longer.'

'Who the hell knows where we are?'

'Uwe Berger, for one.'

'He's not going to tell anybody.'

'He lives by telling people things for money.'

'All right, forget it,' Marit said. 'We'll eat here.'

The clamour of conversation and clatter of crockery carried up the stairs, together with the smell of food. The chances of their being found in the outskirts of Stuttgart were small. But Dwight's training had not only been directed at minimizing chances, but avoiding unnecessary ones. 'We'll eat up here,' Dwight said.

'You can. I'm going down there!'

'And afterwards, you could spend a lot of time thinking if a ten per cent chance was worth taking. It's not important *where* we eat. What's important is that they do not find you.'

Her face momentarily whitened. Then she said, 'All right, have it your way.'

'Your room or mine?' Dwight asked.

'Yours,' she said and gave him a half smile. 'After all, it's your idea.'

Dwight spent the next hour bathing, thinking and reading Marit's newspaper. A Titan 2 missile – Jiminy Cricket! Were they still around! – had exploded near Damascus, Arkansas. The German elections looked like a victory for the coalition of Social and Free Democrats, the dollar was falling and gold was firming up. In the Mid-East the border conflict between Iran and Iraq was increasing in size and frequency. Dwight wondered if Dr Rasul Quassim had inside knowledge of that conflict before he'd made his switch from dollars to gold.

He read the item on Topf's death last of all. Okay, he'd go along with Marit. Topf's death smelled of a cover-up, but one way or the other it did not affect what he and Marit had to do. Their job was to get the processes. And stop the cartel getting rights of ownership over them. He didn't have any idea yet how he was going to do that. But he had no doubt it would come.

Meanwhile, he wished he had a clean shirt.

Marit came exactly an hour later, looking younger, fresher, with all signs of strain gone. She was wearing the clothes she'd worn to Vaduz, a patterned white blouse and a grey skirt which had just a hint of green, and though both skirt and blouse had been wrapped inside the rucksack all day, she had managed to make them look as if they had been freshly laundered and ironed. Some women were like that, Dwight thought. Give them an hour with an old sack and they'd produce something that looked a million dollars. For some reason it pleased him that Marit was like that.

Dwight had slipped down and given the owner a hundred marks to ensure that everything went well. When Marit came, there was a large gin and tonic waiting for her with the menu, and compensating for being forced to eat in a bedroom, they ordered lavishly. Marit insisted they try the local specialities, *saiten* – a juicy sausage served with lentils and balls of browned flour called spatzle, *Kasafladle* – a pancake made with rich Allgau cheese, and just to show they didn't have a care in the world, a small portion of *Schlachtplatte*, a combination of sauerkraut, spatzle, mashed peas, liver sausage and bits of boiled pork. Dwight said he wanted a steak afterwards, with French fries. Marit ordered grilled trout and a green salad, and they decided that Dwight should drink a Mâcon while Marit stayed with the local Uhlsbacher white. By unspoken assent they avoided all talk of anything to do with the Manninger inheritance.

'Khouri,' Marit said, sipping the gin and tonic. 'What kind of a name is that?'

'Part Arab,' Dwight said. 'The poorer half. My father was Lebanese.' He told her how the Khouris had emigrated from the Lebanon three generations ago and grown from being traders to moneylenders, and from being moneylenders to bankers. The difference between moneylending and banking, he assured her, was in the size and volume of the transactions and the amount of paper work. The Khouri moneylending business, the Imtra Bank, was small compared to any of the better-known American banks. They had only seven branches in the United States, but there was a Khouri bank in every major European capital. The Khouris had always thought internationally and believed in spreading their risks.

Relaxed, Marit was an attentive listener, with a disconcerting knack of imperceptibly directing the conversation. With the help of the *saiten* and the Mâcon, Dwight found himself telling her about the three-tiered Lebanese family structure, about his brother, Sami, and the way his father, Mark, the oldest and toughest of the Khouris, ran the family business. He was telling her about his father being a tank commander under Patton, when discreetly she changed the subject.

'What did you do in Vietnam?'

He told her about the SIAF, how they'd gone out in small patrols of twelve to fifteen men and infiltrated remote villages, to control strategic routes or capture hearts and minds, or sometimes both. 'The British did it better in Malaya,' he said. 'They re-located entire villages, and they had more sense than to fight the war for CBS. They established military rule and did what had to be done.'

'And you think if America had fought the war that way, they would have won?'

'No doubt of it.'

'And you think the war was right?'

Dwight looked at her carefully over his steak. She was too young to have paraded up Capitol Hill protesting that war. 'For the answer to that, you must look at those countries now.'

'What did it feel like, the first time you killed someone?'

She was a good journalist, Dwight thought, slipping in leading questions as unobtrusively as a spring-bladed knife. He'd been taught to handle questions like that in 'Nam, and afterwards. But now, what the hell. Who cared, except Henry Kissinger, and a few million Vietnamese peasants who'd been screwed anyway? 'It felt like nothing,' he said. 'It was just another training exercise, another sandbag at the end of a bayonet. You must remember that we were trained to believe that there were no people out there. They were Charlies, gooks, commies; whatever they were, they weren't human.'

Marit leaned back from the table, as if something had been resolved. 'And you still feel like that, do you, Dwight? About people?'

The hell with it. She had no right asking that kind of

question. This was supposed to be a pleasant dinner for the sole purpose of forgetting Manninger. 'Sometimes,' he said.

'The men in the car in Vaduz, the men who came to the house in Tschagguns. You would have killed them?'

'If I had to.'

She had pushed her plate away and was lighting a cigarette. 'You're married, Dwight? You have a steady girl-friend?'

'I was married,' Dwight said. He thought vaguely of Melanie. 'And I don't have a steady girl-friend. That is the price you have to pay for taking life. You cease to believe in the permanence of anything.'

'You poor bastard,' she said. She drew deeply at the cigarette. 'And what about the Manninger processes? What turns you on about that?'

Dwight poured himself more wine. 'I don't know. It seems a good thing to do, as long as one believes that doing certain things are better than doing others.' He sipped his wine and took one of her cigarettes. She was getting close, unnecessarily and dangerously close.

'Smoking's a filthy habit,' she said.

Dwight drew deeply at the cigarette. It made him cough. 'Let's talk about you,' he said. 'You're still in love with this Neumann character?'

Marit laughed. 'Johann,' she said, incredulously.

'Yes, him. You told me you loved him.'

'Johann's much older than me,' she said. 'He's about your age.'

Dwight winced.

'I was twelve years old when I fell in love with him. He never knew about it, and I'm glad he didn't. When I got older and discovered what love was, I realized I didn't love Johann Neumann any more.'

'So whom do you love?'

She smiled, a gentle smile of self-mockery. 'There was a lawyer in Munich, I thought I loved. He came to live with me. He was older than me, and you know what he started doing? He began to wear beads and Indian cotton. He started to smoke dope and grow his hair. I made him leave me.'

They finished eating, passed on the sweet and nibbled at the cheese. Marit moved from the straight-backed chair, taking her wine and cigarette with her, and leaned across the bed. Dwight turned on the radio. It was tuned to the American Forces Network which was playing easy to listen to country and western, with simple lyrics about unattainable women and the men who had done them wrong.

Dwight went and sat beside her on the bed, put his arm around her shoulder.

'If you're going to kiss me,' she said, 'you'd better change the music.'

Dwight turned off the radio. They kissed. A surprisingly passionate and frenetic kiss that had as little resemblance to the sisterly effort of the previous night as a hurricane to a light, summer breeze. Her mouth gyrated frantically under his, and her tongue explored and writhed, sending little trills of pleasure cascading down his spine, each time its searching tip touched. Dwight kissed her with equal passion and thought that little girls learnt more than grain harvesting on those pampas, and then pulled his head away, breathless.

Her eyes fluttered open and locked on his. They were like deep tunnels, full of a hungry intensity. A small, self-satisfied smile tickled her mouth. Dwight lowered his head and kissed her again, feeling the softness and liquidity of that mouth, the snaking excitement of that twining tongue. Holding her close to him, he slipped a hand beneath her blouse. She wore no bra and he caressed her breasts, feeling her nipples come erect under his fingertips. Her arms tightened around him and he felt a little tremor run through her.

He pressed her down on the bed, tore his face away from hers, and buried it in the open V of her blouse. She lay back and smiled and stroked his hair, while he ran his free hand down her body, and stroked the insides of those long thighs that felt as smooth as glass.

She pulled her head to his and kissed his mouth. Dwight

felt he wanted to hold her like this forever, to have her forever trapped beneath him. He wanted to touch and explore all of her, wanted to feel every millimetre of that long body, wanted to keep her mouth against his until the world ended. His exploring fingers reached the tip of her panties and eased down the front of them. She was wet, soaking.

As if embarrassed at the discovery of the extent of her passion, her hand reached down and caught his. Dwight raised his head and for a moment her eyes stared into his, as if she were looking at a stranger. Then she smiled to herself and released his hand, pressed her body against his and allowed her open mouth to enclose his.

Dwight didn't know how long they stayed like that, locked in that lubricious embrace of mouth and hand. All he did know was that he did not want to let her go. And that part of him felt as if it was about to burst.

Suddenly the press of her body against his stopped. She pulled his hand away, and with a quick, lifting, wriggling movement, eased her body from underneath his, pulled her head away from him and sat up, tousled and red faced, her eyes glistening wildly.

She sat on the side of the bed for a moment, fingers flying over her opened blouse. Then she was moving across the room, out of the door, muttering, 'Let's go to my room. It doesn't smell like a kitchen.'

29

Marit lay naked under the bed sheet, her feet and knees pressed together, her stomach taut, holding fast to the surge of electric excitement that washed through her and trying to understand what had made her invite the American to kiss her, invite him back to her room. She wasn't promiscuous.

Four of the five men she'd been with, she had loved, or believed she had, and she'd never, not even after the most outrageous party, woken up beside a man she'd met the previous night.

She told herself it was simply tension, this crazy, nerve-racking situation they were in. Subconsciously, consciously even, she was seeking release. And she knew that was partly true.

So what was the rest of it? She'd disliked the American when she'd met him, disliked his witling friendliness, his evenness of temper and, most of all, his boyish gaucherie. Then, she had seen him act like a primitive warrior and been fascinated by his strength and cold-blooded expertise. Ever since what had happened with Domingo, she'd looked for strength in men and found it in men older than her, and she remembered that after the shooting at Tschagguns, she'd felt dizzy with excitement and convinced herself that it was only relief.

He'd also acted like a bastard. And she'd hated him. Yet, this morning, he'd been so comfortable to be with, and now . . . what had happened now . . . tonight?

She didn't know why, but she knew when. At dinner, when her questions had probed an area of psychic scar, an area marked keep off, do not touch. At that moment, she had felt his vulnerability and she'd wanted to take him in her arms and hold him. To get to know the secret person behind that bland carapace, not only the mister nice guy he projected, not only the coolly violent professional, but the man who was those things and more. She wanted to know what made him angry and what made him cry – know if he could cry. She wanted to discover what that secret man felt passionate about and what he really thought. And she wanted him to hold her, feel the comfort of his strength, feel safe.

At that moment he came in, barefoot and carrying his creased jacket over his shoulder, looking tentative, despite the mischievous glint in his eye and the butt of the Luger protruding from the jacket. For heaven's sake, she still thought of him as the American. She smiled at the ridiculousness of that and watched him drop the jacket on to the floor and slip out of his shirt. His body was hard, tanned, with wide, flat pectorals like a swimmer, with arms, shoulders and chest that had a gymnast's proportioned muscularity. He was strong all right, with a sapling-like litheness. He stepped out of his trousers and with a quick sideways movement, raised a corner of the sheet and slipped into the bed.

She was surprised at the size of him. His feet stretched some way beyond hers, and the bed had groaned at the shock of his weight. Then his arms were around her and his searching mouth found hers and she felt the excitement flow through her like a river. His mouth was firm and mobile. She could taste his skin and feel the hardness of his chest compress her breasts. She felt his hands move along her body, stroking her gently at first and then in a kind of frantic wonder, exploring her, caressing her thighs and breasts and back, stroking her shoulders, her ribs, her calves, the backs of her knees, until they seemed to be everywhere, as if he was trying to convince himself that she was there, that it was really her.

Suddenly he rolled her on to her back and crouched over her on knees and elbows. A hand snaked down her body and parted her thighs. Oh please, don't let it be like that, she prayed. This first time, let him not simply mount me, use me and fall asleep, open mouthed on my shoulder.

He didn't.

He lowered himself on to her, opening her gently, moving away almost as soon as he had touched, moving down on her again, titillating her with swift, delicious movements. She pressed his shoulders to her neck and kissed the stubble on his cheeks, kissed the tiny scar below his left eye, kissed his eyes, his forehead, his mouth. Her pleasure was growing and she felt herself move with him, at his pace. He was never really in her, never really outside her. It was heaven, it was hell, this consummation and non-consummation. She could feel her frenzy growing, her body melting with delight.

She clung to his mouth and ran her hands distractedly

along his back. Don't stop now, my darling, don't stop. She was going mad with it. She couldn't stand it. She twisted her head away, and pulled his body to her, but he resisted and brought his hands between them and caressed her nipples. Oh exquisite, exquisite sensation! Sensation of sensations. Her mouth, her breasts, she was joined to him. She was part of him. They were joined together and not joined. The frustration and the excitement was enormous as she felt him move faster and harder and deeper. She couldn't bear it any more. She was full of molten pleasure that ebbed and flowed and grew and grew.

She tore her head away from his mouth and cried, 'For God's sake, Davy Crockett, do it!'

Dwight felt her rising excitement, as he probed her, saw it in her pleasure-widened eyes staring rapt into his face, and without any warning he thrust deep down into her, heard her cry and felt the breath rush out of him as her moistness engulfed him. His body convulsed with the intensity of it, his mind seemed to shatter into a thousand fragments. For he didn't know how long, he was oblivious of everything except only of that writhing, coiling moistness that was drowning him.

He opened his eyes and saw her spread out beneath him, felt her gyrating hips, and her legs closed tight around him, her whole body riding up and down with his, bucking and rotating, harder and faster, the machine-gun clatter of the bed mingling with the wild pounding of the pulse inside his head. He was aware of her mouth pulling free, her breath against his face, of their bodies pounding in desperate rhythm, and then the exquisite agony enveloped him as he felt her dilate around him in sensational spasms, and she cried, 'Oh Davy Crockett, you've done it!' As he exploded over and over again inside her.

Afterwards they lay side by side, arms draped loosely around each other.

'Who the hell is Davy Crockett?' Dwight growled.

'Someone from a TV show I saw when I was eight. For a long time afterwards I thought all North Americans were like that.'

'I don't like pet names,' Dwight said.

'Oh come on. Didn't your mother have a special name for you? Your father?'

'No.'

'Fine, then I'll be the first.' She snuggled her head into the curve of his shoulder and murmured, 'Davy, I like the sound of that.'

Dwight sighed. Pet names were a symbol of ownership, tangible evidence of a special relationship. He wasn't looking for anything like that. He didn't believe in marriage and living together or unchanged relationships. You met and you humped and you walked away when you felt like it and all you took was a single Kleenex in case there was a speck of dust in your eye.

He looked down at her. She was dozing, her breath stirring the hair on his chest. In repose, relaxed, she was more beautiful than ever. He let his eyes wander over her, over the twin domes of her full breasts now pressed together in front of her, the dip of her waist, the curve of her hip, those long, long legs, with the strong calves and narrow ankles, those well-formed feet, whose toes, even in repose, were slightly splayed like those of a yawning cat. She was beautiful and she was brave and she was intelligent and she was good to be with. He liked her and that was enough.

She stirred in his arms, nuzzled his chest and asked drowsily, 'Are we going to see Brassard and Vickery tomorrow?'

'Tomorrow's Saturday. Tomorrow we clear our heads and make sensible plans about Brassard and Vickery.'

'All right,' she yawned, her voice that of a little girl, content and safe.

Dwight held her close to him and dozed. Once she woke him up and asked him his age.

'Thirty-five,' he said.

She pulled her head away and looked at him searchingly for a moment, before snuggling back against him, saying, 'That's all right.'

They dozed and woke, and he asked her about her life in Munich. They talked about tennis and running and he told her about ski-ing in the Rockies and that she should give up smoking. They kissed each other and fondled each other and slept again.

Then Marit woke and kissed the skin of his chest, beyond the fringe of downy hair, took a nipple into her mouth and kissed it, enjoying his start of surprised pleasure. She kissed his nipples and his chest, the side of his neck, his face, ran her hands down his body and stroked him, moved on to hands and knees and trickled the tip of her tongue down the hard ridge of his stomach. When he had grown hard in her hand, she swivelled, lowered her head and took him into her mouth.

She heard him gasp with pleasure, felt him move against the roof of her mouth. His hands reached down for her, caressed her, entered her. Her body was filled with a delicious, languorous pleasure, slow currents of delight. She felt she was floating, ethereal. Her head was swimming. She'd never known anything like this.

And just when she thought she could not bear any more of it, he reached up and pulled her back on to the bed, his first deep thrust making her cry out. Then he began to move inside her with a steady, continuous rhythm, a joyous unceasing impalement, whilst she writhed and twisted with him and kissed his face and shoulders and begged him not to stop, not now, not ever, never ever. She held him tight inside her, and it took forever until she felt him come, his climactic jack-hammer pounding throwing her into convulsions of pure ecstasy, wave after wave after rapturous wavelet of it that totally engulfed her, so she did not hear his cries or her own and knew nothing except that she had never been so happy before and that she loved him.

The noise blasted away sleep. Dwight came startled into

wakefulness, his mind already analysing the faintly re-membered sound. The clatter of tin on cement, voices, the patter of feet. He tore himself away from Marit and moved swiftly to the window, scooping up the jacket as he went and taking out the gun.

The room was in the back of the hotel, overlooking the car park, beside which jutted out the single-storeyed hotel restaurant. Except for a light over its entrance, the restaurant was in darkness and there were eight cars in the park, none of them lit.

Dwight moved cautiously from the window to the door of the room and checked that it was locked.

'Who is it?' Marit's voice was low and tremulous, from the bed.

'I don't know yet.'

He went back to the window and stood in the shadow of the wall beside it. Two cars now had parking lights on. Dwight clicked back the safety catch of the Luger. Then he heard voices, carrying faintly past the restaurant, through the glass of the rooms, followed by the despairing moan of starters churning. Engines caught and fired, burbled noisily. Broad, yellow-white bands of light splayed out from headlamps. Then with a crushing of cinders the cars were wheeling round the park, and with a rapid blink of brake lights, gone.

Dwight felt the tension ease out of him, his shoulders go limp, his gun hand droop. Suddenly he felt overwhelmingly tired and his breath became shallow and rapid.

'Dwight, who are they?'

Dwight put the gun on the floor beside the bed and rubbed his eyes and face with the heel of his hands. 'Some late-night drunks. They're gone now.'

'You're sure?'

Marit was on her hands and knees on the bed, a sheet pulled over her shoulders, her face a pale moon in the half light, her eyes large and luminous.

'I'm sure,' Dwight said and got into bed.

She waited, crouched above him, not moving.

'It's all right, Marit,' he said. 'They've gone. We've got nothing to worry about.'

A tear wet his chest. He reached out and touched her. Her body was like ice. Slowly he reached up and looked into her face. She was crying silently, not moving, large tears rolling down her cheeks. 'It was nothing to do with us, girl. Forget it. We're safe.'

Numbly she allowed him to pull her down to the bed and drape a blanket over her. He took her hands between his and began to rub them.

'I'm sorry, Dwight,' she said. 'I am just – it's because – I didn't want – oh bugger it!'

'What's wrong, Marit?'

She sighed. 'I didn't want anything to happen, now, tonight.'

He could feel her hands growing warm beneath his. He reached across and kissed her lightly on the cheek. 'Nothing is going to happen, kiddo. No one knows where we are.'

She took her hands away. 'I'm all right, now. You'd better get some sleep.'

She was lying on her side, staring past him into the darkness. 'What's wrong, kiddo? What's scaring you?'

'It's just . . . tonight . . .'

'Why do they scare you, Marit? What have they done to you that makes you so frightened?'

'It's over,' she said. 'It doesn't matter any more.'

'You bet your sweet bippy it does. Look at you, cold as a naked Eskimo and tight as a snare drum. Tell me what it's about.'

'It won't do any good. It isn't important any more.'

'Marit, in New York, I know a couple of hundred guys who'd charge you three hundred bucks an hour just to listen. So why don't you talk and think of the money you're saving?'

She gave a tinny laugh. 'It's got nothing to do with this business,' she said.

'It's got to do with you,' Dwight said.

Her hand reached out and took his. Another hand

meandered thoughtfully along his body. 'I told you, didn't I, that from an early age I knew the processes were to be given to the Gemeinschaft?'

'Yes,' Dwight said.

'Well, it was not only because the Gemeinschaft had done a lot for my family. It was because throughout her adult life, my mother, and to a lesser extent myself, were both assets of the Gemeinschaft.'

Marit explained that Ingrid Manninger had been brought to Argentina when she was nineteen, and installed on von Kassel's *estancia*. 'For a whole year, she never left it. Everywhere she went, she was escorted. Even when, a year later, von Kassel sent my mother to stay with a German family in La Plata, she did not escape his control. She was treated like a sixteen-year-old novice in a convent, and on the rare occasions when she was allowed out alone, she had to account for where she went and what she did.'

Marit began to sob again. Dwight pulled her into his arms.

'There was no one whom my mother could turn to,' Marit said, controlling herself. 'Nowhere she could run.

'When she met my father, she defied von Kassel for the first and last time in her life. When my mother threatened suicide, von Kassel had to relent.'

'What was the objection to your father?'

'He was an outsider,' Marit said. 'He was not *Alte Kamerad*. He was a charming, flamboyant, happy man, who had fought a war because he felt Germany was right and he liked fighting and flying. You would have liked him, Dwight. Honestly.'

She told Dwight how after her parents' marriage, von Kassel had kept in constant touch with them. His unsmiling, rigid figure had been present on every important family occasion, and it was von Kassel who had ensured that she went to a German school, who had advised her parents on her education, sent her lavish presents on her birthday, and watched her progress with avuncular care.

'After my father died,' Marit said, 'von Kassel was able to re-exert his influence on my mother. It was easy for him to do that. My father had invested most of his savings on a process for extracting fuel from alcohol. It was in the development stage when he died, and all his savings were lost. When he died, we were in debt.'

Marit described how von Kassel took control over their affairs. He paid off Paul von Rausenberg's debts, insisted that her mother move to La Plata. He took Marit away from the Spanish paper in Buenos Aires and sent her to Bariloche, where she'd been installed in the all-encompassing cloister of the German community, and where he gave her a job on a German newspaper.

Marit turned away from him, took a cigarette from the pack on the bedside table and lit it. 'It was terrible, Dwight,' she said, sitting upright and folding her hands around her knees. 'You wouldn't believe it. I was treated exactly the way my mother had been. I was watched, spied on, made to tell where I'd been and what I'd done. The only thing that kept me sane was the work on the paper. It was interesting and I was learning a lot. But for the rest of it – I could have killed myself!'

She smoked silently for a while. Dwight reached up and kissed her lightly on the thigh. 'You've got nothing to be afraid of now,' he said. 'I'm here. I'll always be here,' and wondered why he said it.

She reached down and ran her fingers through his hair. 'I was seventeen,' she said, 'and I fell in love. His name was Domingo and he was a ski instructor at Carro Cathedral, a resort about twenty kilometres from Bariloche. Domingo was a lovely boy, lively, very cute and he had large, sad Argentinian eyes and dark curly hair. But it was impossible that I should love an Argentinian.'

She pulled fiercely at her cigarette. 'There was no help for it. We ran away. We went to Buenos Aires, thinking that in the big city they would not find us. We were wrong. They found us and brought us back to the *estancia*.' Marit's hand holding the cigarette began to tremble. Dwight could see the tears welling in her eyes. 'Then they beat him,' she said, hoarsely. 'They beat him in front of me. Three men held me and forced me to watch while they smashed his teeth, scarred his face with a knife and finally broke his knee. And all the time, Domingo kept looking at me with those sad eyes of his, refusing to cry out, until his knee shattered.'

'And you?' Dwight asked. 'What did they do to you?'

'I was punished too, but not like Domingo. I was too valuable to be crippled. They worked on my brain, Dwight. They used a simple technique. The kind Pavlov used on his animals. If I was good, I would be rewarded. If I was bad, punished.

'I was locked up in a room on the *estancia*. Every day, precisely at noon I was taken from it, to von Kassel's study. There, they stretched me over a table and beat me with a cane on my bare back. No one ever said anything to me. No one ever did anything else. But the message was clear. If I would behave like a child, I would be treated like a child. And the daily, certain punishment would continue until I broke.

'I don't know when I broke. It must have been three or four days later. Von Kassel came to take me for my beating. He said he hoped that I had learned enough and that I would forget the foolishness instilled into me by my father. I couldn't help it, Dwight. I attacked him. I beat him with my fists, clawed at his face with my nails. His guards pulled me away, and that day, instead of being beaten on my back, I was given the *bastinado*. Afterwards, I could hardly walk.

'But that wasn't the end of it. They carried me to an outhouse, tied me by the wrists and ankles to a bed and left me. The windows and doors were kept permanently shut and it was always dark. During the day it was hot. At night I froze. The air inside was stale and fetid, and once or twice a day, two women would come and force food down my throat. Once again, no one spoke to me. Once again, the message was clear. When I promised to be a good girl, I would be released. I don't know how long they kept me there, but in the end I would have promised anything just to be able to move, to get away from the smell of my own body.'

She lit a second cigarette from the stub of the first. Dwight reached up to console her, but she pushed his arms away. 'The worst was afterwards,' she said. 'After I promised not to escape again, promised to be obedient and be a good German, I was brought back to the house, given food, a whole wardrobe of new clothes. My bruises were attended to and everyone was very kind. Once again the message was clear. As long as I behaved, I would be looked after. If I misbehaved, I would be punished and sent back to the outhouse.

'And then, for a whole year, I had to spend every day reading and listening to lectures on Nazi history, Nazi philosophy. Twice a week I had to meet with von Kassel and tell him what I had learned. I had to pretend, Dwight, and sometimes pretending was not so difficult.

'In the end, when von Kassel was satisfied that I had been rehabilitated, I was sent back to Bariloche.'

Dwight asked, 'How did you get out of Argentina?'

'Joachim Myrdhal. He was in Argentina at the time I got the training scholarship. He fell in love with me, and Joachim persuaded von Kassel to let me go. Soon after I came to Germany, he made me his mistress, but that didn't last.'

'And you still see him? Work for him?'

'I was a passion Joachim von Myrdhal got over, long ago.' She pulled at the cigarette and inhaled deeply. 'Besides, I happen to be a damned good journalist.'

'And you are frightened that if they find you, they will do these things to you again?'

'They will do anything to make me give them the processes.'

Dwight took the cigarette from her fingers and stubbed it out. 'They won't find you, Marit. They'll never get you. Not as long as I'm around, and that's going to be for a long long time.' He took her in his arms and kissed her. 'Sleep, kiddo. No one's going to take you from me.'

She didn't say anything. But she rubbed her lips against his chest and waited, staring into the darkness.

30

Monday morning. Bright sunlight streamed through the tall plate-glass windows of the Stuttgart Air Terminal, relieving the atmosphere of brisk efficiency that prevailed even at that early hour. His ears deaf to the assault of disembodied metallic voices announcing flights to Berlin, Rome, Frankfurt and Paris, Dwight watched Marit's jean-jacketed figure move with long, easy strides to Passport Control, her heavy blonde hair bouncing off her shoulders, fingers twisted round the soft handles of the flight bag they had bought on Saturday, together with fresh clothes. Dwight had not expected their parting to be such a wrench.

Over the weekend they had assembled a plan to cope with Vickery and Brassard. The plan sought to achieve five objectives, which Dwight had set forth in his best OTC manner. Objective one: to find out if the cartel still existed, and if Vickery and Brassard were part of it. Two: if the cartel was conspiring with the Hoffman Bank to acquire the processes. Three: to discover who the other members of the cartel were. Four: to stop them. Five: to accomplish all this by Friday.

Achieving the first two objectives was easy. All that was necessary was to offer Brassard and Vickery the processes. Immediate acceptance would imply foreknowledge, would confirm their involvement and, with some judicious palaver would reveal the other members of the cartel.

Stopping them was going to be harder. Dwight's plan had been to invite Vickery and Brassard to share in the development of the processes, and suggest that they kept their twenty-five million dollars until the processes were found. Marit had been sceptical. Why would Vickery and Brassard believe such an offer and end their conspiracy with Hoffman? Why would they *accept* such an offer?

Because of the twenty-five million dollars, Dwight had said. Vickery and Brassard must realize that if the processes were not found, they acquired nothing. Instead they lost twenty-five million dollars and continued to lose three to five million dollars a year in potential interest. Therefore it made sense to hang on to the twenty-five million dollars until the processes were found. And Odile Brassard and Sir Alex Vickery were essentially sensible business people.

Secondly, Vickery and Brassard would know that even if their scheme succeeded, there was a risk of litigation, which could mean heavy legal costs and tie up the processes and their investment for years. As responsible business people they would see the advantages of avoiding that.

The next part of the plan was a calculated gamble. If they did not find the processes, that was the end of it. But if they did, they would have to share the processes with the cartel. But, and a very important but, if Mollwo was right and hidden with the processes were certain files, and if those files implicated former members of the cartel like Vickery and Brassard, then, Dwight had pointed out, a little bit of blackmail went a long, long way.

No blackmail, Marit had said. If we do that, we are no better than them. If we don't do it, Dwight had explained, they would be better than us and sometimes it is necessary to do a little evil to obtain a great good. They'd argued about that for an hour and Marit had finally accepted that the consequences of the cartel acquiring the processes were horrendous enough to justify using any means to stop them.

The next problem was how they should deal with Vickery and Brassard. Dwight had suggested they fly to Paris and London together. Marit had said, not. With her journalistic experience she knew that getting to see important people like Odile Brassard and Sir Alex Vickery would not be easy and would take time. And they didn't have time. Therefore, one of them should see Brassard, the other Vickery.

'And what about von Kassel?' Dwight had asked.

That wasn't a problem, a relaxed and confident Marit had assured him. Von Kassel's people would never dream of looking for her in France.

Dwight had tried to dissuade her, but the argument for travelling separately was unanswerable. Time was of the essence. Vickery and Brassard *had* to be neutralized before the meeting in Zurich.

The question of who should go where had been more easily agreed upon. Marit was fluent in French, Dwight was not. So Marit got Paris and Dwight, London. Which only left the business of cover stories.

Dwight's was straightforward. He represented the Imtra Bank which represented the Manninger beneficiaries. But to have the Manninger heiress asking questions and attempting to arrange deals would only arouse suspicion, so, Marit said, she should use the obvious cover – that of a journalist. She could have the paper arrange the interview, perhaps even write it. She would talk to Odile Brassard about the history of Brassards and subtly lead her to talk about the cartel. If Marit was convinced Odile Brassard was part of the cartel, then Dwight could fly over to Paris and do exactly as he'd done with Vickery.

But still, Dwight had worried. The cartel was powerful. The cartel was ruthless. If threatened, they could turn nasty.

'Nonsense,' Marit had said. Even Odile Brassard would not risk harming a journalist. Journalists asked embarrassing questions every day, and the truth was that more of them died from an excess of alcohol than an excess of zeal.

I hope to God you're right, Dwight thought and waited till Marit disappeared beyond the barrier and walked into the snack bar. He had some time before his own flight was called and he felt like coffee and, God dammit, a cognac. He hadn't expected the sudden gut-wrenching emptiness he'd experienced watching her blonde head receding down the escalator. Hell, what was he feeling so upset about? They'd be together in a couple of days, and it wasn't as if he was in love with her.

Yet, as he sipped his café-cognac he kept recalling fragments of their weekend, kept thinking of her; the shape of her bare legs as they ran through the forest, the grim look on her face as she'd forced herself to complete that last mile, uphill and through mud, her expression the first time she'd drunk Lambrusco. He'd remembered she'd laughed that weekend, a rich, pealing sound full of happiness. He remembered when, too, he'd been telling her he'd managed to match her underwear because he'd once spent three weeks on a Quartermaster's detail, issuing new uniforms to recruits. Dwight remembered he'd told her about Jackie and still remembered the enormous concern she had shown. Strange, he'd never told anyone about Jackie before.

He heard his flight called and hurried to the boarding gate, the movement and the urgency putting any more thought of Marit out of his mind.

On the plane, he told himself that such thoughts were only to be expected if two people had been continuously in each other's company for four days. He told himself it didn't mean anything, and tried to work out his strategy for the meeting with Vickery. But Marit still intruded on his thoughts, her face with its helmet of pale gold hair and nervous, grey-green eyes staying with him like a still photograph projected on a screen, all the way to London.

It wasn't summer in London. London was wet. Outside the terminal building, neon signs glowed in grey mid-morning light and a translucent drizzle dampened the tall buildings. Dwight took a taxi to the West End, hissing along a crowded motorway, soothed by the rhythmic clatter of a thrashing diesel. He checked into the Ritz and then took a taxi to one of those side streets off Park Lane, where the Imtra Bank had its London office.

David Goldborne, its manager, was a tall, toothy man with a high freckled forehead, receding sandy hair and a look of challenging cynicism in not quite level brown eyes. An Eighth

Army badge glinted in his lapel and on the wall were two photographs of grinning Tommies gathered around a tank in the desert. Dwight recognized a slighter, toothier Goldborne in both photographs and thought they'd get on fine as long as he didn't mention Patton.

'You must step on dogshit and find gold,' Goldborne said as he waved Dwight to a chair and sat down himself. 'A few days ago, Vickerys approached us for a loan. You'll find all the information you need, here.' He pushed a blue folder across the desk.

Dwight took the folder and asked, 'How much did Vickerys want to borrow?'

'Two million pounds for six months, with a roll over facility, everything secured by company and personal guarantees.'

'And what did you do?'

'I said thanks, but no thanks. Vickerys have been borrowing everywhere. Their factories, their offices, everything has been pledged. When you look at their figures you'll see that all they have is heavy loans and large cash balances.'

'What are they doing with all this money?'

Goldborne said, 'I think they're planning a share raid, a takeover of some kind, a massive deal that needs lots of cash. The whole thing smells wrong to me. What they're doing may not be illegal, but I'm certain it's going to raise a hell of a stink.'

'So they didn't tell you why they needed the money?'

Goldborne shook his head. 'All Sir Alex could tell me was that our money would always be represented by cash or equivalent assets, that there was absolutely no risk of our money being lost, and that we had an opportunity to make a lot of money for very little risk.'

'How intriguing.' In Goldborne's words, Dwight felt that he'd stepped on dogshit and found gold. 'Could you call Sir Alex for me?'

'You're not going to – ' Dwight saw the whites around

Goldborne's lopsided eyes as they froze in an angry stare, his face flush, so that his freckles looked transparent.

'No,' Dwight said. 'I'm not going to authorize the loan. I want to talk to Vickery about something else.'

Vickery came on the phone pretty damn quick. He must have needed that two million bad. 'It's jolly nice of you to call,' he said to Dwight. 'I was wondering if we could get together. As your Mr Goldborne would have told you, we are looking for more friends in the banking community.'

'I'll be free in half an hour,' Dwight said.

There was a slight pause. Then Vickery came back again, still all honey and hyacinths. 'I've asked my girl to rearrange my schedule,' he said. 'I'll see you in half an hour. Your place or mine?'

Dwight was prepared to bet that it was a long time since Vickery had said that to anybody. 'Your place.' Dwight wanted to see what Vickery's offices looked like.

'You know where we are?'

'It's on the file,' Dwight said and didn't wait for Vickery to hang up.

Vickerys was on the south side of the Thames, along the Embankment near Waterloo, an area from whose bombsites enormous concrete and glass structures had sprouted and whose upper storeys were now sheathed in a fine mist. Dwight was met by a large commissionaire, who sported more medals than Montgomery, escorted across the marble floored reception area by a petite receptionist, met at the elevator by a pleasant, middle-aged woman who said she was Sir Alex's personal assistant, and greeted on the twenty-sixth floor by the man himself.

Small, clipped moustache bristling, was Dwight's first impression. An evil-minded son of a bitch. That also was a first impression.

'Your Mr Goldborne is most efficient, most efficient,' Vickery said leading Dwight down the corridor. His voice had a kind of rotund bellow, like that of a sergeant-major making conversation at a dowagers' tea party.

Vickery's office was large, enough to land a two-man helicopter. The floor was ankle deep in carpet, the furniture was Heppelwhite or close to it. There was a reproduction Turner on one narrow wall and through the murk fogging one set of picture windows, Dwight could see the dome of St Paul's, and through the other, the spires of Westminster. Half-way between God and parliament, Vickery seemed to be doing all right.

'You found us without any difficulty. Obviously you've been in London before?'

'Yes.'

'You must be very good at your job,' Vickery said. 'What did Goldborne say you were – Vice-President – that's it. All the Vice-Presidents I've ever met have been my age.'

'My father owns the bank,' Dwight said.

Vickery was smaller than he'd appeared sitting down in the photograph at the back of Manninger's album. The clipped moustache was now silver, but still did little to hide the narrow, curving mouth. Vickery's head seemed to taper, and was dominated by a large forehead, its sparse hair swept back and brilliantined into place. His skin had the floridity and blotchiness that comes from over exposure to the sun, and there was a reddish film to his eyes, as if he'd spent the last hour keeping them open under water. His briskly aggressive military bearing was a sham, Dwight decided. Vickery was too small to have been in any man's army.

Vickery ordered coffee, and after it had been poured, said, 'I suppose you've come to talk about the loan. If you don't mind my saying so, your Mr Goldborne, efficient though he is, misunderstood us slightly. I don't think he quite got the spirit of what we were trying to do, if you know what I mean.'

'I haven't come to talk about the loan,' Dwight said evenly and enjoyed watching the cordiality drain from Vickery's face.

Vickery leaned forward quietly and placed his coffee on the desk, the skin around his mouth and nose pinched, a hard, flat glare in his eyes, like sunlight on stone. 'What have you come to talk about, Mr Khouri?'

'My bank represents the beneficiaries of the Manninger estate. Part of that estate consists of certain valuable industrial processes.'

'What has this got to do with Vickerys?' Sir Alex demanded.

'I was in Europe yesterday,' Dwight said. 'I'm sure you appreciate, Sir Alex, that between bankers the laws of bank secrecy are applied a great deal more flexibly than they are with outsiders.' And if that put Hoffman in the shit, Dwight thought, so much the better. 'We understand that your company has dealt with Manninger Industrie. It is our belief that the processes which will shortly become available to our customers will prove to be of exceptional value once they have been developed. We have been instructed to form a syndicate to develop, market and exploit those processes. I believe you knew Berndt Manninger.'

'Yes,' Vickery said, softly. 'I knew Berndt Manninger.' He was leaning back in his chair, looking at Dwight from under half-lidded eyes, stroking his chin thoughtfully. 'How is this syndicate to be formed, Mr Khouri?'

'We believe that the best way is for the processes to be invested in a holding company in Switzerland. The holding company will then grant exclusive licences to various territories, England, Germany, France, the United States.'

'The world has become a much smaller place, since the days of Berndt Manninger,' Vickery said, carefully.

Dwight shrugged. 'The final form of the syndicate is of little importance to our customers. All they're concerned with is that they should receive an appropriate share of the profits arising from the exploitation of the processes. If, for example, the members of the syndicate wished to create their own holding company and distribute the territories in another way, there would be no objection.'

'I see,' Vickery said. 'Where are these processes, Mr Khouri? Before committing ourselves to what appears to be both a risky and expensive investment, we would like to be satisfied that the processes exist, that they work.'

'Of course,' Dwight said, thinking Vickery was coming along nicely. 'There has been some difficulty in finding those processes. But I have reason to believe that they will be found within the next few days.' Dwight paused meaningfully. 'It is not my customers' intention to expose anyone to unnecessary risk. They seek thirty-five million dollars for the rights to the processes, together with a twenty per cent share in all profits arising from their exploitation. The thirty-five million dollars is to be deposited in a major bank, in a country to be agreed upon. If, at the end of six months, the processes have been found and are accepted by the syndicate, then the capital and the interest is paid over to my customers. If it is not, the syndicate will have the option to renew the agreement for a further six months. The agreement will be renewable at the syndicate's discretion on a six-monthly basis, for a period of three years, unless, of course, the syndicate indicates that it does not wish to avail itself of the processes.'

Vickery steepled his hands in front of him and looked closely at them. 'And you say that your customers are prepared to enter into a valid and binding agreement?'

'Yes,' Dwight said. 'In fact, draft agreements have already been prepared, and are with our branch in Zurich.'

Abruptly Vickery tilted his chair forward and bared his teeth in a jagged smile. 'Let me give you some advice, young man. You're bright, you're sharp, and you're obviously going far.'

Shit, Dwight thought, Vickery's spotted something. But what? Dwight had behaved and talked exactly the way a proper, conservative banker should.

'You've got to look at things from the other man's point of view,' Vickery said. 'Now, I don't know who else you're seeing. But how are you going to convince them that these processes exist? I know you're a banker and your bank has a good reputation, but in this league the word of your bank isn't good enough. If you talk about this to anyone else you're going to get your nose out of joint. And, get a reputation as a confidence man.'

Dwight thought that if Vickery was already fending off mythical competitors, he was hooked. 'But it's true,' he said, rounding out his eyes and looking as innocently outraged as possible. 'The processes exist. You know they exist.'

'I know they exist,' Vickery said, quietly. 'But then, I knew Berndt Manninger. For many years, Vickery Industries had a close relationship with Manninger's company. But would anyone who didn't know Manninger believe you? Would your Mr Goldborne lend me two million pounds if I came to him with such a story?'

Dwight looked down at his feet, shame-faced. 'I see what you mean,' he muttered.

'But I'll help you,' Vickery said. 'I knew Berndt Manninger, and I know he wasn't a fool. Your little scheme exposes the members of the syndicate to hardly any risk. To those who knew Berndt Manninger, it is a gamble worth taking. Will you give me twenty-four hours to see if I can get a syndicate together?'

'I don't know if I can do that,' Dwight muttered. 'I mean, appointments have been made – '

'So cancel them!' Vickery was the sergeant-major again. He relaxed and tried on a persuasive smile. 'There's nothing sacred about appointments. Besides, what have you got to lose? If, in twenty-four hours, I haven't got a syndicate together, you go ahead on your own.'

Dwight nodded, as if he realized that if Vickery got his syndicate together, he'd be saved a lot of work. 'You're right, Sir Alex,' he said. 'I feel as if I've stepped on dogshit and found gold.'

Sir Alex frowned at that. Then almost as an afterthought he said, 'There is something I'd like you to do for me.'

'I've already asked Goldborne to refer the question of your loan to our head office in New York,' Dwight said. 'He should have done that in the first place.'

'I'd very much like that loan, Mr Khouri. I'd very much

like to do business with the Imtra Bank. As you know, Vickery Industries is – '

'It's not a question of your company's credit worthiness,' Dwight said, quickly. 'The problem Goldborne had, the problem our board will have, is that no one seems to have any clear idea as to the purpose of the loan.'

'Mr Khouri, if I may say so, you're acting as if two million pounds is a large sum of money. You're worrying yourself unnecessarily with details. What you should be considering is the financial reputation of Vickery Industries, its history, the acuity of its management.'

'We do not question those things,' Dwight said. 'But we are a small bank. And to us, two million pounds is a lot of money. The Imtra board of directors will want to know where it's going.'

'All right,' Sir Alex said and lowered his voice even though there were only the two of them in the vast room. 'I'm taking a bit of a gamble. I believe the present economic recession is going to get worse. And in recessions, there is no point in holding on to paper. Cash is the only thing that matters. And cash is what I want.'

'And what do you propose to do with all this cash?'

'Make acquisitions. At prices that will never again be repeated. That's what I'm going to do, and now you know, you can appreciate why I was reluctant to talk about this to Goldborne.'

Dwight nodded. Vickery was lying. No sane businessman, least of all someone as experienced as Vickery, would convert to cash on such a scale, for whatever reason. And for Vickery's theory to work on such a scale, it would require the collapse of capitalism, not a depression. The truth, Dwight suspected, was that Vickery was selling his investments in order to buy something else. 'I'll quote you in my report,' Dwight said.

'How long will all this take?'

Dwight shrugged. 'There are a few people still on holiday . . .'

'I need the money in a week. Otherwise, forget it.'

'I'll put that in my report, too,' Dwight said. 'I'll call New York and tell them. I'd like to help you, Sir Alex, and believe me your application will have my personal recommendation.'

Dogshit and gold, Dwight thought elatedly afterwards riding down in the lift with the middle-aged personal assistant, walking across the marble floor with the petite receptionist, striding past the medalled commissionaire. The cartel existed and Vickery was part of it. That was why he had wanted to, that was the only way he could, form a syndicate to acquire the Manninger processes within twenty-four hours. Tomorrow, Dwight thought, he would know who the other members of the cartel were. Meanwhile, he knew that whatever other grandiose scheme Vickery was planning, it would be consummated next Monday.

31

Marit was just finishing her second cup of coffee when Pierre Ducret, the Chief of *Event*'s Paris bureau, entered the café. Pierre was a marvellously handsome man in his early forties, with thick, curly hair just greying at the temples, a lean, square face, and dark, dreamy eyes. The café was in the Rue Balzac and Pierre was intrigued by her insistence that she meet him there, instead of round the corner in the *Event* offices along the Champs-Élysées. Now he took her hand and brushed it lightly with his lips and murmured, 'Marit, it is so very nice to see you,' his voice low and gentle, hinting of murmured remembrances in a moonlit park. 'But why all the secrecy?'

'It's a secret story,' Marit said.

'I was talking to Konrad in Munich this morning,' he said. 'He told me you were on holiday?'

'I was,' Marit said, feeling her smile grow rigid. She'd told Pierre she'd been engaged on a story concerning the history and growth of companies like Brassards. Then she'd heard of Topf's suicide, and knowing of Topf's connection with Brassard had abandoned her holiday to pursue the story.

'But why the secrecy?' Pierre asked.

'Joachim,' Marit said. She knew no one would dare question what she said Joachim had told her. 'He is worried about Topf's death. They were friends, you know. And he thinks Topf may have been murdered. He has someone looking into that in Frankfurt and he wants me to talk to Odile Brassard and find out if there was anything in Topf's past that would indicate why he died.'

Pierre sipped at his coffee, selected a cigarette from a thin, gunmetal case. 'Odile Brassard is one hell of a tough lady,' he said. 'She doesn't usually give interviews. And even if she agreed to see you, and you asked her a question she didn't like, she would throw you out on your pretty little *popotin*.'

'I've got a tough little *popotin*,' Marit said. 'How quickly can you arrange for me to meet her?'

Pierre stared thoughtfully at her. His eyes were large and liquid, dreamy and teasingly suggestive. 'That could take a few weeks.'

'Oh Pierre!' Impulsively she reached out and grabbed his arm. 'You can do better than that.'

Pierre shifted uncomfortably. 'There is another way,' he said. 'Tomorrow night, Madame Odile is giving a little party at her château in Argentuil. I can take you. And perhaps she'll agree to talk to you.'

'Fine,' Marit said. 'I've always said how clever you are.'

'The party,' Pierre said, 'may be a little bit unusual. You might have to put up with a few things you don't like, even maybe do things you don't usually do.'

'I'll do anything,' Marit said excitedly, 'so long as I can talk to her '

*

Raison Tearkes had reversed his normal custom and spent the weekend in New York, in the small, Third Avenue apartment he provided for Samantha Wallace. Sammy, as she liked being called by her friends, came from Hoxie, Indiana, where some twenty-six years ago she had been born as plain Margaret Wells.

Tearkes had first met Sammy three years ago, at a party in Hollywood to launch a horror movie, in which Sammy had played the part of a Transylvanian virgin, and for which SummiTco had put up half the budget. Then Tearkes had been taken by her large, pouting lower lip, and wide, innocent brown eyes; he'd been totally fascinated by her small, delicately formed body with its apple-like breasts, skinny legs and tight ass.

Tearkes had taken her to Hawaii. He had invited her to New York. He had financed her next film. And to his surprise, discovered that Sammy was just as innocent as she looked. For Sammy, the world was divided into nice people and funny people. The nice people were practically everyone you cared to mention. The funny people, those fat two-bit producers and apoplectic agents who got so much enjoyment out of touching her up, calling her a sweet little girl and kissing her everywhere – yes, especially there, when they got her into bed.

Tearkes wasn't like that. He never drooled over her, and sometimes he even frightened her. But she liked him. He was a gruff old bear, but he was kind to her and generous. Some time after she'd starred in 'The Last Enchantress' Sammy discovered that it was much more fun to be *known* as an actress and live as Raison Tearkes's concubine.

Now, she was a familiar figure on Pan Am's five-thirty Friday evening flight to Miami, and their nine o'clock Monday morning flight to New York.

Tearkes had stayed the weekend in New York because he'd invited George Grundsecker to lunch at Sammy's apartment, on Monday. A firm of outside caterers had fixed the lunch and now, as Tearkes speared his prawn cocktail, he smiled across at Grundsecker and said, 'I really appreciate your making the time to see me here, George.'

George Grundsecker was a burly man in his early fifties. His face was large, with a prognathous jaw, topped with tufts of thinning brown hair. He had a nervous smile, and a hesitancy of movement, as if he realized he was awkward and large, and keenly aware that it was a combination of qualities that embarrassed others. Grundsecker was the kind of man who always said excuse me before he interrupted. Which was why, at fifty-two, George Grundsecker was only a Junior Associate at Fort, Levin and Myers.

Fort, Levin and Myers were one of the largest firms of stockbrokers in the world. Twenty years ago when George had moved to them from Merill, Lynch, it had been expected that within ten years he'd become a partner. But twenty years later, George still remained a nice guy and a Junior Associate.

But Tearkes knew that if Grundsecker had begun his career with a smaller firm, his life might well have been different; that Grundsecker had found the internal struggle that exists in every large organization too much; and that like most men who had failed their youthful genius, nursed a secret ambition to go out in the world and beat an enormous drum. Which was why he'd invited Grundsecker to lunch.

'I've got something to tell you,' Tearkes said, launching as usual directly into business.

Grundsecker tore his eyes away from Sammy, which though he didn't know it, was yet another reason why Tearkes had invited him to the apartment.

'What I have to tell you is highly confidential,' Tearkes went on when he was satisfied that he had all the attention Grundsecker was capable of giving. 'I am changing SummiTco into a straight investment company. And I want you to handle the SummiTco account. I don't give a shit about Fort, Levin and Myers.'

That got Grundsecker's undivided attention. Tearkes could see him figuring that the SummiTco account on a straight investment basis was worth some two, three hundred million dollars, could see him reckoning the broking commissions on that.

'Can you handle it?'

Grundsecker swallowed nervously, his large Adam's apple bobbing above his shirt collar. 'For the present, I'll have to do it through Fort, Levin and Myers.'

'That's fine,' Tearkes said. He didn't give a damn how Grundsecker did it, as long as he did it.

'I want to start small,' Tearkes said. 'Safe. I want to get myself a piece of some banks.'

Grundsecker took a large gulp of iced water, then arranged his face into a proper, dignified, professional expression. 'I wouldn't recommend that,' he paused before he added, 'Raison. Many of our large banks – '

'I was talking to David Rockefeller the other day. I think you people are too conservative. I think banks are undervalued. You people have exaggerated the risk on the Third World loans. You're all getting desperate about Poland, because you guys make a habit of looking on the dark side of things. Poland's not going to go belly up. We won't let it. The Russians won't let it. I think banks are a good investment. In these times of recession and high interest rates, their profits must zoom.'

'Perhaps you're right, Raison,' Grundsecker said, dubiously.

'I'm glad you agree,' Tearkes said quickly. 'Now look, I want to go into banks in a big way, but not too big, if you know what I mean. I'm not looking for control. I'm not looking for participation. All I want is to know that my money is safely tied up, that I will get a regular flow of dividends and reasonable capital appreciation.'

'I'm glad you told me that,' Grundsecker said. 'As soon as I get back to the office I'll work out a list of potential investments.'

'I've already done that,' Tearkes said drily, and handed him a sheet of paper. 'Those are the banks and those are the amounts.'

Grundsecker's eyes popped.

'I know the market in bank shares is a restricted one,' Tearkes continued. 'That kind of money going into them, could well jump up prices. I want you to handle it so that I don't end up bidding against myself. Also, I am counting on you to see that this is handled discreetly. And that means, no private calls to other clients, no word of it in your advisory letter to investors. Is that clearly understood?'

'Of course,' Grundsecker said. 'I'd never dream of – '

'I'll want you to arrange these purchases through your people in Boston, Houston and Los Angeles. I'm keeping a low profile in all this.'

'You could work through our nominee company,' Grundsecker said.

'I have my own,' Tearkes said and gave him another list.

For the next two hours they worked out exactly how the shares would be acquired, and when Grundsecker finally left he was elated but exhausted.

Tearkes was elated but not exhausted. In the hour he had left before he took the five-thirty Pan Am to Miami, he made sure that Sammy knew it.

32

The next morning, Dwight discovered he was being followed. He'd first seen the man at breakfast, seated alone at a table overlooking the park; a stocky, bull-necked, beetle-browed character packing a lot of muscle underneath his charcoal business suit. The man was not one of Vickery's people. A copy of *Frankfurter Allgemeine* had been propped against a coffee pot, and the man had divided his attention equally between that and his food.

After breakfast, when Dwight had walked over to Jermyn

Street to buy some shirts, he'd spotted the man lingering twenty yards behind. When he'd gone to Piccadilly Arcade and bought a gold bracelet for Marit, the man had been there examining a stack of second-hand books. Later, when he'd come out of the Imtra Bank, he'd seen the man looking ostentatiously into the window of a restaurant. And afterwards, when he'd returned to the hotel, the man had been seated at the front of the lobby, facing the large revolving doors into Piccadilly.

Waiting for the lift, Dwight wondered whether to confront the man or not. Whoever had hired the man, had done so cheaply. The man wasn't any good. He'd been too close and too obvious. To carry a copy of a German newspaper so ostentatiously was –

Dwight stepped into the lift. The man *meant* to be obvious. He'd wanted Dwight to know he was being followed. Perhaps he wanted a confrontation.

Not yet, Dwight thought, walking along the corridor to his room. The important thing was his meeting with Vickery. If the man was still around after that, then he could have his confrontation.

Dwight stayed in his room and went through the papers Goldborne had given him. They only confirmed what he already knew about Vickerys. Vickerys was liquid. Vickerys had sold most of their investments. Vickerys had borrowed heavily. Vickerys had also got out of dollars. Now why would they do that? True, the dollar was weakening, but not at such a rate as to cause Vickerys, Brassards and Topf to sell them in such a hurry. He tried to think what Brassards, Vickerys and Topf were planning. A large acquisition obviously, but what? And whatever it was, it certainly wasn't American.

Dwight looked at his watch. The previous day he had avoided telling Vickery where he was staying, and had promised to telephone Vickery at noon. He reached for the phone, and then thought better of it. If, for any reason, Vickery had got suspicious, he could have made arrangements to have the call traced. And in a hotel like the Ritz, with three separate entrances, Dwight knew he was vulnerable.

Dwight decided to call Vickery from a public call box in the underground station, about a block away from the hotel. He took the stairs down to the lobby, hoping to surprise the German.

The German wasn't there.

Dwight went out of the hotel, ran quickly down the steps of the subway, crossed underneath the road and emerged into the cavern of the underground station's semi-circular ticket lobby. Ahead of him were wooden barriers, waist-high automatic gates beyond which escalators trundled into the depths. On one side of the barriers was a pill box from which a uniformed attendant collected tickets. The phone booths were to the right. Dwight looked carefully round before stepping into one of them. There was no sign of the German.

Vickery's bellow was confident. 'I have good news, Mr Khouri. The syndicate has been formed. Why don't we meet for lunch and finalize the arrangements? There are a few other members of the syndicate who would like to meet with you . . .'

Dwight did not hear the rest of it. Alarms were ringing in his head. Lunch! A few other members of the syndicate! But the syndicate was international, its members scattered throughout the world. They would not have rushed to London to meet him. No, the normal procedure would have been to authorize Vickery to complete the negotiations, to forward the final documentation for their approval. And anything that was abnormal, like the awkwardly broken twig or uneven patch of earth over a mine, was to be avoided.

No, Dwight decided, not lunch. There were too many opportunities at a meal for drugging food or drink and no excuses were necessary when an inebriated guest was helped away by sympathetic friends. 'I already have a lunch engagement,' Dwight said.

'Let's say my office then . . .'

Out of a corner of his eye, Dwight saw the German

standing directly behind the booth, his body turned sideways to it, his coat held open, looking as if he were pointing something at Dwight. Not a gun, Dwight thought. If it was a gun, he would have been dead by now. The German was holding a directional microphone.

'I'll call you after lunch,' and cut off Vickery's startled protest by tapping his finger on the cradle. Still holding the receiver to his ear, he turned his head to get a better look at the German. The German was fastening his coat. Dwight replaced the receiver and turned to leave the booth.

Vickery heard the phone whir in his ear and slammed down the receiver. The previous night when he'd called Raison Tearkes about forming the syndicate, he'd been told that Khouri did not represent the Manninger estate, that he was a CIA agent who'd gone over to the Gemeinschaft and that he'd disappeared from Switzerland with the Manninger heiress. Last night, Tearkes had ordered Vickery to locate Khouri and hold him.

Khouri obviously suspected something. Why else had he been so hesitant about meeting over lunch? Why else had he run off so abruptly? But suspicious or not, Vickery knew Khouri would have to meet with him. There was no other way he could discover if the syndicate had been formed and who its members were. Vickery knew that if he were Khouri, he'd arrange a meeting, on his terms.

He looked across his desk at the expectant face of his eldest son, Reginald. 'Khouri's going to call back with a time and place for a meeting,' Vickery said. 'Have the boys stand to. We'll collect him then.'

As he opened the door, Dwight caught the German's eye. Quickly Dwight looked both ways. The booths on either side of him were empty. He raised his finger and beckoned to the German.

Hesitantly, the German approached.

Dwight stepped out of the booth and held the door open.

'This one's working,' Dwight said, and moved as if to allow the German to enter.

The German nodded and smiled, turned sideways to edge past Dwight into the booth.

Dwight grabbed him by the lapels and pulled him inside. Before the German could recover from his surprise, Dwight jabbed him in the stomach, his fingers bent over, a blow that travelled hardly any distance but had all the force of a trip-hammer. The man gasped, twisted forward, the smell of a rather esoteric aftershave filling Dwight's nostrils. Dwight hit him again. The man flopped against the side of the booth. Dwight held him at arm's length, took his wallet and shook the contents out on to the battered metal shelf holding four grubby telephone directories. The man's name was Fritz Schulze and he worked for the Four Star Detective Agency which had offices in Frankfurt, Berlin, Hamburg and Munich.

Dwight dropped the empty wallet on the floor, caught the man and hit him again, crossed his wrists in front of the man's throat, grabbed his coat lapels and pressed the edges of his wrists into the sides of the man's neck. Schulze's face turned puce.

'Who the hell's your customer?' Dwight asked. Schulze's eyes bulged, his mouth opened. He gasped for air.

'What the hell is –' Dwight looked down at the contents of the man's wallet scattered on the metal shelf, 'Four Star –' Dwight froze. A photograph of the man had dropped upside down, and now peeped up at him from behind an American Express card. Dwight stared at the photograph, at the spread lapels of the man's coat. On the lower right-hand corner, just over the coat pocket was a small red streak, the kind that could have been made accidentally with a felt-tip pen. Except Dwight knew that the mark was no accident. It was an undercover recognition signal of a KGB officer on covert duty.

Dwight loosened his grip, then slammed the insides of his wrists against the man's neck. Despite the thick muscle, the neck arched back. 'What's the fucking KGB got to do with this?' he demanded, then hit the man again with his wrists.

Breath exploded from Schulze. Shiny spittle sprayed Dwight's face.

'Talk, or I'll kill you.'

The man shook his head, red faced.

Dwight tightened his grip. The man's flesh folded over the edge of his wrists. He could feel the bones he would have to break. 'You know the rules, comrade. Make it easy on yourself. Who are you?'

The man said nothing. His sweaty face was purple. His eyes looked as if they would squirt out of his head like orange pips. Shit, Dwight thought, he didn't want to kill the man. He wanted to find out what the man was doing. He told the man called Schulze that.

The man remained silent. His body started to sag. His legs trembled against Dwight.

Dwight placed his lips to the man's ear and whispered, 'If I kill you, comrade, there is no come back. No one's going to bother about a spy who got caught on the job.'

The man yanked helplessly at Dwight's wrists. Dwight tightened his grip. 'You're going to die, comrade. Now.'

The man tried to shake his head. Then he raised a hand and tapped Dwight's shoulder lightly.

Dwight eased his grip.

The man sucked air, choked and coughed. The pressure was still there and he took great wheezing breaths.

'Who the fuck are you?' Dwight asked.

'Viktor Tretiak,' the man coughed. 'Deputy Resident Director, Zurich Station.'

Deputy Director Zurich! The guy was a fucking high-up! 'You're a long way from home, buddy boy,' Dwight said.

Tretiak asked if Dwight would remove his hands from around his throat.

'No bloody way, Charlie. You talk like this.'

Tretiak went silent, translating his thoughts from Russian.

'I know you,' he said at last. 'You were a soldier. You worked for the CIA.'

'Come on, Charlie. Tell me something I don't know.'

'But you were never political. You were always administration. You pushed money around.'

'Okay. So you know about me. What's with the tail?'

Tretiak sighed and said, 'We have orders to kill you when you return to Zurich.'

It was insane! Crazy! *He'd* invented the KGB to scare Marit. Dwight had the eerie sensation of being in a trance, of meeting his *doppelgänger* face to face. Then he thought, if Tretiak had orders to kill him in Zurich, what was he doing in London? If Tretiak had orders to kill him, why hadn't he done so already? 'Your origination is unclear,' he said.

Tretiak's chin touched Dwight's hands as he nodded.

'What's your origination? What's your source?'

'I can't tell you that.'

'But it is irregular?'

'It is irregular,' Tretiak said. He tapped Dwight's wrists placatingly.

Dwight eased his grip.

'Look, Mr Khouri. You are CIA agent. I am KGB. No matter we work on different sides. We both work for the same system, you get what I mean? We have superiors to answer to, promotions to obtain, families to look after. You have the same problems, no?'

'More or less.'

'So last week, we get an all-stations alert to look for you and a woman. We get no background, no reasons. So I think, what the bloody hell, someone is doing someone a favour. Then I get instructions, not through regular channels, not traceable, you know what I mean? Please arrange a *mokrie dela* – a wet job – arrange it quietly, I am told, discreetly. They say I have unlimited funds. And I must use outsiders.' He looked mournfully at Dwight. 'I am eighteen years in service. I don't trust it.'

'Quite right, Viktor,' Dwight murmured.

'Look, Mr Khouri, we have many operations in Zurich, important operations, like your CIA does.. And Zurich's a quiet station. The Swiss don't like funny business. They don't like *mokrie dela*. So if we're going to play silly games in Zurich, we could screw up many important things.'

'And you could end up shovelling snow in Siberia.'

'More likely Afghanistan,' Tretiak said, mournfully.

'What are you doing in London?' Dwight took his hands away from Tretiak's throat and waited to see if Tretiak would run.

But Tretiak didn't run. He massaged his throat and said, 'Our people in British Immigration informed London Section that you are here, staying at the Ritz. Deputy Director London calls me. He does same job I do, but London is more important that Zurich. He is Colonel, I am only Major. Tretiak, he says, your man is in London and what the bloody hell do you want me to do? You see, suddenly you are *my* man. The Colonel asks me, the Major, what he should do?'

'So you came to London?' Dwight said.

Tretiak nodded. 'I come to London to find out what you are doing. Why you are so important, no one wants to touch you.'

'Viktor,' Dwight said, softly. 'You're being set up.'

Tretiak frowned. 'Maybe. But now you tell me, Mr Khouri, are you political? Or is this something else? You see, if it is political, if you're working against the interests of Russia, then fine, they say you must be killed, and I will see that you are killed. But if you have been sleeping with someone's wife, if this is revenge – then I must know.'

Dwight said, 'You listened to my telephone call. You know I was talking to Sir Alex Vickery, a good friend to Russia. You heard what I said. No code words, just business. You know who I am. You know all about me. You know I am a director of the Imtra Bank in New York. I am here on bank business.'

Tretiak's beetle brows lowered. 'Who is the woman you were with?'

Dwight shrugged and smiled. 'Women,' he said, 'you know how it is. They come, they go.'

'So why do I get these orders?' Tretiak asked, perplexedly.

'Viktor,' Dwight said, 'have you stopped to think it isn't me they're after. It's you.'

Tretiak stared at him with dazed incomprehension like a man seeing a lamp-post walk.

'You should check back with the Centre,' Dwight said. 'You mustn't act until you have a clear, attributable directive.' He could see Tretiak thinking of Siberia or Afghanistan or both.

Tretiak scooped the contents of his wallet from the shelf. 'I will go to embassy and talk to Moscow,' he said.

'Right, Viktor. You do that.'

Dwight watched Tretiak leave the station before he walked thoughtfully back to the hotel. If the situation was as bungled as Tretiak said it was, it would take him weeks to get a clear directive. Meanwhile, Marit was in no danger from the Russians. This was a personal investigation of Tretiak's. Nothing would happen without his authorization, and in any case, the Russians had only traced him through the immigration form he'd completed. Marit, travelling on a German passport, wouldn't need to complete an immigration form to enter France. Dwight decided to shelve the lunatic episode with Tretiak and concentrate on what was important now. On what he was going to do about Vickery.

He had to meet Vickery, somewhere neutral and safe. So, not the offices of Vickery Industries. The Imtra Bank then? No, that would make Vickery suspicious. Dwight had lost the initiative by seeing Vickery at his offices, and it was normal when many equals were meeting one, for the one to travel to the many. So where? The hotel? No, that would reveal his base. A café? A park? Both too unusual and likely to put Vickery on his guard.

A car! That was it! A car! Vickery's car! Vickery must have at one time or another held meetings in the backs of cars. And in a car he would naturally sit next to Vickery, so if an attempt was made to grab him, he could create a stand-off by taking Vickery hostage.

Dwight dialled Vickery's number and apologized for being cut off previously. 'Could we meet at three?' he enquired.

'Of course, Mr Khouri. Will you come here?'

'No, Sir Alex. There are reasons why, for the present, our relationship should be secret.'

'What reasons?' Vickery barked.

'I'll explain when I see you. Could you pick me up in your car outside the Green Park underground station at precisely three o'clock?'

'I could, Mr Khouri, but there are other people who wish to meet with you. Is all this melodrama really necessary?'

'Yes,' Dwight said.

He heard Vickery snort angrily. 'Very well, then.' He told Dwight his car was a black Daimler limousine and that it would be outside the Piccadilly north exit of the underground station at precisely three o'clock.

Dwight asked the hotel to make a reservation for him on a flight to Paris that evening, had them arrange for his flight bag to be put in a locker at Heathrow Terminal and the key left at the British Airways desk. Then he had lunch in the hotel, paid his bill and went into the lobby.

There was no sign of Tretiak. The Russian was obviously in his embassy firing off telexes demanding more background information on Dwight. Dwight went out of the hotel, through the subway and into the station.

The station was quiet, the lunchtime rush over, the evening rush not yet begun. Three people thrust tickets into the slots beside the automatic gates and hurried towards the escalators. A scruffy-looking young man in jeans and sandals occupied one of the call boxes. A trim, blue-suited, sandy-haired man with square-lensed sunglasses loitered near the pill box, staring beyond the barriers at the escalators, obviously waiting for someone.

The hands of the large clock above the ticket office moved

to three o'clock. Dwight hurried across the lobby, past the man waiting at the barrier, and ran up a short flight of steps.

Behind him, the man with the square-lensed sunglasses turned.

Dwight reached the landing. To his left was the flight of steps leading to the street, divided down the middle by a metal rail. A news vendor sat beside the drawn-back grille of the exit. Across the pavement from him, Dwight could see the gleaming black bonnet and fluted radiator of a Daimler. Six or seven people emerged from the sunlight and pattered down the steps into the station, the sound of their feet drowning the scrape of leather on cement behind him.

'Mr Khouri!'

Dwight whirled. The blue-suited man with the square-lensed glasses was standing on the landing below him. His feet were spread evenly apart, his right arm was raised, wrist supported by his left palm. Clutched in his fist was something that looked like an ancient flintlock pistol with a peculiarly bulbous barrel. The pistol was pointing straight at Dwight.

But it was not the gunman who had shouted. Backlit by the fluorescent lighting of the station was Viktor Tretiak.

Tretiak hurled himself at the gunman. The gunman turned, pulled the trigger. There was a faint, cork-popping plop. A small, silvery dart embedded itself in Tretiak's shoulder. Tretiak twisted in mid-stride, hand reaching for his shoulder, then his legs turned to rubber and he sprawled full length on the floor.

The gunman was reloading. Tretiak's head twitched. His face was covered by a shiny patina of sweat and was the colour of industrial soap. His eyes were fixed on Dwight in a rapidly glazing stare. His mouth sagged open, worked desperately. He fought for breath. 'Behind you,' he gasped.

Dwight turned. Two men in grey suits were running down the station steps, their faces shielded behind sunglasses, hands reaching inside coat pockets.

Dwight charged them, caught them unbalanced, their

hands trapped inside their jackets. He shouldered them out of the way and bolted up the steps, ran past the news vendor on to the pavement. The black Daimler was still there, its door open. There was no sign of Vickery, but two more men bounded from it.

'Khouri!'

Arms grabbed at his shoulders. Dwight turned, ducked, felt his body tear free.

'Khouri, wait!'

'All we want to do is talk to you!'

Dwight ran down the street. People stepped hurriedly out of his way. He shoulder charged someone in a commissionaire's uniform, oblivious to the shouts of anger and protest, determined to put as much distance between him and the men with the dart guns. He'd been shown how to use a dart gun once, and had found it effective only at very close quarters. So unless the men had more conventional weaponry, and he kept bobbing and ducking and weaving, he'd get away.

He ran past a car showroom, raced up to a corner, turned and ran down the side of the showroom. Behind him the shouts grew fainter. Not so the patter of running feet. He raced past a book stall, a florist's with baskets of flowers on the street. Wreaths. There was a sharp pop above him as the florist's neon sign shattered. He dodged and weaved, trying to make sure his movements didn't fall into a pattern, but the pavement was narrow and he knew all they had to do was wing him.

Tretiak had gone down quickly from the dart in his shoulder. Whatever they were using was certainly powerful, if not fatal.

He raced past a travel agency, another corner. He skidded and turned, knowing he was outrunning the men, knowing also he couldn't keep up this frantic pace much longer. The street ahead of him was short, quiet, with a wooden walkway and scaffolding half-way along it. He ran for the gap, pounded over the walkway, the wood threatening to collapse under him, reached the pavement, ran. The men were still behind him.

Another corner. He turned. There was no way he could outrun a gas-propelled dart. With a stomach-twisting spasm he realized he was running back towards Piccadilly. He'd run round three sides of a square. A red and blue sign glowed in the street ahead of him in confirmation. He was running back to the tube station.

Dwight reached the sign, his pursuers' noise barely audible. It was a different entrance. He plunged down the steps, raced along a corridor, raced into the ticket lobby.

Two large men built like linebackers for the Rams had Tretiak's arms round their massive shoulders and were dragging him to the exit. At Dwight's approach they turned. Dwight glimpsed menacing, close-set Slavic features, the bulge in one of the men's pockets where a free hand was locked on a gun. Dwight accelerated. Tretiak's eyelids fluttered as he rushed past and then Dwight was speeding through the gap before the ticket collector's pill box to an escalator moving steadily upwards at him.

Behind him someone shouted in protest. Dwight hurdled the chain separating the up from the down escalator and took the moving staircase, three steps at a time. The shouting grew louder.

He reached the foot of the landing and skidded to a stop, panting. A train was drawn up to the platform on his left. Dwight turned and darted for it. As he reached the platform the doors hissed shut. He stood there, sucking lungfuls of stale air, frightened and desperate. The shouting behind him seemed to grow louder, echoing wildly under the cavernous roofs. Someone was getting closer.

The train made a hard chocking sound. Repeated it three times, moved inches and stopped with a grating of metal. The doors opened momentarily. Dwight launched himself through them. The doors shut behind him.

The train began to move.

*

Dwight slumped in his seat, sweaty and breathless, nearly choking as he gorged huge gulps of dry air. He had a line of seats to himself, the only occupants of the carriage spread out amongst the rows of seats in the middle, which faced back and front. Dwight mopped his face with a handkerchief and tried to think.

Vickery had reversed the trap. He'd spoken to the other members of the cartel and one of them had warned Vickery about Dwight; a warning Vickery had taken seriously enough to attempt an abduction right in the middle of London. But who in the cartel could have known about Dwight? Not Vickery, not Brassard. Hoffman?

Yes, that was it. Vickery had called Hoffman, and Hoffman told him he'd met Dwight the previous week. That Dwight was . . . Why had Hoffman met with him anyway? Why had Hoffman discussed the Manninger inheritance with a complete outsider when he could just as easily have refused to talk at all? Hoffman had said he was concerned about protecting the good name of Swiss banks. Crap! There were enough dirty stories about the fortunes buried in Switzerland, and one more wouldn't make any difference. Besides, Hoffman wasn't the kind of person to care about the reputation of Swiss banks, unless he was paid for it.

Suddenly, he remembered Mollwo. *Mr Khouri, I believe your Agency has been infiltrated!* Dwight pressed his handkerchief to his face. That was it. There was another member of the cartel, an American member, influential enough to control Hoffman, powerful enough to infiltrate the CIA and put a man like Sam Kamas into place. Which meant that he would have known who Dwight was, that he would have told Vickery exactly what Dwight was doing. Which was why today, Vickery had tried to bring him in and make him talk.

What the devil was he to do? Dwight felt utterly alone, utterly helpless. For the first time in years, he was mentally terrified. For all he knew, Jeb Anderson might be involved. The President! An alliance between big business, government and the intelligence community had been struck, a ghastly alliance that could hold the world in fee! The implications of that were horrible, the consequences unbearable.

And he was the only one who knew! He was the only one who could stop it! Stop it, how? He had no contacts, no resources. The only people he could trust were Mollwo and Marit.

Marit! Paris! If Vickery knew, so did Odile Brassard. He had to warn Marit. He had to prevent her meeting Odile Brassard.

Lights flashed past the train windows, the train slowed, stopped. Leicester Square. Dwight rushed out and raced along a narrow corridor, ran up the escalator two steps at a time to the top. 'Hey man, you got no ticket!' A large West Indian in the dark blue uniform of London Transport was blocking his way.

Dwight thrust a five-pound note at him and ran into the station.

Leicester Square was busier than Green Park had been; the phone boxes were full, and those that were empty, unusable. Dwight waited impatiently till one came free and dialled the operator. After an interminable time she answered.

'I want to make a credit-card call to Paris,' Dwight said and gave her the number of the hotel and his credit card.

Another interminable wait with lots of clicking and purring and frail voices gabbling in foreign languages. Then an unmistakably French voice said. 'Hotel Regis.'

Dwight exhaled a sigh of relief. 'I want to speak to Miss von Rausenberg. I am calling from London.'

'She is staying in this hotel, monsieur?'

'Yes, yes. Room number 236.'

'One moment.'

The moment dragged on forever. The phone began to utter a series of burbles. Dwight waited, praying the connection wouldn't be broken.

'I'm sorry, monsieur, she does not answer.'

'Have her paged.'

'Of course, monsieur.'

Another gnawing wait. Dwight could feel the receiver wet in his hands.

'I'm sorry, monsieur. She does not answer the paging.'

Dwight's eyes glanced over his watch. She had to be in her room. It was just after four and she'd told him she was meeting Odile Brassard at five. She would want to look her best for that meeting. She must be in her room, getting ready.

'Monsieur, I said she does not answer the paging.'

Dwight had another thought. His watch had been damaged in the chase. It was early and Marit had not returned to the hotel yet. 'Do you have the right time?'

'Yes, of course. It is twelve minutes past five.'

'Past five!'

'Yes, monsieur. Here in France we are on double summer time.'

Numb with shock and despair, Dwight replaced the receiver. Marit was already with Odile Brassard.

An hour later when he got to Heathrow he found that all flights to Paris were delayed by a baggage loaders strike.

33

Feeling very relaxed and assured, Marit sped westwards out of Paris in Pierre's pale green Citroën Maserati. She'd spent that morning in the library of the Faculty of Business Studies at Sorbonne University, poring through back numbers of *Fortune*, *Time*, the *Wall Street Journal*, *Business Weekly* and the *Financial Times*, piecing together a history of Brassard & Cie.

The company had been founded nearly a hundred years ago by Joseph Brassard, a retired *colon*, and dealt mainly with the import of raw materials, agricultural produce and textiles from the colonies and the export of light machinery and finished goods from France.

André, Joseph Brassard's only son, had taken over the business in 1908 and moved the company into manufacturing – automobile components and industrial goods for the railroads – and into dyestuffs. André Brassard had been trained in the laboratories of Topf Industrie and the Aktiegesselschaft and soon after the First World War, had begun to produce revolutionary dyestuffs. No one knew the source of these dyestuffs, though it was hinted that André Brassard had secret agreements with the Germans. However he had obtained the processes, their contribution to the company's profits was immeasurable and by the mid 1920s, Brassards were one of the largest industrial-chemical companies in France.

A quarter of a century later, his German connections appeared to have stood André Brassard in good stead after the fall of France. While a number of leading French industrialists were interned and had their factories dismantled, Brassard's factories were undisturbed throughout the Second World War, in the occupied territories as well as the France of Laval and Pétain. And after the war, Brassards had participated in the post-war European boom and were now one of France's most prosperous and stable companies.

Marit saw Pierre eyeing the Cardin designed silk shirt and narrow pants she'd bought in the Faubourg St Honoré. 'Will it do?' she asked.

'Exactly right,' Pierre said. 'Odile will be overcome.'

'How do you know Odile Brassard so well?'

Pierre smiled. 'I was working on *France Soir* when Odile succeeded her father. She needed friends in the press. I was one of them.'

After they had been driving for about an hour, Pierre slowed and turned through a narrow opening on to a paved road that led into a forest of tall, straight trees. The road twisted through the forest, and the foliage was thick, turning the florid brilliance of the setting sun to sombre shadow. As they came round a corner, Marit glimpsed the pale yellow boundary walls of the chateau, appearing as if from nowhere, in the middle of the forest.

They drove up to tall wrought-iron gates flanked with obelisks. A bucolic guard peered into the car, recognized Pierre and waved them into a paved courtyard.

The chateau was a comfortable size, two geniculated wings spreading from the main building to the gate, forming the perimeter of the courtyard; a main building in early baroque, the Italian influence emphasized by a frieze running between the archiform windows of the first and second floors. The buildings were of the same yellow stone as the boundary walls and an open, curving stone staircase flowed from a balcony on the first floor to a courtyard. Underneath the staircase was a row of tall, rectangular doors behind Ionic pillars.

The Citroën was driven away and they were ushered across a magnificent ballroom into a large, ordered garden beyond. Gravel paths stretched between lawns and flower beds to the woods. Fountains played over stone statuary. Formally attired waiters and waitresses served canapés and champagne to the elegantly informal guests strolling about the gardens.

Pierre was obviously well known to many of them. They were greeted with cries of recognition and invited to join small groups.

Pierre pointed out Odile Brassard at the far end of the garden, a stubby, stoop-shouldered woman in a brown trouser suit, flanked by two unsmiling matrons who looked like wardresses. It was not somehow the kind of gathering Marit had expected. Most of the people were young and brash, connected with design, public relations, the theatre and the arts; most of them had the wary predatoriness and facile good looks of those accustomed to sunning themselves in the South of France at another's expense. There was no one connected with finance or industry, no members of the aristocracy or government.

As darkness fell they were moved to the Chinese room on the first floor, its panelled walls lacquered with Asian landscapes, elegant gold and white chairs spread around the room and a huge chandelier dominating the centre. From a long table at one end of the room, waiters served cold cuts and salads, white Loire wines and clarets. Marit had seen rooms like this only in museums. She had never before seen a room like this actually being used.

At some time over dinner, she'd been separated from Pierre. Now she saw him across the room from her, part of a group of seven young men, his arm thrown caressingly round the shoulders of one of them. A chilling thought struck her. Most of the beautiful men and women in the room were homosexuals.

She became aware of a tall, slim, dark-haired girl standing beside her. The girl had a marvellously fine-boned face, an exotic beauty emphasized by the black eye patch she wore. Marit recalled seeing her earlier with Odile Brassard.

'Do you have a cigarette?' the girl asked.

Marit made to take out a pack from her bag.

The girl motioned her towards the doors that led on to a balcony. They went out and stood looking at the garden. The girl accepted the cigarette and stood in silence, sucking smoke deeply. Marit felt embarrassed by the girl's silence, which bordered on rudeness.

'My name's Marit,' she said. 'I came with Pierre.'

The girl smiled tightly and took another long pull at the cigarette. 'He is very good looking, isn't he.'

'Yes,' Marit said.

'You're not the first one he's brought here,' the girl said.

'What do you mean by that?'

The girl pulled again at the cigarette, her palm cupped around its glowing end as if to shield it from a non-existent wind. 'You'll find out.'

'Francine!' Odile Brassard stood in the doorway behind them, her stubby figure silhouetted against the light of the room. 'Put out that cigarette! Go inside!'

With a deliberate show of defiance, the girl took one more drag at the cigarette before stubbing it out on the stone balustrade. Then she brushed angrily past Odile Brassard and went into the room.

Odile Brassard came out on to the balcony and stood beside Marit, fitting a Gauloise into a long, black holder. She had a strong, almost masculine face with a sharp, beaked nose and heavy-lidded black eyes. The perfume she wore wafted over Marit. 'Francine has just recovered from pneumonia,' Odile Brassard explained. 'The doctors have forbidden her to smoke.' Her gaze wandered appraisingly over Marit. 'You must be Pierre's friend. I'm sorry we have not spoken earlier. Have you had enough food, enough wine?'

'Yes, thank you,' Marit replied. There was something prehensile about Odile Brassard, that made Marit feel uneasy.

'You want to talk to me.'

Marit forced herself to smile. 'Yes. I work with Pierre on *Event* magazine. We intend running a series about companies like Brassards, which have been in existence for a long time. We'd like to show people how these companies have changed and developed and how they have adapted over the years.'

'What other companies are you writing about?' There was a hint of suspicion in Odile Brassard's tone.

'Oh,' Marit said and trotted out the first names that came into her head. 'Jardines in Hong Kong, BASF in Germany, Rolls-Royce in England, and we're hoping to do Ford in America.'

'Such impressive company. I'm flattered.'

Marit wasn't sure whether Odile Brassard was being sarcastic. 'Brassards is an impressive organization,' she ventured and was rewarded by a small smile from Odile.

Odile Brassard drew closer to her, the combination of perfume and black tobacco smoke overpowering. 'Well then, we must do it properly. I shall tell Pierre you are staying the weekend.' A finger ran over Marit's knuckles pressed to the balustrade. 'Before you are ready to receive information about Brassards, you must get the proper historical perspective, you must read my father's biography. I shall leave a copy in your room.'

Marit hadn't come across a biography of André Brassard in her researches. Therefore, it had either been privately printed, or was a fiction to keep her at the chateau. In any case it was too dangerous to say she had already read it. Odile Brassard's finger was playing suggestively with the back of her hand. Marit remembered Pierre saying the party would be different; remembered telling Pierre she'd do anything to interview Odile Brassard. Anything looked pretty gruesome right now.

'I wouldn't dream of taking up so much of your time,' Marit said, and freed her hand from Odile's touch – to take a cigarette. Lighting it she decided she had to lead Odile Brassard into the interview now. Her mind raced frantically, searching for a question that was sensational enough to make Odile Brassard want to defend herself, yet not outrageous enough to make her angry. 'Your father worked very closely with German industrialists, didn't he, Madame Brassard? Wasn't he very close to men like Bruno Topf, Berndt Manninger and the Aktiegesselschaft?'

Odile Brassard stiffened. 'That is correct. And we still work closely with German industry, as do Ford and General Motors and almost every major company you care to name.'

'I'm talking about 1936,' Marit said.

'The relationships of Brassards with German industry in 1936 were as close as they are today, in 1980.'

'And what about 1941, Madame Brassard? Is it not true that André Brassard maintained relationships with the Germans during the war? That the reason his factories were not destroyed by the Nazis and that he was allowed to operate freely in occupied France was because of those relationships?'

Odile Brassard drew herself up to a not very full height. Her face twisted, she clenched her hands against her thighs. For a moment, Marit thought that Odile would strike her. 'How dare you ask questions like that in my house!' Odile hissed fiercely. 'You print one word of that and I'll sue. I'll break you and your foul paper!'

Bingo! Marit thought. She'd got Odile Brassard just where she wanted her. Odile Brassard now had to stand and defend herself. 'What was your father's real relationship with the Germans?' she asked. 'You must appreciate that his relationship with the Germans is an important part of the Brassard company history. That even now it is a matter of legitimate public interest.'

Odile Brassard looked about her. For a moment, Marit thought she would go and confront Pierre, or that she would summon her servants and have Marit expelled. '*Event* is a responsible paper,' Marit said. 'I am a responsible journalist. I'm not interested in sensational stories. All I want is the truth.'

Odile Brassard looked at her, the fire dying from her eyes. 'My father was awarded the Legion d'Honneur for the services he rendered to France during the war. That was not the reward of a traitor!'

'Tell me more,' Marit said.

Mollified, Odile Brassard went on. 'My father was ordered to co-operate with the Germans.'

'Why?'

'Because there were those amongst us who knew that the Third Reich would not last forever. That one day France would be free. It was essential that when France became free, she did not become someone else's slave because her industry had been ruined. Some of us had to survive so that France could live. My father was one of those.'

'Did he, do you still detest Germans?'

Odile Brassard gave her a small smile. 'Don't be silly, child. We hated the Nazis, and we hated what the Germans did to us. But that was a long while ago, and no one can hate a whole nation because of a few lunatics. We have and will continue to work with Germany. After all, our two countries are now nearly one.'

'It's true, isn't it, Madame Odile, that your father's

association with the German dyestuffs industry, helped build up Brassards?'

'That's true,' Odile Brassard said.

'Would you say that without these cartel arrangements, Brassards could not have grown to its present size?'

'Cartels!' Odile Brassard was annoyed again. 'There were no cartels.'

'I'm sorry, Madame Odile, there were cartels. IG Farben and the General Aniline Corporation, the various companies involved in the manufacture and distribution of aluminium, Manninger Industrie and the US Styrite Corporation. There were big cartels and little cartels. That was how business was done, or are you going to tell me Brassards were not part of it?'

'You're talking of business arrangements,' Odile Brassard said quietly. 'Cartels are something else.'

'So these business arrangements contributed substantially to Brassards's growth?'

'As similar arrangements have contributed to the growth of other companies.'

'Quite,' Marit said. 'Would it be correct to say that over the years these relationships have not changed? That they form the basis of business today?'

'This is really too complex a matter for discussion with someone so ignorant of business,' Odile Brassard said. 'Go back to Munich and tell your editor to send me an experienced person.'

She turned on her heel.

'Madame Odile,' Marit called after her. 'Can you confirm that Brassards still has close relations with Vickerys and Topf Industrie?'

Odile Brassard turned. 'The business of Brassard et Fils has always been international,' she said, tightly. 'We have good relations with companies in every part of the world. Now, enough of your interrogation. I must go and see to my guests.'

'One last question,' Marit said. 'How do you account for the close similarity in the financial affairs of Brassards, Topfs and Vickerys?'

Odile Brassard advanced threateningly towards her. 'What do you mean?'

'Your most recent accounts show the most outrageous similarities. You have all recently disposed of investments. You are all inundated with cash. And you are all borrowing heavily.'

'I know less than you seem to do about the affairs of Vickery and Topf,' Odile Brassard said.

'Why is your company in this unusual state?'

'It's none of your damned business!' Odile Brassard spat into Marit's face.

Marit wiped away the saliva. She was enjoying this. She had Odile Brassard on the run. She was on the verge of a great story. 'Would the remarkable coincidence in your financial affairs have anything to do with the death of Bruno Topf?'

'You're mad!' Odile Brassard cried. 'You're a raving, dangerous lunatic!' She swung her hand at Marit's face.

Marit sidestepped easily and caught it. 'No more questions, Madame Brassard,' she said. 'You've already told me enough. Thank you for your hospitality. I'll leave now.' She walked past Odile to the door.

'Wait,' Odile Brassard said. She came after Marit. 'What are you going to write? Are you going to publish those lies?'

'No,' Marit said. 'No lies. Just the facts, as I know them. Just the truth that the cartels still exist.'

'That story could ruin Brassards,' Odile Brassard said softly. 'How can I persuade you not to write it?'

'You can't,' Marit said.

'What if I told you the whole truth? What if I gave you the entire story about the cartels?'

Marit lit another cigarette thoughtfully. 'As I told you before, Madame Odile, neither I nor my paper are interested in mere sensationalism. The truth would be a different matter.'

For a long while Odile Brassard stared at her. Then she said, 'You are right. The cartels existed and exist now. My father was part of it. He had to join them or be ruined.' She looked furtively around her and turned back to Marit. 'But we can't talk about this here. I am followed and watched. There are people in this house who work for the cartel, who will do anything to preserve its secrets. Go outside and take the path to the left. You will come to a small maze surrounding the Galileo Fountain. I will meet you there in ten minutes and tell you about the cartel and tell you why Bruno Topf died.'

Marit watched Odile Brassard go and leaned against the balcony, her heart pounding. Odile Brassard had already revealed that the cartel existed, had confirmed the link between Brassards, Vickerys and Topfs. But in order to save Brassards, would she tell all? Or was it a device to get her out of the house, out of sight?

Marit moved towards the door and hesitated. She should take Pierre with her. She'd do the sensible thing and leave. But if Odile Brassard was going to talk to her, what a story!

She walked uncertainly into the Chinese Room.

The maze was more ornamental than abstruse, three concentric circles of tall hedges radiating from a small paved square on which stood a stone fountain underneath a marble statue of Galileo. Why Galileo, Marit wondered, sitting on the cold edge of the fountain. In the bright moonlight that washed over the maze she could see both entrances clearly. And the sound of voices and laughter carried from the Chinese Room.

Marit heard footsteps beyond the hedge to the left and turned, suddenly nervous. The footsteps were lighter than Odile's could be and less brisk. One person, so it couldn't be lovers seeking seclusion. She got to her feet and moved to the side of the fountain.

Francine, heels dragging sloppily across the stone, walked into the square and came up to Marit.

'Waiting for Odile?' Francine asked scornfully.

'As a matter of fact, yes.'

Francine placed her hands on her hips and swayed gently

back and forth. 'I thought so,' she said. 'Pretty bloody romantic, isn't it?'

'Odile and I have something private to discuss,' Marit said.

'Very private, I'm sure,' Francine said. Behind the sarcasm, there was menace in her tone, something threatening in her stance.

'I'm not going to share Odile's bed, if that's what's worrying you,' Marit said. Somehow she had to get rid of Francine before Odile came.

'You hope. If Odile wants you, she'll have you. Just be careful she doesn't blind you while she's doing it.'

'I'm interviewing Odile for my paper,' Marit said. 'Then, I'm leaving.'

'If,' Francine said, 'you can find Pierre.'

There were low voices from the right side of the maze, hurried footsteps. Marit turned. The two matrons she had seen earlier with Odile entered the square, two dark, bulky, sinister figures, looking in the half light like birds of prey.

'Odile wants to see you in her office,' one of them said in a chill voice. 'Come.'

It was a trap. Heart pounding, Marit moved away from the women towards the opposite exit.

'Where are you going?'

From behind her, Francine giggled.

'I'll be back . . . I need my notebook . . . it's upstairs.'

The women closed up to her, one of them carrying a loose bag.

'Tell Odile I'll come straight to her office.' Marit moved away. Suddenly Francine ran round her, stood between her and the exit. 'Got a cigarette?' Francine extended her hand, smiling.

Automatically, Marit reached into her bag, took out the packet. 'Keep it.'

Francine grabbed her wrist and yanked her forward, grabbed the free arm Marit thrust out for balance. There was a rapid movement of feet behind her. Marit felt Francine pull her arms down in front of her. Then a square of white silk floated before her face and was pulled tight across her mouth. She tried to pull her hands away from Francine, tried to turn her body as something soft rushed through the air behind her. Then the moonlight was blotted out. Darkness enveloped her. Her hands, suddenly freed, fell to her sides and a rope pulled tight around the sack that enclosed her, pinioned her arms to her sides.

It had all happened so quickly, Marit had no time to react, let alone scream or struggle. Hands grasped her shoulders, propelled her forward, turned her left, turned her right, marched her through the maze. She lost all sense of direction. She felt her shoes scrape on gravel, she was turned, pulled, pushed. A door opened in front of her. She was marched up a narrow staircase. At the top of the staircase, light seeped through the sacking. She was made to walk across a landing, through another door.

She felt the boards underneath her feet undulate, smelt Odile's perfume. 'We shall have our little talk later,' Odile Brassard said softly. 'Now, I must attend to my guests.'

She heard Odile walk away. A door shut. An unseen hand wandered over her face, settled in front of her throat, pulling the sacking roughly against her cheeks. The hand explored, tightened. Marit gasped, choked against the gag, felt her breath grow hot against the sacking. The hand tightened increasing the pressure on both sides of her neck. Other hands went round her body, holding her rigid, upright. She felt the pulse begin to beat in her head, her face grow hot, her lungs begin to burn. She couldn't breathe, she couldn't open her mouth, she couldn't cry out. She moaned, struggled feebly as the pressure on her throat grew tighter, tighter, squeezing out air. She wanted to cough. Her stomach heaved, she felt her legs collapsing, felt herself falling into a deeper blackness, felt a sudden surge of warm air into her lungs, then nothing.

When she woke, she was in semi-darkness. Her neck ached and there was a damp piece of cloth in her mouth. When she tried to move, she found she couldn't. She was fastened by her

277

wrists and ankles to the four posts of a large bed, a pillow thrust underneath her neck, her limbs raised so that she lay helpless on the small of her back. Underneath the sheet that covered her, she was completely naked.

34

In the room next to which Marit was held, Odile Brassard sat before the Empire *Bureau-Plat* which she used as a desk and thoughtfully fitted another Gauloise into her long-stemmed cigarette holder. She was certain the girl was an imposter. No journalist would dream of writing a story comparing the history of Brassards with that of Jardines, Ford and BASF. Brassards simply wasn't in that league yet and no story based on that comparison, was possible. Further, most of the girl's questions had been concerned with the old cartel, with the relationship between Brassards, Vickerys and Topfs. What had that to do with Jardines, Ford and BASF? No, the girl was after something else. She might well be a journalist, she probably worked for *Event*, but the story she was writing had nothing to do with the comparative history of Brassard and Cie.

So what story was she writing? The girl was German. *Event* was based in Munich. Bruno Topf had been German. The connection was obvious, the girl's line of questioning conclusive. Marit whoever-she-was, was investigating Topf's death. Enquiring into Topf's affairs she had come across the connection between Vickerys and Brassards, probably through the Russian aromatic factory consortium. The question was, how much did the girl know? Did she know of something that connected all of them to Topf's death, or had she merely been following her nose when she'd persuaded Pierre to bring her to the chateau?

Odile looked at the phone and hesitated. She did not want Sir Alex Vickery patronizing her, telling her not to worry her little head with these things and to go out and buy some perfume. She didn't want Raison Tearkes's irascibility either. But if the girl had found a trail, sooner or later someone else would. And none of them could afford even rumours of a conspiracy to murder, when they were gambling their entire fortunes on the Andronov plan.

She decided Tearkes's irritability was preferable to Vickery's saloon bar gentility. Tearkes was on the line in two minutes. 'Raison, I have here a journalist from *Event* magazine asking questions about the relationship between Brassards, Vickerys and Topf Industrie. She wants to know why our financial statements look so similar.'

'Put her off, Odile. Tell her you need to speak to your accountant. Better, tell her you'll arrange for her to see your accountants, next week.'

'Raison, I do not think this woman is interested in our financial affairs. I think she is interested in Bruno.'

'Bruno!' Tearkes's laugh sounded brittle. Nervousness, Odile wondered, or a distortion on the line? 'No one can trace our connection to Bruno,' Tearkes said, confidently.

'Your connection,' Odile said. 'Remember, I was not involved.' She hadn't known of Tearkes's involvement in Topf's death until afterwards.

'Odile, we've got too much at stake to fight amongst ourselves.'

Odile clicked her tongue angrily. It was all very well for Raison to sound statesmanlike now, after he had nearly ruined everything. 'If you'd talked to me first, I would have told you to leave Bruno alone.'

'There wasn't time – '

'There was no reason to – '

'He was threatening everything. He'd sold out to the Gemeinschaft.'

'The Gemeinschaft!' Odile laughed scornfully. 'You stupid man. Bruno has been working with those Gemeinschaft

279

people for years. What else do you expect from a German of his age? But Bruno was with us too. And he was loyal to us. As he was loyal to them.'

'Not this time,' Tearkes said. 'This time he sold out. What makes you think this woman is interested in Topf's death?'

'She is German,' Odile said. '*Event* magazine is German. Her questions are based on our association with Germany, with Bruno.'

'It's libellous,' Tearkes said. 'Tell her, if she prints a word, we'll sue the ass off her.'

Odile Brassard said, 'I've tried that. It won't work.'

'Have you talked to her about a job on another newspaper? A present? A new car or a fur coat?'

'She's a dedicated journalist,' Odile said. 'She wants to print the story.'

'Who is she?' Tearkes asked.

'Her name's Marit von Rausenberg.' Odile thought she heard Tearkes gasp.

'Marit von – how did she get to see you?'

There was a strange note in Tearkes's voice, a mixture of excitement and anxiety. 'I'm having a small party at the chateau. She was brought here by an old friend, Pierre Ducret, who also works for *Event*.'

'And no one else came with them?'

'No.'

'Is there anyone at your party you haven't met before? An American?'

'No,' Odile said. 'Why do you ask?'

'Odile, this von Rausenberg gal is working for the Securities and Exchange Commission. She is not concerned with Bruno. She is concerned with *us*. Look, can you keep her at the chateau till breakfast time tomorrow?'

'Why?' Odile asked.

'It'll take me till then to get my people to you. We'll persuade her not to write this story. And don't worry, Odile. I promise you, there won't be any comeback on you.'

Odile hesitated, confused. She didn't believe Tearkes. 'How do I get her to stay?' she asked.

'Oh, come on, Odile. Make her drunk, dope her drink, seduce her, but keep her until my people get there. If she gets away, she could ruin all of us.' Tearkes sounded very frightened.

'Don't worry, Raison,' Odile said. 'She won't be going anywhere.'

When she finished the call, she fitted another cigarette into her holder and thought, she didn't believe Tearkes's story about the girl being with the SEC. They'd been dealing cautiously so far, through nominees, and in any case, they'd only been speculating in gold and dollars, which had nothing to do with the SEC. No, there was something between Tearkes and this girl. Had he shoved his wretched *quequette* up her and talked too much afterwards? No, that couldn't be it. The girl was too independent to allow Tearkes to use her and Raison preferred stupid child-whores like that Sammy or Cindy or whatever her name was.

If it wasn't that, what was it? Why should Raison get concerned over a German journalist? What new, devious scheme had he thought of? Odile looked at the door behind which Marit lay. No sound came from it. Odile decided she would get rid of her guests and then she and Marit would have a little talk.

She stubbed out her cigarette. *Merde!* She'd finished another pack. She walked to her bedroom on the further side of the study and threw open the door. She heard a rustle of movement in the darkness by the bed and turned on the light.

'Francine! What are you doing here?'

It was obvious what Francine was doing. Hurriedly she leaned over to the ashtray by the bed and put out her cigarette. 'I wanted to smoke,' she said. 'And no one there,' she gestured behind her to the main part of the house where the party was being held, 'will give me any, because you've told them not to.'

'It's for your own good,' Odile said. 'You shouldn't smoke, especially when you've just recovered from a serious illness.' She shut the door behind her and moved into the room. 'How long have you been here?' she asked, taking the freshly-opened packet of cigarettes Francine had left on the bedside table.

'Oh, I don't know. Ten minutes. I only smoked one cigarette.'

Odile looked at the pack. 'Liar,' she snapped. 'Two.'

Francine looked down, raising her hands beside her head as if expecting a blow. 'I'm sorry, Odile. I can't help myself.'

'Put your hands down, child. I'm not going to hit you.' She took Francine's arm and led her round the bed towards the door that led to the corridor. 'I've told you before, you mustn't come in here uninvited.'

Francine withdrew her hand. 'And I suppose tonight, I don't get invited. Tonight, you have a new German friend.'

Odile reached and turned Francine towards her, drew Francine's head down to hers and kissed her on the lips.

'There,' she said, when she had finished. 'I've always told you that jealousy is a sign of inferiority. And don't forget, that you get more of me than anyone else. Others come and go but you're always here, aren't you, Francine?' She reached up, kissed Francine on the cheek, then said brightly, 'Now, let's go and join our guests.'

Marit waited, her body stiff and aching from the unnatural posture in which she had been fastened to the bed, listening to the sounds of the party die, the last goodbyes and the rumble of the last exhaust fade into the night. God, how had she got herself into this? Don't worry, she remembered telling Dwight cheerily, Odile Brassard won't harm a journalist. More journalists die from an excess of alcohol than an excess of zeal. Stupidity! So here she was, trussed, suspended, gagged, unable to move, unable to cry out . . . alone.

A blinding shaft of panic split her brain. She forced her breath against the gag, feeling her head swell. She heaved furiously at the ropes till the bed groaned at the desperate flailing of her body. But it was useless. Her bonds had been expertly tied and the manner in which she was suspended across the bed made it impossible to exert any force. All her struggles had achieved was to chafe her wrists and ankles raw.

Marit sagged against the ropes, allowed her body to rest upon the bed. There was nothing she could do to free herself. She was completely at Odile Brassard's mercy.

Idiot! She'd been so invigorated by the interview, so excited that she'd ignored all the danger signs and thrown away all caution. She'd talked too much about the relationship between Brassard, Vickery and Topf, revealed too much of her own knowledge, possibly even threatened some other coup the cartel was planning.

She knew Odile would by now have sent Pierre away. That soon, Odile would come to interrogate her. And afterwards — she couldn't stand the thought of those stubby fingers exploring her body, of those rubbery lips pressing themselves on hers. Tentatively, she tried to wriggle a wrist free, an ankle. It was hopeless. The bonds were too tight, too secure. Oh God, someone, please help me, she prayed into the darkness, fighting back the tears of panic that erupted into her eyes. Oh God, someone, please help me!

Marit heard feet tread firmly across the floor of the next room, felt the floorboards vibrate gently. Then the door was flung open, a light turned on. Marit blinked.

Odile stood in the doorway, carrying a glass of champagne and smoking a cigarette through the long, black holder. Her brown suit, Marit unaccountably noticed, was an original Raphael. Transferring the champagne to her left hand, Odile strode across the room and pulled away the sheet that covered Marit. Marit forced herself not to cower as Odile examined her spreadeagled body with gloating care.

'That Francine,' Odile said, clicking her tongue in mock annoyance. 'Who'd have thought she could be so jealous.' She leaned over Marit and unfastened the gag. 'And now, my little, inquisitive journalist. We shall continue our interview, but first – ' Odile stood away from the bed, raised her hand above her head and clicked her fingers loudly.

One of the women who had helped capture Marit came into the room, sinister in her long black gown, her face averted, her head covered in a black shawl. In her hand, she carried a long, thin cane.

The cane zipped through the air. A blinding stream of liquid fire streaked across Marit's belly. Her body came off the bed. Her wrists and ankles blazed. She had just time to bite down on her lips before her body crashed down on the bed again, shock waves jarring her head. The cane was zipping through the air again. What were they doing? For God's sake – her stomach was being ripped open. Her wrists, her ankles torn. The bed creaked and she felt a dull pain in the small of her back as her body floundered against the bed. Tears burned behind her fast-shut eyes and there was a warm wetness where her teeth had bitten her lip.

She lay tensed waiting for the next blow. When it did not come, she opened her eyes and saw the woman had gone. She tried not to flinch as Odile's hand ran up the inside of her thigh.

'Now,' Odile said, smiling down at her. 'Tell me who you are, and what you are doing here.'

'My name is Marit von Rausenberg. I am a journalist with *Event* magazine. I am doing a story on the history of Brassards.'

Odile leaned forward and wiped the blood from her chin. 'You don't seem to have heard me, child. I asked you who you are and what you are doing here?'

'My name is Marit von Rausenberg. I am a journalist with *Event* magazine. I am doing a story on the history – '

Odile's fingers closed fiercely around her nipple. 'The truth, child! The truth!'

'Of the Brassard company,' Marit sighed.

Odile released her nipple and leaned over her, placing her hands on either side of Marit's head. 'There is no story,' she said, her brown eyes flat as buttons, 'I have checked with Munich. Your managing editor says you are on leave.'

Marit closed her eyes to hide the hopelessness in them. 'My name is Marit von Rausenberg. I am a journalist –'

'Marit,' Odile said. 'Open your eyes. Look at me.'

Marit looked into that square, mannish face with the little tendrils of hair on either side of the lips, the pronounced nose and the swollen chin.

'No one knows you're here. You can scream as much as you like. No one will come. You will not leave here until you have told me everything.'

'I have already told you everything,' Marit said.

Odile's purse-like mouth crumpled in a smile. Then her hands clamped down on either side of Marit's head as she pressed her mouth against Marit's.

Marit gave a subdued scream and tried to wriggle her head free. But Odile's grip was massive. She closed her mouth. Then felt Odile cup her chin, press her fingers into her cheeks. Oh God, she couldn't stand it, not the pain, not this obscenity. The pressure against her mouth, against her face was unbearable. She went limp, felt Odile's lips encircle her mouth, her tongue move round, rest against hers. Then Odile was drawing her head away, her eyes glowing with baleful triumph. 'You see, my dear, there's nothing you can do.'

Marit sucked her bruised cheeks together, pursed her mouth and spat. '*Gouine!*' she shouted. '*Salope! Va te faire voir!*'

Odile looked down at her and laughed.

'Go get yourself some balls and a shave,' Marit said.

Odile's expression changed. Her face flushed, became tight and pinched, her pupils dilated. With an awkward, plunging movement she lurched across the bed and slapped Marit.

Marit's cheek stung, her head rocked, her body sawed at the ropes.

Odile strode to the door and shouted.

The two women came in. 'Now,' Odile hissed. 'I'll make you talk.'

The two women stood on either side of the bed. Marit

caught the pungent aroma of surgical spirit. Then they poured it over the raw skin of her wrists and ankles.

The pain was searing. A million red-hot needles were being drawn through her wrists and ankles. She tried to pull them away and the pain flared. Then there was a quick, whizzing hiss above her that was part of the pain, and yet not of it. A light, wet-sounding smack, a tendril of fire extending across her body as the cane laid her open from hip to hip. Another hiss, another blow. She saw the stripes stand out across her stomach, felt as if her flesh was being incised by a razor dipped in acid. Desperately she tried to twist her spread-eagled body away and felt the ropes catch in rings of blazing fire. She screamed.

She couldn't help it. She screamed and screamed again, her whole body full of molten, stinging pain. She screamed as the canes descended on her in demented unison, striping the soft flesh of her stomach and thighs. She was burning, her whole body was on fire. Her wrists and ankles were being severed with a close-toothed, rusty saw. And she locked her jaws and jammed her teeth together and forced herself not to scream. Forced herself to lie back sweating on the bed, throat dry and rasping, forced herself not to move and to think.

Her stomach and thighs felt as if the flesh was being peeled from them. The whole area was a suffused red and her stomach muscles were cramped from the repeated flexing. She must not flinch. She must not move. Each movement only increased the pain. She gasped with the shock of each blow and through her tears saw Odile Brassard, standing beside her, a rapt smile on her face. The bitch was enjoying the spectacle. The bitch would stand there smiling while they beat her to death.

Somehow she had to stop them. She had to tell them something. What? A story that would fit the known facts. Think, girl, think, think, despite the molten lava cauterizing your stomach, the manacles of red-hot steel branding your wrists and ankles. A story, as close to the truth as she dared. Blood was spurting down her raised legs and hands. They were tearing out her stomach, sawing at her thighs, they were flaying her to ribbons. She had to tell –

'Stop! Please stop! I'll tell you everything.'

She couldn't believe she had cried out. She couldn't believe the devastating rain of blows had ceased. Her wrists, her ankles, her stomach, her thighs, were suffused in a burning glow. She slumped against the ropes, covered in sweat, her mouth dry from crying out so much. She heard the two women move away and Odile approach the bed.

'Now, my child, what do you have to tell me?'

'I'm a journalist. I am also Berndt Manninger's granddaughter. I am the sole beneficiary of the Manninger estate.' She told Odile about the processes, how Hoffman had told her they were lost and how she'd have to find the *Zessions* before she could claim the estate. She'd discovered that Manninger had been friends with André Brassard, Sir Alex Vickery and Bruno Topf. She'd been on her way to meet Topf when she'd learned of his death. So she'd come on to Paris and used Pierre to get in touch with Odile, hoping that by going through the history of Brassards, she might find where Berndt Manninger had hidden the processes and the *Zessions*.

Odile Brassard looked down at her sympathetically, stroked her hair and wiped the sweat from her forehead. She had the women apply ice to Marit's stomach and thighs, had them unfasten her bonds and apply a soothing salve. She made them bring food and wine, and when Marit had eaten and drunk asked, 'Do you know a man called Raison Tearkes, my dear?'.

'No,' Marit said.

'Have you ever *heard* of a man called Raison Tearkes?'

'No,' Marit said.

'You look tired, my child,' Odile said. 'Why don't you sleep. I have some things to think about. I will see you later.'

Odile Brassard poured herself a large Cointreau from the tulipwood secretaire and carried it over to her desk. She remembered her father talking about the Manninger processes. Once or twice he had even spoken about leading an expedition to find them, but the task of rebuilding France after the war had been more urgent and more immediately profitable. The Manninger processes had to do with . . . energy, with agriculture.

She picked up the phone and dialled. 'Hello, Alex.'

'Odile! Do you realize what time it is?'

'Yes, it's quarter to eleven in England. What do you know about the Manninger processes?'

'Quite a lot actually. They were – '

'Are they to do with energy?'

'Yes, I believe those processes could solve our present energy problems.'

'Are they valuable?'

'Yes.'

'Who has them?'

'That's a bit of a problem, you see. No one's really seen them since Berndt died.'

'Is Raison looking for them?'

'Yes, why – yes, in a manner – '

'And you?'

'I'm giving Raison a hand. There's a couple of things he's asked me to do for him, here. Raison was going to bring this up at the next meeting.'

'So that we could share in the expenses, I suppose, if he didn't find the processes.'

'No, Odile, it isn't – '

'Goodnight, Alex.'

Damn Raison Tearkes! Odile poured herself another slug of Cointreau. Double damn Raison Tearkes! So that was why he'd been so anxious to collect Marit von Rausenberg. Tomorrow his men could go away empty handed. She was sick of the cartel, sick of Raison Tearkes's domination, of Raison Tearkes's double dealing. Tomorrow, she could start looking for the Manninger processes, she would find them for Brassards and for France.

35

Dwight came into Paris around midnight, a volcano about to erupt. He bubbled and seethed with a terrible knowledge and a terrible helplessness. For the first time in his life he was faced with problems he couldn't handle. The American government was involved in a massive conspiracy with big business. And he had lost Marit.

The taxi screeched to a stop outside the Hotel Regis. Dwight thrust a five hundred franc note at the driver.

'Pardon, monsieur, I have no change.'

Dwight stared wordlessly at the man. For a terrible moment, the taxi driver was a broken neck away from eternity, then Dwight relaxed. 'Keep it,' he said thickly and ran into the hotel.

'Von Rausenberg,' the clerk looked at the keys dangling from the pigeon holes behind him. 'No. She is not in.'

Dwight leaned forward, pressing clenched fists on the counter. 'What time did she leave?'

The clerk shrugged. 'It was before I came on duty, monsieur.'

'What time was that?'

'Seven o'clock.'

'Has she been back while you've been on duty?'

The clerk shook his head. 'No, monsieur. If she has been back, she hasn't been to her room.'

Dwight pushed himself away from the counter, took out his wallet and laid three one hundred franc notes before the clerk. 'I need a car very quickly. Any kind of car will do. I want directions to the Chateau Brassard in Argentuil.'

The money disappeared under the clerk's hand. 'It's difficult, monsieur. But I shall try. I have friends . . .' The clerk walked to a corner of the reception area and picked up the telephone.

'Pardon me.'

Dwight turned. A tall, distinguished-looking man was advancing on him, full of Gallic superciliousness and Gallic charm. Dwight eyed his vaguely nautical blazer and white slacks with distaste. 'I heard you asking for Marit von Rausenberg, for directions to the Chateau Brassard.' The perfectly elliptical eyebrows twisted slightly in enquiry.

'That's right.'

'My name is Pierre Ducret. Earlier this evening I took Madamoiselle von Rausenberg to a party at the chateau.'

'You left without her?'

Ducret winced at the harshness in Dwight's voice.

'Yes. Madame Odile told me that Marit had completed her interview and returned to the hotel to file her story.'

'Do you have a car?' Dwight demanded.

'Yes. It's outside.'

Dwight grabbed his arm, shoved him towards the hotel entrance. 'Let's go. We must get to the Chateau Brassard.'

Ducret tried to pull his arm free.

'What is this – who are you – '

'I'll explain in the car. Now move, man, move!'

Hardly aware of the scrape of the chair leg which had disturbed her, Marit woke slowly. She lay with her eyes closed feeling the light on her face bright behind her lids. There was a dull ache that ran through her back and shoulders, a stiffness that petrified every muscle. She tried to stretch and felt the ropes pull her wrists tight against the bed posts; remembered that though her wounds had been dressed she was still cruelly suspended across the bed: she was still a prisoner.

What did Odile Brassard want with her now? She'd told Odile as much of the truth as she'd dared, and Odile had believed her. She'd been left alone, allowed to sleep. She wished she could move her hands, move her feet, walk. And why had they left the light on? She opened her eyes and froze with shock.

A grotesquely made-up Odile Brassard was seated in an armchair some distance from the bed, looking at her with an expression that was partly coy and partly gluttonous. Her cheeks were heavily rouged, her mouth a weirdly artificial carmine. Her eyes were shaded and pressed to her head was a garish blonde wig. Odile had changed her trouser suit for a brocaded night gown which revealed sagging breasts and fleshy, freckled arms.

As Marit watched, the mouth broke. Odile spoke in a soft, little girl voice. 'How do you feel, precious one?'

Marit turned her head away. Odile Brassard was mad. Odile Brassard was perverted. Marit looked at the ceiling and said in a small voice, 'I feel fine. Please untie me. Please let me go. I've told you everything.'

Odile leaned forward in the chair, unable to take her eyes from Marit's body. 'You were a good girl,' she said, thickly. 'You told the truth. Now let us be friends.'

Marit realized that Odile had been seated by her, all the while she'd slept. Oh God! It was horrible. It was sick. Didn't Odile realize how disgusting she was? 'Please let me go,' Marit repeated.

'No,' Odile said, moving towards the bed. 'I can't do that. You're far too precious, in every sense of the word. I'll be a good friend to you, Marit. I'll be the best friend you've ever had. And believe me, you need a friend.'

Marit felt the bed sag as Odile sat beside her, breathed the familiar odour of strong perfume and harsh tobacco. 'Leave me alone,' she muttered. 'For God's sake, leave me alone.'

Odile's mouth broke, the sagging skin beneath her jaws trembled. 'You're such a lovely child,' she murmured, 'so very, very lovely.' Slowly she ran her hand, all the way from Marit's foot to her shoulder. 'Such a beautiful, strong body, such wonderful skin. You're perfect, dear child, do you know that? Divinely, exquisitely perfect.' She leaned forward, kissed Marit's arm, placed her lips close to Marit's ear. 'I'll be your friend,' she said, softly. 'And believe me, Marit, you need friends. The cartel exists,' Odile said. 'The cartel has always existed. It is because of the cartel that we have become what we are. Because of your grandfather. And they want your grandfather's processes, Marit.'

She swivelled her head. 'No!'

'Marit, listen to me. I've told them about you. I had to tell them. You were asking so many questions and I didn't know what you were getting at. I thought you were investigating something else. I told them you were writing about Bruno Topf's murder.'

Marit looked emptily at Odile. Too numb to feel shock. Thoughts formed in her brain. Her mouth spoke words. 'Bruno Topf was murdered?'

'Yes. The cartel killed him. They found out he was working with the Adler Gemeinschaft.'

Marit closed her eyes, feeling the tears sting behind the closed lids. Oh God, when would it stop! Would the killing and the violence never end?

'And they're sending men for you,' Odile continued. 'They'll be here in a few hours.'

It was useless, Marit thought, sagging against her bonds, feeling the ropes hold her fast to the bed. Everything she'd done had been ineffectual, pathetic, futile. If it was not the Adler Gemeinschaft it was the cartel. If not them, someone else. But always someone stronger, cruder, more ruthless, more violent. She remembered Dwight. Good guys don't win ball games, he had said. There's no point being good and being second. But what was the point of it all if the good guys always lost? Oh Jesus, let them have the bloody processes. Let them take everything as long as they left her alone.

'Don't worry, dearest one. I won't let them take you. I'm going to keep you here and look after you. And together we'll find the processes.'

'Go away, Odile! Leave me alone!'

Odile thrust that crimped, meringue-like face over hers, twisted those carmined lips into a horrible smile. 'In the morning I'll hire the best private investigators in France and have them start looking for the processes. I'll have my lawyers draw up an agreement. Everything will be divided equally between us. Brassards will bear all the costs of finding and developing the processes. You'd like that wouldn't you?'

There was a gruesome streak of lipstick across Odile's tobacco-yellowed front teeth. 'Fuck off, Odile, or go and find a man to teach you how to!' If she made Odile angry, perhaps she'd leave, or perhaps she'd have her beaten again. Marit didn't care. Anything was better than this.

But Odile was in a world of her own. 'The processes will be ours, Marit. Yours and mine. And we'll be together, my darling, for always and always.' Odile lowered her head, her mouth rounding into a soggy, red circle.

Marit twisted her body away. She couldn't stand it, she couldn't bear to think what this obscene woman was trying to do to her. 'Leave me alone, Odile,' she cried, feeling the ropes bite into her wrists and ankles. 'I'm not like you. I don't want to be like you. Go away, please!'

Odile placed her hands on Marit's shoulders and pressed her on to the bed. 'You're lovely, Marit,' she said, 'so lovely.' The words seemed to be torn out of her. She was panting, spraying saliva over Marit as she spoke.

Marit writhed under Odile's desperately searching mouth, under those ceaselessly exploring hands. She pulled furiously at her bonds. 'Leave me alone! Stop it! Go away! Stop – '

Odile's mouth closed over hers, her hands caressed Marit's breasts and thighs, seeming to be everywhere at once. Marit tried to pull her head away, but it was firmly wedged between Odile and the pillow. She struggled, choked.

Suddenly there was the crash of a door being flung open. Odile lifted her head, turned. Francine stood in the doorway, smiling, her left hand resting arrogantly on her hip, her right clasped behind her back.

'Francine! What are you doing here?'

'Spying on you, you despicable old dyke.' In an eerie imitation of Odile's voice, Francine said, 'I'll always be your friend, Marit. You need friends. Tomorrow we will talk to my lawyers. And the processes will be ours, yours and mine. Oh please, let me love you.'

'Go to your room at once, Francine!' Odile Brassard shouted. 'I will speak to you in the morning.'

'No you won't, you revolting cow. You'll speak to *them* in the morning.'

Odile got to her feet, her face, under the rouge and garish lipstick, white. 'What do you mean? What were you really doing in my bedroom, you ungrateful child? What have you done?'

'I called them.'

'You evil, evil girl!' Odile advanced towards Francine.

'Stay where you are!' Francine brought her hand out from behind her back. Clenched in her fist was a small gun. 'Don't come near me, you slut!'

Odile stopped, her mouth working furiously. 'Whom did you call?' she asked, hoarsely. 'America?'

'No, you stupid bitch. I called them.' She pointed the gun momentarily at Marit. 'Her friends. The Adler Gemeinschaft. They're coming for her. And they're coming for you too, Odile. You are going to pay for Bruno Topf's death.'

'You foolish, ungrateful child,' Odile said and advanced unsteadily towards Francine. 'You don't know what you have done.'

'On the contrary, I know exactly what I've done. I've been doing it since I first met you, you miserable fart. Do you think I *liked* lying in your arms? Do you think I liked you making love to me? Do you think I enjoyed your sadistic games? Do you think I enjoyed being chained and beaten? Do you think I liked being blinded?'

'It was an accident,' Odile muttered, tightly. 'We didn't mean to hurt you.' She held out her hand. 'Give me the gun, child.'

Francine stepped back. 'No.'

'I'll let you go,' Odile said, softly. 'I'll find you a place in

Paris. I'll make you an allowance. I'll never see you again. Now give me the gun.'

'No,' Francine said. 'I want to see what they'll do to you and to her.'

'How much are they paying you?' Odile demanded.

Francine laughed. 'They were paying me one thousand francs a month.'

'I'll double it.'

'No,' Francine said again. 'You see, Odile, it's not possible to leave them. Ask Marit, she knows. She knows that the Gemeinschaft is everywhere. That wherever we go they will find us. That we, the children of the damned, have nowhere to run.'

Johann's words! Marit felt her body turn to ice, a solid, unyielding block of ice, immobile, senseless.

Then she heard a rustle of skirt, saw Odile throw herself at Francine, face twisted in anger, eyes filled with madness. 'Thief!' she shouted, 'traitor! Ingrate! Stupid – '

There were three short flat cracks, three yellow-white flashes. Odile wheeled. Marit saw blood gush from an eye socket, stream down her face, mingling preposterously with the rouge and the lipstick. Bright circles of blood gleamed on her chest and stomach. Her mouth sagged open in anger and disbelief. She moved towards the bed, staggered, her eyes staring uncomprehendingly at Marit. Then her eyes seemed to roll up inside her head and she fell forward, slid off the side of the bed and fell heavily on to the floor.

Francine walked into the room, smoke curling from the barrel of the pistol. She stood over Odile and turned her over with her foot. 'The bitch is dead,' Francine announced and looked thoughtfully at Marit. 'I should kill you too,' she said and raised the gun, pointing it at Marit, 'but they have plans for you, traitorous slut!'

36

Dwight hung on to the grab handle as the Citroën bounded along the forest track, and skidded to a stop before the tall, iron gates of the chateau. A guard came out through the narrow entrance beside the gate post, waving a torch.

Pierre lowered the window, allowed the man to shine the torch into his face and into the car. 'Good evening, Jacques. It's me, Pierre Ducret.'

The guard stared blankly at him. 'The party's over. My orders are not to let anyone in.'

Pierre smiled. 'No one but me. I've just picked up a very special friend of Madame Odile's from Orly. She is expecting us.'

'She told me no visitors.'

'This gentleman has just flown in from America,' Pierre said. 'Madame Odile asked me to go out to Orly and meet him, to bring him here after everyone else had left. They have urgent business to discuss.'

Jacques flashed his torch over Dwight. 'No visitors,' he repeated. 'You'll have to come back tomorrow.'

'Don't be ridiculous,' Pierre was saying as Dwight got out of the car and walked round the hood. 'Madame Odile will be very angry with you – '

Dwight stepped in front of the man.

'If she knows that you prevented – '

There was no movement in the guardhouse behind the gatekeeper, no sign of a second guard.

'Your name Jacques?' Dwight asked.

Jacques turned. He was in his mid-fifties, and years of good eating and sitting in the guardhouse had reduced his once muscular body into hunks of fat.

Dwight said, 'I have a letter . . .' He took out his notebook and held it out.

Jacques extended his hand.

Dwight hit him twice, once with the edge of his hand, once with the notebook. Jacques's knees folded under him, his body sagged like a collapsing tent. Dwight waited till he hit the ground, then looked in his pockets for keys and opened the gate.

They raced up the gravel drive without lights. Dwight glimpsed the bulky shadows of a vast building as Pierre edged the car around the side of the house. The chateau was in darkness, except for a faint glow of light behind the drawn curtains of a room on the second floor.

'Odile's awake,' Pierre said. 'That's her bedroom.'

He edged the car around the side of the chateau and stopped at the back. 'I know a way in from here.'

Then they heard it, three faint, unmistakable cracks. Pistol shots.

Together they leapt out of the car, raced along the gravel, heedless of noise. Pierre skidded to a stop before a door, twisted it open. 'Up those stairs and to the right,' he said.

Dwight pushed ahead of Pierre, pounded up the stairs, skidded on the topmost landing. There was a faint rim of light underneath the door to his right. He seized the knob, flung it open, stood in the doorway, momentarily petrified at what he saw.

Marit lay naked, spread out on a bed, wrists and ankles bound to each of the bed posts. At the foot of the bed, a stubby, middle-aged woman lay on her side, blood still welling out of wounds in her eye, chest and stomach. In the middle of the room stood a tawny, sun-tanned young girl, wearing an eye patch and holding a gun.

She turned at the noise of Dwight's entrance, swinging the gun away from Marit to cover him. 'Thank God you've come,' she said.

Dwight felt Pierre press behind him in the doorway, saw the girl's expression change, saw the finger tighten on the trigger, hurled himself sideways. The gun spat flame. He heard Pierre gasp. Then he was launching himself off the floor in a headlong dive at the girl. She turned, but wasn't quick enough to level the gun at him before he crashed into her. She staggered back under the weight of his body, cannoned into the wall. Dwight felt his arms slip round her, felt her gun arm drop to her side, felt himself slide forward.

He braced his arms against the wall for balance, landed on one knee, aware that the girl's gun arm was free, aware that this time she needn't take aim. He reacted instinctively, primitively, pushing himself up at her, swinging his left hand up in a furious angled swipe that had all the weight of his body behind it.

The edge of his hand crashed into the side of her throat. He felt bone crack, heard her strangled gasp. Then he was falling off her, reeling across the room. He cannoned into a table and regained his balance.

The girl was sliding down the wall, an arm raised to her neck, her head lolling at an impossible angle on her shoulder, her eyes staring glassily at Marit. For a moment she seemed to squat before the wall, then her body tilted sideways and she rolled on to the floor, releasing the gun as she fell.

Dwight picked up the gun, raced over to Pierre. He was lying on his back, half in and half out of the room, his arms flung above his head, blood gouting from a huge wound in his throat. The bullet had torn through flesh and ruptured an artery. Pierre was already dead.

Dwight hurried back to the room, took out his Swiss army knife and cut Marit's bonds. She sat on the side of the bed, rubbing her wrists. Dwight put his arms around her. 'Can you walk? Where are your clothes?'

Marit pressed her head into his chest. 'I don't know. I'll try . . . look in the wardrobe.'

Dwight walked across to the wardrobe.

Behind him Marit said, 'There, that's mine.'

He followed her pointing finger, gave her the Cardin shirt and trousers, helped her into them.

'Let's get out of here,' he said.

Marit nodded. 'Yes, there are others coming.'

As soon as she was dressed, he helped her on to the landing, down the stairs, into the car. Without a word he started it, drove it round the side of the chateau and raced up the drive, through the open gates.

All the way to Paris, Dwight listened while Marit talked, forcing himself to think not of what had happened, but why; trying to make himself believe it had happened to someone else, not Marit. When she'd finished, he concentrated on the road, knowing as long as his mind was fixed on something, he wouldn't have to think about the scrawny-legged girl with the eye patch who was now dead.

He'd felt it as soon as his blow had connected, the sweetness of timing, a lethal ease of movement, the perfect kill. His hands shuddered against the wheel. His reaction had been instinctive, a defence against the gun in her hand. But he'd never killed outside a war situation. What the hell was he thinking about? She'd been trying to kill him, hadn't she? She'd killed Pierre. And if that wasn't a war situation, what was? But still he felt the trembling, like a pulse beneath his skin, and the nausea rise in his throat.

He stopped at the Hotel Regis and waited while Marit paid the bill and collected her flight bag. Then he left the car in a side street off the Avenue McMahon, wiped it as clear of fingerprints as he could and took a taxi to Orly.

Their arrival at the Orly Hilton caused little comment. The hotel was used to airline passengers arriving in the small hours of the morning and taking rooms for only a few hours. He'd chosen Orly, because it was near the airport, and tomorrow they would take the first flight to anywhere.

In their room, over sandwiches and coffee and wine and brandy, he told Marit what had happened with Vickery in London, how he had met Pierre at the Regis and driven to the Chateau Brassard. 'He was only double checking that you were all right,' Dwight told Marit.

Marit sighed. 'Poor Pierre.'

The wine slopped out of Dwight's glass. A series of rapid convulsions ran through his body. He couldn't hold the glass, goddammit. He couldn't hold – the glass sprayed wine over the carpet, fell and rolled under the table. His whole body was vibrating. He was like a derelict building by a railroad track where the trains went on forever. He pressed shaking hands to his face, as the bile rose in his throat.

'Darling, what is it?'

Marit's arms were around him, her cheek pressed to his sweaty head.

'Dwight, for God's sake, say something! What's happening?'

She was trying to pull him from the chair, move him to the bed.

'Leave it,' he chattered, through rattling teeth.

'Lie down, darling. I'll get a doctor.'

'No doctor. It'll pass.'

His body shook helplessly in her arms. He buried his face in her and waited, hoping, praying. His body was clammy with sweat, he could hardly breathe. He pushed her away, ran for the bathroom and was sick.

When he came back, wiping his mouth with a towel, Marit asked anxiously, 'Are you all right?'

'I guess so.' He slumped in a chair.

'What is it, darling?'

'Reaction. Most combat veterans suffer from it, one way or another.'

'Talk about it,' Marit said. 'Why here? Why now?'

'The girl,' he said. 'Francine.' He stared vacantly at his hands, those lethal palms with that killing edge. 'I didn't want to do it. I didn't know I was doing it. It was instinctive.'

'She would have killed you,' Marit said, harshly. 'Killed me. You couldn't help it.'

He raised his head and stared at her in surprise.

Later, he didn't know how much later, he said, 'I was

frightened. Ever since I got away from Vickery's people, I was frightened for you.'

She cupped his face in her hands and kissed it.

He ran his hands over hers, kissed them. 'I didn't want to lose you,' he said. 'I couldn't have borne that.'

'We're here,' Marit said. 'We're together. We're safe.'

They waited in silence with their arms around each other, drawing comfort from each other's presence. Finally, Marit asked, 'What are we going to do now?'

'I don't know,' Dwight said. He told her about Vickery's American connection, a connection which had been confirmed by Odile Brassard. 'Government and business,' he said. 'An invincible combination. And there's only the two of us. I don't know anything, except that I am scared. I think we should walk away, Marit. I've never been this scared before.'

'You've never dealt with this kind of problem before,' Marit said. 'All the other times you could fight or shoot your way out. Now, you've got to do it another way. We've got to do it another way.'

'I thought you said – '

'When I was tied to that bed with Odile Brassard groping me, knowing I was helpless, that no one knew or cared where I was or what happened to me, I felt like giving up. But not any more, Dwight. Look at the kind of people they are. Look how they have treated us, how they treat each other. We cannot let them take the processes. Just think what will happen if people like that take over, if they run the world.'

Dwight eased her arms away, stood up and paced about the room. He felt helpless, lost.

'We have to do something, Dwight.'

'Sure, what?'

'Why don't we go to America and find out who runs this cartel?'

Dwight stopped his pacing and looked at her. Her head was raised, her chin pointed towards him, those green eyes were bright with challenge. After all she'd undergone, she wanted to fight. Wrong. She'd become a fighter. He was the one who had lost his *cojones*.

Dwight sat down opposite her, took a cigarette from the pack he'd had brought up for her.

'Smoking's a filthy habit,' she said as she lit it for him.

Dwight coughed and pressed the glowing end of the cigarette against the back of his wrist, watching the hairs singe, keeping his flesh pressed against the burning spark until it turned brown. Then he took it away.

'What the hell are you doing?'

'That's just to remind me of something,' he said. 'Now, tomorrow, we'll fly to Stuttgart. I want Mollwo to find you a lawyer who will get you some kind of writ or injunction to prevent Hoffman selling the processes.'

'Lawyers!' Marit said contemptuously. 'Is that all you're going to do?'

Dwight shook his head. 'Herren must know your grandfather's American connection.'

They caught an early morning flight to Stuttgart, picked up the Porsche and were outside Mollwo's stockade by noon. The old man was delighted to see them, insisted that they partake of an enormous meal of boiled ham, sauerkraut, black bread and cheese and wine.

He listened with barely concealed horror to Dwight's account of his meeting with Vickery, to Marit's more harrowing experiences at the hands of Odile Brassard.

'I told you they're evil,' he said. 'They're evil, vile people.' He told them he'd heard a news broadcast a few hours previously. There had been an accident at the Chateau Brassard, a massive explosion. An entire wing of the chateau had been destroyed and it was feared that Odile Brassard and a number of her guests and servants had died in the explosion.

The cartel, the Gemeinschaft, whoever they were, had been remorselessly efficient, Dwight thought. All traces of what had happened the previous night had been eliminated. He asked Mollwo what he knew about Manninger's American involvement.

'Nothing,' Mollwo said. 'Berndt dealt with America himself.'

Dwight buried his head in his hands. It was hopeless. To trace existing links between corporations frequently took weeks. Even if he went back to America, even if he could raise the help he needed, everything to do with Manninger and the cartel had happened thirty-five years ago. Since then files had been scrapped, documents deliberately or accidentally destroyed. To find Manninger's American connection could take months. And he didn't have months. The bank meeting was on Monday.

'Raison Tearkes,' Marit said.

'What's that?'

'Raison Tearkes,' Marit said again. 'Last night, Odile Brassard asked me if I knew a man named Raison Tearkes. It seemed important to her that I knew him.'

'What's this – '

'There was a Willard Tearkes,' Mollwo said. 'He was the head of the US Styrium Corporation. He worked closely with Berndt.'

'You're sure Odile Brassard asked you about Raison Tearkes, not Willard?' Dwight asked.

'It was definitely Raison,' Marit said. 'I couldn't invent a name like that.'

Mollwo said, 'Willard Tearkes was involved in a big scandal some twenty, twenty-five years ago. I believe he killed himself.'

'But you're sure he worked with Berndt Manninger?'

'I'm sure,' Mollwo said.

Dwight picked up the phone and asked to be put through to the Imtra Bank in Zurich. Like all Swiss banks, the Zurich branch of the Imtra Bank had excellent sources of financial information. Within minutes the manager told Dwight that

Raison Tearkes ran SummiTco, that he'd created SummiTco from the shell of the US Styrite Corporation, that he'd built it into a large conglomerate and converted it into a personal holding company some years previously, and that he'd been involved with Topf Industrie in Russia.

And that wasn't all, the manager continued. The Zurich branch of the Imtra Bank was holding a stack of SummiTco paper. SummiTco was buying gold and selling the dollar short, on margin. And he believed Vickerys and Brassards were doing the same thing.

'I feel as if I've stepped on dogshit and found gold,' Dwight said and asked the manager to have all sixteen branches of the Imtra Bank cable any information they had on SummiTco to him in Washington.

'Washington?' Marit asked nervously when Dwight had finished.

'Yes,' Dwight said. 'The cartel's planning a massive raid against the dollar. I've got to talk to Jeb Anderson. I've got to notify the American government.'

'And the processes?' Marit asked.

'Don't you see, if they're in trouble over this, they couldn't take a chance on anything else. They'll have to let the processes go. They'll have to cancel the meeting.' He went up to her, took her hands in his and kissed her lightly on the forehead. 'Don't worry. I'll get a flight back tomorrow evening.'

37

Dwight reached Washington at eight o'clock that evening, Eastern Standard Time, fighting the urge to stretch cramped limbs and close eyes whose rims seemed lined with specks of burning coal. The Washington branch of the Imtra Bank had sent the coded telexes to his hotel and Dwight spent the next hour de-coding them.

Ten of the banks had no information on SummiTco. Los Angeles said that SummiTco had once wholly financed a motion picture – somehow no one in Los Angeles spoke of films or movies – called 'The Last Enchantress'. New York reported that SummiTco was a prestigious, wealthy and diversified company with an excellent credit rating. Cayman and Nassau, like Zurich, were all holding a lot of SummiTco paper. A little plaintively they enquired if anything had gone wrong.

Not yet, Dwight thought grimly. All three banks had sold dollars and bought gold for SummiTco on margin. All three banks were in countries where it was normal for banks to act as stockbrokers. All three were awaiting SummiTco's instructions to buy large quantities of shares, the following Monday. All three banks confirmed that they would take profits on the gold and dollars that day.

The three Imtra Banks were handling fifteen million dollars' worth of sales and purchases and they all confirmed that other banks in those cities were handling at least equivalent amounts.

Over half a billion dollars, Dwight thought, and that only in cities where the Imtra Bank had been used. What about other cities where there was no Imtra Bank? London? New York? Luxembourg? Only the death of a President and one or two Chiefs of Staff coupled with a European declaration of war on America, could reduce the value of the dollar to an extent sufficient to justify speculation on such a scale. What the devil was going to happen next Monday?

Despite time differences, Dwight called the managers of the Zurich, Cayman and Nassau branches. None of them had any idea of what event was expected to occur the following Monday. Zurich said if it was any help, there were rumours that the Russians were preparing to unload a large shipment of gold, far more than they would need to meet their payments for wheat.

Dwight put the phone down, exhausted. Coincidence or conspiracy? Was Tearkes working with the Russians? Had the cartel's involvement with Soviet Russia gone beyond mere investment? He suddenly remembered his lunatic meeting with Tretiak in London. And that wasn't so lunatic any more. Tearkes *was* working with the Russians. They weren't interested in the processes. The cartel had been worried he would discover their plot against the dollar.

Any time of the day or night, Jeb Anderson had said. Dwight picked up the phone and called him.

At 9.30 the next morning Dwight stood outside the Sheraton-Carlton, beside the brown-uniformed commissionaire and stared to his left down Sixteenth Street to Lafayette Square and the White House. The morning rush had already quietened. Traffic moved easily along Sixteenth Street and the broad pavements on either side of it were deserted.

Last night Jeb Anderson had sounded strained, had been positively angry when Dwight had insisted that he would only see him alone, only meet him at the coffee shop of the Statler Hilton, and then only if he walked there. Dwight sighed with relief as he recognized Anderson's dejected-looking figure dart across H Street and hurry towards him past the restrained edifice of St John's Church. Dwight waited, watching Anderson for a moment. No one had crossed H Street behind him, no one was keeping pace with him on the opposite side of Sixteenth. As he had promised, Anderson was coming alone.

Dwight slipped into the lobby and waited until he saw Anderson's figure hurry past the driveway of the Sheraton-Carlton, then he went out into the street and took Anderson's arm.

Anderson started, turned. 'What the – '

'In here,' Dwight said.

'What the hell kind of game are you playing – you said the Hilton coffee shop.'

The Hilton was further up the street, at the intersection of

Sixteenth and K. Anderson's eyes were angrily fixed on its yellow and brown awnings.

'We're going to talk here,' Dwight said. 'In private, in my room.'

Tight lipped, Anderson allowed himself to be led into the Sheraton-Carlton and followed Dwight up the stairs to his room. He refused a chair and leaned his shoulders against the door. 'All right, Dwight. Now give it to me and give it to me fast. I haven't got a lot of time, and I'm on a terribly short fuse.'

Anderson's eyes were reddened as if he hadn't slept much. There were deep pouches under them, and the flesh beneath his jaws seemed to sag. Despite the neatly-pressed suit and the fresh shirt, he somehow managed to look tousled.

'SummiTco,' Dwight said, sitting down. 'What the hell has SummiTco got to do with the Manninger processes?'

Anderson sighed and shifted irritably against the door. An expression of long-suffering forebearance flitted across his face. 'Is that what all this assing around is about?' He shook his head tiredly. 'We needed an industrial cover. That happens to be SummiTco, right.'

Dwight sat back in his chair and stared at Anderson.

Anderson ran a hand down his face. 'Okay, you didn't know, so you found out. So what's the big deal, Dwight? Haven't you heard of an industrial cover before?'

'Maybe you can tell me why we need an industrial cover.'

'Because of Manninger,' Anderson said. 'Berndt Manninger was part of that industrial-political establishment that supported Hitler's war plans. We, the American government, cannot be seen to deal with his heirs. Just think what would happen in Israel, in New York, if word got out that we were collaborating with Nazis, especially in an election year.'

'If we needed an industrial cover,' Dwight asked, 'why SummiTco?'

Anderson looked quickly at his watch. 'Because

SummiTco is autocratically run. Raison Tearkes doesn't need to get board approval to go after the Manninger processes. That satisfy you, Dwight? Now tell me what are you doing here? Why aren't you in Zurich?'

'It doesn't satisfy me,' Dwight said, ignoring Anderson's questions. 'There are hundreds of independently run companies in America. Why SummiTco?'

'If you must know, the project originated with SummiTco. Tearkes brought it to us.'

'Why?' Dwight asked.

'How the hell would I know why? He was feeling generous. He's a loyal American. Why he did it doesn't matter. The main thing is that he did, the DOE went crazy for it, the Chief felt if he could promise the people a solution to the energy crisis he'd be home and dry and meanwhile over at State they were wetting their pants about this Iraqui-Iranian thing blowing up into a war and cutting off our oil supplies. So everyone wants the Manninger process, right. Does that satisfy you? I'm sorry you weren't told about SummiTco before. But you know the intelligence mind better than I do. And that's it, Dwight. Now, for goodness' sake, get on with why you've brought me here.'

'This is why I've brought you here,' Dwight said. 'To find out if I am working for the government or the greater profits of SummiTco?'

'Don't be absurd. We have an agreement with SummiTco signed and sealed, agreeing to license the processes at a nominal cost to all companies approved by the Department of Trade.'

'So what's Tearkes getting out of it?'

'I don't know, and I don't bloody well care. Have you located the processes?'

'Sam Kamas?' Dwight asked. 'Tell me about him?'

'Kamas works for Tearkes. He used to be with the Agency. The Agency wanted a cut off. If anything went wrong, they wanted SummiTco to carry the can. So, Sam Kamas.'

'You make SummiTco sound like a charitable foundation.

Did any of you guys ask yourselves why Raison Tearkes was doing all this?'

'Suppose you tell me,' Anderson said.

'I believe that at the same time that Manninger secreted the processes, he also hid some files. Files that implicate Raison Tearkes and a few of his buddies like Sir Alex Vickery and the late Odile Brassard.'

'Okay, so Tearkes wants the files. He can have them.'

'Those files implicate governments. They could be more valuable than the processes to someone who is prepared to use them.'

'And those files, if they deal with governments at all, deal with governments of thirty-five years ago. No one can use them to blackmail this government.'

'So why does Tearkes want them?'

Anderson sighed, walked into the room and sat down. 'Okay,' he said, 'let me tell you. You know about Germany's post-war economic miracle. What you may not know, is that after the First World War, there was another economic miracle. By the 1930s, Germany was technologically light years ahead of any other country in the world. In synthetic oil, fertilizer, dyestuffs, sulpha drugs, atabrine, optical glass, photographic materials. You name it, the Germans had it and we needed it. American companies worked hand in glove with the Germans and even after the German invasion of Poland, it was vital that they continued to do so.'

'And during the war?'

'That was necessary. Raison Tearkes worked for the OSS. Part of his job was to keep in touch with his industrialist counterparts in Germany. Contacts such as that provided us with vital intelligence about the state of the German economy, but they also provided us with information on Germany's industrial secrets. And the men who undertook to maintain those contacts, were patriots, Dwight, true patriots. They loved their countries so much, they took the risk of being branded as traitors. Raison Tearkes was one of those men. So if he wants the files implicating him in those manoeuvres, he gets them.'

'Tearkes is no patriot,' Dwight said. 'Tearkes wants those files for another reason.' Dwight paused and studied Anderson's tired countenance closely. Anderson had been irritable, Anderson had been harried, but he had not so far kept anything from Dwight. Dwight decided to chance it. 'What would you say,' he asked, 'if I told you that Raison Tearkes, patriot and double agent, was trying to screw the dollar into the ground?'

Anderson's look of surprise was followed by a sharp intensity. 'How do you know that?' he asked.

Dwight handed him de-coded transcripts of the telexes.

Anderson read them carefully, then looked up at Dwight, all traces of tiredness and irritability gone. 'How did you get involved in this?'

'Coincidence,' Dwight said. He told Anderson everything that had happened since he'd left for Zurich ten days previously, told him of his encounter with Tretiak and of the cartel's involvement in Russia.

Anderson picked up the de-coded cables. 'Mind if I keep these? I'd like to show them to the Treasury.' He ran his hands tiredly along his face. 'I don't know if with all your moving around, you've had time to read any newspapers. Over the past few days the dollar has taken a hell of a bashing, and our friends in the Mid-East could well refuse to take dollars for their oil.'

Dwight asked, 'So what are you going to do now?'

Anderson sighed. 'I don't know if we can do anything. There is nothing illegal about speculating against the dollar. Unless we can prove Tearkes is in cahoots with the Russians, we're stuck.'

'I suppose I'll have to find the Manninger files,' Dwight said, 'and blackmail Tearkes.'

'You do that, Dwight. I'll arrange to be in Zurich over the weekend. If we're going to save the dollar, we'll need the Swiss.'

He walked across the room and placed his hands on Dwight's shoulders. 'And I'm going to put that thank you sign in neon over the White House,' he grinned.

It was already Thursday afternoon in Hellenthal and Marit sat in the small office in Mollwo's sawmill, the bible and photograph album spread out on Mollwo's desk. Herbal poultices had done wonders for her wounds. Her stomach and thighs were now a dark mass of bruises that felt stiff but gave no constant pain. Already healing scabs were forming around her wrists and ankles.

That morning, Mollwo had accompanied her to Stuttgart, introduced her to the son of a friend, Dr Arne Becker, a partner in a large firm of corporate lawyers. Marit had been relieved that Becker was too young for the name Manninger to mean anything. He was brisk and gave an impression of great efficiency and made scrupulous notes as Marit talked.

Her problem raised interesting legal questions, he said when she'd finished. Usually, inheritances were distributed under the law of the country in which the assets were situated or where the deceased was resident. In this case it appeared that the assets, if they existed, were in one country, the deceased in another. It would take considerable time and considerable expense to decide which country's laws applied.

Normally, Becker had continued, estates had to be distributed under the exact terms of the will. But recently, courts had taken to adjudicating on the reasonableness of a deceased's wishes, and in many instances, the courts had held that when the deceased's requirements were unreasonable they should be set aside.

This could be one of those cases, Becker had said. If the documents evidencing the title could not be found, if it was unreasonable to expect that they could be found, then the courts would set aside this aspect of Berndt Manninger's will and order that his only living descendant be entitled to the estate without producing proof of ownership. Becker had gone on to emphasize that this was only a likely outcome, that there would be no certainty until the matter came to trial.

Meanwhile, he advised her to seek an amicable compromise with the bank, and wrote a letter on her behalf setting out the basis of her claim, and warning the Hoffman Bank, that any attempt to dispose of Berndt Manninger's directly or indirectly owned property would be strongly opposed, and if necessary a court order obtained to restrain them. Becker assured Marit that the letter would give her enough time to find the evidence of ownership that was necessary, or to arrive at a settlement with the bank. If litigation became necessary, he advised she should commence action in Switzerland and gave her the name of a firm of Swiss lawyers.

Marit turned over the pages of the bible, studying each page carefully for a note in the margin or a sidelined passage that might be relevant to Manninger's legacy. She could smell the food from the large room at the back, where one of Mollwo's sons was preparing dinner. They were looking after her like a queen, refusing to allow her to cook or clean or help about the mill in any way. She heard the giant mechanical saw stutter to a stop, the ensuing silence punctuated by the drum of Mollwo's boots as he walked across the building to the office.

'Found anything yet?' he enquired, placing a glass of white wine on the desk.

'I've been through it twice. There's nothing except the writing on the fly leaf, and that doesn't make sense.'

Mollwo sipped at the glass of wine he carried in his calloused hand. 'Berndt was always very logical,' he said. 'He wouldn't have left these with me, unless they had some significance.'

Marit turned over the pages of the bible, holding each page between thumb and forefinger, scanning each page quickly, moving from back to front.

'There's nothing here,' she said, 'nothing, nothing, nothing. Perhaps we're on completely the wrong trail. Maybe all these have is sentimental value.'

'It's possible,' Mollwo admitted, and sat down, watching her turn the pages.

'Did my grandfather collect bibles?' Marit asked.

'Not as far as I know. He had no hobbies outside his work.'

Marit turned the last few pages quickly, snapped the bible shut, paused frowning, at the memory of something vaguely inconsistent. Something was wrong with that bible. She could *feel* it. She'd *felt* it. It was there between the tips of her fingers, the feel of a page.

Slowly she opened the bible, turned back the pages from the third chapter of Genesis. Yes, she felt it again, a difference in the paper. The title page felt different from the rest.

Slowly she ran the tips of her fingers along it, along the next three pages. There was no doubt of it. The title page had been printed on different paper.

She looked at it carefully. The paper was yellowed like the others, but less so and it definitely felt smoother to the touch. The printing looked similar though. She peered closely at the binding. The title page had been inserted separately from the rest.

So there could have been an accident, the binding may have split. The insertion might have been made, not by Manninger, but by some previous owner. She peered at the page with its large Gothic printing, 'The Holy Bible containing the Old and New Testaments, translated out of the original tongues.' That was as it should be. Her eyes roved down the page. The bible had been printed by one Johannes Bruckner in Geneva.

Geneva! But this was a German bible, and at the time it had been printed, Geneva had been part of France, not Switzerland. Then as now, the main language of the canton of Geneva had been French, not German. This bible could never have been printed in Geneva.

Excitedly Marit asked Mollwo if he had a street directory of Geneva. He returned with a map and Marit saw that the address of Johannes Bruckner still existed. She picked up the telephone, called directory enquiries, asked for the phone number of Bruckner's at the address. When she'd got it, she called.

A mellifluous voice answered in French, 'Jacob Bruckner, *privatbankiers.*'

'Thanks,' Marit breathed into the phone. 'A million thanks.'

Marit reached Geneva three hours later and took a taxi to the address given on the title page of the bible. As he had agreed Jacob Bruckner was there to meet her. He took her upstairs to an empty boardroom.

'I have come concerning account number M459L4813 opened in February 1945 by Berndt Manninger,' Marit said formally. She showed Bruckner the bible.

No further questions were asked. No further questions were necessary.

Bruckner took the envelope away and returned a few minutes later. He handed her a bank statement showing a sum slightly in excess of a quarter of a million francs. 'You may withdraw it, if you wish,' he said.

Marit said she would leave the money there.

He gave her a small packet. Inside was a map of the Grissons. Nothing was marked on it, nothing written on the envelope containing it. The only thing of any significance, she noticed, was that the map had been printed in March 1936.

When she got to Zurich, she found Mollwo at the Hotel Bellevue with the Porsche. He was relieved to see her and told her he'd been able to talk to Dwight before he left Washington and divert him to Zurich.

38

Dwight emerged bleary-eyed into the bright, early morning freshness of the Arrivals area at Kloten. He'd got a flight the previous afternoon from Dulles, but with time differences it was already breakfast time in Zurich. The flight hadn't been full and he'd been able to grab some sleep, but he felt creased and confused and fuzzy-headed, his body clock insisting it was two o'clock in the morning, perhaps.

At the Bellevue he took the stairs two at a time to a room, knocked lightly on the door. 'Marit, it's me, Dwight,' hearing her footsteps patter across the boarded floor, the clank of a bolt being drawn back. He wanted to beat on the door in his impatience, lift it off its hinges. Then the door was open and she was standing there. Marit! He was nearly suffocating with excitement. Marit. His heart, dammit, was going like a trip-hammer. Hi, kiddo. He couldn't bring out the words. He shrugged and held his arms out helplessly, then she folded into them and buried her face in his shoulder, and he kissed the top of her head and kicked his flight bag into the room.

Her. Marit. Her shoulders against his arm, her body beneath his hands, her fingers twisting the back of his jacket. The silly girl was crying – he yanked her face upwards, saw the relief and the happiness and the wonder in the misty grey-green behind those trembling tears. He kissed her. Her mouth stiffened, broke in a stifled sob, then she was kissing him too, her mouth warm, soft, alive and he knew they were together, that he had come home.

Afterwards, while he showered, she called Mollwo and ordered breakfast. They ate and told each other what had happened, and Dwight couldn't keep his eyes off her or stop himself touching her. Then they talked about what they should do and decided that first of all they should give a copy of Dr Becker's letter to Gerhardt Hoffman.

They called the bank and checked that Hoffman was in, got to the bank shortly before ten o'clock. Dwight smiled cheerfully at the commissionaire, went and stood in line, till he had worked out the pattern of the elevators. Then avoiding Hoffman's matronly appointments secretary, he suddenly broke from the line, walked quickly to the elevator and went up to the third floor. He led Marit along the carpeted corridor to Hoffman's office, knocked and in response to the gruff *Herein*, opened the door.

Hoffman's eyes bulged and took on the look of red veined marbles. His face turned a choleric magenta. Before Hoffman could say anything, Dwight pushed Marit through, shut the door and leaned against it. 'This won't take long,' he said.

He nodded to Marit who walked across and placed Dr Becker's letter on Hoffman's desk. Hoffman stared angrily from the letter to Marit to Dwight.

'Once you've read that, we'll go,' Dwight said.

Hoffman placed two thick white fingers on the envelope and drew it towards him, distastefully. He was less than his usual suave self today and there was a carelessly-shaved patch beneath his nostrils. He tore open the envelope with a snap and crumpled it noisily in his hand while he read. His jaw tightened. He looked up balefully at Dwight, then at Marit. 'This letter has no legal significance,' he said and pushed it contemptuously across the desk with a flick of his hand.

'What the hell do you mean, no legal significance? That letter clearly sets out Fraulein von Rausenberg's claim. If you do not voluntarily agree to cancel the proposed sale of the Manninger companies, we will get a court order forbidding you to proceed with the sale.'

'I understand that,' Hoffman said, quickly. 'I understand exactly what you are trying to do. But the point is not whether your legal procedures would be effective, but whether Dr Becker should be writing this letter on behalf of Fraulein von

Rausenberg. The point is whether Fraulein von Rausenberg has a valid claim to the Manninger estate.'

'Fraulein von Rausenberg is Berndt Manninger's granddaughter, his only living descendant.'

Hoffman steepled his hands in front of his face. 'There seems to be some doubt about that?'

'What doubt?' Marit snapped. 'Has another descendant of my grandfather's been found?'

'No,' Hoffman said, now staring closely at his steepled fingers. 'Nothing like that. But we have reason to doubt that you are Berndt Manninger's granddaughter.'

'Don't be absurd! My mother was Ingrid Manninger. My father was Paul von Rausenberg. They were married in La Plata in February 1955.'

'We have been reliably informed that your mother was not Ingrid Manninger, but one Ingrid Muller.'

'Ingrid Muller! That was the name under which my mother was taken to Argentina. Surely you must understand the reasons for that. It was the end of the war. Germany was defeated. Manninger was a well-known name. It was necessary to – '

'According to evidence I have seen, Ingrid Manninger died at Ravensbruck on the 27th February 1945.'

'Evidence from the same reliable sources, I suppose! Those documents were forgeries, necessary for my mother's escape. I have seen an order for Ingrid Manninger's release from Ravensbruck and an exit permit allowing her to leave Germany dated 12th April 1945.'

'You have these documents?' Hoffman asked, indifferently. 'No.'

Hoffman shrugged helplessly. 'Then, there is nothing I can do.'

'But my mother was Ingrid Manninger,' Marit burst out. 'Everyone knew she was Ingrid Manninger. Berndt Manninger was my grandfather. From the time I was a child, I knew about the Manninger inheritance and that one day I would inherit it.'

'Opinions, hearsay, rumour,' Hoffman said. 'Not a single fact. If you want me to accept this letter from Dr Becker, you must first prove to me that you are Ingrid Manninger's daughter.'

'But how can I? If I bring anyone here who knew my mother you would say that all they knew was what she'd told them, and that isn't proof. How can I find proof?'

'It is not for me to tell you what you have to do,' Hoffman said, sanctimoniously. 'You could start with the records at Ravensbruck and perhaps the Immigration Office in Argentina.'

'But that would take ages!' Marit cried. 'Before I've even begun, you would have sold the companies.'

'That,' Hoffman said, cruelly, 'is a possibility.'

'I'd better talk to Johann,' Marit said. They were back in the hotel room, Marit seated erect on the bed, Mollwo looking unusually helpless perched at the foot of it, and Dwight straddled across a chair, opposite them. Marit explained that in order to prevent discovery by the Allies, records of Ingrid Manninger's death at Ravensbruck had been forged, and she had been taken to Argentina under the name of Muller. Proof of Ingrid Manninger's identity was in Argentina. Johann and the Gemeinschaft had it. 'Either someone's found the false documents or Johann's trying to tell me I can't get the processes without the Gemeinschaft. In either case, I have to talk to him.'

'No,' Dwight said.

'Why not?'

'Because if he passed the false information to Hoffman, that's exactly what he'll be expecting. Let him sweat. Let's not make a deal until we have to, and if we have to make a deal, let's make sure he doesn't have too much time to argue.'

'I still think I should see Johann now,' Marit said. 'You two can come with me, if you're worried they'll kidnap me.'

'Remember one thing, Marit,' Dwight said. 'Johann wants

those processes far more than you do. When it gets nearer to sale time, he's going to come looking for you. He's going to want to make a deal.'

'I don't know,' Marit said. 'Johann is unpredictable and obsessive. If he's thwarted, he may substitute his obsession for the processes with an obsession for revenge.'

'We have three days to find the processes and the *Zessions*,' Dwight said. 'Without them, there's no point in deals with anyone. Besides,' he added, in order to convince Marit, 'we may be lucky and find that the *Zessions* are made out to bearer. Which means that anyone who possesses them, becomes the owner of the companies; which means that anyone who possesses them can turn up at the meeting and object to the sale of the companies.'

'You're forgetting the will, Dwight. Under the will, only a direct descendant of Berndt Manninger can inherit.'

'Okay, so when the time comes to inherit, we'll talk to Johann, or we'll subpoena him to produce the evidence. But the important thing right now is to stop the cartel. To find the processes.' As if that determined the matter he got up and walked to the breakfast table. 'Where's that map you got from the Bruckner Bank, the bible and the photograph album?'

For two hours they pored over the bible and the stamp album, pored over the map Manninger had left of the Grissons, that vast area of straggling, snow-capped mountains that spread over three thousand square miles of Switzerland. The map was unmarked, and while the figures on the fly leaf of the bible could have been map references, they did not tally with this particular map.

'Perhaps Berndt Manninger left something else with the Bruckner Bank,' Dwight suggested.

Marit said, 'Jacob Bruckner was positive that all my grandfather left was the money and this map.'

'Perhaps somewhere there is another map,' Mollwo said.

The three of them studied the map again. Somewhere amongst those thousands of square miles of rugged mountains and silvery alpine lakes, somewhere amongst those valleys threaded with twisting passes and tumbling rivers, somewhere in that area where Romansch and esoteric Italian dialects were still spoken, lay the Manninger inheritance.

'Skiing,' Dwight said, suddenly. Davos, St Moritz, Klosters, Arosa, these were the only names that were familiar to him.

'Berndt was fond of skiing,' Mollwo said. 'But no German took skiing holidays in Switzerland during the war.'

Dwight asked, 'But he skied in Switzerland before the war?'

'Yes. Almost every year.'

'Perhaps he made a friend there, someone he trusted.'

'As far as I can recall,' Mollwo said, 'Berndt went to a different resort every year.'

'1936,' Marit said. 'Where did he go in 1936? The map is dated 1936. That must be the clue.' She was already opening the photograph album, rapidly turning its pages. 'Here,' she cried, pointing to a photograph of Manninger and two other men standing outside a hotel. Manninger and one of the others wore the baggy trousers, calf length socks, ungainly caps and bulky jerkins fashionable at the time. They were leaning forward on their ski poles and between them was a man in evening dress, smiling embarrassedly at the camera. The name of the hotel was clear in the background. The Hotel Waldhaus.

'It's in Davos,' Dwight said. 'I skied there three years ago.' He turned to Mollwo. 'Do you recognize the other men?'

'The other man on skis is Willi Frisch, Berndt's accountant. He was killed in the bombing raid over Ludwigshafen soon after Berndt's death. I don't recognize the man in evening dress.'

'From what he's wearing,' Marit said, 'I would imagine he was the owner of the hotel, or worked there.'

They lapsed into silence, relieved that they had found the answer. In February 1945, Berndt Manninger had left Germany to settle his affairs. He hadn't trusted the Hoffmans, he'd needed someone he did trust outside Germany. Who better than an inn keeper whom he knew, who could be relied on to keep a packet of documents until Berndt returned after the war.

'Let's go to Davos,' Marit said.

39

They reached the Hotel Waldhaus in time for a late lunch. It had not changed much since Berndt Manninger had stayed there. A wood and glass exterior had been added, the basement converted from a wine cellar to a disco and a neon sign had replaced the old Gothic lettering. There was no sign however of the man in evening dress who had been photographed with Manninger.

Midway through lunch, Mollwo asked to speak to the owner, and a few minutes later, a tall, pasty-faced man wearing striped trousers behind a chef's apron came up to the table. He was about forty, with signs of grey in his thick, brown hair. Dwight looked in vain for a resemblance to the man in the photograph.

'Anything wrong?' the owner asked.

'Everything's fine,' Mollwo said. He showed the owner the photograph. 'We're trying to check when this photograph was taken, if anyone here remembers this man.' He pointed at Berndt Manninger.

The owner took the photograph and looked closely at it. 'This was taken many years ago,' he said. He placed the photograph on the table, his finger on the man in evening dress. 'That is my father.'

Is, not was, Dwight thought. The owner's father was still alive. 'Is it possible to talk to your father about this?' Dwight asked.

The owner looked across the room at a clock on the wall.

'He usually has a sleep about this time. If you care to wait, I'll ask him to talk to you.'

Two hours later, they sat in the restaurant, lingering over coffee, the only guests. At a table in the far corner, the owner ate with the kitchen staff. Suddenly he looked up and walked to the door, leading a man of about seventy to where Dwight and the others sat. The man was the person who had been photographed with Manninger, wearing a neat, dark suit and leaning heavily on a cane as he walked. His son led him up to the table and introduced him, drew up a chair for him and went back to his meal.

Mollwo showed him the photograph, asked him what he would like to drink. The old man ordered wine and mineral water, held the photograph close to his eyes. 'It was taken many years ago,' he said. 'I had more hair then and fewer wrinkles.'

They all smiled politely. 'Do you know when that photograph was taken?' Mollwo asked. 'Do you know who the people with you were?'

'It was taken many years ago,' the old man said, 'and we have had many guests. A lot of them like to take pictures like this. I am sorry, I don't remember.'

'Does the name Berndt Manninger mean anything to you?' Mollwo asked.

The old man frowned. 'Manninger ... Manninger. Oh yes, of course. Wasn't he the German businessman. I recall he stayed here once. Yes, of course, that is Berndt Manninger. I don't remember the other man, though.'

'Do you remember when Berndt Manninger stayed here?'

The old man screwed up his face in concentration. 'It was before the war,' he said. 'Sometime before the war. After the war few Germans could afford to come here. Yes, definitely, before the war.'

'1936?' Marit asked.

'I couldn't be sure,' the old man said. He sipped his wine and water. 'If it is important, I can look in the old registers, that is, if my son hasn't destroyed them.'

'Did Berndt Manninger come here regularly?' Mollwo asked.

'Regularly? Let me see now. Once, definitely. Perhaps twice, perhaps not.'

'But this is the only time you met Berndt Manninger?'

'I only met him when he stayed here.'

'And you did not meet him after this picture was taken? You did not meet him in 1945?'

'1945! We had no German visitors then. It was the war. I remember, there were only a few lifts open. In 1945 it was only the Swiss who skied here.'

'Berndt Manninger may not have come to ski,' Dwight said. 'He might have been escaping from the Nazis.'

'No one like that came here,' the old man said.

'Did Berndt Manninger ever leave anything with you, or with anyone else in this hotel?'

'No,' the old man said. 'Why would he do that? And, if he'd left anything behind, we would have posted it back to his address. We were always particular about things like that.'

'I'm sure you were,' Dwight said.

They sat round a table at the Café Sport, the map, the bible and the photograph album spread out before them. Patiently they studied Manninger's holiday photographs. Apart from the photograph taken outside the Hotel Waldhaus, few places were clearly identifiable, and those that were, not precise enough. Then they checked the locations of the other photographs. None of the places they identified were anywhere near the Grissons. They looked at the map, they turned over the pages of the bible. They looked at the photographs again. Nearly two hours and innumerable cups of coffee later, they had to admit defeat. Berndt Manninger's secrets were buried forever.

Dwight closed his eyes in weariness and thought for a while about Manninger. The image of a mud-spattered red Duesenberg flickered through his mind.

Manninger had left Germany on the 21st February, two days before his meeting with the Hoffman Bank and the Allied agents in Zurich. Two days before . . . a mud-stained car . . . Manninger obviously had not visited Switzerland solely for meeting with his bankers and the Allied agents. Manninger had gone somewhere else in Switzerland, about a day's journey from Zurich over snow-packed winter roads. The Grissons. Here.

Zurich is not the source. The source is Hellenthal. And the scriptures, the devil in the scriptures. What had Manninger meant? Zurich is not the source. That was obvious. Whatever he had was not with the Hoffmans. The source is Hellenthal? Had Manninger collected the processes, the files and the founders certificate from the Hoffmans or someone else in Switzerland and taken them back to his house in Hellenthal? No, that was absurd. Germany in February 1945 was no place for those secrets. He would not have taken them back to Germany for fear of being stopped at the border. So Manninger had gone somewhere in Switzerland, seen someone.

And the scriptures. So, he meant the bible. The devil in the scriptures? What could he have meant by that? A curse on his enemies? A clue to his heirs?

'Was Berndt Manninger a religious man?' Dwight asked Mollwo.

Mollwo finished stuffing his pipe with tobacco and pressed the tobacco down into the bowl with stubby fingers. 'His father was very religious, High Church. But Berndt went to church only when it was necessary. He once told me he'd attended enough services as a child for anyone's lifetime.'

'Where was he educated?'

Mollwo got his pipe going and puffed smoke contentedly. 'Now there's something interesting. Berndt received his early education at a Catholic school. It was run by a small Catholic Order.'

'What was the Order?' Marit asked.

'I don't remember. I know they were not Dominicans or Benedictines or any Order that is well known.'

'Why was he educated there, if his father was High Church?'

'Money,' Mollwo said. 'Old Manninger was a book keeper at Krupp. He could not afford to send his son to a good school. Berndt only went to the Catholic school because he won a scholarship.'

'But he was not a Catholic?'

Mollwo smiled. 'Berndt told me he'd put his religion down as Catholic on the application form. The monks were astounded when they discovered that he was not a Catholic. But he did so well in the scholarship papers, that they felt it would be wrong to deny him the opportunity. So they took him.'

'Did he ever talk about his school days to you? Was he happy at the school?'

'I think so, but I don't recall him ever attending prizegivings or anything like that. Sometimes he sent them money.'

'Does the school still exist?'

Mollwo shook his head. 'It was bombed during the war. The monks disappeared. I don't believe they ever returned.'

Dwight remembered the old Jesuit saying, give me a boy till he is seven . . . had Manninger been a secret Catholic? Had Manninger taken his secrets to the monks? But the school was in Essen and had been bombed. The monks had disappeared. And Berndt Manninger had not been especially religious. But religion had been instilled into him. He had married Sophie in church. Dieter and Ingrid had been christened. At the customary times in his family life, he had turned to the church. What about in a crisis? Whom had he gone to when he'd heard of Dieter's death?

Dwight asked Mollwo the question.

'He went away. For two, three weeks, something like that. And when he came back he was different. Quieter, more controlled, as if what had happened to Dieter had been accepted, placed in perspective. It was then he went to live in Hellenthal. That was when he started working on his new processes.'

'Do you know where he went in those four weeks?'

Mollwo was smiling now. 'Bernard Menz. I remember, sometime after Berndt went to Hellenthal, I had to authorize a payment of seventy thousand Reichsmarks to the Order of St Ulrich. I remember asking Berndt about it, because the payee was so unusual and I didn't know there was a St Ulrich.

'Berndt told me that Ulrich was a little-known German saint, who lived about the sixteenth century, a strange combination of preacher and recluse.

'When I asked Berndt the reason for the payment, he told me he'd been approached by an old school friend, Bernard Menz, who was now a monk in that Order. They had a monastery near here.' Mollwo looked at them , his eyes bright with excitement. 'Near Zernez.'

'There could be no safer place to hide something than a monastery,' Marit said.

Dwight looked at both of them, smiling. 'Well, what are we waiting for? Let's go.'

Mollwo looked at his watch and said, 'No. It's about an hour and a half from here and it's starting to snow. We'd better go there tomorrow morning.'

They decided not to stay in Davos, to find somewhere more secluded. They left the Café Sport and drove towards Zernez.

A few minutes later, a green Peugeot moved quietly out of a car park a few yards away from the Café Sport, drove quietly through the town and took the twisting road to Zernez.

Half-way across the bare saddle of the Fluela Pass, they came across a desolate Gasthof, a tall, wooden, barn-like building with shuttered windows and an empty wooden balcony. It was situated just off the road in the middle of a corner, and there was a good view of the traffic coming down the pass and the small town at the foot of it. Around it, the snow-covered hills were devoid of buildings.

'It's closed,' Marit said with disappointment as they pulled off the road into its gravelled courtyard.

Mollwo struggled to get out of the car. 'Leave this to me,' he said confidently, striding towards the back of the Gasthof. 'Sometimes they take visitors in summer.'

And they did.

They left for the monastery after breakfast the next morning. The monastery was marked on Manninger's 1936 map of the Grissons by a tiny cross on a mountain peak beyond Zernez. Mollwo, in his tweed, leather-patched jacket, warned them it would be cold, that they would be up near the snowline. Dwight had been on mountains in summer before, where the sun only softened the upper layers of crusted snow. He said they'd be all right if they didn't have to walk too far and looked again at the map. The road to the monastery was a wavy blue line, if it still existed, if it wasn't blocked by snow, if it was a road.

Despite being mid-summer, a damp, chill mist hung over the pass, transforming the steep, winding turns into opaque emptiness, blotting out the mountains above and the valley below. Marit drove, wipers scrubbing against the screen, headlights reflecting spirals of grey damp. They wound slowly down the pass to the bare valley of the Susasca, through woods and across an ancient stone bridge to the little village of Susch. They were travelling in a vacuum, isolated by mist, glass and steel from the terrain they were moving through. They spoke little, each of them rapt in their own thoughts, lulled by the steady drone of the engine and the constant, gentle movement. Other vehicles swept up the pass, headlights glowing a murky yellow, damp, live shadows looming through the mist.

They pottered through Zernez at the bottom of the valley where the mist was trapped and thicker. The stone of buildings gleamed damply and the roofs of buildings jutted, seemingly suspended on cloud. Dwight asked Marit to stop, walked through the clammy moistness and returned with two parkas and a detailed map of the area.

'What do you want another map for?' Marit asked as they drove on.

'Makes it easier,' Dwight said, but that was not the only reason. If Manninger had only skied in the Grissons, he only knew certain resorts well, not the whole area. If he had been wandering around, hiding things, he would have needed a more detailed map.

Dwight looked at the map he had bought. The monastery was clearly shown, depicted by a little church, and the turn-off to the mountain was clearly marked, between Zernez and Brail. The road was shown in yellow, the turns clearly marked and it ran all the way to the monastery, which was on a mountain appropriately called Piz Christian.

As they drove, the mist thinned. They found the turn-off without difficulty and began to climb past farms and empty pastures. The road was a mixture of asphalt and mud, where the hard surface had been broken by neglect and weather. The car bounced along the uneven surface and from time to time snaked through patches of mud. Marit handled the car skilfully, driving out of the skids without losing momentum, sometimes using the loss of traction to steer the car into a turn. When they reached the trees, the mixture of mud and leaves made the driving more difficult, the slides more frequent. Marit experienced wheel-spin, the car shuddering and twisting as if it would turn about on itself. Their headlamps scythed through the gloom, illuminating trees packed closely together, interspersed with columns of mist. The atmosphere grew oppressive and ominous as they struggled upwards, the sound of the straining engine filling their ears, their bodies lurching with the movement of the car.

They began to drive over patches of crusty snow, stained with mud. For no discernible reason the track became easier, climbing straight through the trees, the road surface good. They crested the brow of the rise, cleared the mist and were surrounded by snow, the track running white and smooth ahead of them flanked by gentle, white hills.

The car began to slip beneath them, an insidious twisting movement that brought them almost to a standstill. Somehow, Marit kept going, with roaring engine and madly-churning wheels. Dollops of wet snow smacked against the large rear window, momentarily darkening the inside of the car until Marit got the massive rear wiper going. Desperately she struggled for momentum, inching the car forward until they reached a small incline and began to move more easily. She kept the car going fast into the dip, skidded it up the rise afterwards, slid it round a corner and up another hill, until beneath the shadow of the peak, they stopped.

On one side the mountain fell steeply away. On the other it sloped gently over a wide expanse, then soared magnificently upwards to a peak with a massive rock-strewn summit.

On the slope, where the monastery should have been, there was nothing. They got out of the car, pulled on their anoraks and walked along the slope. Dwight felt the snow cold and powdery, rise over his shoes and the bottoms of his trousers. They'd come to the wrong place, he thought, before he heard Mollwo's shout and lumbered through the thigh-deep snow to where Mollwo stood on a small rise.

Rubble. When he got to where Mollwo stood, he could see that Mollwo was perched on a mound of brick and mortar. Below them fragments of brick and plaster peeped through the snow and the remnants of a wall stood, barely distinguishable against the all pervading whiteness.

The monastery had been abandoned, destroyed. Whatever Manninger had left here was lost forever.

Mollwo pointed at the massive peak, its angry sides piled high with snow jutting out over the valley.

'An avalanche,' Mollwo said. 'That's what happened here.'

Despondently they plodded back to the car, helped Marit turn it round. They took off wet shoes and socks, rolled up damp trouser legs and drove back down the mountain.

The journey back was easier, the only risk that of sliding off the road. Dwight took out the number of the Basle bank account and checked it against the map. No, that wasn't a map reference. M459L4813. What was the significance of that number? Those initials? Manninger had opened the account before banks had used computers. He could have chosen any combination of figures and letters that he would have wanted. Why these? Why the initials M and L?

M for Manninger, that was obvious. But L? His first wife was Sophie, his children were Dieter and Ingrid, his second wife, Elisabeth. Dwight turned and asked Mollwo if Elisabeth Manninger had ever been known as Liz.

Mollwo looked surprised. 'Certainly not,' he said.

'But why did Manninger choose the letter L? Did he have a girl-friend, someone else he cared deeply about?'

'No one whose name began with an L,' Mollwo said.

They reached the open snow field before the forest. Dwight tried to visualize himself in Manninger's place, a man moving in a hurry, leaving a trail for people he did not know. Manninger had left the bank account number in the scrap book. He'd left a map. What if the numbers on the fly leaf of the bible were map references and the number in the scrap book, a biblical reference?

'Stop!' Dwight shouted.

Startled, Marit braked harshly, the car swinging round in a swift semi-circle.

'What's happened?' Marit asked, anger covering her nervousness.

'The bible.' Dwight said turning round to Mollwo, 'pass me the bible.'

He took the heavy book on to his lap and looked. M for Matthew, M for Mark, L for Luke. Matthew, chapter four, paragraphs five to nine. 'Then the devil taketh him up to the Holy City and sitteth him on a pinnacle of the temple, and sayeth unto him, if thou be the Son of God, cast thyself down: for it is written, he shall give his angels charge concerning thee: and in their hands they shall bear thee up, lest at any time thou dash thy foot against a stone.'

Dwight skimmed the rest of the passage and turned to Mark. The parable of the sower and the seed ending with he that hath ears to hear, let him hear. Dwight turned to Luke. The same incident as Matthew, the temptation of Christ by the devil.

The source is Hellenthal and the devil in the scriptures! Manninger had left a message. But what message? Casting people down, the kingdoms of the world, if thou shalt worship me? Had Manninger sold his soul to the devil? No, the message had to be something else. Matthew had said the devil had taken Christ up to an exceedingly high mountain and shown him all the kingdoms of the world. Luke also referred to a high mountain and all the kingdoms of the world. The devil, mountain, kingdoms.

He passed the bible to Marit. Mollwo read the passages over her shoulder. The devil, mountains, kingdoms. The kingdoms were obviously the processes. Who was the devil? And what was the mountain?

'It's over there,' Mollwo said, pointing across the valley.

Dwight and Marit looked out of the car window at a jagged range of snow-covered mountain peaks, little different from the mountain they had already climbed.

'The Piz del Diavel,' Mollwo said. 'The Devil's Peak. Many years ago there used to be a monastery there. It too was destroyed in an avalanche. But there is an ancient burial ground. I don't believe anyone has climbed that peak for years.'

'Not since 1945,' Dwight said with sudden certainty. The Devil's Peak was where Manninger had hidden everything.

40

They spent the afternoon hiring equipment for the climb,
clothes, boots, snow shoes and skis. The climb was not
difficult, they were told. There was an old trail that led to
within a thousand feet of the summit, where there had once
been a monastery. They wouldn't need ropes or pitons, unless
they were going to scale the summit itself. However, though
the climb was easy, it was long and arduous. If they were very
fit and could ski well, they could get to the summit and back
in around ten hours.

Mollwo asked about the monastery. There was no trace of
it now, he was told. It had been built by monks over two
hundred years ago and the trail was now the only evidence of
their habitation. They were curious as to why he wanted to go
up the Piz del Diavel. It was an ugly place, barren, constantly
swept by chill winds and composed of slabs of rock and ice.
The place was haunted, they said, and strange things had
happened to people who had gone there. No one went there
any more, despite the existence of the trail.

Mollwo asked about the monastery on the Piz Christian.
The owner of the equipment rental store said that had been a
tragedy. He'd been a young man at the time, and he'd gone
up the mountain afterwards to help. It had happened in the
bad winter of 1953. The snow had been late that year, not
falling till two days before Christmas, and then it had been
light and slushy. In February, as if to compensate for its
earlier mildness, the weather turned savage. Snow fell
continuously in heavy, driving sheets that blocked the roads
and passes, cut off farms and villages. That winter, many
farmers had slaughtered their livestock in order to survive
and a family had frozen to death in their car on the Stelvio.

In March there had been avalanches throughout the mountain chain, which was inevitable with so much snow piled on such an infirm base. One night in March, the monastery had been swept away, swept down the side of the mountain into the plateau below. Everyone had been killed. The shop keeper was certain of that. He'd gone up the Piz Christian to help recover the bodies.

They agreed that Dwight and Mollwo would climb the mountain, that Marit should stay behind, partly as a base contact, but mainly to effect the alternative plan. If Dwight and Mollwo didn't get back to the Gasthof within twenty-four hours, Marit was to inform the police of their disappearance and leave immediately for Zurich, where she would have Dr Becker's Swiss lawyers subpoena Johann's evidence, and use that evidence to obtain a court order restraining the Hoffman Bank. Marit would have much preferred to have gone mountain climbing with Dwight, but she knew she was the only one who could put the fall-back option into operation.

To: S.K.

From: Temporary Field Agent Otto Geier.

Yesterday, while the subject's vehicle was parked outside the Café Sport in Davos, we succeeded in attaching a radio device beneath its left rear wing, the location being chosen due to the vehicle's rubberized bumpers. This location exposes the component to road dirt, and in view of the present adverse weather conditions, the component is not expected to function satisfactorily for more than seventy-two hours.

However, since affixing the device, keeping watch on the subjects has been easier and safer. We are using a three vehicle surveillance and are confident that we have not been detected.

Today the subjects visited a local mountain called Piz

Christian. This mountain is largely uninhabited and there is hardly any traffic on the road to its summit. Consequently we did not follow the subjects to the summit, but having ascertained their destination, awaited their descent.

After their visit to the Piz Christian, the subjects returned to the village and hired equipment for a day's climbing and skiing from a local store. A subsequent conversation with the store keeper revealed that the two men intended to climb a nearby mountain called the Piz del Diavel, tomorrow.

The Piz Christian is the site of an old monastery which was destroyed some years ago by an avalanche. The Piz del Diavel is uninhabited and avoided by the local people. We have not been able to ascertain the purpose of the subjects' visit to this mountain, tomorrow.

O.G.

To: Otto Geier.

From: S.K.

Jerry Vaslav and friend arriving tonight.
Arrange accommodation, skiing and climbing equipment.

Kamas.

The next day, Dwight and Mollwo left before sunrise. It was still dark when they reached the foot of the mountain, but the climb was easy, the trail wide and clear. For about an hour they climbed steadily, watching the sky turn to silver, the sun rise bloodily through the trees. It was going to be a fine day and they were pleased there was no mist.

They moved slowly, not speaking, their pace slowed by the equipment they carried and the unbalancing effect of the skis strapped across their backs. At eight o'clock they stopped, ate a portion of the sandwiches Marit and Frau Winkler had prepared and went on. The clothing they wore was too heavy for the lower reaches and they sweated freely. The climb was still easy, though the trail had narrowed and both men began to feel the first soreness in their backs and shoulders from the unaccustomed weight.

An hour later they reached the snow. At first, it lay thinly under the trees, and they only donned snow shoes when they came to a gap in the forest, and found the snow thick under foot. Now the journey became harder. They were more tired and each step called for more effort. But grimly, they plodded on, stopping only when they had cleared the tree line.

Now they could see the mountain in all its fierce magnificence. Warped upwards by a giant eruption of the earth's crust, honed by the sharp thrust of glaciers, the cloven peaks which gave the mountain its name rose savagely above them, jagged and saw-toothed, a massive, frozen explosion of snow, rock and ice. A biting wind chilled their sweat-drenched bodies, flung stinging particles of snow into their raw, exposed faces. Dwight took one more look at the map, against which he'd checked the figures on the fly leaf of the bible. They had proved to be map references, they had fitted this large-scale map of the area around Brail, identifying the location of the monastery on the Piz Christian and a spot high up on the Devil's Peak.

It must be the burial ground, Mollwo had said. He hadn't seen the one on the Devil's Peak, but he'd seen a similar place further south, on the Italian border. The monks had buried their dead in holes cut into the walls of ice caves, the openings sealed with slabs of rock.

From the fact that Manninger had identified both locations, they had surmised that he had not left the documents at the monastery. Perhaps Father Bernard had not wanted to keep them, perhaps Manninger had wanted the documents where he could get at them without anyone else's knowledge. Perhaps they had been concerned about a situation like the present one, where both of them had died before the inheritors could be told where the documents were.

They went on in dogged silence, the terrain becoming more difficult with each step. The thin air made them feel exhausted, and as they climbed higher the snow became mixed with layers of ice that caused them to slip and forced them to travel more cautiously.

Immediately after their next stop they came across their first ice field, a narrow expanse of glistening white that offered no foot hold, no grip for their feet. They slipped and slid. They fell. They dragged themselves on all fours. They swore and cursed as their bodies were bruised by the unyielding ice and the equipment they carried.

As they climbed higher there was less snow and soon there was only a treacherous blanket of ice spread across the fold of the mountain. In some places it was over eighty feet thick and scarred with crevasses, punctuated with rigid hillocks like the waves of a frozen sea. Sometimes, as they moved, they could feel the whole pack shift beneath them and by now the wind was stronger, a continuous arctic blast that threatened to hurl them off the mountainside into the steeply shelved valley below.

But still they kept going, moving slowly and steadily upwards, fighting the wind, fighting the cold, fighting the ice that surrounded them. When they came to a small plateau, they stopped. Above them, the peak rose sheer and awesome. Dwight pulled out the map and looked. Somewhere on this plateau was the burial place where Manninger had hidden his secrets.

They celebrated the climb with sandwiches and coffee, then checked Manninger's reference and slithered across the ice to a wall of rock.

There was nothing there. No burial ground, no grave markers, just ice and rock and a desolate vastness.

Marit sat in her room smoking restlessly. She'd gone back to sleep after Dwight and Mollwo had left, had a late breakfast with Frau Winkler and gone for a walk in the hills behind the house.

Now she'd come back, there was nothing to do but wait. And waiting was the difficult part. Nearly eight hours of waiting. Dwight and Mollwo would not be back until early evening. She'd tried to read an English paperback Dwight had brought with him from America, a German romantic novel she found in Frau Winkler's parlour, but it was hopeless. She couldn't concentrate. Her mind was on the mountain and on Dwight and Mollwo struggling up it.

What if they found nothing? What if they found that the burial vaults had been destroyed, or that the documents were damaged or missing? What if they had an accident? Summer snow was notoriously unreliable, and could vary in texture and depth over as short a distance as thirty yards. If they'd had an accident, she'd have to go to Zurich, see the lawyers Becker had recommended and subpoena Johann.

She'd never been keen on the idea of subpoenaing Johann. Johann was a lawyer and probably knew a hundred ways to avoid being subpoenaed, or he might have left Zurich. And what if Johann, resentful at her attempt to compel him to produce the documents, came to court and said he had nothing?

Another thought struck her. What if Johann didn't know of the cartel's scheme to buy the processes? If it wasn't Johann who had shown Gerhardt Hoffman the forgeries? She had a duty to inform Johann about the cartel, warn him of the consequences if she was unable to prove she was Ingrid Manninger's daughter. Whatever Dwight and Mollwo found on the mountain, she'd have to contact Johann. And it would certainly be better to talk to him, before threatening him with lawyers.

She looked at her watch. Dwight and Mollwo wouldn't be back for hours yet. In any case, there was little point waiting for their return, before talking to Johann. In fact, the sooner she knew Johann's attitude, the better. If he was hostile, they could leave for Zurich as soon as Dwight and Mollwo returned, and see the lawyers first thing in the morning. With a subpoena to serve and two sets of court procedures to go through, the difference between seeing the lawyer at eight o'clock or eleven o'clock could be vital. She picked up the phone and dialled.

The man who answered seemed surprised when she gave her name, but he got Johann right away.

'Marit, where are you?'

'That isn't important. There's something you must know.' She told Johann about the cartel and the conspiracy to acquire the processes, told him of her visit to Hoffman and his demand for proof of who she really was.

'Marit,' Johann said mildly, when she had finished. 'Heinrich is here. He'd like to see you.'

A shudder of apprehension ran through Marit. 'I don't want to see Heinrich. Are you going to help me or not?'

Johann took so long thinking about her request that she wondered if the phone had been cut. She was about to jiggle the receiver rest when he said, 'Why should we help you, Marit? If the Gemeinschaft does not get the processes, it doesn't matter who does.'

'What about the community, Johann? What about the things we spoke about? If I get the processes, I will help the community get the things they need. Now, isn't that better than letting men like Raison Tearkes and Sir Alex Vickery have the processes?'

'You'd better talk to Heinrich,' Johann said.

Marit hesitated. Then she thought, what the hell. She was hundreds of miles from Zurich and von Kassel didn't even know where she was. 'All right, put Heinrich on.'

'It'll have to be in person,' Johann said.

No, Marit thought, not without Dwight and Mollwo, her own private bodyguards, a battery of lawyers and a host of guarantees. She pressed her finger on the cradle and cut Johann off.

Though he'd only known them a few hours, Otto Geier was

pretty sick of Jerry Vaslav and his raw-boned companion who answered to the name of Cary, and who in addition to having an easily provoked, high-pitched, scornful giggle, suffered from pyorrhea.

Because it was Swiss and not American, they'd complained ceaselessly about the skiing and mountaineering equipment he'd provided. The previous night, when they were told that the inn did not have two rooms with baths, they'd wondered loudly if the fucking Krauts ever washed. Over dinner, they'd attempted to fondle the waitresses and afterwards, drank loudly and too much. Now, driving to the Piz del Diavel, they made it clear to Geier that they expected him to find them women afterwards, explaining loudly in pidgin English, 'We want to fuck fraulein, understand?'

The radio device he had stuck on the Porsche had packed up. But the Porsche was there, parked in the brush at the foot of the mountain. Geier got out of the Opel and stood with them by the Porsche, taking care to remain upwind of Cary.

'What do you think those bastards are doing up there?' Vaslav asked.

'Climbing a mountain,' Geier replied.

'But what the fuck's up there, Otto?'

'Mostly snow and ice. There's also some rock.' He caught a whiff of mould and stale sweat.

Cary said, 'You know something, Otto, you're stupid. This is your fucking country, right? And you don't know the first thing about it.'

Geier didn't think there was any point telling the American that it wasn't his fucking country, that he was Austrian and not Swiss, and that they were in Switzerland, not Germany. 'If you want to find out what they're doing at the top of the mountain,' he said, 'you should climb it yourself.'

Cary lowered his head level with Geier's. Otto tried not to blanch at the smell.

'Don't get shirty, Otto. You step out of line,' Cary placed two fingers beneath Otto's nose, 'bang, bang. No head. You're dead. Arsehole.' And he giggled.

'Come here, Otto,' Vaslav said. Otto stepped cautiously round Cary and went up to him. Vaslav pointed up the mountain. 'That the way those bastards are going to get down?'

Otto felt like saying yes, but then reminded himself, that whatever the provocation, he was still a professional. 'There are lots of ways down,' he said. 'If you want to make sure of meeting them, you've got to go up high where there's only one trail.'

'You mean climb that fucking thing?' Cary was with them again.

Otto edged so that Vaslav's body was between them and said, 'Yes.'

'I'm not going to climb any fucking mountain,' Cary said. 'Hey, Jerry, call us a chopper.'

Vaslav laughed. 'Where do you think you are? Da Nang?' But he walked to the Opel, picked up the radio and asked for a chopper.

Ice and rock and desolate vastness. Dwight and Mollwo stared at the rock. There was nothing. *Nothing!* There was no trace of the monastery, no trace of the vaults, no trace of the processes. In the end, Dwight thought bitterly, they'd been defeated by simple human error. Manninger had been tired, Manninger had been frightened, he'd been a hunted man and his final map reference was wrong. He looked about the plateau, looked down at the stepped fall of rock and snow. Without precise directions, there was no hope of finding anything on this mountain.

Nothing. Their whole search had ended before this bare rock. There was nothing else to look for, there were no more clues. The search for the Manninger inheritance was over.

'We'd better be getting back,' Mollwo said and pulled out a flask of brandy from inside his voluminous anorak.

Dwight stared angrily at the implacable rock. 'Damn you!' he shouted. 'Damn you! Damn you!' His voice sounding childlike and tinny as it echoed down the mountain, hating

340

the feeling of having lost, hating Manninger for having been too clever and too careless. He took the proferred flask and poured brandy directly on to the back of his throat. Jesus Christ! After all this effort, nothing!

'We'll find another way,' Mollwo said, soothing him.

The brandy hit Dwight's stomach, sending steady waves of warmth radiating from the centre of his body. His eyes began to water from the sting of the spirit and the cold.

'Don't worry,' Mollwo said. 'We'll do something.'

Dwight followed Mollwo to where they had left their skis and packs. 'Sure,' he said, 'sure.' But he didn't believe it.

He stooped down, pulled off his snow shoes and took his ski boots out of the pack. The journey down the mountain would be faster and Dwight found some consolation in that. Now that it was over, he wanted to get away. He felt drained, diminished by the realization of failure. Oh hell, stop thinking! Forget everything! Forget you were here! Forget you were born! Try not to think where you are or what you've done or what you've been through. Forget everything and just skate down the mountain and try to enjoy the scenery.

Dwight turned and saw Mollwo standing very still, staring down the mountain with eyes that seemed frozen open. 'The sooner we leave, the sooner we'll get down,' Dwight said. They'd better get down as quick as they could. They had to get Marit to Zurich and he had to see Anderson and tell him that Tearkes's wish had been fulfilled, that the files were lost for ever.

Mollwo was still standing looking down the mountain as if frozen to the hillock on which he stood.

'Snap out of it,' Dwight shouted. 'Let's get going.'

Mollwo remained immobile.

'Come on, Herren. Get your arse in gear. Let's get down this fucking hill while we can still see.'

Only Mollwo's lips moved. In a voice that seemed to come from deep inside his belly, he said, 'Ice moves.'

'What?' Dwight got up and stomped over to Mollwo. Mollwo had gone mad. The cold and the altitude had got to him. The failure to find the processes had got to him. His age, his involvement with Manninger, all the events of the past few days, had curdled his brain. 'What the hell did you say?' Dwight asked.

'Ice moves,' Mollwo said again.

'What the hell has that got to do with anything? Never mind about ice moving, let's get the hell out of here.'

Mollwo turned and stared at Dwight with the far-seeing gaze of a sleep walker. 'The processes are here,' he said, fiercely. 'Don't you see, they are here. Ice moves. You felt it this morning. The earth moving under our feet.'

'It always happens,' Dwight said. 'At the right time, in the right place, with the right woman. Now let's go.'

'Dwight, don't you see? You're standing on ice, ice which has formed upon ice. You are standing on layers of ice, of different textures, formed at different times, exerting different pressures. Because of that pressure, ice moves. Don't you realize what I'm saying, Dwight? Ice moves. The whole mountain moves!'

Dwight looked from Mollwo's passionately flushed face down to his feet. Nothing was bloody moving.

'Look at those sticks.' Mollwo pointed past Dwight to a row of surveyors poles planted in a large U along one side of the plateau. 'That shows you how much the mountain has moved. When those poles were planted, they were in a straight line.'

Mollwo was already shambling past Dwight towards the poles. Dwight turned and went after him. 'You mean the vault is here, on this plateau? You mean the vault has moved since Manninger placed the documents in them?'

'Yes,' Mollwo said. 'If we can work out how much those poles have moved and when they were planted, we'd get some idea how far the ice has moved in thirty-five years.'

'Holy shit,' Dwight breathed.

41

Marit was lying on the bed, finding some distraction in Dwight's paperback, when she heard Frau Winkler's shout. 'Fraulein – you can't go – ' followed by the thump of feet running up the stairs.

She leapt off the bed.

Running feet and Johann's voice! 'It's all right,' Johann was shouting. 'I am her brother.'

Marit ran to the window. A long, black Mercedes stood outside with three men in it. She felt her legs tremble with the shock, had a moment of sheer panic. The back door, she thought. If only she could get to the back door. But there was only one way out of this room, only one flight of stairs. Heart yammering, she raced for the room door. Opened it. Johann stood in the open doorway and she felt the blood drain from her face.

His bronzed features were split in a dazzling smile. In his pale blue suit he looked elegant, relaxed, casual, friendly. But the cold amethyst eyes bored into her. 'Time to come home, little sister,' he said and took hold of her wrists.

He lowered his head to hers, brushed her cheek with dry lips. 'Get rid of the old woman,' he hissed. 'We don't want to involve outsiders.'

Marit knew that if Frau Winkler got involved, she'd only be hurt. 'It's all right, Frau Winkler,' she said over Johann's shoulder. 'This is my brother, from Zurich.'

Frau Winkler stood in the doorway, staring doubtfully at both of them. Then gathering up her long, black skirt, she went down the stairs.

Johann kicked the door shut, his hands still firmly locked

around Marit's wrists, careful not to break the healing scab of her wounds.

'Johann, I want you to understand something,' Marit said, tremulously. 'If you take me from here against my will, you will never get the processes, not one tiny part of them.'

Johann studied her face carefully. 'Heinrich wants to see you in Zurich,' he said. 'You can come quietly, or you can compel us to use force.'

And that was no choice at all, Marit thought. If she resisted, she would be dragged to the car, Frau Winkler and her husband hurt, perhaps even killed in the struggle.

'I'll come,' she said, feeling her whole body start to tremble.

A black cross on black rock. A black cross carved the entire length of it. Dwight stared at the slab of rock. He couldn't believe it. He couldn't believe that he was staring at the last impediment between him and the Manninger inheritance.

For two hours they had quartered the plateau, Mollwo returning time and time again, to look at the sticks, to measure their movement, to suggest they look more to the right, more to the left, to suggest they look in a different direction.

An hour ago, Dwight had given up all hope. It was just another damned manoeuvre, another convolution of Manninger's distorted brain. There was no Manninger! There was no inheritance! There was nothing!

This was all a dream, a nightmare. He'd wake up and find himself back in his brownstone, back in the bank waiting for Dr Rasul Quassim.

But the rock was there. HE was there. Dwight felt he could jump for joy if only his legs weren't so tired, and the snow shoes so cumbersome. He looked triumphantly across at Mollwo. 'Let's get this bastard out of the way. Then we can go home.'

Getting the bastard out of the way took longer than he thought. For over an hour they prised at the rock, with the crowbars they had brought in their packs. They prised at the rock and dug at the snow. They pulled at it and pushed at it. They leant against it and heaved. Then they prised some more, dug some more. They didn't stop to rest, but kept on working furiously, ignoring the chill wind that snapped snow into their faces, but did not cool the perspiration on their frantically moving bodies.

After an hour and a half the rock moved. Not completely away from the mouth, but enough to let Dwight and Mollwo sidle through. Inside it was dark, cold, colder than it had been outside on the mountain, a cold that was of the mountain and a cold of something more than the mountain.

Death.

Dwight moved his flashlight along the walls. Dark slabs of stone stared at him from the shiny ice. Here and there a stone had come away from its support and fallen, revealing the pale wood of a coffin. At the back of the vault, where the movement had been greatest, he saw that the coffins had come away too, and lay exposed, half in, half out of their niches, except for one which had fallen open, revealing a marvellously preserved body dressed in a pale, woollen shroud. The hands, Dwight noticed, were still clasped together, the head twisted round as if looking at the intruders.

Dwight ran his flashlight round the walls. There were over forty of them. In which one had Manninger placed the documents? Where would *he* have placed the documents, if he were Berndt Manninger?

Dwight tried to recall the trail that Manninger had laid. The bible, the photograph album, the bank account in Bruckners. The map of the Grissons and the monastery on the Piz Christian. The devil's temptation, the Devil's Peak, the gospels of Matthew and Luke.

He moved closer to the wall, shone his flashlight on the grave stones. Brother Martin, Brother David, Brother Joseph. All the gravestones were identical, carved with a name, a small cross, the dates of birth and death. Brother Thomas,

Brother Calixtus, Brother Paul. Brother Peter, Brother Pious, Brother Anthony.

Brother Matthew!

Dwight pulled Mollwo to the grave and asked him for the crowbar. Quickly he prised it into the small gap between the rock and the ice. Desperately he levered it, felt it move. Together with Mollwo he eased it away and lifted it from the coffin it covered.

For a wild moment he stared at the pale wood. He hoped it wasn't *in* the coffin. He ran his hands along the sides. Nothing. Then along the top. His groping gloved hand hit something. He heard it fall off the coffin, on to the side. He reached out and took it. A bulky packet, wrapped in oilskin and as pristine as the day it had been interred.

There was a larger packet on the coffin of Brother Luke. Dwight collected both packets and crept through the opening in the rock outside.

'We've got it!' he cried out to Mollwo. 'We've got it!'

Heedless of the cold, heedless of the risk of frostbite, he tore away his gloves and tugged at the oilskin. The packet opened easily enough. Right at the top were three share certificates, the *Zessions* of Perpetua, Sopadep and Augusta. They were, Dwight saw, made out in the name of Berndt Manninger. Which meant that the assets of the companies could only be disposed of under the terms of Manninger's will; that the only person who could use them to stop the meeting was Marit, if she could prove she was Berndt Manninger's granddaughter.

Underneath the certificates were a mass of papers, covered with writing and figures. They'd been torn from an old foolscap pad and clipped in separate batches. Dwight stared at the headings in total amazement.

Design of a Low Temperature Heat Engine, Formulae for the Production of Liquid Hydrogen. A Paper Concerning the Extraction of Power from a Combination of Water and Sodium, Notes on Improved Coal Gasification, a thick bundle of notes on Geo-Thermal Power, a series of processes for the artificial manufacture of leather, plastic paper and synthetic fibres, a technique for strengthening plastic with mineral particles to make parts as resistant to wear and tear as metal, the detailed plans for a Hydrogen Engine and a method of storing hydrogen under pressure, and, wonder of wonders, a thick wedge of notes headed 'Mass-energy Conversion'.

Dwight came aware of Mollwo slapping him round the shoulder, insisting that he put his glove back on. Dwight did so and opened the second packet.

In it were the files describing a conspiracy which had existed since the First World War.

After the First World War, the Allies had gathered at Versailles to dismember Germany. Germany must never rise again, not because she was naturally war-like, but because she was too industrious. The Germans had no soul, but they controlled the processes for synthetic fertilizer, for dyestuffs, for manganese and certain metal alloys. They were trying to develop synthetic rubber and synthetic oil, they were developing new and wonderful drugs and a cure for malaria.

The Germans had to be stopped. They had to be defeated. They had to be absorbed.

Allied businessmen had gone into Germany, providing plant and providing capital. All they wanted in exchange was cheap German labour and the end product of German inventive genius.

Deals had been made, processes had been stolen. Lunatic inflation had been greeted with suppressed glee. It was only when the Weimar Republic had collapsed that people began to get concerned.

Germany couldn't go Communist. Communists didn't believe in profit or the rights of private property. The Communists would not deal with industry and self-serving governments. Communists, everyone had said, sagely, would ruin Germany.

So they had looked for a strong man, someone strong enough to bring order out of chaos, but not too strong to want

Germany to rise again. And they had found such a man, a former corporal in the German Army, an untalented painter who sold pictures to tourists. But the man had charisma, the man had a following. To the Tearkeses and Vickerys, to certain powerful people in the governments of America, England and France, Adolf Hitler seemed to be the right man to run Germany.

But in the end, everyone had been proved wrong. Hitler may have been uneducated, may have been no more than a corporal and an unsuccessful painter of kitsch, but he believed in Germany, he believed that he could make Germany great. More than anything, Hitler believed in himself, believed in an intuition that was superior to intelligence or rational thought. When Hitler ordered the German Army into the Rhineland, the conspirators knew they were finished.

Germany would be for the Germans. Germany would not be exploited. Germany would not provide the cheap labour foreign industry required. Hitler came out with import controls, with blocks on foreign exchange, with an irresistible appeal to all Germans to unite, wherever they were.

Hitler had to be stopped. Germany had to be defeated once again. Hitler had to be made to fight, even if it was over a country like Poland, which no one wanted and the Allies couldn't really defend.

And the Tearkeses, the Vickerys and the Brassards had played their part. They had conspired. They had profited. They had conspired for profit. There were whole pages setting out the deals that had been done before and *during* the war. Whole pages naming names, citing evidence, stating incontrovertible fact.

And there was a deed of secret trusteeship. At the outbreak of the war, Manninger had transferred his foreign assets to his friends, to Willard Tearkes, to Andre Brassard, to Sir Alex Vickery. And they had jointly and separately agreed that within six months of the war ending, they would procure the transfer of those assets back to Manninger, for a consideration no more than fifteen per cent above the price they had paid for them. Dwight stared at the grey German type, the signatures at the foot of each page. So this was why Manninger had been killed. His friends had sought to keep the processes they had leased, to keep what was never theirs.

'Dwight, let's go before we freeze to death.' Mollwo was insistent and Mollwo was right. It was nearly three o'clock in the afternoon and they would now never get down before dark. Dwight put the documents away, fastened his skis and set off across the ice.

42

Skis juddered on ice, edges fought for grip. The ice was ridged and gave no traction. They had to move slowly in clumsy traverses, with shoulders hunched forward, their arms hanging wide like the wings of wounded birds. They had to turn frequently, edges sawing for grip, every movement accompanied by a thin clatter, like that of pebbles shaken in a soft bag, every movement threatening to unbalance them and send them skidding helplessly over the ice.

They moved slowly, cautiously. A fall now could tear ligaments, could wrench ankles, could fracture bones. A fall now could prejudice the success of the whole operation.

Dwight now knew how he could stop both Hoffman's sale and Tearkes's massive speculation against the dollar. All he had to do was inform Tearkes he had the files. All he had to do was inform Tearkes that unless he was a good little boy, the contents of those files would be published. Raison Tearkes had been named in those files. Willard Tearkes had been named. A large number of people in industry and government had been named and no further proof was necessary. Those files and the documents they referred to, would damn everyone ever concerned with the real Operation Brunhilde.

Dwight wished it was safe to move more quickly. He wanted to get down, he wanted to talk to Marit. He wanted to tell her all that had happened, he wanted to tell her they had won.

He heard the chatter of a helicopter overhead and looked at it puzzled. It was flying low and bore the markings of a Swiss charter company. Dwight told himself not to be silly. The Swiss were very concerned about the state of their roads, the condition of mountain passes and the volume of traffic. The helicopter was obviously on standby for the police or the road traffic information people.

They pressed on downwards, moving as quickly as they dared, worrying about the imbalance caused by their back packs and what was left of their equipment. Four hours more and it would be over. Four hours more and he'd be soaking in a hot bath, with Marit fixing him a proper drink. Four hours!

Dwight thrust his weight on his outside ski, tilted the ski inwards, felt himself turn slowly. Slowly the sky and the rugged fall of the mountain turned. Slowly the ravelled line of trees disappeared. Then he was plunging down the hill in the direction he had come. Dwight braked, leaned his weight on his upper foot and turned again.

The helicopter had disappeared behind the trees. Dwight could hear its staccato chatter, as it hovered out of sight. Marit couldn't have sent a search party yet, he thought.

He pressed on, twisting and turning over pinnacles of ice, twisting and turning towards the tree line. Mollwo was keeping up surprisingly well. Watching him come down the slope, one would never have thought he was nearly seventy, or that he was fit enough to climb up the mountain and afterwards, ski down it.

They threaded their way through a clump of trees, shivering momentarily at the sudden chill underneath the thick branches. They turned slowly and gracefully as the path wound between tree trunks, then left the path and made for the open field beyond.

The field was vast, covered with ice. It would still be a slow journey down. They twisted and turned and burst out of the forest, threw their weight forward and tilted their skis to brake harshly.

Standing in the middle of the clearing, by the track along which they should have emerged, were two men. They were both dressed in black from head to toe, with heavy, yellow goggles pulled down over their faces, underneath the tight-fitting, woollen ski hats. Cradled in their arms were two automatic rifles.

'Split!' Dwight shouted to Mollwo. 'Go like hell for the bottom!'

He twisted his skis sideways and forward, throwing his weight forward on to bent knees, angling the skis flat. He streaked over the ridged ice.

From the corner of his eye he saw Mollwo turn the other way, head directly for the clump of trees at the edge of the open basin.

Dwight kept his head down, his body low. He was forced to make wide turns, nearly pulled over each time by the weight of his back pack. He reached below his waist and took out a knife, turned behind him and severed the strap of the snow shoes and boots. He would go quicker without them. He inclined his head slightly to check on his pursuer.

The gunman was coming after him like a frenzied bat, his body rising and falling as he turned and twisted down the slope, lifting his body, collapsing on his knees, looping and swooping, moving, despite the ice, with an effortless grace.

Christ, he was good, Dwight thought. He skied like a bloody angel and he was catching up, fast.

Dwight forced himself to keep his skis pointed down for longer, allowed himself to take wider, skidding turns, reached out behind him and cut away the shovel and the crow bar.

He risked a glance back to look for Mollwo. There was no sign of Mollwo. The last time he had seen him, Mollwo had been heading into the trees. At that moment, Dwight heard the sound of a shot, a flat, slapping sound that rent the air like tearing cloth. There was a flurry of snow under the trees and then nothing.

Dwight skied on. Somehow he had to avoid the man with the Armalite. The man was a killer, a specialist.

Dwight concentrated on his skiing, concentrated on keeping his tips together, concentrated on ignoring the scraping, high-pitched chatter, as he flung himself down the side of the hill.

Once more he turned, in time to see Mollwo rush out of the clump of trees in a flurry of snow. Mollwo was alive. Mollwo had dealt with his assailant.

Dwight bounced and turned. His calves were aching, his eyes were aching, his body felt as if it had been buffeted against a brick wall. But still he kept on. He had to keep on. There were two of them and only one of the enemy. But the enemy must not get him. The enemy must not get the Manninger secrets.

Desperation gave his skis wings and made him forget the pain and the wind searing his face. He had to get down before his pursuer. He looked over his shoulder. The gunman had gained ten yards on him, was gaining every second.

Jesus Christ, what the hell should he do! Dwight pointed his skis downwards, thrust himself forward to cope with the sudden acceleration. He would go straight down if he had to, straight down without a single turn. The skis jumped and buckled under him, juddered along the uneven ice. He could feel the wind snatching at his face, snapping his hair back, stretching his clothes tight against his body. His teeth chattered as he bounced over a series of ridges. His head felt as if it was coming loose. He risked a look behind him and saw the gunman had gained five yards.

Dwight threw himself into a turn, skidded to take off some of the pace, and launched himself into the forest. He twisted and turned round the trees, rising up now, lowering himself, planting his poles, riding the edges, knowing that this was no friendly contest. If he fell, if the gunman got up to him, he was dead.

He burst out of the trees into a clearing. He felt his skis catch on snow. A fine layer of it spread over the ice, it gave him grip and allowed him to move faster. He flung himself into a long controlled slide, turned and saw the gunman emerge from the trees.

Dwight rocketed down, rising on his toes, feeling the boots cutting his shins. Up, down, plant pole, turn, traverse, check, plant pole, turn. His legs were growing heavy, his lungs dry of air. He could hardly breathe and he could feel the sweat wetting his forehead, hot and sticky against his back.

But he kept going. He had to keep going. He'd even gained two yards.

As he dropped lower and there was more snow, his lunatic journey became easier. But he couldn't let up. Not now. Not with such an expert skier behind him.

He saw a mound and braked for it, a shoulder-high boulder covered in snow. Twisting his skis inwards, he made a large turn, skidding in a wide arc round the boulder and behind it.

He stopped in a flurry of snow, crouched behind the boulder, peeped over the top, glimpsed a dark, cavorting figure, gun raised now, coming straight for the boulder.

Dwight reached behind him, reached for his pack, took out the Luger. He flicked off the safety catch and placed the Luger on top of the rock.

The gunman was turning more quickly, zigzagging in small, tight turns, as if he realized what Dwight was doing. Dwight checked the frequency of the turns, absorbed the rhythm of the man's corkscrew motion, kept the gun pointed at empty space, then as the man filled it, fired.

It was a clean shot, and caught him high in the chest. The man flung up his arms, but his body continued corkscrewing down. Then it tilted sideways, the skis skidding from underneath in a streaming wash of snow. He hit the ground on his shoulder, rolled over and over, sideways and forward, rising and falling as the tips of the skis cartwheeled down the slope.

353

Dwight watched until the skis broke free and the man's legs dragged on the snow, until the man swivelled and lay still.

Painstakingly he crabbed his way up to the man, looked down at that placid, bovine face, with those muddy brown eyes, that stared sightlessly up at him. He opened the man's parka and took out his wallet. His name was Jerry Vaslav. He was American and according to Samir Achmet, he'd worked for Sam Kamas. At last it was over, Dwight thought. They'd tried to stop him and they'd failed. They'd tried to get the processes and the files, they'd tried to get the *Zessions* and they had got nothing. He looked down at Vaslav, feeling no regret for his death. It had been kill or be killed, and he had survived.

This time he felt no reaction.

It was three hours later when they reached the Gasthof. They were bone tired, their bodies punished to exhaustion, their muscles aching as if they'd been through a mangle. Dwight couldn't wait to see Marit's face when he told her everything was over. That all they had to do was go to Zurich.

He stopped the car outside the rear entrance, lumbered heavily up the wooden steps, crossed the landing and ran across the kitchen. Frau Winkler was saying something to him, but he wasn't interested. He rushed down the corridor and through the small lobby, rushed up the stairs to their room. The door was unlocked and he flung it open.

'Hi, kiddo,' he carolled into the darkness. 'We're back. And we've got the processes. We've got everything!'

He turned on the light. She wasn't there. Perhaps that's what Frau Winkler had been trying to tell him. That Marit was in the lounge, or in the bar.

But the room had a peculiar emptiness to it. Then he saw that Marit's suitcase had gone, that the wardrobe was open and her clothes weren't there.

He took two lumbering steps into the room, walked dazedly to the bed. At the same time he heard Frau Winkler's heavy footsteps behind him, the wheeze of her breathing.

'The fraulein, she is gone. She is gone with her brother to Zurich.'

Zurich! Brother! Marit did not have a brother! Dwight wheeled to face Frau Winkler. 'What did her brother look like?'

'Oh, he was tall, youngish, very good looking. He had very strange eyes.'

Johann Neumann, Dwight thought, and asked, 'Was he alone?'

'He was the only one who came into the house. There were other men outside, in the car.'

So Neumann had come and forced Marit to accompany him, forced her to make a show of going willingly, by threatening to harm Frau Winkler and her husband. But how had Neumann discovered where they were? Dwight looked carefully around the room. The bed was rumpled. A paperback lay face down on the coverlet. Marit had apparently been lying reading when Neumann had arrived. His gaze rested on the telephone beside the bed. The receiver was angled off its rest.

Dwight turned back to Frau Winkler. 'Did the fraulein make any telephone calls?'

'I don't know. I can check.' Frau Winkler padded over to the phone and spoke to the operator. Cradling the receiver on her shoulder, she turned to Dwight and said, 'Yes. The fraulein did make a call to Zurich.'

Dwight took the phone from her and asked the operator for the number and the address. The operator was most efficient. She gave Dwight the number immediately, and the address of a house on the Dolder, a minute later.

So that was how Neumann had found out where they were, Dwight thought as he replaced the receiver.

'You want anything more?' Frau Winkler asked.

Dwight shook his head.

'Then I will go and get your dinner ready.'

Dwight sat for a while, thinking. Then he called the manager of the Imtra Bank's Zurich branch and asked him to

355

be outside the bank in approximately three hours. Then, his mind made up, he packed and went down to the dining-room. Mollwo was already half-way through his dinner.

Frau Winkler stood up and rushed to the kitchen to bring Dwight his food.

'Better eat something,' Mollwo said. 'We could have a long night ahead of us.'

Dwight sat down. Frau Winkler placed a steaming plate in front of him. Before he started to eat, he told Mollwo, 'Can you call your sons in Hellenthal and ask them to meet us at the Hotel Bellevue in Zurich, as soon as possible?'

Mollwo grinned and got to his feet. A few minutes later, Dwight heard him shouting to his sons, and telling them to hurry.

The moment Marit entered the house she was engulfed by a vast swooning helplessness. The house was like a fortress, isolated, set back from the road, surrounded by high walls, its narrow entrance barred by tall, iron gates and guarded by two armed men. Inside, there were more men, their eyes scanning her in silent approval, automatic weapons slung over their shoulders. There was no way Dwight and Mollwo could rescue her.

She was led through a lobby, along a small corridor into a large room that ran down the side of the house.

The further part of the room was some kind of a library, its walls covered with glass-fronted book cases that reached to the ceiling, comfortable armchairs and a small writing table arranged around the Chinese rug before the fireplace. The remainder of the room was the living area, an artfully careless arrangement of vinyl-covered chairs and sofas, scatter rugs, a beechwood table and a mirrored cocktail cabinet. The division between the room was emphasized by a large desk. Heinrich von Kassel sat behind it.

He was wearing his usual informal attire, a black cashmere turtle neck under a brown sports jacket. His face had a meaty, freshly-scrubbed appearance, and the scar along his cheek seemed unusually puckered. He rose to his full height as Marit entered, a huge intimidating slab of a man, towering over her and Johann. His narrow lips parted in the semblance of a smile. 'Marit, my dear, it's so good of you to come,' as if he were receiving her at some state reception. He waved graciously at the armchairs opposite the desk.

Marit remained standing. 'I didn't come here,' she snapped. 'I was forced.'

'Sit down, my dear.' Von Kassel's voice was low-pitched and persuasive. 'We have no time for mutual recriminations. There is much I have to tell you.'

Marit flounced into an armchair and took her cigarettes from her bag.

Von Kassel picked up a smouldering cigar from the ashtray on his desk and looked thoughtfully at her through the curtain of smoke. He said, 'At ten o'clock tomorrow morning, the assets of Sopadep and Perpetua, the Manninger inheritance, will be sold by your grandfather's trustees, the Hoffman Bank. The purchaser will be Raison Tearkes, the man who once worked with your grandfather and later had him killed.'

Marit drew deeply at her cigarette, forcing herself to remain calm. 'The only way you can prevent Raison Tearkes buying the inheritance is by giving me the documents that will prove who I am.'

Von Kassel threw her a humourless smile. 'But you need certain other documents, isn't that so? What are you going to do about the documents your grandfather hid?'

Marit went silent.

Johann asked, 'Has the American got them? Was he out looking for them when we came to you in Zernez?'

Marit felt a sudden surge of confidence.

Without both her and Dwight, they could do nothing. 'He was looking for the documents,' she admitted. 'If you hadn't brought me here, I'd know by now whether he'd found them or not.'

'Where is he – '

'Tearkes must be stopped,' von Kassel interrupted. 'First, he had your grandfather killed. Then, when it seemed that Elisabeth Manninger would inherit, Tearkes had her murdered, and arranged her killing in such a way that it would look as if *we* were responsible.'

Marit swivelled to face Johann. 'And who killed Ilana Jarusovic?'

'We did,' Johann replied, his cold, amethyst eyes boring into hers. 'It was necessary, Marit. Ilana Jarusovic believed we had hired her. If she talked, if the Swiss investigated Elisabeth Manninger's death, we would have been implicated. And more important than that, your claim to the inheritance could have been prejudiced.'

'We did it for you, my child,' von Kassel said.

A blazing streak of anger convulsed her. 'You did nothing for me!' Marit shouted. 'Everything you did was for yourselves!'

Von Kassel was looking at her, shocked. Softly, he said, 'Hear us before you judge us. You know of this cartel headed by Tearkes?'

Marit nodded.

'You know what they are planning to do?'

Marit shook her head, not trusting herself to speak.

Gently, in a voice devoid of any inflection, von Kassel told Marit of the cartel's association with Pyotr Voskov, of the cartel's scheme to make vast profits from the collapse of the dollar, of their conspiracy to effectively control the world's largest banks.

'Bruno Topf worked with the cartel,' von Kassel continued. 'But he refused to participate in this. So they killed him.' He paused, as if shaken by the memory of Bruno Topf's death. 'Now do you see why Tearkes has to be stopped, my child? In the next twenty-four hours his cartel will have quintupled in value. It will control the banks, it will control money, with your grandfather's processes, it will control the forces of energy, and with the files, it will control governments. By tomorrow night, Tearkes's cartel will become the world's most powerful and influential entity.'

'Then goodbye Gemeinschaft,' Johann murmured. 'Goodbye community.'

'And goodbye everyone who has ever opposed them,' von Kassel echoed. 'Everyone who has ever dared to compete with them.' He leaned forward across the desk, his large face covered by a shiny patina of perspiration. 'So you see, Marit, why we need your grandfather's files.'

'And what about the processes,' Marit asked. 'Don't you want them as well?'

Von Kassel's eyes widened in surprise. 'The processes are yours,' he said. 'They've always been yours.'

That was incredible! Untrue! All they had ever wanted – Marit looked from one to the other of them in confusion.

Von Kassel was pushing some papers across the desk. 'There is the proof you require. Take it.'

Heart pattering, Marit looked at the papers. Ingrid Manninger's exit visa dated 23rd April 1945. The release from Ravensbruck dated two weeks previously. A copy of her registration with the Argentinian Immigration Authority.

'Now do you believe us?' Johann said. 'Now will you have the American bring what he has found?'

And that way, both the inheritor and the means to the inheritance would be in the one place, surrounded by armed guards in a house that looked like a fortress. 'No,' Marit said, stuffing the documents into her handbag. 'You see,' she held up her wrists, 'we already know about the cartel. We are going to stop them. Dwight works for the American government, and the American government is very concerned about the dollar.' She smiled at both of them and got to her feet. 'So if you will allow me to leave now, you will achieve your ends.'

From beside her, Johann said, softly, 'We can't let you do that, Marit. You may love and trust this American. We don't.'

Marit turned to look at him, her face set. 'Do you let me

leave,' she demanded, 'or do you let Tearkes take everything?'

'Those aren't the only alternatives,' Johann said.

Von Kassel asked, 'Is this American in love with you?'

Marit felt angry at herself for colouring. 'That is irrelevant,' she muttered.

'Then why don't we let him prove his love,' Johann said, standing up in front of her. 'Why don't we see if he will exchange the Manninger documents for you?'

'Don't be stupid, Johann,' Marit snapped. 'To claim the inheritance you need both me and the documents. There is no sense in exchanging one for the other.'

'Ah,' Johann said. 'But we need not complete our part of the exchange.'

She heard a buzzer sound from beside von Kassel's desk. The door opened. Three men stood there. Marit turned towards the window. No way of escape there.

'You've got nowhere to run,' Johann said from behind her. 'You've got nowhere to hide. Wherever you go, we will find you.'

She felt hands grasp her shoulders and arms, turn her round, march her to the door. She knew that to struggle was useless, to escape was impossible. Yet as she passed von Kassel, she sucked her cheeks together and spat full in his face.

Johann leading them, the men took her out of the library, up the stairs, to a small room along a corridor. The curtains in the room were drawn, admitting not a speck of light and the narrow iron bed had been freshly made. The men laid her on the bed and Marit remained passive as they fastened her wrists and ankles to the bedposts.

'You know, Johann,' she said as soon as the men left. 'Now, you will never get the processes. When I see Gerhardt Hoffman alone, I shall insist he arranges for police protection before I leave the bank.'

Johann gave her a pitying smile. 'Once we've destroyed the cartel, I think you'll find that Gerhardt Hoffman will be less pedantic about Swiss banking regulations.' He turned out the lights and left.

Marit stared into the darkness, fighting the terrible fear, the terrible scream that welled inside her, and threatened to tear her apart.

43

It was after midnight when Dwight and Mollwo reached Zurich. The manager of the Imtra Bank was waiting for them. He took custody of the Manninger documents and agreed to hold them to Dwight's sole order. With the documents safely stored away, Dwight set off for the Dolder and the address the telephone operator had given him.

The house was large and set back from the road, with two sentries at the front gates and most of it surrounded by a high wall. Dwight was glad they'd left Frau Winkler's so hurriedly they still had the climbing equipment they had hired.

When an hour later, they got to the Bellevue, Mollwo's sons were waiting. Dwight sketched a plan of the house and explained what he wanted them to do. Then he called the number he had traced through the telephone operator and got through to Johann Neumann right away.

'Well, Mr Khouri, how did your expedition go?'

'Very well. I have the Manninger documents.'

'In that case, we should meet. We may not have a lot to talk about, but there are some things we could exchange.'

'Let me speak to Marit,' Dwight said.

'I'm sorry, but she is unable to take telephone calls at present. But don't worry, Mr Khouri. She is well, suffering only temporary discomfort.'

Bastard, Dwight thought, but he kept his voice very

controlled as he said, 'I suppose you want to exchange the documents for Marit.'

'Quite right, Mr Khouri.'

'Right. Have you got a map of Zurich?'

'Just a moment.' Dwight heard voices in the background, a rustling, before Neumann said, 'Go ahead, I have a map.'

'Can you see the Zurichberg?'

The Zurichberg was a vast wooded park to the north east of Zurich, near the Dolder. Dwight traced the route with his finger as he explained it to Neumann. 'You will come only with Marit,' Dwight said. 'You will see Marit's Porsche parked facing the wrong way. You will approach the car and park ten yards in front of it and identify yourself by flashing the headlights of your vehicle once. If you leave now, you could be there in forty minutes.'

Neumann started to protest, but Dwight put down the receiver.

He turned and told Mollwo to take Marit's Porsche to the meeting place as soon as possible, to leave the car and return to the Bellevue as soon as he could. Neumann wouldn't bring Marit to the meeting place, he told Mollwo and his sons, instead, he would bring the security men from the house, hoping to take the processes by force and not make the exchange.

As soon as Mollwo left, Dwight drove with Mollwo's sons to the house on the Dolder. It took them twenty-five minutes to reach the house, using a circuitous route that brought them round behind it, without alerting the guards in front. They parked in the darkness and waited. Over the high walls they could see lights on in the upper storey, but there was no sound from the house, no sounds except those of the night and the occasional sigh of a vehicle climbing the hill.

Dwight waited staring at the luminous dial of his watch, watching the minute hand move in agonizing slowness. The palm gripping his wrist was clammy with sweat. Fear seeped through his brain. What if Neumann had been suspicious and sent someone to cover the site? What if his plan had been discovered? What if Neumann had spotted the empty car and was already speeding back to the house?

Dwight climbed out of the car and gestured with his thumb towards the wall. Noiselessly, two of Mollwo's sons picked up the rope ladders laid out beside the cars, and carried them silently across the road. Dwight looked right and left, then stepped across the road and joined them in the shrubbery.

There was a faint whirring, a slight clanking as the ladders were flung on to the wall and made secure. Dwight went up quickly, drew his head level with the top of the wall, and looked.

The house was an imposing two-storeyed affair, situated diagonally in the middle of lawn and cultivated garden. The driveway and the tall iron gates in front were blocked out by the mass of the house, and Dwight was looking side on at its vertical rear, which consisted of a large kitchen on the ground floor, and two bedrooms at the top. There was an entrance to the kitchen from the side of the house, and Dwight decided they would get in through that.

The area at the foot of the wall had been left uncultivated, and beyond it were a line of shade trees, then lawn. There was no cover between the trees and the house and Dwight noted that one man in the kitchen could cover almost the entire rear approach.

He waited, watching, looking from time to time at his watch. He had to get in and out before Neumann and his men returned. He also had to reach the house without being spotted. They didn't have a hope in hell against one man in the rear of the house.

Three minutes passed. Four. No movement at all from the back of the house. No lights turning on and off, no stealthy cigarettes glowing in the dark, no sign of life. His second hand moved round agonizingly. To go or not to go? Were they using stationary watches or patrols? If patrols, what was their frequency? Was the area beyond the trees wired? Was that kitchen door alarmed? Five minutes and twenty seconds. Zurichberg was less than fifteen minutes away if one drove quickly, and without doubt, Neumann would be driving quickly.

Dwight stared at the house. Would Marit be in one of the bedrooms upstairs, or surrounded by guards in a room downstairs? Was she even now being interrogated, tortured? If she was, would she be able to react correctly to their appearance, be able to run back and climb the wall with them? So many problems and so little data. He should have had more time to plan this. Six minutes. There was no time. He had to go.

With a low whistle to the others, he heaved himself over the wall and dropped noisily into the shrubbery, heard the sound of bodies falling through the air, the crumpled thump of their landing. He turned and looked at them. Everyone on his feet, everyone crouching slightly, cradling their weapons. No twisted ankles or broken legs. So far, so good.

Dwight moved out from the shrubbery into the trees, stopped in their shadow and waited. No movement from the house, no indication that their intrusion had been observed.

'Go!' Dwight whispered and broke into a run, hearing the pad of the others' feet, slightly behind him.

Then there was a sharp crackle! Automatic fire! Instinctively Dwight flung himself on to the grass. The sound of glass breaking. Another burst of fire. Two more bursts, longer, sustained. But where the hell were the flashes?

Shouts carried on the night air. Whatever was going on was at the front of the house, Dwight realized, and in that split second of realization, got to his feet and ran crouching to the wall. Quickly he unhooked the ladder, coiled it and ran past the prone figures of Mollwo's sons, going like hell for the back of the house.

Two of Mollwo's sons took the ladder from him and looped it. Dwight went up quickly, bouncing and swaying, kicking himself away from the brickwork. He reached a window, leaned across and smashed it with the butt of his gun, cleared the glass, went in quickly in a shower of glass and wood. He hit the floor, rolled and lay prone for a moment, the M-16 cradled on bruised elbows in front of him. He was in a room of some kind, a bedroom. He could distinguish the outlines of a bed and dressing table, the refulgent glow of a mirror. He moved back to the window and opened it. Like four shadows, Mollwo's sons joined him.

The noise of the firing was louder now. It was downstairs. Dwight opened the bedroom door. A corridor, to the left a window, to the right a flight of stairs. Opposite, another bedroom door. No light seeping out from around or beneath it. He reached across and tried the door. It was locked.

He moved to his right, down the corridor. An open door on his left. Bathroom. Five paces further down. Doors to his right and left. Both unlocked. Both bedrooms. He stopped. Two of Mollwo's sons bumped into him.

'The room at the back, on the left,' he whispered.

The man nearest to the door, charged it. He heard the lock shatter, heard Marit's scream. A rectangle of light washed across the corridor, at the same time as a burst of fire sprayed the landing in front of him.

Dwight hurled himself forward to the stairhead. A man was already on the landing directly in front of him, his gun sweeping the top of the stairs. Dwight flung himself to the floor. A gun chattered into life behind him. Bullets sizzled over his head. When he looked up, the man on the landing was lying sprawled over the stairs. There had to be a second man covering the first. Dwight spotted him, crouched beside the banister. Dwight fired. Wood splintered. There was a startled shout, a glimpse of a black hooded figure, sprinting from behind the shelter of the stairs, disappearing down the corridor.

One of Mollwo's sons was beside him.

'Cover me,' Dwight said. 'I'm going down.'

He moved to the head of the stairs, reached the first landing in two giant leaps, saw a movement in the corridor beneath him, fired.

The sound of running feet, a door slamming. Dwight leapt down on to the next landing. Below him, a body on the stairs, two more lying on the corridor that led past an open door to the rear of the house. Dwight came up from his crouch, leapt past the man sprawled on the stairs, to the corridor. There was the sound of running feet from the room to his left. Dwight stopped by the open doorway, pressed his shoulders to the wall, stole a sideways glance into the room. The body of a large man wearing a black turtle-neck and brown sports jacket sat slumped in a chair behind a desk, a row of bullet wounds stitched across his chest.

There was no sound from the room. Dwight edged around the door, went in quickly, gun thrust out before him. The body of a younger man lay on its back between two armchairs opposite the desk. Across the room from Dwight, tattered curtains moved before shattered french windows.

Dwight heard shouts from outside the house, the sound of a car starting. He rushed across the room, whipped aside the curtains, as a man ran up the drive and climbed into a car already moving along it. As the man got in, the car moved away, without lights and accelerating rapidly. Dwight watched it go, a faintly gleaming shadow in the darkness, was about to turn from the window when it happened.

There was a gigantic, metallic thunderclap. A massive, globular, orange eruption. A deep kerwumph of an explosion that rocked the house, a harsh, sizzling crackle of flame.

Dwight stared horrified at the gate, at the dark skeleton of two cars wrapped in a final, fatal embrace. A dark figure moved in the flames, seemed to wave its hand in crazy goodbye, then all there was, was the sound of fire, the smell of burning rubber and burning flesh.

Dwight stepped back, turned away, saw Marit standing between two of Mollwo's sons, staring at him white-faced. The scabs on her wrists had opened and the back of one of her hands was covered with a dark streak of dried blood.

'My God, Dwight! You did this!' She looked horrified at the figure slumped behind the desk. 'You didn't have to kill him, damn you!'

Dwight hurried to her. She tore her arm away from his grasp.

'Who is he?' Dwight asked.

'Heinrich von Kassel! Who else? Or did you just kill for the hell of it?'

'We didn't do it,' Dwight said. 'It was Tearkes's men.'

'Johann?' she asked tremulously. 'Where's Johann?'

Dwight pointed beyond the shattered window to where the two cars blazed.

'Oh God! Oh God!' She raised her scarred hands to her face and began to sob.

Mollwo's eldest son came into the room. 'There's no one alive here,' he said. 'We'd better get out, before the police and the fire brigade come.'

Dwight took Marit's arm and led her out of the house, hurried her across the lawn and helped her up the ladder and into the car.

She lay motionless in his arms, while Mollwo's sons put the equipment away, and they drove back to the Bellevue.

44

Mollwo and his sons left soon afterwards, anxious to get to the border before news of the shootings spread beyond Zurich. Marit waited, pale and shocked, occasionally breaking into fits of near hysterical sobs.

'Take it easy,' Dwight said, thrusting a glass of brandy at her. 'We've got the processes, we've got the files. It's all over.'

'It isn't over, Dwight,' she said. 'It'll never end. Tearkes isn't interested in the processes.'

'What the hell do you mean?'

She shook her head. Tears welled out of her eyes. 'Heinrich ...' She shook her head helplessly. 'Heinrich ... was trying ...

to stop them. Tomorrow morning . . . at nine o'clock . . . the Russians will make an announcement . . . suspending payment of all loans and interest.' She took the brandy from him and gulped it fiercely, shivered as the raw spirit hit her. She pressed a damp handkerchief to her nose and blew. She lit a cigarette and fought to control herself. 'Tearkes and the cartel have been amassing gold and selling dollars forward. When the announcement is made, they stand to make a few billion dollars.'

Marit paused and took another sip of brandy. 'That isn't all,' she continued. 'They're ploughing the profits into buying banks. Can you imagine it, Dwight? They and the Russians will control the world's most important resource, money. Can you imagine what they will do with that power, that influence?'

'How do you know all this?' Dwight demanded.

She blew her nose again and wiped the tears from her cheeks. 'Bruno Topf,' she said. 'He was part of the cartel. He didn't want them to become so powerful. He pulled out of the cartel and told Heinrich. That is why they were both killed.'

Dwight got to his feet. 'Jeb Anderson is in town. We'd better talk to him now. Do you think you can cope?'

'Yes,' Marit said and taking a compact out of her bag started to tidy her face.

Two hours later, the Soviet Ambassador listened with growing apprehension as his American counterpart informed him of the details of the Russian attempt to devalue the dollar, an apprehension that increased as the American Ambassador outlined the steps that the United States were taking, together with Britain and Switzerland, to counter Andronov's plan – a massive sale of gold, a freeze on Russian assets in their respective countries, a trade and cultural boycott that would last until the loan repayments were reinstated.

As soon as the American Ambassador left the Soviet Ambassador to Switzerland got on the phone to the

Chairman of the Politbureau and Economics Minister Feliks Andronov.

Forty minutes later a Zil limousine drew up outside one of Zurich's most magnificent hotels, the Dolder Grand. Three men got out, marched into the lobby and having ascertained a room number, marched solemnly into the lift and went up to the third floor. There, they pounded on a door.

'Who is it?' Pyotr Voskov demanded sleepily.

'Viktor Tretiak. Open the door, comrade, or I'll smash it down.'

Voskov opened the door angrily. 'What is the meaning of this?' he demanded.

Viktor Tretiak smiled. 'I have orders for your recall, comrade Voskov.'

'This is ridiculous. I have vital business in Zurich tomorrow. Business vital to the interests of the USSR.'

Tretiak's grin widened. 'I think you will find, comrade,' he said, 'that the USSR has made other arrangements.'

Precisely at eight thirty the next morning, Marit and Dwight were at the Hoffman Bank. They were taken up to Hoffman's office straight away.

Hoffman looked liverish and there was an unhealthy yellowness about his face. He had difficulty arranging his face into a smile.

Marit placed the documents on his desk. 'The *Zessions* of Perpetua and Sopadep,' she said. She shuddered as she showed him the documents von Kassel had given her. 'Here is all the evidence you will need concerning my mother's release from Ravensbruck and emigration to Argentina.'

Hoffman looked listlessly at the documents.

'The assets of Perpetua and Sopadep will not be sold,' Marit said. 'The meeting you have called will be cancelled.'

Hoffman looked up at her, tiredly. 'Anything you say, Fraulein von Rausenberg. The Hoffman Bank is always at your service.'

'And that's another thing. I want everything transferred to the Imtra Bank.'

'There are three gentlemen downstairs who will help you,' Dwight said, smoothly.

Hoffman looked down at his desk. 'Anything you say,' he repeated.

When at five o'clock that evening, Raison Tearkes and Sir Alex Vickery left the house on the Uetliberg, they had about them that air of desperate gaiety which sometimes affects men facing ruin. All day they had waited, surrounded by an array of television screens and the huge communications console, all day they had waited with telex and teleprinters at the ready and their attention focused on a radio tuned to Moscow.

But the announcement hadn't come. Voskov hadn't come. And twenty minutes previously they had heard that Gerhardt Hoffman had been arrested and charged with economic espionage.

They were so occupied with their moods of alternating gaiety and despair that they only noticed they were being taken to the airport by an unfamiliar route, when the car suddenly pulled off the road, drove down a secluded, muddy track.

'Where are you taking us?' Sir Alex demanded, leaning forward and taking the driver by the shoulder.

The driver turned, and as he did so, they noticed the revolver clutched in his fist.

'What –' Sir Alex started to say and the driver fired twice.

45

Pulling her dressing gown tightly around her, Marit closed the bedroom door quietly and walked into the lounge. The coffee she had ordered barely ten minutes ago stood steaming lightly on the low table between the angular sofas. Except for the quiet hum of the air conditioner, the lounge was absolutely still.

She poured some coffee and lit a cigarette. In the last four days, her life had been unalterably changed. She could no longer be a carefree bachelor girl, living in a tiny apartment, running a second-hand Porsche and doing a job she loved. She would spend the rest of her life as she had spent the last four days, surrounded by lawyers, bankers and accountants, isolated by a cordon of assistants and bodyguards, pandered to by people anxious to gratify her every whim, and who gave total attention to every word she spoke. Over the past four days, she had ceased being Marit von Rausenberg, and become Manninger Industrie.

She picked up the envelope that had been brought in with her coffee. The processes had been verified by two independent firms of industrial chemists, who confirmed the processes would work, provided time and money was spent developing them. Then, after lengthy meetings with various officials, Jeb Anderson had informed her that the United States government was not constitutionally able to bid for the processes or develop them. However they would arrange for certain American companies to get in touch with Marit.

Marit tore open the envelope. As she'd expected, the letter was from Dr Arne Becker, the lawyer who had advised her over her claim against the Manninger estate and who now headed the team of lawyers advising her how to exploit it

Becker's letter contained a list of fourteen major American corporations, all of whom jointly or severally wished to help Marit develop the processes. In addition, there was an agglomerate of European bankers and industrialists, a large British company with substantial investments in the Third World, a Swiss-German consortium, two Swiss and four German chemical companies, who wanted the same thing. He stressed that meetings should be set up as soon as possible and a suitable partner found.

Marit sighed and put down the letter. She didn't want any more long, tedious meetings, she wanted to go back to being Marit. But she couldn't. She was the Manninger heiress.

Thoughtfully, she lit another cigarette.

Dwight came out of the bedroom, rubbing his eyes. 'Ah, there you are,' he said sleepily, leaned over and kissed her. 'What have you been doing?'

'Thinking,' Marit said, quietly.

Dwight sat on the sofa opposite her and poured himself some coffee. 'You really should quit smoking,' he said.

'I'll be all right.'

He pointed to the letter. 'Offers?'

She nodded.

Dwight read it. 'Christ!' he said. 'We'll be here for three months.'

'There's no need for you to stay,' Marit said.

Dwight put down the letter and looked at her. 'What the hell do you mean?'

'I can handle the meetings. You don't have to stay.'

'And what about advice?'

Marit laughed, harshly. 'I can't even tie a shoelace without someone telling me the best way to do it.'

'Be serious, Marit. These meetings are important. They're going to turn up with all kinds of lawyers and financial experts. You've got to have proper advisors.'

'And I have a number of very proper advisors.'

'You are also a client of the bank. An important client.'

'And the Imtra Bank has here in Zurich, a number of excellent people who will help me. Really, Dwight, there is no need for you to stay. You don't want to sit around and talk to me about money. You're not interested in money. You're not even interested in banking. Why don't you leave professional advice to those who really want to give it?'

'You mean there's nothing more you need me for. There's nothing left for me to do. You mean everything's over, thank you and goodbye.'

Marit got to her feet and walked across the room. She stopped at the window, turned, lit a cigarette and drew fiercely at it. 'That's about it,' she said. 'Don't make me feel guilty. Don't make me feel any worse than I do.'

'Sure,' Dwight said. 'Let's not upset you, right. Let's not make you feel bad.'

Marit looked past him at the wall. Her voice was mechanical. 'I'm grateful to you, Dwight. Very, very grateful. Without you, I wouldn't have got the processes,' she waved a hand around the suite, 'or any of this. But now I've got to work things out for myself. I've got to decide what I am and where I am going and who with. Don't you see, Dwight, the processes have changed everything.'

'They bloody well have.' He walked to the bedroom. 'I'd better get packed. There's a flight leaving Kloten at noon.'

Marit turned and watched him go. She started to say something and stopped. She couldn't find the words.

46

The Ambassador was wearing the happy coat he had bought some years ago when he had been an attaché in Singapore. It was a magnificent affair of pure silk resplendent with dragons. The Ambassador looked like a Chinese mandarin,

Jeb Anderson thought, and wondered what could be so urgent about the Manninger affair that required a meeting at twenty minutes after midnight.

The girl, surrounded by advisors and a wall of bodyguards was immersed in negotiations with various contenders for the processes. Dwight Khouri had returned to America, and Jeb himself was taking tomorrow's Pan Am flight back to Washington.

'Extraordinary, these KGB people,' the Ambassador remarked pouring out a brandy for Jeb. 'But then I suppose you meet them every day.'

Jeb sipped the brandy cautiously and didn't say anything. He would have preferred bourbon.

'Had someone round here called Viktor Tretiak,' the Ambassador continued. 'All he wanted to do was assure me that the USSR had punished the principals in the dollar raid. He suggested that we should not concern ourselves too much about them and hoped that this trivial incident would not upset the cordial relations between our two countries.'

'Did he say anything about Tearkes and Vickery?' Anderson asked.

'No.' The Ambassador sipped his whisky. 'Do you think the KGB murdered them?'

'I know they didn't,' Anderson said. He told the Ambassador the Swiss Police had found the limousine which had taken Tearkes and Vickery to the airport. Embedded in the upholstery was a sliver of metal, which had come from a dart. Analysis had shown that it was coated with a disabling but non-fatal soporific.

'But why would the KGB want to take men like that to Russia?' the Ambassador asked.

Anderson smiled. 'To punish them or to use them. We'll just have to keep our eyes and ears open for another share raid.'

47

His name was Alec. He had wide shoulders and supple legs and moved with relaxed grace. With his long, straight hair trapped beneath the wide head band, his bronzed face and sculpted features, he looked like an Indian warrior. 'Watch me,' he said, dropping the ball, twisting his body sideways, stepping forward and swinging at it with an easy, rhythmic loop.

The ball rocketed across the net and pounded into the court, inches inside the baseline. 'You've simply got to take it easy,' Alec said. 'There's no need to swipe.'

'I know,' Dwight said.

Dwight walked across to his side of the court. Alec hit the ball wide and deep to his forehand. Before even realizing it, Dwight's feet skipped towards it, his body turned sideways, his knees bent, he stepped forward. The ball sang off his racket, looped high, cross court, the top spin bringing it down sharply.

Alec returned it down the line.

Dwight hit it back, deep, using lots of slice.

'Here it comes.' Alec chipped the ball. It barely cleared the net, dropped four feet from the service line.

Dwight was already there, lining up for it, weight on his rear foot, preparing to step forward. He could feel his arm going back, back. He looked up to see if Alec had noticed. He swung. The ball trickled between the racket and his legs.

'You've got to keep your head down,' Alec said, coming up to the net. 'Hey, Dwight, what's the matter?'

Dwight was staring past him at the slim figure treading the paved path between the courts. Dwight's lips moved. 'Can I take five?'

Alec turned and whistled softly. 'Take twenty, man, take as long as you want.'

Dwight ran off the court, hurried along the path towards her. He couldn't believe it. Marit. Here. Yes it was her, walking towards him, familiar golden helmet of hair bouncing off her shoulders. Marit. His heart was thumping in his chest and he knew it wasn't from the exercise. It was catching in his throat. 'Marit,' he said and stopped, reached out his arms to her, then dropped them, embarrassed. 'I'm all sweaty,' he said. 'What are you doing here?'

'What does it look like?'

He couldn't believe she'd come looking for him. He'd thought it was all over, and now it wasn't, and he wanted it to be over and didn't. He couldn't think what to say. 'You're looking for a banker,' he said.

'Wrong. I'm looking for a friend.'

Suddenly her complacency, her certainty irritated him. 'You've come to the wrong place,' he said. 'Now that you've sold the processes, why don't you buy yourself a friend?'

She flinched, as if he had struck her. 'I'm sorry about Zurich,' she said. 'I didn't handle myself very well, did I, Dwight?'

'Zurich was a long time ago,' Dwight said. 'As you said, things have changed.'

'I didn't sell the processes,' she said.

'You what?'

They began to walk towards the building. 'I couldn't,' she said, looking down at the path. 'I couldn't make the giants even bigger. And that wasn't the only reason. Oh hell, I'm getting confused again. They're my processes, Dwight, they're all that's left of my family. I want to keep them. I think it will be better that way. If I sell them, I wouldn't have any control over who used them and how they were used, who exploited them and who used them to exploit others.'

'So no sale,' Dwight said. He put his arm around her

shoulders. 'You're crazy, kid. If I'd been there, I'd have told you to take the money and run.'

She stopped, turned and looked at him. 'Would you, Dwight? Honestly. Would you also have tried to turn me into Manninger Industrie?'

Dwight shrugged.

'I've been in Washington with Jeb Anderson,' Marit said. 'I've made an agreement with him. Under existing legislation for development of alternative sources of energy, the government will loan me part of the costs of development.'

'And the rest?'

She smiled up at him. 'That's why I need a friend who is a banker.'

'I know nothing about industrial processes,' Dwight said.

'We'll learn.'

'It doesn't make sense,' Dwight said. 'It could take us years to develop the processes.'

She tilted her head back. 'I know,' she said and smiled happily.

Helen MacInnes

Born in Scotland, Helen MacInnes has lived in the United States since 1937. Her first book, *Above Suspicion,* was an immediate success and launched her on a spectacular writing career that has made her an international favourite.

'She is the queen of spy-writers.' *Sunday Express*

'She can hang up her cloak and dagger right there with Eric Ambler and Graham Greene.' *Newsweek*

FONTANA PAPERBACKS

Eric Ambler

A world of espionage and counter-espionage, of sudden violence and treacherous calm; of blackmailers, murderers, gun-runners—and none too virtuous heroes. This is the world of Eric Ambler.

'Unquestionably our best thriller writer.' *Graham Greene*

'He is incapable of writing a dull paragraph.' *Sunday Times*

'Eric Ambler is a master of his craft.' *Sunday Telegraph*

JOURNEY INTO FEAR £1.25
DIRTY STORY £1.35
THE LEVANTER £1.25
PASSAGE OF ARMS £1.25
THE CARE OF TIME £1.50
DR FRIGO £1.50
THE SCHIRMER INHERITANCE £1.50

FONTANA PAPERBACKS

Desmond Bagley

'Mr Bagley is nowadays incomparable.' *Sunday Times*

THE ENEMY   £1.35
FLYAWAY   £1.65
THE FREEDOM TRAP   £1.50
THE GOLDEN KEEL   £1.35
HIGH CITADEL   £1.25
LANDSLIDE   £1.50
RUNNING BLIND   £1.50
THE SNOW TIGER   £1.50
THE SPOILERS   £1.50
THE TIGHTROPE MEN   £1.50
THE VIVERO LETTER   £1.50
WYATT'S HURRICANE   £1.50
BAHAMA CRISIS   £1.50

FONTANA PAPERBACKS

Fontana Paperbacks

Fontana is a leading paperback publisher of fiction and non-fiction, with authors ranging from Alistair MacLean, Agatha Christie and Desmond Bagley to Solzhenitsyn and Pasternak, from Gerald Durrell and Joy Adamson to the famous Modern Masters series.

In addition to a wide-ranging collection of internationally popular writers of fiction, Fontana also has an outstanding reputation for history, natural history, military history, psychology, psychiatry, politics, economics, religion and the social sciences.

All Fontana books are available at your bookshop or newsagent; or can be ordered direct. Just fill in the form and list the titles you want.

FONTANA BOOKS, Cash Sales Department, G.P.O. Box 29, Douglas, Isle of Man, British Isles. Please send purchase price, plus 8p per book. Customers outside the U.K. send purchase price, plus 10p per book. Cheque, postal or money order. No currency.

NAME (Block letters)

ADDRESS